THE
GIRL
FROM THE
TYNE

Melody Sachs

ZAFFRE

First published in Great Britain in 2017 by

ZAFFRE PUBLISHING
80-81 Wimpole St, London W1G 9RE
www.zaffrebooks.co.uk

A CIP catalogue record for this book is
available from the British Library.

ISBN: 978-1-7857-6287-1

also available as an ebook

1 3 5 7 9 10 8 6 4 2

Typeset by IDSUK (Data Connection) Ltd

Printed and bound by Clays Ltd, St Ives Plc

MIX
Paper from
responsible sources
FSC® C018072

Zaffre Publishing is an imprint of Bonnier Zaffre,
a Bonnier Publishing company
www.bonnierzaffre.co.uk
www.bonnierpublishing.co.uk

THE
GIRL
FROM THE
TYNE

Melody Sachs was born in Newcastle. As a child, she appeared regularly in pantomime at the Theatre Royal. At 18 Melody moved to London where she spent time in West End cabaret and in provincial repertory theatres.

In 1960, she married the actor and writer, Andrew Sachs, and they have three children. Melody wrote short stories and sketches for the BBC and once appeared in an episode of *Fawlty Towers* along with her husband.

Melody went on to study antique textiles and design and opened her first shop in the eighties in Hampstead, specialising in wedding gowns. Her creations frequently featured in *Tatler*, *Brides* and *Wedding* magazines. She designed for celebrities, including Boy George for his Japanese tour, and Barbara Kelly for the entire series of *What's My Line*. One of her most memorable designs was the gown she created for Lady Glenconner to attend a ball at Buckingham Palace in honour of the King of Spain.

The Girl from the Tyne is her first novel and she is currently working on the second book in the Tyneside series.

In loving memory of my husband Andrew Sachs
who encouraged me to write this book

Prologue

Jack smoothed back his dark brown hair and applied a touch of Brylcreem. His sister Ena wouldn't approve, but what the heck, all the lads were using it nowadays. He took his new blue blazer from the wardrobe and tried it on in front of the mirror. Mam was right, it went well with his stone grey trousers and crisp white shirt. He smiled at himself in approval, stepped back from the mirror and straightened his tie. Yes, he thought, that'll do nicely.

He splashed on the fancy aftershave his mother had given him for Christmas and patted his face. Just wait till the girls smell this, he told himself, they'll be queuing up to dance with me!

He whistled as he took the stairs two at a time, stopping in the hall for a moment to wink at himself in the mirror. Music was coming from the sitting room and he quietly tiptoed inside. His mother was sitting in her favourite chair engrossed in her needlework while tapping her feet to Bing Crosby singing 'Star Dust' on the radio. Jack cleared his throat, stepped forward and bowed low. 'May I have the pleasure of this dance, Mother?'

She put down her embroidery and looked him up and down. 'Oh son, you look a real bobby dazzler!'

He waltzed towards her, took hold of her hands and pulled her to her feet. 'What do you think?' he said, as he spun her around the floor.

'Oh don't be silly!' she said. 'I'm not a young girl any more!' But Jack noticed the sparkle in her eyes. She was on the heavy side, but it was no effort to whisk her around. As they came to a halt, she leaned forward to plant a kiss on his cheek and breathed in his aftershave. 'You smell good enough to eat, son!'

'Get away, Mother, you're biased! Now how about a nice cup of tea before I go? The bus into town doesn't get here till seven.'

'All right, Jack, you can read the paper while I'm gone. Now where did I put the *Herald*? It was around here somewhere.'

'It's on the sideboard, Mother.' He picked up the paper and waved it at her.

'Oh yes, there it is. Have a good read while I get the tea. I won't be long.'

Jack perched on the edge of his mother's armchair and began to read. A truck driver had found the Lindbergh baby dead in a wood in America and the news wasn't much better at home. The *Herald* was still full of violent details from that Dartmouth prison revolt, but at least the convicts had been sentenced now – and not before time either.

Mrs Wood picked up the tea caddy and thought about her son as she spooned his favourite Lipton's tea into the pot. He'd always been considered the baby of the family, especially by his sister, Ena, but now here he was, running his own joinery business and providing work for four men. Finding work in this Depression was no mean feat in Tyneside and, in striving to keep his business open, Jack was helping folks worse off than himself to scrape a living. She was proud of him and, if only his father had lived, he would have been proud of him too.

She took the butter and sliced ham from the pantry and cut two slices of bread. It's best he has something in his stomach if he's having a drink, she thought. She picked up the mustard pot. Now, I know he likes a bit of this on his ham. When she was satisfied everything was ready, she straightened her back and carefully carried the loaded tea tray into the sitting room.

Jack put down the newspaper. 'It's depressing news in the *Herald*, Mother. We're nearly halfway through 1932 and all we read about is trouble.'

'Stop it, Jack, you don't want to be thinking things like that when you're off to a dance. Here, have a sandwich. I know what you lads are like when you're let loose. You need to have something inside you before you go gallivanting.' She set the tray before him with a smile.

He was not in the least hungry, but there was no refusing his mother when she had made up her mind. Besides, his mouth was already watering from the smell of the ham.

He picked up the sandwich and took a healthy bite. 'That's delicious, you always know the right amount of mustard, Mother. But I can't stay here stuffing myself all night – I'll just finish this, then I'll be off.'

'That's right, son. You don't want to miss the bus.'

He polished off the rest of the sandwich and stood up, brushing the crumbs from his blazer as he did so. 'Now, don't wait up for me,' he said, as he bent over and kissed her. 'You never know, I might be late.'

She stood at the door and smiled as she watched her handsome boy striding down the gravel path with a spring in his step, whistling all the way.

⌐⌐

Jack winked at two young girls waiting at the bus stop and grinned as they nudged each other and giggled. They were dressed to kill, in bright red frocks Jack guessed could be their mothers'. He bet they were going to the dance in the nearby town centre of Blaydon.

It was a chilly night and Jack was beginning to feel cold. He paced up and down, stamping his feet and rubbing his hands, chiding himself for not remembering his overcoat, but he cheered up when he saw the headlights of the bus lighting up the hedgerows at the side of the road. When it pulled up at the stop, he stood aside to make way for the girls. They giggled again as they climbed inside. Jack followed behind, looking for an empty seat. He nodded at the conductor, but was rewarded with a bad-tempered scowl.

Just as he bent to sit down, the conductor pulled the bell-cord and the bus took off with an almighty jolt, throwing Jack into the lap of a plump old man. 'Whoops!' he said. 'Are ye drunk already, lad?'

Jack wondered if the tetchy conductor had done that on purpose, but the old man was laughing so Jack joined in. At last it was time to have some fun, especially now there was no big sister at home to ruin it for him. He could hear Ena's voice now. 'It's too rowdy at those dances for the likes of our Jack.' Honestly, just because he'd let her teach him a few steps in the kitchen, she seemed to think she could keep him indoors like some kid, wet behind the ears. Thank heavens she'd married Peter and moved a few miles away to Dunston.

There was nothing to beat the excitement of a dance hall on a Saturday night. Jack had been to one or two before, but never at Blaydon. He wondered if it would be anything like the Oxford Galleries in Newcastle. He looked at the other passengers. It looked like most of them were heading to the same place. Lots of them were young lads like him, geared up for a good night out, and were in raucous mood – some had been at the drink already and were laughing loud enough to raise the roof. Jack had his eye on the conductor – the louder the lads shouted, the more grumpy he looked. Lads in the seats over the aisle from him had dark rings around their eyes and he noticed coal dust behind the ears of the ones in front. He bet they were miners who'd hurried home from day shift to clean themselves up for the dance. Thank God I'm lucky enough not to have to dig around in the dark, just to keep somebody's coal house filled, he thought. Mother always says they don't pay the men enough for what they have to put up with down there.

One of the lads across from him caught his eye and grinned. To Jack's surprise, he got to his feet and turned round to address the others. 'Come on!' he yelled.

The bus conductor marched up the aisle and glared at him. 'Sit down!' he shouted.

'Keep yer wig on!' he yelled back, then turned again to the others. 'Yas ahl kna' this!' He threw back his head and burst into song.

'Ah went to Blaydon Races, 'twas on the ninth of Joon, Eighteen hundred an' sixty-two, on a summer's efternoon . . .'

His voice was deep and gritty and the lads cheered him on. Jack stole a quick look at the old boy beside him, wondering how he was coping, but he was smiling from ear to ear. The conductor, on the other hand, looked ready to explode.

As the lad reached the chorus everyone joined in the Geordie anthem:

'Ah me lads, ye should see us gannin',
Passin' the folks upon the road just as they wor stannin';
There was lots o' lads an' lasses there, al' wi' smiling faces,
Gannin' alang the Scotswood Rooooooad, to see the
Blaydon Races!'

The old man was singing along with the best of them, his voice easily as loud as Jack's.

Jack grinned at him, but he couldn't help noticing the conductor's face – it had turned dangerously red and a vein was pulsing in the side of his neck. 'Keep the noise doon!' he yelled. 'Ah divvn' want to be had up for carryin' a load a drunks!'

Fair enough, Jack thought. But the bus was pulling into the main square at Blaydon and the lads were already on their feet, almost falling over each other in the rush to get out. I'll wait until the crush dies down, he thought, and stayed put in his seat, but the conductor was having none of that. He stood over Jack. 'If ye divvn' wanta get off,' he said, 'ye can mind the bus while we have wor tea.'

Jack got the message, quickly got to his feet and stepped down onto the busy pavement. Darkness was falling, the air was crisp and the street lamps were shining on the merrymakers as they headed towards the dance hall. Jack put his hands in his pockets and sauntered past a group of girls in their special Saturday night dresses. The heavy scent of their perfume enveloped him as he glanced surreptitiously in their direction. But he wasn't alone – lots of lads were gaping at them, weighing up their chances. Expectation filled the air and Jack quickened his pace. He patted the wallet in the inside pocket of his new jacket and looked forward to a nice brown ale.

As he had never been to a Blaydon dance before he thought it best to keep up with the others. He followed the noisy crowd to the end of the street and stayed with them as they crossed over the road into a narrow pathway along the side of St Joseph's Catholic church.

Iron gates opened on to what seemed like a small recreation ground. For a moment, Jack wondered if he had come to the right place, but he could hear music drifting in the air and the crowd was surging forward, so he hurried after them. At the far end of the tarmacked ground stood a rambling building, with an impressive arched doorway. 'Blaydon Church Hall' was lit up in flashing lights around the arch.

Jack joined the queue to buy his ticket. He stamped his feet on the tarmac to warm them up and a young man in front of him turned around. 'Cahd, isn' it?' He held out a packet of Woodbines. 'D'ye fancy a tab, bonnie lad? Go on, help yersel', Ah've got a whole packet.'

'Thanks all the same, but I don't smoke.' A look of disappointment crossed the young man's face and Jack added hastily, 'But I wouldn't say no to a nice beer.'

They moved through the arched doorway into a mosaic-tiled hall. It wasn't much warmer in here, but at least they were at the front of the queue. The young man winked at Jack as he went up to the ticket counter. 'It winnit be lang till ye can wet yer whistle, Geordie, Ah'm next.' He took out a shilling, slapped it on the counter and picked up his ticket. 'Gan on,' he said, 'it's your turn and mind ye divin' get drunk.' He slapped Jack on the back and disappeared inside.

Jack paid for his ticket and joined the crowd squeezing through the doorway at the end of the hall. As he pressed forward, a wave of heat and noise surrounded him and he felt a heady rush of pleasure. At last he was in!

The ballroom was completely packed. Dancers filled the floor and every seat at each small round table surrounding it was full. He elbowed his way across the floor to reach the stage at the other end of the room. The band that night had a great reputation and the crush was even greater near the front as people jostled to get close.

The musicians certainly looked the part in their smart black suits and bow ties, belting out the latest tunes for all they were worth. A pretty girl sang into the microphone trying her best to be heard above the noise. Jack thought her a knockout, with her long black hair and slender figure. She wore a flimsy dress in black and silver, cut low at the front, with shoe-string straps. A glitterball hung from the ceiling, covering her in delicate snow-like flakes. She reminded Jack of the Snow Queen at his first pantomime. He had been just six years old when his mother had taken him to the Theatre Royal that Christmas and he could still recall the magic of it.

But now it was time for a drink. He pushed through the dancers again to reach the crowded bar. Four hard-pressed waiters, with shirt sleeves rolled up to their elbows, were pouring out Dutch courage to lads who looked like they needed it. Jack had to admit he was one of them. He waved a ten bob note to get the barman's attention. 'When you're ready,' he called.

'Had on, hinny, can ye not see Ah'm run off me feet?'

'In your own good time. And have one yourself.'

That did the trick. The barman was with him in seconds. 'Cheers, bonnie lad, what's yer poison?'

'Newcastle brown ale, what else?'

'Good choice.' The waiter poured the clear, cold liquid into the glass and placed it carefully on the counter. 'That'll put the lead in yer pencil, lad!'

Jack took a deep gulp of his favourite beer. He needed that! But there was no use standing here all night – this wouldn't find him a lass to dance with. So he pushed back through the crowds, careful not to spill his drink down some bonnie lass's best new frock. He stopped at the edge of the dance floor – there were a lot of bonnie lasses, he'd never seen so many! Some of them were dancing together so it looked like men were in short supply and if that were the case, he shouldn't have a problem.

A loud burst of hysterical laughter made him turn. A group of girls were huddled around one of the tables at the side of the dance floor. Should I try my luck, he wondered, as he moved closer to the table. One of the girls caught his eye and smiled at him. 'Ah'm Ruby,' she said. 'They're playing a foxtrot. D'ye fancy a dance, canny lad?'

Could she be talking to him? For a moment he wasn't sure, but then she slipped her arm through his. 'Well!' she went on. 'What aboot it?'

'Why not?' he heard himself say.

Ruby steered him towards the floor. 'What's yer name, bonnie lad? Ah've never seen you here before.'

'My name's Jack Wood. Pleased to meet you.' He looked her up and down. Ruby was a pretty girl, with long brown hair. She was wearing a dress that accentuated the colour of her green eyes. It was just the right length to show off her shapely legs as he took her in his arms and began whirling her around the floor.

He was racking his brain for something to say, something sharp but not too clever, when a line from a film came into his head and he decided to try it out. 'Do you come here often, Ruby?' He smiled at how easily her name had slipped from his lips.

'Ah come 'ere every Sat'day. Why d'ye want to know anyway? Are ye tryin' to get off with us?'

Jack flushed. 'I'm sorry. I hope I wasn't too forward.'

She gave him a knowing smile. 'Divvn' worry, pet, yer alreet. Ah like a man wi' manners.' She nuzzled up to him. 'Ye divvn' get many in this place.' Then, without warning, she tightened her grip around his neck and kissed him on the cheek. Jack stumbled in surprise and missed his step, landing heavily on Ruby's foot. She cried out and they came to a halt so suddenly the couple behind bumped into them. The man glared at him. 'Watch what yer doin', ye dozy bugger!'

Only a moment ago, Ruby had been smiling at him, but now she screwed up her face and pushed him away. 'Bloody hell!' she yelped. 'Ye've laddered me best stockin's. What've ye got on yer shoes? Hob nails?'

Jack tried to hide his humiliation as he held his hand out to Ruby. 'Please, let me help you.'

She snatched her hand away and limped off to find a seat. Jack followed behind, hoping to make amends, but Ruby pushed him away again. 'Yer no bloody good, are ye? So bugger off and ye needn't bother asking us again either!'

Jack slinked back to the bar with his tail between his legs. He pulled his wallet from his pocket and rummaged inside for a note, looking out for the barman he'd charmed earlier. A man standing next to him nudged his arm. 'Never mind the drink,' he said, 'just wait till ye get a load of what's comin' on next!' He nodded towards the floor. 'She'll knock yer bloomin' eyeballs out, lad.'

'Who's she then?'

'Keep yer shirt on,' the man said, 'ye'll find out soon enough. She's hot stuff, Ah can tell ye.'

The room quietened as the band stopped and the MC ran up the steps on to the stage. He was a tall, thin man in a tight black suit, his hair parted in the middle and flattened to his head with Brylcreem, reminding Jack of a mannequin in Burton's window. 'Good evening, boys and girls!' he said. 'You won't have to wait much longer to see the main attraction! They've just won their latest competition and here they are to celebrate at their favourite venue, with their greatest fans!

'So, Ladies and Gentlemen, please welcome our ballroom champions for the North East, none other than Earl Dixon and Alice Rooney! Let's hear it for them – Alice and Earl!'

The band struck up with the staccato rhythm of a tango, and as the audience broke into applause, Jack turned away from the bar and moved back to the ballroom. He was curious to see what a champion dancer looked like.

He joined the crowd as they formed a circle around the edge of the floor. The lights went out and a hush fell over the room. A drum roll began, quietly at first, then built to a crescendo as a spotlight lit up a couple in a striking pose. They stood as still as statues, reminding him of a figurine on his mother's sideboard. Their heads were at sharp right angles to their bodies as they looked down the length of their outstretched arms to their firmly clasped hands. Earl Dixon had one arm around his partner's slender waist, her hand resting on his broad shoulder. Jack noticed her long, slim fingers with the nails painted bright red. His mother had never allowed his sister to wear that colour.

He had never seen anyone like Alice Rooney before. She looked like a model in his sister's *Vogue* catalogue. Maybe it was the crimson flower she wore in her hair or perhaps it was the bright slash of scarlet lipstick. Whatever it was, he would have to get closer. He began to ease his way to the front. He couldn't wait to see what this woman would be like in action. As the dance began, he pushed his way through the cheering crowd until he found an unrestricted view. Alice Rooney was as glamorous as a film star. She looked like she had been poured in to the red dress she wore: it clung to her slim body, dipping low at the back, showing off her flawless skin. The shoulder straps were flimsy and sparkled with diamanté. Her golden blonde hair rippled over her shoulders and her eyes lit up as the rhythm of the tango took possession of her, and she allowed Earl Dixon to lead her through a series of perfectly rehearsed steps.

Jack couldn't take his eyes off her. She was as light as a feather in the arms of Earl as she followed his every move. Earl was good-looking enough and a strong dancer, but Alice's raw magnetism drew every eye to her performance. Jack could tell she was all woman, whereas the girl whose toes he had trodden on earlier had been just that – a girl. He cringed when he recalled his clumsiness, but all thoughts of the girl were chased away again instantly by Alice. He hardly noticed Earl Dixon, except that he was Alice's partner, the lucky man who held her close or flung her away from him before reeling her back in to his arms again. I'd give anything for just one dance with her, he thought, imagining himself in Earl Dixon's shoes.

He was brought back to earth as the music suddenly stopped. The dance had ended and the couple were holding their final pose, Alice leaning seductively backwards over Earl's strong, outstretched arm. For a moment or two they remained still, until Alice moved slowly and gracefully to an upright position. When Earl led her forward to take their bow, the audience went wild. The applause seemed to go on forever.

And now Alice and Earl were smiling and stepping, in separate directions, from the centre of the floor. Jack's eyes followed Alice. The audience parted like the Red Sea as she threaded her way through the crowd and sat down at a small table on the edge of the dance floor. She had hardly taken her seat before she was surrounded by a throng of admirers. Jack hung back and watched as she acknowledged the compliments. Then, when the last of her fans had melted away, he gathered up his courage and walked slowly over to her table.

He cleared his throat. He had never felt so nervous, but he wasn't going to let a chance like this slip through his fingers. 'I hope I'm not intruding, Miss Rooney,' he began, 'but I just had to tell you how much I enjoyed your performance and how lucky Earl Dixon is to be your partner.'

Alice looked as if she was about to laugh at his formality, but then seemed to think the better of it.

'Thanks for the compliment, pet! D'ye like dancin'?'

He nodded. 'I do like dancing. But I'm nothing special – I mean, I'm not up to your standard.'

'It takes a lot of practice,' she said. 'What's yer name, anyway?'

'Jack Wood. And I know yours. It's Alice, Alice Rooney, isn't it?'

'That's right.' To his surprise, she stood up. 'Well, now we know each other, come with me, Jack Wood. They're playing a nice slow foxtrot. Let's see what you can do.' She took his hand. Well, she's not backwards in coming forward, he thought.

He tried to keep his nervousness from showing as they walked on to the floor. Pray to God he didn't make a fool of himself and tread on her champion toes – he'd be thrown out of the hall for sure.

But he needn't have panicked. It was wonderful dancing with Alice. Her vitality was infectious, and after a few tentative steps, he felt a burst of energy flood through him and he began to pick up the pace. He knew they made an attractive couple, and soon realised that the nerves had vanished and he was actually enjoying himself. It would have been impossible not to have a good time, when she danced so expertly that some of it rubbed off on him, and instead of feeling like he had two left feet, he felt so right in his skin. He breathed in her scent as she leant her head on his shoulder. It was Coty, just like his sister Ena wore.

They stayed on the floor for two dances in succession, a foxtrot and a quickstep. When the music stopped, she gave him a provocative look that was far from sisterly.

He would have had to be stupid not to read the blatant signal, the flare of interest in her eyes. Jack was sure it had nothing to do with dancing. All of a sudden, he felt ill at ease. She wasn't his type, he realised – too forward and too hot to handle. His type were sweet and shy. And when it came to girls, he preferred to do the choosing.

Alice snuggled up against his chest. 'You're not that bad, you know. Ah think Ah could do somethin' with you.'

Jack didn't like the sound of that. No, this lass was definitely not for him. He would have to find a polite way to excuse himself. At that moment the band leader announced the last waltz. Saved by the bell, he thought. A last dance and he'd be off.

Alice spun in his arms to the strains of the waltz. He had to admit, she was an amazing dancer and, to be fair, the evening had had its moments. Even so, he knew it would be wise to make a swift exit. When the waltz ended, he let his arms fall to his sides, took a step back and looked around. The crowd in the hall was thinning as couples trickled out into the night.

'It's time I was off,' he said. 'Thanks for the dance.'

But Alice held on to his arm. 'Just a minute,' she said. 'Wait till Ah fetch me shawl.'

Taken aback by her pushiness, he missed his moment to escape. He had planned to leave alone, but now that he found himself nodding his head, he felt obliged to do as she asked and wait for her. That would be the polite thing to do.

Alice headed to the ladies' cloakroom, returning in no time with her shawl over her arm and her face covered in smiles as she saw him still waiting for her.

Once outside, Jack sighed with relief. The cold air had cleared his mind and he was thinking of a polite way to say goodbye to Alice, when her voice broke in to his thoughts.

'If you're walking me home, pet, let's go by the canal.' She cast him a sideways look, which might have served as a warning if he'd caught it.

He was walking with his hands in his pockets, striding ahead of her.

'What's the hurry?' she asked, and linked her arm through his to slow him down, humming one of the tunes they had danced to.

They made slow progress along the tow path, Alice looking at the houseboats moored by the bank. Most of the occupants seemed to have gone to sleep already, although one or two still had lights showing in the cabins.

They were at a point beyond the houseboats, when Alice stopped suddenly and reached down to fiddle with her ankle.

'Would ye believe it, the strap's snapped on me shoe!'

She made a show of hobbling a few paces to the shelter of some willow trees, set back a little from the bank, and sat down under a leafy canopy of trailing willow branches, practically inviting him to join her. Jack crawled in beside her and knelt at her ankle to see if he could help.

'Looks like a buckle's come undone,' he said, but as he fumbled at the strap, she took his face between her hands, and tilted her face towards his.

And in that fateful moment, Jack obliged by kissing her. Where was the harm in it, he asked himself. He'd give her a kiss goodnight, and then be off.

But the kiss was more than he'd bargained for, a kiss that she took control of and deepened. After a while she pushed him, playfully, so that he lost his balance and was no longer kneeling, but lying beside her on the grass under the willows. She eased the straps of her dress from her shoulders, revealing the top of her milky white breasts, the breasts which had been pressed against his shirt front while they were dancing. She pulled him towards her, guiding his hand under the flimsy red fabric of her dress on to the cool, bare skin of her thigh. Desire swept over him.

The moment it was over, he was struck with remorse. He already regretted his weakness. And prayed there would be no consequences.

PART 1

Chapter 1

Newcastle upon Tyne, 1933

Jack walked along the depressing street looking for number 14. His boots felt like lead as he made his way through the cheerless, rundown neighbourhood. He felt the urge to turn back, but no matter where he went, there'd be no escape from the predicament that awaited him. To think this was only a short walk from his own house, yet a whole world away from what he was used to.

His heart sank when he saw the house. It was just like all the rest, with paint peeling from the doors and window frames. Water was dripping steadily onto the pavement from a loose gutter and as he jumped back it splashed on to his boots. A scraggy cat came from nowhere and nuzzled up to him, before lapping water from a hole in the pavement.

He wanted to turn and run, but as he paused for a moment, the door opened. A young girl, about fourteen, with a tousled mop of limp brown hair, smiled shyly at him. 'Ah'm Peggy, Alice's sister,' she said.

Jack wondered if he had heard right. She didn't look a bit like Alice.

'Come in,' she said.

He followed her through a narrow hallway into a shabby front room. 'Sit down,' said Peggy. 'Mam won't be long.' She smiled shyly at him once more and disappeared.

Jack gritted his teeth and lowered himself onto a frayed and sagging sofa. As his eyes got used to the gaslight, he couldn't help noticing that the carpet and curtains were begging to be cleaned.

'Well, well, Jack Wood!'

He jumped at the sound of the grating voice. A thin elderly woman stood in the doorway, holding a bundle in her arms. She stared at him through piercing blue eyes, tightening her lips as though ready for battle.

Jack stood up. 'You must be Alice's mother.'

'So! Ye got my message then. Ye thought ye'd show yer face, did ye? And not before time either! Ye should be ashamed of yersel'. Have you any idea what my lass has been through? Here – take yer little bastard. An' Ah hope yer proud of yersel, Jack Wood!'

Jack could hardly register he was being handed a new-born baby. He stared at the cream shawl, but the baby was so tightly swaddled he couldn't tell what it looked like. He felt sweat prickle under his collar.

Mrs Rooney glared at him. 'Have yer nowt to say for yersel'? My lass nearly died havin' that bairn! Did ye know she's got a bad heart? A fat lot you care! Your bairn's that little she could fit into a bloody pint pot – it's lucky she wasn't any bigger or she coulda killed wor Alice!'

Jack lowered his eyes. 'I'm sorry Alice has suffered so much, Mrs Rooney, and I hope she soon feels better.'

'Ye cannat pull the bloody wool over my eyes by comin' the gentleman, with "Ah'm sorry", oh no, yer not foolin' nobody. Ah know your kind, buggerin' off when ye've had yer way!' Mrs Rooney's words poured out like scalding water from a kettle.

To Jack's relief, the door opened and a small, stout woman came into the room. 'Ah'm the midwife,' she said. 'Ah thought Ah'd better come for the bairn, seein' as you've matters to sort out. Besides, she'll be needin' a feed now her daddy's seen her.'

Jack blanched at the word 'Daddy' just as he had at the harsh sound of 'bastard.' He handed the baby over gratefully. She was in capable hands now – more capable than his. When the midwife left the room, he felt the urge to follow her and make a bid for freedom, but his conscience had obliged him to come, to put a proposition to Alice, so he stayed where he was and forced himself to look Mrs Rooney in the eye.

He took a deep breath. 'I'd like to see Alice. There's something I've got to say to her.'

Mrs Rooney glowered at him. 'She's not fit for visitors, you daft bugger! Ah've already told ye that bairn was nearly the death of her.'

Jack's temper began to rise. He had come out of decency, not to be lectured at, but to be fair and businesslike, and to deal with Alice, not with this battleaxe. But after listening to

her ranting, his idea of saying a few kind words and handing over a cheque to Alice, seemed naive.

Mrs Rooney stood with her arms folded, scowling at him.

'I'll be going then if I can't see Alice today. Maybe
another time.'

'Oh yis! Ye'd like to run away with yer tail between yer
legs and never be seen again, wouldn't ye? But my son
wants a word wi' ye first.' Mrs Rooney opened the door and
shouted upstairs. 'Martin! Get yersel' doon 'ere!'

Jack felt like a fly caught in a web, his heart beating a
little faster as he heard heavy footsteps lumber down the
stairs.

Martin Rooney filled the small room with his hulking
presence. He was the same age as Jack and as tall as Jack's
six feet but broadly built. His black, curly hair was unkempt,
and his face looked as if it wouldn't recognise a razor. He
looked Jack up and down.

'Why! If it's not Alice's fancyman showin' up at long last!'

Jack cleared his throat. 'I'm just off as Alice isn't well
enough for me to see her.'

'And are ye takin' yer squealin' little bastard with yer? Or
are ye just creepin' off, leavin' us to cope?'

'Well . . . as a matter of fact, I was going to give Alice
something.'

'Ye've givin my sister somethin' already and ye'd better
not try an' get away wi' it! Flashin' yer money to get yersel'
outa trouble! That bairn and my sister'll need a roof over
their heads!'

'And how do I even know the bairn's mine?'

The moment the words left his lips, Jack knew he had given Martin Rooney the excuse he had been itching for. 'You callin' my sister a whore?' He pushed Jack against the wall, ramming an elbow against his throat and pinioning him there. Jack pulled at the muscled forearm to stop himself from choking but Rooney leant on him, breathing into his ear.

'Ah know ahl aboot what went on 'tween the two o' you doon by the canal!' he whispered. 'An' now ye'll pay for the fun ye helped yersel' to!'

He gave another vicious shove at Jack's windpipe before allowing his mother to pull him off.

'Divvn' be daft, Martin, that's no way to fettle things,' she said as she watched Jack spluttering to regain his breath.

He rubbed his throat and straightened his twisted shirt collar, trying to recover his dignity, but his breathing was coming fast, rasping in his throat.

'Leave him to me,' said Mrs Rooney. 'Ah'll mak' sure he makes an honest woman of your sister.'

Suddenly she was pushing and shoving at Jack, manhandling him towards the door. 'Gan' on, then, since you're in such a hurry to leave. Bugger off! Jus' mak' sure you come back and tell us your plans for Alice and the bairn. Think on! She's your little bastard and don't you forget it!'

Martin opened the front door and Mrs Rooney pushed Jack in the small of his back, sending him stumbling over the threshold and into the street.

He scrambled to his feet, breathing in the icy February air, his chest rising and falling rapidly as he limped away from the ugly scene more shaken up than he'd like to admit.

What a pair those two were, he thought. Rough as badgers! So they were Alice's family, the hard-bitten mother and brother, and the shy little sister who looked like she wouldn't say boo to a goose.

'How have I got myself entangled with the likes of them? What a mess I'm in,' he muttered to himself. He pulled his jacket collar up over his ears against the cold, jammed his hands in his pockets, and lengthened his stride. He couldn't wait to get home away from this nightmare.

⁂

Jack's father had bought The Lilacs, a large solid brick-built house just outside Blaydon, when he was a young vet so that he could run his practice there and nurture the family he and his new wife had looked forward to. They'd had three children, but Mr Wood had died when his youngest son Jack was only six.

The lilac trees on either side of the gate, which gave the house its name, seemed to beckon to Jack, their branches waving him on down the path, with every crunching step on the gravel leading him home. He turned his key in the lock, shut the heavy front door behind him, and rested with his back against it for a few moments, almost weeping with relief. Then he took a grip of himself – lights were on in the kitchen, and when he heard the murmur of friendly voices, he knew the family was here.

'So, Jack, how was it in the lion's den?' It was his older sister Ena who spoke first, her brown curls framing her plump cheeks as she scraped back her wooden chair. She stood on tiptoe to give him a peck on the cheek.

'It was awful. I regard myself lucky to come back in one piece.'

'I warned you,' said Ena. 'I knew . . . '

'Come on, Ena.' Her husband Peter peered out from behind his wire-rimmed glasses. 'Let the lad get himself a cup of tea and sit down before you start on him.'

Jack nodded at his brother-in-law gratefully. Everyone listened to Peter's opinions, always delivered in the same measured tones. He could be mistaken for a school teacher in his old tweed jacket with the leather-patched elbows, but in fact he was a well-respected GP.

Jack's siblings and their spouses were gathered round the oak table in the kitchen, with Mrs Wood at the head. Her usual kindly composure had obviously been shaken, and she was frowning as she presided over the big brown teapot. It looked like a council of war. His older brother Joe looked especially grim, his arms folded in front of him. His wife Annie squeezed his hand.

Mrs Wood cleared her throat. 'As you know, Jack, I asked everyone here tonight to ask what they think we should do, as a family, to help you in your difficult situation.'

'Thank you, Mother.' He reached up to the kitchen dresser, and unhooked a cup.

'I don't believe for a minute that bairn's yours,' Ena burst out. 'That family just want to get their claws into you, a nice boy from a respectable family. God knows who the father really is!'

'Well, we don't know.' Jack looked away. 'It could be mine.'

'So what the hell were you thinking?' A muscle twitched in Joe's jaw. 'Had you thought of the consequences?'

Jack raked his fingers through his hair. 'I didn't have time to think.'

'Anyway, you should have known better than to consort with the Rooneys and their like. I've heard they're a rough lot.' Joe thumped the table with his fist. 'All right then! Is it a question of money or are we in for a shotgun wedding?'

At the mention of a shotgun wedding, Mrs Wood put a hankie up to her mouth and stifled a sob.

'I thought about giving Alice some money, Mother, but I didn't even get to see the lass. I had to contend with the mother and her thuggish son.' Jack tugged at his shirt collar. 'Take a look, can you see the bruising? He damned near choked me!'

'That's no surprise to me,' said Joe. 'I was told in the Cross Keys that Martin Rooney's been charged with assault in his time.'

'But it doesn't mean his sister is in any way like him, does it, Jack?' his mother asked hopefully.

'I know nothing about her if I'm honest, except she has a reputation as a dancer. Everybody at the dance seemed to know her and she's won loads of cups. But I haven't seen her since that night, so I just can't say.'

'I'll bet it's not just her cups she's known for,' Ena said.

Peter gave her a disapproving glance.

'Anyway,' said Jack, 'they say it takes two to tango. She wasn't in the least backwards at making her intentions clear.'

'I'm sure she wasn't!' Ena said heatedly. 'I'll bet she knew she was on to a good thing! Alice Rooney is taking you for a ride. I know her type. You should have steered well clear.'

Mrs Wood wiped away a tear. 'But what if it is your bairn, Jack? Is it a boy or a girl, son?'

'It's a little girl, Mother.'

'Just listen to yourselves!' Joe barked. 'If you hadn't mollycoddled him all his life, Mother, he'd have had more sense than to land himself in this mess.'

Jack leapt to his feet. 'There's no need to take it out on Mother, Joe, and you can all stop talking about me as if I wasn't even here – I'm not a child.'

'Sit down,' Joe said, 'and listen to what I have to say. What's done is done. It's what you do now that you need to decide.'

Jack nodded and sat down slowly. 'I tried to offer them money to help with the bairn, but the brother and the mother want more than that. They want me to marry Alice.'

'Rubbish!' said Joe. 'That's just a negotiating tactic. There's always a price to men like Rooney. Trust me.' Joe was one of the town's leading insurance brokers and prided himself on his ability to drive a hard bargain.

'We want to help,' said Ena. 'Just tell us what we can do. We won't let you be pushed around by the Rooneys.'

'Perhaps I should just do the decent thing . . . ' Jack put his head in his hands.

'I won't have my son go like a lamb to the slaughter. The Rooneys will make his life a misery.' Mrs Wood dabbed her eyes again.

'What about the bairn?' asked Peter. 'Let's say she is yours, Jack. Do you want to leave her upbringing to the Rooneys? From what I hear it wouldn't be the best start in life.'

'Peter is right,' Joe said. 'And do you want your bairn to grow up without a father?'

'You've changed your tune,' said Jack. 'A moment ago you were dead against me marrying the lass, you wouldn't even contemplate an association with the likes of the Rooneys.'

'Well, I'm beginning to think you might be in too deep already, Jack.'

Mrs Wood straightened her back. 'Perhaps we should at least ask the Rooneys round and talk to them face to face. Anyway, I'd like to meet Alice.'

'Hang on a minute! Why would you want to meet the Rooneys, Mother? That would be as good as admitting I'm responsible for the bairn. And what if I'm not ready for marriage and fatherhood?'

'You might just have to grow up, our Jack,' said Joe briskly.

Jack's head was reeling. He looked at their faces, all focussed on him, all expectant. He thrust his chair back as he stood up and it fell over with a clatter.

'I didn't ask you to make my mind up for me,' he said bitterly. 'How about you all go to hell and let me make my own decisions!'

Chapter 2

Ena spun round from the window. 'They're here!' she said. 'There's only two of them. Three, if you count the pram!'

Mrs Wood took a last look round the room. Jack – now resigned to what was to come – and Ena had told her not to fuss, but she couldn't help it – she liked to make people feel welcome in her home, whoever they were, and part of that was making sure it was neat and tidy. She checked the spread on the dining table and when she was sure everything was to her satisfaction turned to Jack. 'You can let them in now, son.'

But it was Peter who went to the front door. Jack had just poured himself a shot of whisky to steady his nerves; now he downed it in one and wiped his mouth with the back of his hand. His mother's invitation had only extended to Alice and Mrs Rooney, but Jack had been worried that Martin Rooney might turn up. And he was nervous about setting eyes on Alice for the first time since that night by the canal.

Mrs Rooney walked ahead of Alice and the pram, mostly blocking Alice from view. She looked as though she had dressed up for the occasion in a green wool dress with an ancient fox stole draped around her neck. Peter helped Alice out of her belted brown mac and hung it up in the hall. She was dressed demurely in a cream blouse, an olive-green cardigan and a sensible skirt which fell below the knee. Her hair hung loose, a honey coloured ripple which curled round her shoulders. She was slender for a woman who had given birth only three weeks ago, Peter noticed.

Alice smiled at Peter. 'The bairn's asleep,' she said. 'I'll just leave her where she is.' She parked the pram in the hall.

'Come this way, ladies.' He showed them into the dining room, where Mrs Wood, Ena and Jack were standing in line as if ready for inspection.

'This is Mrs Wood,' said Peter, introducing her to Mrs Rooney. Mrs Wood put out her hand, but it was ignored. She took it back and fiddled with her beads. Trust the Rooney woman to snub her! What a downright lack of manners!

'And this is my wife, Ena.'

Mrs Rooney ignored her, too. Peter hastily gestured towards Jack. 'And of course, you know who this is.'

'Ay, we do, but Alice knows him better than me. You's ahl know who we are and why we're here an' ahl.'

Alice had made up her face with care. She obviously wanted to appear a different kind of woman this afternoon and she had chosen a coral pink lipstick and pale powder for her cheeks. She was wearing a 'butter wouldn't melt in her mouth' expression, like a vulnerable woman in need of a man to protect her.

There was nothing meek though, in the way she deliberately walked straight up to Jack, and planted a kiss on his cheek, claiming him in front of his sister and mother. Jack flushed red.

'Hello, Alice. You look well.'

'Hello, Jack.' She stood beside him and looked round the room. 'Ah see you've got a piano – Ah play the piano, ye know.'

'Oh, do you?' Jack said politely.

'Do make yourselves comfortable,' Mrs Wood said quickly, 'and I'll bring in the tea.'

'Won't you sit down?' said Peter, pulling out a chair for Mrs Rooney. He turned to Ena. 'Give your mother a hand in the kitchen, pet.'

Alice made sure she sat next to Jack. He was highly conscious of her, of the rustle of her skirt as she sat down, and as the faint scent of Coty revived the memory of his indiscretion on that fateful night, he flushed red again. Unable to think of anything to say to break the awkward silence, he looked at Peter, calmly polishing his glasses with his handkerchief, but he said nothing either. Mrs Rooney was scowling, while Alice fidgeted with her napkin. Jack was relieved when Mrs Wood and Ena bustled in to the room with freshly made tea and a plate of hot toasted teacakes.

Mrs Wood took her place at table, then settled to pouring the tea and handing it around. Passing a cup to Mrs Rooney, she enquired, 'Shall we be meeting your husband?'

Mrs Rooney gasped in surprise. 'Ah should hope not! He's gone to his reward.'

'What reward would that be?' Mrs Wood innocently asked.

'Are you tryin' to be funny, missus? My husband's long dead.'

Mrs Wood flapped a hand in front of her face. 'I'm so sorry, my dear. I didn't know you were a widow. My own husband died many years ago. I know how hard it is bringing up a family on your own.'

Mrs Rooney looked around the comfortable room, with its tasteful furnishings. Her eyes took in the porcelain birds and little figurines on the mantelpiece, her eyes lingering on a large marble bust on top of the piano.

'By the looks of your place, it couldn't have been that hard.'

Mrs Wood gave a genteel cough. 'Am I right in thinking you have three children, Mrs Rooney?'

'Martin, Alice and Peggy,' she replied tersely. Then blurted out: 'You've no idea what it'll be like for me if your lad doesn't do the right thing.'

'And what's that?' asked Ena.

'You's ahl know what's right. Your precious Jack should marry Alice.'

Ena laughed and shook her head. 'Why should he when he hardly knows her?'

Mrs Rooney turned to Ena, her face pinched with anger. 'He knew her well enough to get her pregnant, didn't he?'

'And how do we know it's his bairn?'

Mrs Rooney ignored the question.

'It's time he got to know 'er, an' ahl,' she said stubbornly. 'Fetch her here, Alice.' It came out like an order, and Alice

37

did as she was told. She came back and stood in the middle of the room, as stiff as a shop mannequin, with the baby in her arms.

She didn't look a natural mother, Mrs Wood thought, but perhaps it was just the awkwardness of the occasion.

Ena bent forward as if addressing someone hard of hearing. 'As I was saying, how do we know it's his bairn?'

Mrs Rooney pushed aside her tea and rose to her feet. 'Ah told you, Alice, we shouldn' have come here without wor Martin. I'm off to fetch him.'

Jack sincerely hoped she was bluffing – he wouldn't let Martin Rooney over his threshold, now that he knew what kind of man he was.

'Please stay,' said Peter, who had also got to his feet. 'I'm sure Ena didn't mean what she said.'

Ena's brown eyes were flashing. 'I meant what I said all right, even if it doesn't suit Mrs Rooney to give me an answer.'

'It is his bairn, I'm tellin' you.' Mrs Rooney glared at Ena. 'An' everybody knows it.'

'Hush, the both of you,' said Mrs Wood. Her voice was quiet, but there was an authority in it which made both women turn and look at her. She stood up, and walked over to Alice, holding out her arms. 'Can I hold the bairn?'

Alice looked at her mother for guidance.

'Gan arn then. Let her hold her.'

Mrs Wood cradled the child in her arms and looked down at the little peaceful face. 'She looks just like you, Jack,' she said quietly.

Jack heard Ena's sharp gasp, but he said nothing.

'Did you hear that, Jack?' Mrs Rooney goaded him. 'If your own mother can see the likeness, why the hell can't you?'

Jack remained dumbstruck. His mother's words had suddenly brought home to him that he was in all likelihood the baby's father, and that she might look like him took his breath away.

Mrs Wood smiled kindly at Alice. 'Is she a good baby? She looks a little pet.'

'I'm worn out. She kept me awake all night.'

Ena got up from the table to look at the baby. She scooped her from her mother's arms, and handed her to Jack. 'Here, it's about time you held the bairn – it looks as if you're going to be landed with her, whether she's yours or not!'

'Behave yoursel'!' said Mrs Rooney sharply. 'The bairn's not a bloody parcel.'

Alice spoke up. 'It's all right for her dad to hold her. He's got to get to know Lizzie, after all.'

Jack stared at the baby as if transfixed. He was holding his daughter, his very own flesh and blood. She lay in his arms and he studied her delicate features, the rosebud mouth, the waxy eyelids, the miniature hands with elegant fingers and nails like new moons. The other day at the Rooneys', that was exactly what he had felt, that he'd been handed a parcel, a burden. But now with his mother's words in his ear, it was as if a new possibility was unfurling in his mind. He could come to love this baby if he chose to allow this new feeling to grow.

Perhaps his daughter would have green eyes like his own, and her mother's slender figure. An inkling of pleasure, of pride, surprised Jack. Until now a baby had meant being trapped and unhappy. But what if he walked willingly into that trap?

The baby chose that moment to open her eyes and gazed straight at him. The brand new feeling of fatherhood stirred in him again. For the first time, he felt an urge to protect the baby flood through his veins.

'Lizzie, is that her name?'

'Yes,' said Alice. 'Ah hope you like it.'

Mrs Wood watched as Jack touched the tiny hand, and the baby's grip curled round his finger. The Rooneys might well be dreadful – Mrs Rooney certainly was – and it was too early to judge whether Alice could make her son happy or not. Alice was a mystery, standing there looking strangely detached while others held her baby. But Lizzie was just a little scrap of innocence, purity and hope – yes, the baby was a fresh start, a new life. From the besotted look on his face, her son would love his baby daughter, of that she felt sure.

Mrs Rooney, far from being pleased that she had proved her point, seemed infuriated. 'We're off,' she said abruptly. 'An' if you've any decency, Jack, you'll know well enough where your duty lies.'

He didn't answer her, but handed the baby back to his mother while he stepped into the hall and busied himself with the coats. Peter helped Mrs Rooney into hers, while Jack held Alice's for her to slip her arms in. Mrs Wood tucked Lizzie under her blanket in the pram, and gave her soft pink cheek a final stroke.

༄

The Wood family gathered at the window in the dining room and watched the Rooneys walk down the road. When they were out of sight, Ena spun round to confront Peter. 'How dare you tell that old witch I didn't mean what I said? And how can you be encouraging my brother to marry that girl? She's sly and manipulative, but Jack's too green to see what's in front of his nose.'

Peter shrugged. 'Now, Ena, you have to watch that temper of yours. Alice is an attractive lass, there's no denying that, and you're exaggerating. How can you judge the poor lass so harshly on one meeting? Where's your evidence of slyness?'

'Didn't you notice the way she smacked those lips on him, bold as brass in front of us all, then snuggled up to him at the table? It's all an act – womanly wiles.'

'Come along, Ena, we mustn't be uncharitable,' said Mrs Wood.

'And as for you, Mother,' Ena mimicked Mrs Wood's voice, "She looks just like you, Jack." What a lot of nonsense that was!'

Jack had to say something. 'Hush, Ena, none of this is Mother's fault. Just calm down, will you. I know you mean well, but you'll just have to trust me to do whatever's necessary.'

Peter decided it was time to go, and fetched Ena's coat. He held it out for her. 'Come on, dear, we're off. Your mother looks tired and Jack's got a lot to think about.'

'You're right,' said Ena. She kissed her mother. 'Well, Jack, all I can say is be careful.' She pecked his cheek, too, and Peter patted him on the shoulder.

As the front door closed behind them, Mrs Wood sighed. Jack looked at her face and could tell that the tea party had been a strain on her. She looked pale and tired.

'Perhaps you need a little lie down, Mother.'

'Ay, perhaps I do. It's given me one of my headaches.' She stroked her son's hand, and made her way to the foot of the stairs. Jack watched her climb them, and on the landing she turned to look at him as he had known she would. 'Such a dear little bairn,' she said.

❧

As the Rooneys rounded the corner, Alice turned to her mother and grinned. 'Ah told you Ah could handle him, didn' I?'

'Why are you so pleased wi' yoursel? Ah didn' hear a proposal.'

'Ah reckon there'll be one soon enough, Mother.' Alice nodded confidently.

'If there isn', Ah'm sendin' wor Martin round. We'll not let Jack Wood get away wi' the shame he's brought on our family!' Mrs Rooney tugged on her ragged fur collar.

'Keep Martin away,' Alice said sharply. 'You almost spoilt everything, the two of you. Leave it to me – and to little Lizzie.'

As she thought of the way Mrs Wood had fussed over the baby, and how dopey Jack had looked too, she smiled to herself. It was only a matter of time before she would be wearing Jack's ring.

Chapter 3

Mrs Wood looked at the clock on the mantelpiece and, catching a glimpse of her sad reflection in the mirror, straightened the new hat she had bought especially for the wedding. She forced a smile.

The hat was moss green velvet covered in tiny feathers, secured by a fine tulle veil. It was not the kind of hat she would normally wear, but at least the veil was long enough to cover her face if necessary.

She was beginning to feel the strain of the occasion already and the hastily-arranged day had hardly begun. She was glad Ena had come round and agreed to hold the reception, as well as taking in the newlyweds until they moved into their new home; it was beyond the call of duty. She hoped Alice wouldn't take advantage of Ena's generosity; she knew Ena longed for children and maybe her niece would be the next best thing.

Her thoughts were interrupted by Joe's voice calling from the hall. 'The best man's here and he hasn't forgotten the ring!'

She held out her arms as he came into the kitchen. 'Thank God you're here, son. Your brother's in a terrible state.' She held on to him like a drowning woman.

'Don't worry,' he said, planting a kiss on her cheek. 'It's only nerves.'

He stood back and looked her up and down. 'That's a hat and a half, Mother! I've never seen you wear anything like that before.'

'That's right,' she said, 'and you never will again. It's already earmarked for the church jumble sale.'

Joe looked at his watch. 'Where's Jack? We're due at the register office in half an hour.'

Mrs Wood walked wearily into the hall and, with a lump in her throat, called upstairs, 'Hurry up! Your brother's here!'

Jack was pacing up and down like a prisoner on his way to the gallows. He would miss his old room, his comfortable bed and the quilt his mother had made for him many years before. It had become a reliable friend on cold winter nights. He still had his old collection of planes that he'd loved when a boy. Time to say goodbye to that kind of thing. Taking a last look around the room, he resigned himself to the inevitable and went downstairs to meet his fate.

He heard a clatter of cups in the kitchen and went in. Seeing the strain on his brother's face, Joe patted him on the back. 'Cheer up, you're not going to a funeral. It might not be half as bad as you think.'

Mrs Wood poured Jack a cup of tea and Joe laced it with brandy. 'Get this down you, lad. Dutch courage. It's worked for me many a time.'

Mrs Wood frowned. 'Is that a good idea? I don't want him turning up drunk at his own wedding.'

'What about Mother's hat?' said Joe. 'What do you think?'

Jack put down the cup and took her hand. 'You look lovely,' he whispered, 'but can we go now? I just want to get it over with.'

He picked up her coat and placed it round her shoulders as he led her to the car. Joe hurried after them and pinned a carnation on Jack's lapel. 'There we are,' he said, 'you look more like a bridegroom now.'

Mrs Wood thought Joe's remark insensitive and squeezed Jack's hand as they piled into the car. Jack sat in the back, white-faced and silent before turning to watch the house he was born in slowly disappear from sight.

Mrs Wood saw the look of despair on his face and nudged Joe. 'How's Annie?' she asked.

'My wife was like a cat with two tails this morning. She's gone to Ena's to look after Lizzie until we get back from the wedding and she couldn't wait to get her hands on the bairn.'

'Sounds like she's broody, Joe. Isn't it time you made me an uncle? Time's marching on.' Jack raised his eyebrows at his big brother.

Mrs Wood caught the look on Joe's face and glared at Jack. 'It'll come when they least expect it.'

'You're right,' he said, knowing he was in no position to joke about such things. 'They certainly don't come when it's convenient, do they?'

'Ena's made a lovely spread, I hear,' Joe said hurriedly. 'Annie reckons she's been up half the night preparing a buffet that would make your eyes water.'

Mrs Wood took out her handkerchief. 'My eyes will certainly water, Joe, but it won't be over the buffet.'

She looked out of the window as the car pulled up outside a dreary, soulless building. This wasn't how she'd imagined her youngest son's wedding.

Jack watched as Joe helped her from the car and she studied the grey stone heap. 'Remember, this used to be the old town hall,' he said, 'but I'm afraid it's past its prime now.'

She looked up at the sad, grimy windows. They were badly in need of a shammy leather to rid them of the coal dust clinging to the glass. It all looked so gloomy. Even the sun was hiding and it looked like rain.

'We'd better get inside before there's a downpour,' said Jack.

They helped their mother up the countless steps and waited until she had got her breath back. She gasped when she stepped inside. The reception area was extensive. My goodness, she thought, it must have been a sight for sore eyes before they let it go to seed. A huge circular table boasted an attractive vase displaying what must have been proud lilies when in their prime. She peered inside the vase. 'Just look at this, Jack. Not a drop of water!' She sniffed the lilies. 'What a shame,' she said, 'they're going the way of all flesh, just like everything else around here.'

Joe pointed to a sign, REGISTRAR THIS WAY. They followed him down a long corridor with rooms on either side. It seemed endless to Mrs Wood but just as she was thinking about sitting down on a bench to rest, Joe turned round and smiled at her. 'We've found the room!' he said. So she straightened her coat, picked up her pace, and joined her sons outside the door.

'I think they've already started,' Jack whispered, 'we'd better not go in.'

Joe laughed. 'Don't be daft! They can't start without you!' He opened the door as quietly as he could and they tiptoed inside.

'Are you sure we're in the right place?' said Mrs Wood. The room was dark and dreary, without a flower in sight. Brown benches facing a large table seemed to dwarf a small man sitting behind it – Joe thought he looked more like an undertaker than a registrar. His hair was sparse and parted at the side in an effort to cover the expanse of baldness on top. His black jacket was shiny from wear and, as for his white shirt, Joe was sure his wife had never heard of Persil.

His eagle eye spotted the latecomers. 'I hope you know you've kept us waiting,' he shouted.

A group of people were gathered at the front of the room. Alice and Ena were there, with Peggy standing next to them. Alice waved at Jack and he reluctantly waved back. If only he could escape. The only good thing was that so far, at least, there was no sign of Mrs Rooney.

Alice caught Joe's eye and smiled. He thought she looked a picture in a silver satin dress cut on the bias that showed off her slim figure and a cloche hat with tiny rosebuds scattered around the brim, framing her face. All eyes were on her and Joe bet she was the envy of every woman in the room.

The registrar stood up. 'Just another five minutes,' he said, 'and I would have asked you to come back next week. So if you're ready let's get on with it.'

Jack took a few steps towards them and hesitated. The registrar raised his voice. 'Would the groom kindly come forward, please!'

Mrs Wood nudged Joe and whispered, 'Go on, you're the best man – do something.'

Grimly, he took Jack firmly by the elbow and glanced around the room before ushering him to the table to join Alice.

Ena's husband Peter was hovering at the back of the room with a small group of strangers. They must be Alice's friends, Joe thought. They had clearly begun to celebrate before they arrived and Peter looked uncomfortable – as if he might have to step in to control them at any moment. Then one of them noticed that something was about to happen and nudged the others.

A hush fell over the room as Alice and Jack held hands. The registrar cleared his throat. 'The bride and groom are now ready to make their vows. Is the best man ready with the ring?'

Joe nodded his head and stepped forward.

'Now Mr Wood, please repeat after me: I solemnly do declare that I know not of any lawful impediment why I, Jack Wood, may not be joined in matrimony to Alice Rooney.'

There was really no way out of this. Jack pulled himself together and repeated the words.

'I call upon these persons here present,' the registrar continued, 'to witness that I do take thee to be my lawful wedded wife.'

Ena's eyes were fixed on her brother, but this time, she was powerless to help. And now the registrar was turning to Alice, who looked as though she'd just won the pools.

Alice fluttered her eyelashes and stared adoringly at Jack as she repeated her vows. When she reached the part, 'I do take thee, Jack Wood, to be my lawful wedded husband,' Joe nudged Jack and passed him the ring. Alice held out her hand and, anticipating her new title, smiled at Jack. But he stood frozen to the spot. The registrar raised his voice. 'In your own time, Mr Wood, if you please.'

A feeling of foreboding came over Mrs Wood and she feared the worst, but Ena caught Joe's eye and he tapped his brother on the shoulder. Jack jerked forward and thrust the ring on Alice's finger.

'Now you can kiss the bride,' said the registrar. Alice closed her eyes and puckered her lips. Jack leaned forward and kissed her dutifully.

She looks like she's just died and gone to heaven, thought Ena. Jack turned away from the registrar and took

Alice's arm, escorting her back through the dingy room, past her cheering friends. Ena turned round and looked at her mother. Her heart sank at the sight of her, sitting on her own like a lost parcel. 'Come on, Peggy,' she said, 'let's rescue my poor mother.'

Peggy held up a box of confetti and began to cry. 'Look,' she said, 'Alice didn' wait for me and Ah wanted to throw this at 'er.'

'I'd like to throw something heavier than that at her,' said Ena. 'Come with me, pet.'

But Joe reached his mother first and by the time Ena and Peggy got there, he was sitting next to her, holding her hand. 'She's not well, Ena. I'll take her straight to the house, she could do with a cup of tea.'

Ena hugged her mother. 'Go with Joe, dear. Peter will run us back with Jack and Alice.'

As Joe helped his mother to her feet, Ena put a consoling arm around Peggy. 'Come on,' she said, 'let's see if you can throw your confetti outside.' They followed Joe and Mrs Wood out of the dingy building and into the fresh air. There was still no sign of sun.

Alice was surrounded by her laughing and jostling friends. 'Just look at them,' said Ena, 'it's more like throwing out time at the pub than a wedding. Thank God your sister didn't invite them to the reception, Peggy.'

As they watched, Joe helped his mother into the car and slowly drove away, down the gloomy street. Ena stood still for a moment then she drew Peggy over to the newly married couple. Peter was tugging at Jack's elbow. 'Try and get your wife into the car,' he muttered. Jack took Alice by the arm, but she snatched it away. 'Give us a minute,' she said, 'can't ye see Ah'm talkin'.'

Ena stepped forward. 'Never mind about them, Peter. Take us home – I've got a party to see to. Come on, Peggy, get in the car with me.'

'But what about Jack and Alice?'

'I've had enough. They can make their own way back.'

⚭

Mrs Wood sat in the dining room sipping her tea. What could be keeping Ena, she wondered. It's only a ten-minute drive from the register office. And what about our Jack? Young people have no manners today, but it's a bit much to be late for your own wedding reception. She sipped her tea again and looked around the room. It was filled with flowers, and the buffet was a work of art. It was laid out on a long table down the centre of the room, dressed in Ena's best lace tablecover and trimmed with silver horseshoes and white satin bows. She had even managed to find a wedding cake in time, which was a miracle considering how the marriage had been arranged in only a few short weeks. Mrs Wood admired her daughter's generosity, especially knowing how she felt about Alice.

Annie brought the cradle into the room and put it next to her mother-in-law. 'I've just fed the bairn,' she said. 'Keep an eye on her while I soak her bottle.'

Mrs Wood leant over the cradle and cooed at Lizzie. 'I wonder where your Auntie Ena's got to, pet.'

No sooner had the words left her mouth, than the door flew open and Ena rushed into the room with Peggy.

Mrs Wood sighed with relief. 'Thank goodness you're back. I was worried about you. The room looks lovely. Thanks for making it so nice for them.'

'I only did it for Jack, Mother. Try as I may, I can't take to that woman.'

Little Peggy sat next to Mrs Wood and shook Lizzie's rattle.

Mrs Wood smiled. She had taken to this adolescent girl. She found her demeanour gentle and her affection for Lizzie was plain to see. It was hard to believe she was Alice's sister – they were opposites in every way.

But this tender moment was abruptly interrupted as Alice burst into the room with Jack trailing behind.

Ena's eyes were like daggers as she glared at Alice and Mrs Wood shuddered. If looks could kill, she thought, our Ena would be up for murder.

Peggy ran to her sister. 'Come and see Lizzie! She's smiling!'

'It'll be wind,' said Alice. 'Ah'll see her in a minute.'

Jack bent over the cradle. 'You're right, Peggy,' he said. 'Lizzie is smiling.'

Alice sauntered over to Joe. 'Be a good lad and get me a drink. Jack's far too busy playin' the doting daddy.'

Annie bristled. How dare she treat my husband like a waiter! As Joe left to get the drink, she stalked over to Alice. 'Aren't you interested how the bairn was while you were gone?'

'Oh yes, Annie, how was she?'

'As good as gold . . . why don't you pick her up and give her a cuddle?'

At that moment Jack took Lizzie from the cot and placed her in his mother's arms while Peggy played 'little piggy' with her toes.

'See what Ah mean?' said Alice, pointing to the happy group. 'Ah'd have to join the queue to get a look-in. Anyway, she'll have to stay in the cot while we eat. Ah don't know about you but Ah'm starving.'

Peter sensed trouble brewing. 'Shall we eat?' he said. 'Come on, Alice, you sit here at the top of the table. And Jack, you're next to Alice, of course.'

Mrs Wood was watching Ena's stormy face. She walked over to her and took her aside. 'What's done is done,' she said. 'Whether you like it or not Alice is part of the family now, so for God's sake try and get on with her, even if it's only for Jack's sake.'

Ena scowled, but Mrs Wood knew her well. Ena might not like it, but she was going to do the right thing, she was sure. The bride and groom took their seats and waited as the rest of the family came to the table. Once they were settled, Ena began. 'As you all know, Alice and Jack will be staying with us while they save up to furnish their new home. We hope their stay will be a happy one. Let us all welcome Alice, the newest member of our family.'

Alice looked surprised at this, but said nothing.

Mrs Wood smiled gratefully at Ena, then stood up and put her hands together. 'For what we are about to receive,' she said, 'may the Lord make us truly thankful.' She glanced over at the wonderful spread on the table. 'And in this Depression, let us think of those who are not so lucky.'

Alice had to admit that Ena's food was delicious. There were different sorts of sandwiches, salads, cheese straws and little iced buns as well as the impressive wedding cake. She tucked in hungrily, in spite of the fact that Jack hadn't touched a thing. She was about to help herself to seconds, but before she knew it, Ena was passing a knife to Jack. 'Come on, you two,' she was saying, 'cut the cake and we'll make the toasts!'

Jack shuddered at the thought but the knife was already in his hand, with Alice – her arm outstretched – waiting to place her hand over his. Together they pushed the knife downwards through the soft layers of cake. Then Ena took over, cutting it into portions and passing them around, while Peter filled the glasses with champagne. He stood up and tapped the side of his glass. 'Can we have a little hush, please! It's time for some of us to say a few words. I'll volunteer to be first. When I was a medical student I lived with Jack's mother as a paying guest. You could say I married the landlady's daughter and you'd be right. In doing so, just like you, Alice, I became part of a loving family. The youngest member of the clan was

Jack, my six-year-old brother-in-law. I've watched him grow up and feel proud to see him here today with his new wife and their lovely little daughter. Please raise your glasses to the happy couple – Jack and Alice!'

Jack was a bundle of nerves. He was expected to speak, but had no idea what to say. He got to his feet and searched for words. Ena watched her brother struggling and when she could bear it no longer, stood up beside him and whispered in his ear. 'Do your duty, Jack. It'll be fine when you get to know each other better. We're all behind you.'

He stared at the familiar faces, all waiting for him to speak. 'I . . . I just want to say . . . I will take good care of Alice and the baby. I'll look after them and see they want for nothing.' He paused and looked at Alice. She avoided his eyes as he struggled for something more to say. He shuffled his feet and stared at the ceiling for inspiration. None came. Finally he shut his eyes and blurted out the only thing that came into his mind. 'Um, Alice and I don't know each other that well but I'm sure we'll get along just fine. Please raise your glasses to Alice and Lizzie!'

The colour drained from Alice's face. Peter raised his glass rapidly and said once more, 'To the happy couple! Jack and Alice!'

As they raised their glasses, Lizzie gurgled. Peggy lifted her from her cot and gave her to Alice, who kissed her on the cheek and passed her straight to Jack. 'Stay with Daddy,' she said. 'Yer mother's got a nasty headache an' she's goin' upstairs to rest.'

Annie took Lizzie from Jack. 'It's time for her feed. I'll see to it.' She waved at Peggy. 'Come on, pet, you can help.'

Alice stood up and glared at her new relatives. 'Ah'm honoured to belong to such a loving family that cares so much for themselves,' she said tartly. 'Thanks for the party.' She stalked out of the room and slammed the door.

The atmosphere turned chilly in an instant.

Mrs Wood burst into tears. The weight of the day hung round her like a ball and chain. She turned to Joe. 'When Annie's finished feeding the bairn could you take me home?'

'Take her home now, Joe,' Ena said. 'I'll see to Lizzie.'

Jack was filled with remorse. What would his family think, he wondered. Why hadn't he tried to stop Alice from walking out? He knew he'd made a dreadful speech. If only he'd thought before he opened his mouth. He watched in grim silence as Annie helped Mrs Wood with her coat.

Joe stood up to fetch his own coat but before he did so he gripped Jack's hand and looked directly into his eyes. 'Keep your chin up,' he said, 'it'll all work out in the end.'

Annie put her arm around Peggy, who was reluctant to say goodbye to her small niece. 'Come on, pet, we'll drop you off on the way. Goodbye, Jack. Don't be a stranger.'

Ena watched her brother's face as the others left. She had never seen him look so down. She touched his arm and patted his face. 'I'll put the kettle on, our Jack. You're still my little brother. Now sit down and Peter'll keep you company.'

As Jack sank into the chair next to Peter, the phone rang. Peter rolled his eyes. 'No peace for the wicked,' he said as he picked up the receiver, but his face grew serious as he listened to the call. He looked grave as he put down the phone. 'I'm afraid I have to leave,' he said. 'Old Mrs Clasper has taken a turn for the worse. I'll get back as soon as I can.'

'Shall I wait up for you, dear?' said Ena, coming back in with her tea tray.

Peter smiled wearily at his wife. 'Don't bother, pet, I might be late.'

❧

By ten o'clock, Peter had still not returned and Alice was still upstairs. Lizzie was asleep in Ena's arms. 'Take the bairn's cot to my bedroom, Jack. I'll look after her tonight. You'd better go to bed, Alice will be wondering where you are.'

He shook his head sadly. 'I know I've made a mistake but I made my bed and I suppose I'll have to lie in it.' He kissed his sister. 'Thanks for everything, Ena, especially taking care of Lizzie.'

He climbed the stairs and stole into the bridal chamber like a thief. The light was out and he prayed Alice would be asleep. His prayer was not answered but he got the next best thing.

'Is that you?' she said. 'Well divvn' think you're havin' your way with me after the way you behaved tonight!'

Jack sighed deeply and thanked the Lord for his reprieve.

Chapter 4

Newcastle upon Tyne, 1934

Alice loved her new home. She enjoyed living in a style so far removed from the one she had left behind.

Now here she was, a married woman, with her husband at work and the baby asleep, drinking coffee on her new sofa in the comfortable sitting room. She admired the curtains hanging on a proper curtain rail, unlike the tatty drapes held up by a piece of string in her mother's house.

She was proud of her home with its proper dining room, three bedrooms, a telephone and an indoor toilet and shuddered at the memory of the closet in her mother's back yard. She had come a long way in the months since Lizzie had been born.

But she could hardly describe her marriage as harmonious. It hadn't taken long for her and Jack to be at each other's throats, and now it was most of the time. The biggest bone of contention was her mother. Despite her insistence that they marry, she had ignored their invitation to the wedding and Jack had never forgiven her. On top of that, he couldn't stand her disgusting language. Things had got so bad he had put his foot down, forbidding her mother to cross their threshold.

Now, in retaliation, Mrs Rooney had stopped Peggy coming to the house and there'd be no one to help with Lizzie. Alice sighed. How could she cope without Peggy? There was only one thing for it – she would swallow her pride and pay the old cow a visit.

Next morning, after Jack left for work, Alice put on her smart brown belted mac, fastened Lizzie in her pram and set off for her mother's house. It would be hard breaking the ice on this first visit, but she would bow and scrape if necessary.

She was standing outside the rundown house she had once called her home when an uncommon feeling of gratitude crept over her. Thank God, she thought, this is only a visit. She straightened Lizzie's bonnet before knocking and almost at once the door swung open. Alice cringed at the sight of her mother. She was standing in the doorway, tight-lipped, with her arms folded. 'Well,' she said, 'just look what the cat's dragged in!'

Alice ignored the jibe and forced a smile. 'Hello, Mother. I've brought the bairn to see her grandma.'

'So at last you decided to pay yer poor ahld mother a visit, did ye? What an honour, Mrs Wood!' She looked in the pram. 'My God!' she said. 'They can never deny she's Jack's. She's the bloody spit of him!'

Alice struggled to remain sociable. 'How are you, Mam? You look well.'

Mrs Rooney glared at her. 'A fat lot you care,' she snapped, 'when your ahld man winnit even have me in his hoose. It'll be his la-de-da mother put him up to that, Ah'll bet!'

Alice slid her arm around her shoulder as she edged inside, pulling the pram in after her. 'Ah do care, Mother. Ah'll work on Jack, Ah promise, and Ah'm sure he'll change his mind.'

Mrs Rooney grinned. 'Stop his rumpy-pumpy – that'll do the trick.'

Alice ignored the remark and cast around for something to change the subject. 'How's our Martin, Mam? Has he got a girlfriend yet?'

'How the hell should Ah know? 'E tells me nowt. The only time Ah see him's when he wants his dinner. Nobody cares aboot me. You'se ahl be glad when Ah've gone to meet me maker; and the way Ah feel Ah divvn' think it'll be lang.'

Depression hovered over Alice like a black cloud. She couldn't wait to escape and return to her own home, but then she thought about Peggy and decided to stay. She'd come this far; it would be like admitting defeat to give up now. She needed to get this right.

Lizzie woke up and started to cry. Mrs Rooney rushed to the pram and began to undo the harness.

'Leave her in,' said Alice, 'we can't stay long.'

'Canna not give me grandbairn a cuddle? Divvn' worry, me hands are clean,' she added sarcastically.

Alice pulled her mother away. 'Stop it, will ye? Ah've already told ye we can't stay lang!'

Mrs Rooney ignored her and continued to struggle with the buckle. Alice pulled it from her, but Mrs Rooney held on to the hood and the pram fell over, tipping Lizzie onto the floor. Alice panicked as she scooped Lizzie up in her arms. Her lip was cut and her nose was bleeding. She ran with her into the kitchen and Mrs Rooney hurried after her.

'You auld bag!' Alice yelled. 'Ye've done it this time. Jack'll gan mad if he sees this!'

She picked up a tea towel, soaked it under the kitchen tap and dabbed Lizzie's face.

'Here! Let me look at 'er,' said Mrs Rooney.

'Get out o' my way, Mother, ye've done enough damage already!'

Alice put Lizzie back in the pram. She was still crying as she fastened her inside and made for the door. Mrs Rooney called after her. 'Ah hope ye divvn' blame me for this!' Her answer came as the front door almost left its hinges.

Alice hurried home, trying to think of an excuse that might exonerate her from blame. But knowing how Jack felt about her mother, she would be forced to conceal her visit and accept responsibility for Lizzie's accident. Then they'd have another row and things would be worse than ever. She needed to come up with something fast. Perhaps she could distract him, stop him from paying the baby much attention until the cuts had time to heal?

She had an idea and stopped at White's butchers. She would make Jack a special dinner that night. She went inside and chose the best cut of steak before stopping at the greengrocers for fresh vegetables. After putting the shopping in the pram, she looked at Lizzie. She had calmed down now and was almost asleep. Alice convinced herself there was nothing to worry about and quickened her pace on the way home.

Her spirits lifted as she turned the key in her own front door. Lizzie was asleep now. Alice took the pram into the kitchen and carefully removed the shopping. She missed Peggy but why did she have to visit the bloody old scarecrow? Jack was right. She's nowt but trouble, she thought. I'll see to the bairn tonight and with luck she'll still be asleep when he gets home.

But Lizzie suddenly woke up again. Her face didn't look so bad, Alice reasoned. The blood from her nose had dried and the cut on her lip wasn't quite as big as she'd first thought. If she could stop Jack from going up to her cot to say goodnight as he usually did, there was a chance she'd get away with it. The child shifted and snuffled a little. Maybe she was just hungry.

She changed her nappy and began to feed her, but as she held the teat to Lizzie's lips, the baby screamed and pushed it away. After several attempts to coax her, Alice gave up. She held her in her arms and walked up and down until she fell asleep again, then she managed to place her carefully back in her pram. I'd better start on Jack's special dinner before she wakes up again, she thought. She unwrapped the steak and picked up the tenderizing mallet. As she pounded the meat, she thought about her mother. Losing control, she thumped the meat harder and harder until it was so pulverized it looked like a pancake.

The noise woke Lizzie up. Alice glanced at the kitchen clock. It was six thirty and Jack would be home in an hour. She took Lizzie upstairs and got her ready for bed, but as she laid her in the cot she began to cry again. It was clear to see she was still hungry. Alice hurried downstairs and returned with a jar of condensed milk. Dipping her finger into the sticky milk, she held it up to Lizzie's lips. Lizzie licked her mother's finger hungrily and cried for more. Alice kept on feeding her until she fell asleep, then removed her finger from Lizzie's mouth and tucked her down for the night.

Alice tiptoed from the room hoping she would stay that way throughout the night. She went to her bedroom and rummaged through the wardrobe for something suitable to wear. Nothing gaudy, she thought, something more refined – more wife and mother style. She found the very thing. The cream shirt, olive cardigan and sensible skirt she had worn on her first visit to Jack's house. It still retained a slight smell of Coty, the perfume Jack had seemed so fond of.

She dressed and brushed her hair until it fell around her shoulders just the way Jack liked it. Then, once the mirror had approved her efforts, she went downstairs to cook her husband's dinner.

So far things were working out just the way she had planned – except for the steak. The juicy meat had been battered to death. Never mind, she thought, it wouldn't taste so bad with a spot of gravy.

She went to the dining room and laid the table using part of the dinner service Mrs Wood had given them as a wedding present, and to please Jack she would serve the vegetables in their proper dishes just like his mother did.

Alice was excited as she polished the glasses Joe and Annie had given them on their wedding day. She had bought a bottle of wine, hoping to put Jack in a good mood. This would be the first time they'd used the special glasses and she was sure Jack would notice.

She wound up the gramophone and placed one of Jack's favourite records on the turntable.

Jack arrived home to the sound of Richard Tauber accompanied by Alice singing 'You Are My Heart's Delight', and with the unfamiliar smell of something tasty coming from the kitchen, wondered if he was in the right house.

He tiptoed into the dining room and stood open-mouthed watching Alice dance around the table as she sang. She froze when she saw him, then smiled shyly.

Jack examined the table. 'This all looks so lovely, Alice, but what's it in aid of?'

She looked fretful. 'When Ah make my husband a special dinner, does it have to be in aid of something? You noticed the table but you haven't noticed how nice Ah dressed up for ye.'

'You don't have to compete with the table. You look lovely, Alice.' He threw his head back and sniffed the air. 'What's that wonderful smell coming from the kitchen?'

She smiled. 'Well ye'd better get yer coat off. It'll be on the table in five minutes.'

Alice rushed into the kitchen to camouflage the steak. She covered it with onions and for good measure almost drowned it in gravy. That should do the trick, she decided, and carried on singing as she spooned the vegetables into their proper dishes.

Jack was baffled by his wife's behaviour. When he had left for work that morning, Alice was all on edge and couldn't wait to get rid of him. Now here she was, killing him with kindness. Maybe she's had a change of heart, he thought. From the smell in the kitchen it had certainly seemed like it. He combed his hair, straightened his tie and hurried to the dining room. It felt so welcoming with the candlelight and the gramophone down low.

Alice came in and kissed him. 'D'ye remember this tune, Jack?'

'No, but it sounds familiar.'

She pretended to be hurt. 'They played it the first time we danced together. Fancy not remembering that! But Ah'll forgive ye. Open the wine while Ah get yer dinner. You're in for a surprise.'

How many more surprises could he take, he wondered. He noticed Alice had used his mother's china and smiled when he saw the glasses from Joe and Annie. They hadn't stinted: they were Irish crystal.

Alice came in with the dinner and placed it in front of him. Her eyes were focused on him as he picked up the knife and fork. He didn't disappoint her. After chewing a piece of steak with difficulty, he smacked his lips and said what he knew she needed to hear. 'It's lovely, Alice. And I appreciate all the trouble you've taken.'

She sighed with relief and sat down opposite him. He poured the wine and passed her a glass. 'Here's to us, Alice, and let's hope this becomes a habit.' They were clinking glasses when Lizzie woke up and started to cry.

Alice leapt from her chair. 'Carry on with your dinner, pet. Ah'll see to her.'

'No, no,' he said, 'I'll go up.'

He was halfway upstairs before she could stop him. Oh my God, she thought, this could be the end of my marriage. He'll go bloody mad when he sees the bairn. She tiptoed after him and stood on the landing. Lizzie's bedroom door was ajar and she quietly peeped inside to see him pacing up and down with Lizzie cradled in his arms. He turned and saw Alice standing in the doorway.

'Jack . . . ' she said.

'What have you done?' he hissed. 'Get out of here.'

'Should Ah put your dinner in the oven?'

He was white with rage. Without replying, he edged her out and closed the door behind her.

Alice was shaking like a leaf as she crept back to the dining room. The cold remnants of what should have been her greatest triumph were staring at her as though mocking her effort.

She looked at the wine and remembered Jack's words. 'Here's to us,' he had said, 'and let's hope this becomes a habit.' What was in store for her now, she wondered. Reaching for the wine they were meant to share, she filled a glass and took it with her into the sitting room. She slumped into a chair, allowing her eyes to take an inventory of her favourite things while contemplating her future without the comfort of her lovely home, when Jack walked in. His eyes were cold and he stood so close she could feel his breath on her face.

'Lizzie's asleep now,' he said. 'Is that what all this is in aid of? Did you think you could hide her until her face healed!'

'Ah can explain everything, Jack. It was an accident,' she began.

He held up his hands. 'I haven't finished yet. Did you think you could keep her out of sight until I left for work in the morning?'

Alice raised her voice. 'Stop it! Ye may as well know, ye'll only find out later. It wasn't my fault. Me mother caused the accident. She undid Lizzie's harness and the pram fell over. That's how she fell on her face.'

Jack struggled to keep calm. He lowered his voice. 'Did I hear right? You took the bairn to your mother's even though we agreed she was a bad influence on Lizzie with her swearing and troublemaking. I've heard enough, Alice. I'll take care of the bairn tonight. Get out of my sight before I do something I might regret.'

She didn't try to stop him as he made for the door and headed up the stairs.

Jack crept back into Lizzie's room, to find she was still asleep. He pushed an armchair to the side of her cot, covered himself with a blanket and tried to settle down for the night.

His head was spinning. How could Alice think of food with the bairn in this state? And how could she dance around the table as though nothing was wrong? How had he got himself trapped in this situation? He fell asleep asking questions to which there were no answers.

He woke up early next morning and packed a bag with what Lizzie would need for the day, then made his way to his mother's house, his daughter wrapped up warmly in her pale yellow blanket. His mind was in turmoil. Would his mother be asleep and would it be fair to involve her in his troubles. But what else should he do?

He paced up and down outside the house with Lizzie in his arms. There was nothing for it – he would have to wake his mother up. He was about to knock when Mrs Wood opened the door in her dressing gown and slippers. 'I saw you from the window,' she said. 'Is something wrong? Where's Alice? Anyway, bring the bairn inside. You look fit to drop. Do you know what time it is?'

He sat down with Lizzie. 'I'm sorry to come so early but –'

'Just give me the bairn, Jack, and make a pot of tea.'

She looked down at Lizzie's face and gasped. 'Oh my God,' she said, 'what on earth's happened?'

'Let me get the tea, Mother, and I'll tell you all about it.'

When he came back with the tea, he found Lizzie in his mother's lap, completely undressed. 'What are you doing, Mother?'

'Checking for any other damage to the bairn, that's what I'm doing. I'm sure there's plenty to tell, but let's make her comfortable before you start. Go upstairs and get the big drawer from the bottom of my wardrobe and bring down the little quilt and pillow from your old room.'

He watched as his mother turned the drawer into a comfortable cot for Lizzie. She lulled her to sleep, then gently laid her inside. 'There we are!' she said. 'Now pour out the tea and tell me all about it.'

Jack told the whole story from start to finish. There was a long pause. 'So what do you think, Mother?'

She sipped her tea and stood over Lizzie, choosing her words carefully. She could see how upset he was, and she was struggling with her own horrified disbelief at the state of her granddaughter's face, but giving in to that would help nobody. 'I'm thinking of this bairn, Jack. I know you'd like me to blame Alice, but if I do that I'd have to blame her mother too. Alice is a product of the way she's been brought up and I don't envy the kind of childhood she must have had.'

Jack looked shocked. 'But why did she hide the bairn from me?'

Mrs Wood put her arm around him. 'Calm down, son. It was fear. After you had forbidden her to see her mother, she was scared in case you found out that she'd defied you. Can't you see it's wrong to stop a girl from seeing her own mother? And can't you see Alice loves you and she's scared of losing you.'

Jack laughed. 'She's got a funny way of showing it, don't you think?'

Mrs Wood raised her voice. 'You committed yourself to Alice and Lizzie and you can't run off after the first hurdle. She deserves a chance to change – and we can help her. It costs nothing to show we care or give her a bit of praise now and then. It's something her mother never gave her.'

Jack tried to absorb what she was saying. It ran contrary to how he was feeling and yet he could see that it made sense. 'Well, if you think it would do any good, Mother, I'd give it a try. But how would we start?'

Mrs Wood saw a chink in his armour and smiled. 'I'll tell you how. First, ask Alice to invite me over for lunch on Sunday. Let's help her to feel she's got a family around her. But before that, you have to make it up with her. She's probably out of her mind with worry. Leave the bairn with me while you sort things out and bring Alice with you when you pick her up. Give the girl a chance.'

Jack hugged her. 'You don't know how much you've helped me, Mother.'

'Yes, I do!' she said. 'Now go and do your bit and remember the lass wasn't as lucky as you. You were loved from the moment you were born, and you'd better make sure you both give this one the same thing.'

Chapter 5

It was Sunday but as far as Jack was concerned this wasn't just any old Sunday. This was the day Alice had invited his mother to lunch. He was proud of the way she had set about her task with such enthusiasm, making sure everything was just right. The new crockery was out, the cutlery had been placed just so and the crystal glasses had been polished in readiness.

There had been a noticeable change in his wife. She spent more time with Lizzie and seemed more relaxed and understanding since he'd asked for his mother's help that day at The Lilacs and she had decided to take Alice under her wing. Mrs Wood had been especially kind to Alice since then and Alice was better as a consequence.

Alice was in the kitchen preparing the roast for the oven, when Mrs Wood put her head around the door.

'I hope I'm not too early, Alice, but our Joe gave me a lift.'

'Come in, Mother,' she said, as Mrs Wood had told her to call her. 'Ye can never be too early. Sit down and Ah'll put the kettle on.'

Mrs Wood scrutinised the meat. 'That's a nice piece of topside, pet.'

Alice's face lit up. 'Nothin' but the best for you, Mother. Ah'll be servin' it with roast potatoes, parsnips and carrots. And Ah can do a few peas if ye like.'

'For goodness' sake, Alice, by the time I get through that lot you'll have to wheel me home!'

Jack smiled as he listened to their happy banter. 'You two are getting on like a house on fire,' he said. 'How about I take the bairn for a walk while you're making the lunch, Alice? Then the two of you can talk behind my back!'

She laughed. 'Why not? It would do Lizzie good. What do you think, Mother?'

There was no need to reply. Mrs Wood's face spoke volumes.

Jack fastened Lizzie in her pram and set off. It was a lovely day. On the way, he stopped to admire the neat gardens in the neighbourhood and felt the urge to tidy up his own patch. Maybe, like his dad, he would plant a lilac bush one day. But for now, there were more important things on his mind.

Lizzie stirred in her pram and Jack bent over her. 'Guess who we're seeing today, pet?'

The baby beamed when she heard his voice.

'Who's my pretty girl?' he was saying when he felt a tap on his shoulder. It was Peggy. 'Where are ye goin'?' she said. 'Can Ah push the pram?'

'What a surprise,' said Jack. 'We're just on the way to see your mother.'

She pulled a face. 'Really? But she hates ye! She says 'orrible things about ye.'

'Is that right, Peggy? What sort of things?'

'She says yer stuck up an' selfish an' ye only pretend to like Alice because o' yer bairn. An' anyway, she says one o' these days she'll swing fe' you.' She leaned over to kiss Lizzie and noticed the bunch of flowers on top of the blanket. 'Who are these for?'

'Your mother, to sweeten her up.'

But as they approached the house, Jack's heart began to sink. Although he wanted to follow his mother's advice and build bridges with Mrs Rooney for Alice's sake, this wasn't going to be easy.

Peggy pushed open the door and shouted, 'Jack's 'ere. With Lizzie, Mam!'

Mrs Rooney lumbered into the hallway. 'Ah don' believe it! What the 'ell are you doin' 'ere?'

Good grief, Jack thought, her clothes are so creased it looks like she's slept in them. He held out the flowers.

'And what's this?' she said. 'On yer way to a bloody funeral, are ye? Ah'll bet yer sorry it's not mine! Anyway, Ah suppose you'd better come in now yer 'ere.'

Jack manoeuvred the pram into the hallway and followed Mrs Rooney as she shuffled into the living room. 'Don't look at the place,' she said. 'Peggy 'asn't lifted a finger ahl day and Ah'm too poorly to do the 'ousework. The doctor said to rest.'

Jack turned to Peggy. 'How would you like to take Lizzie for a walk, while I talk with your mother?'

Peggy's face lit up. 'Come on, Lizzie,' she said. 'Yer goin' fer a walk wi' yer auntie!'

They were hardly out of the door before Mrs Rooney squared up to Jack. 'So,' she demanded, 'what brings ye 'ere? Ah suppose ye want somethin'.'

'You're right,' he said. 'I do want something and don't worry, it won't cost you a penny. What I want is peace between us. Whether we like it or not, we're related through marriage.'

She took her usual pose, folding her arms ready for battle. 'Ah don' know aboot that! If ye could've got away wi' it ye'd never 'ave married ma lass. Ye didn' even believe the bairn was yours till yer mother said she looked like you!'

'All right, Mrs Rooney, you may think I behaved badly towards Alice in the beginning, but please try to understand,' Jack said, trying to keep a level head even though he was being provoked. 'I wasn't prepared for fatherhood or marriage – we weren't even a couple. I only knew Alice from dancing with her. And on that night I made a mistake, never thinking of what the outcome could be. But that's all in the past. The reason I'm here today is because Alice can't stand the hostility between us.'

Mrs Rooney softened a little. She put her hand in her pinny pocket, drew out her snuff box and took a pinch. 'Ah'm sure ye'd like a cuppa tea, Jack. Ah'll put the kettle on.'

Her nostrils were stained from the snuff, her fingers a dirty dark brown. The last thing he fancied was drinking her tea but he knew that sacrifices had to be made. He was about to sit down on the grubby sofa when he heard the front door open. 'We're back, Jack!' Peggy called cheerfully. 'She's fast asleep.'

He helped her in with the pram. 'That was a quick walk,' he said, 'you've only been gone five minutes.'

'Well, Ah didn' wanna miss anythin', did Ah? Where's Mam?'

'You won't believe it! She's in the kitchen making me a cup of tea. Who said miracles could never happen?'

Peggy widened her eyes but said nothing.

Mrs Rooney returned with two cups and gave Jack the one without the crack. 'Well, it looks like yer playin' the game by wor Alice. We'll just 'ave to see how we get on, won't we? Ah suppose Ah'll be welcome in your house now, won't Ah?'

'Why not?' he said, as he sipped the tea. Mission accomplished, he thought, and winked at Peggy.

⁂

He returned home to the sound of laughter. Alice leapt from her chair when she saw him. 'Ah've just trumped yer mother!' she shouted, waving her cards at him.

'What about that!' said Mrs Wood. 'I've been teaching her to play whist and she's taken to the game like a duck to water. She'll soon be playing in one of my whist drives.'

Alice grinned like a Cheshire cat. 'Can we play again after lunch?'

Jack could scarcely believe the warm atmosphere he'd walked into, but before he could comment his ears pricked up. 'Hang on,' he said, 'I think the bairn's awake.'

Mrs Wood held out her arms. 'Give her to me, Jack, I'll feed her so Alice can get on with things.'

He watched as she tenderly picked up her grandchild. Mother was right, he thought, giving Alice a bit of praise now and then had worked wonders.

Alice had laid the table just like she had done on the night of Lizzie's accident, but this time it was different. She felt secure now, knowing Mrs Wood appreciated her – and Jack seemed to be becoming the ideal husband.

She went to the kitchen and looked in the oven. The roast was just perfect. She drained the parboiled potatoes and placed them around the beef. If it hadn't been for Mrs Wood understanding her troubles, she might have lost Jack. Now here she was in the bosom of a happy family.

In the dining room, Lizzie was making the most of having her grandmother feed her and gulped happily from her bottle of milk. When finally she finished, Mrs Wood settled her in the pram. 'My goodness,' she said, 'that bairn's got a healthy appetite!'

Jack helped Alice carry in the meal. 'Come an' sit doon, Mother,' said Alice. 'Ah'm sure ye must be starvin'.'

'I don't know about that, but my mouth is watering at the sight of that roast,' Mrs Wood told her kindly. 'Now, if we're all ready, I'll say grace.' They put their hands together and bowed their heads.

'For what we are about to receive may the Lord make us truly thankful. And thank you for the loving family at this table. God bless us all.'

She complimented Alice on her table setting while Jack carved the meat. 'You're such a clever girl,' she said, 'and Jack's a lucky boy.'

Alice almost burst with pride.

cﾞ≤

After lunch, with Lizzie sleeping peacefully in her pram again, they took her into the living room and continued their game of whist.

'Deal me in,' said Jack, 'it'll make for a more interesting game. Shall we play seven-card this time, Alice?'

'No,' she said. 'Ah'm playin' much better now. Let's play thirteen.'

Alice cut for trumps and dealt out the cards. She nudged Jack and laughed. 'Ye'll never guess how many trumps Ah've got!'

'Don't let me see,' he said playfully, 'or I might trump you.'

Mrs Wood sat back, relishing their good humour, but there wasn't time to enjoy it for long – their peace was interrupted by a loud knock at the front door. She stood up to answer it.

'It's all right,' said Alice, 'Ah'll go. Just mind Jack doesn't look at me cards!'

She bounced out of the room. Mrs Wood smiled at Jack, but her smile soon faded as she heard raised voices coming from the hall. Suddenly the door swung open and Mrs Rooney charged into the room, followed by Alice with a face as red as a beetroot. 'Who the 'ell invited 'er?' she shouted.

'That's right!' said Mrs Rooney. 'Why don't ye show 'em yer real true colours!'

'I invited her,' said Jack. 'I thought you'd be pleased that we've buried the hatchet at last.'

'And when was this, Ah'd like te know?'

'It was earlier today when I took the bairn for a walk.'

Alice turned and glared at her mother. 'Well it didn' take ye long to show yer face, did it, ye bloody auld troublemaker!'

'Did ye 'ear that, Mrs Wood? Did ye 'ear the way she speaks to 'er poor auld mother?! Divvn' let 'er pull the wool over your eyes, because – just mark ma words – ye'll be next!'

'Shut yer gob, ye bloody auld windbag!'

'Did ye 'ear that, Mrs Wood? Well, just wait till you get to know wor Alice like Ah do! Your lad must be a bloody saint to live wi' 'er! And Ah kna what Ah'm talkin' aboot! She's a right little madam!'

Mrs Wood held up her arms and raised her voice. 'That's quite enough! You're behaving like fishwives!' She pushed Lizzie's pram towards the door. 'The bairn doesn't need to hear this, Jack. Take her in the dining room while I make a pot of tea. I think we could all do with one.'

She was glad to get to the kitchen, away from Alice and her mother. She put the kettle on and lowered herself into a chair. Her head was throbbing from their screeching voices and she felt a headache coming on. Alice's behaviour had surprised her. Maybe I got it wrong, she thought: she certainly didn't act like a girl who missed her mother. On the contrary, she seemed to regard her as an intrusion.

The kettle boiled and Mrs Wood mashed the tea. She was confused. This didn't seem like the same girl who had been the perfect hostess at lunchtime. Then she recalled how Alice had behaved at her wedding reception, apparently feigning a headache to leave Lizzie with Ena for the night. What a state of affairs, she thought. She picked up the tray and, making sure she hadn't forgotten anything, went back to the living room. Jack was pacing up and down with Lizzie in his arms, but there was no sign of Alice and her mother.

'Where is everybody?' she said as she put down the tray.

He shook his head. 'I wish I knew. Mrs Rooney stormed out and Alice ran after her, screaming like a banshee. Anyway, you look worn out, Mother. Don't go home. Stay here for the night.'

Mrs Wood smiled briefly and then told him; 'thanks, son, but I think I'll make my way home. It's not that far and the walk will do me good. And don't fret, I'm sure Alice will be back soon.' She kissed Lizzie, put on her coat and left with a heavy heart.

On the way home, she wondered if she had done the right thing. Should she have waited until Alice came back? But then again, the last thing she wanted was to be caught in the middle of a row between her and Jack. She couldn't afford to fall out with Alice, and the way she felt at the moment, that was something she couldn't guarantee. There had been a kind of detachment – coldness even – in Alice's response to Lizzie today and she'd been shocked by her uncontrollable temper towards her mother. Mrs Wood worried about her state of mind when it came to looking after Lizzie. Would the baby be safe?

Perhaps Ena could pop in to see the bairn while Jack was at work? She'd soon tell if there was something amiss. Mrs Wood quickened her pace. I'll talk to Ena in the morning, she thought, I'm sure she'll be happy to help. It was far from a solution to the problem, but a second opinion couldn't hurt. And Alice might appreciate the company.

～

Peter helped Ena on with her coat. 'Give Lizzie a kiss from her uncle and give her this.'

Ena fingered the parcel and wondered what it could be. Peter tapped her hand. 'Naughty, naughty,' he said. 'You'll just have to wait until she opens it. Now run along and enjoy yourself with Alice and the bairn.'

Ena had every intention of doing so, even though she knew she was doing her mother a favour by keeping an eye on Alice. Still, it was no hardship to spend more time with her niece. She tucked her gloves back into her pocket, as it was too warm for such thick ones now. The weather was improving as every week went by and she turned the corner into Jack and Alice's road with a spring in her step.

When Ena arrived at her brother's house, she was surprised to find the front door open. 'Is anyone in?' she called. 'It's Ena.'

'I'm in the sittin' room! Come in and shut the door.'

Ena did as she was told. She went inside to find Alice shouting down the phone as though the recipient was deaf while Lizzie sat in the playpen banging on a biscuit tin with a spoon.

'Keep her quiet,' said Alice. 'Ah can hardly hear what he's sayin'.'

Ena took the spoon from Lizzie and helped her to open her present. It was a box of building bricks in pretty colours. She scattered them onto the floor and watched as Lizzie picked one up and put it to her mouth. Ena couldn't help overhearing Alice's conversation. It sounded quite heated.

'Ah'd love to, Earl,' Alice was saying, 'but you know Jack won't stand for it.'

There was a long silence as the person on the other end clearly spoke at length. Alice lowered her voice. 'Ah know, Earl, an' how d'ye think Ah feel? But there's no way he'll agree. Ah'm sorry, but Ah'll have to go now, my sister-in-law's just popped in to see the bairn. Ah hope ye can find somebody in time.' She put down the phone and sank into a chair.

'Whatever's the matter, Alice? I hope it wasn't bad news.'

'No, not for me, but Earl Dixon's in a hole. Ah've had to refuse to do him a favour – and after he's been so good to me.'

'What a shame,' said Ena. 'Wasn't he your dance partner at one time? What did he want if you don't mind me asking?'

Alice lowered her eyes as she spoke. 'His new partner's broken her arm and he wanted me to stand in for her. Ah had to tell 'im it's out of the question.'

'Why? Wouldn't you like to do it, Alice?'

'Of course Ah would! Ah'd love to. Ah miss it so much. But Jack thinks ma place is here with the bairn so ye can see how Ah'm placed.'

'How many competitions are there likely to be?'

At that moment, Lizzie began to cry. Ena picked her up and cuddled her. 'Were we neglecting you, my little pet? Never mind, Auntie's here.'

'About the competition,' Alice hastily continued. 'There shouldn't be more than three, so there wouldn't be much rehearsin'.'

Ena bounced Lizzie up and down. 'Who's my lovely girl, then?' she cooed. 'Why can't I look after the bairn, then?'

Alice glanced at her sister-in-law to see if she was serious and then tried to hide her glee. 'That would be wonderful, but are you sure you could cope?'

'Of course we can cope, can't we, Lizzie? Why don't you ring Mr Dixon and tell him you've changed your mind?' Lizzie gurgled contentedly on her aunt's lap, clutching one of the bright new bricks.

Alice wasted no time in picking up the phone. She was so happy at Ena's offer. She fussed over her for the rest of the day, even persuading her to stay for dinner.

When Jack came home that night he was surprised to see his sister.

'I've been invited to dinner,' she said. 'As a matter of fact I've been here all day!'

'Where's the bairn, Ena?'

'She's fast asleep. Alice let me bath her and tuck her in for the night. We've had such a lovely day, Jack.'

Alice called from the kitchen. 'Dinner's ready! Sit down. Ah'm just fetching it.' She placed a large casserole on the table and began to serve the stew. 'D'ye remember, ye gave us this dish on our wedding day, Ena. Ah use it all the time.' She smiled at Jack. 'Pass the veg around, dear, Ah've forgotten the pepper. Ah won't be a minute.'

When Alice was out of earshot, Ena leaned over to Jack. 'Now don't go mad with what I have to tell you,' she said, 'but I've offered to look after the bairn while Alice does a friend a favour. Earl Dixon's new partner's broken her arm and Alice is going to step in.'

'Is that right?' he said. 'Well let me step in, Ena. There's no way I'll let Alice start that game again!'

'Oh come on, Jack, it's just a dance or two.' Ena glared at her brother in irritation.

'That's what you think, but I happen to know that once she starts she'll never stop.'

'But I've promised to look after the bairn, Jack – it's all agreed.'

Alice rushed back in and put the pepper on the table, oblivious to the turn the conversation had taken. 'Ah hope Ah didn' keep ye waitin'?'

'Did you hear that, Alice? It's all agreed? What right did you have to agree, before asking me what I think? You're a married woman with a bairn now. What do you think you're playing at? And you're no better, Ena, for letting her take you in.'

Ena's heart sank. What have I done, she thought, my brother knows her better than me. Even though I love having the bairn, I shouldn't have interfered.

Alice looked at Jack through veiled lids. 'Ah'm so sorry we've upset you, but it's not Ena's fault, it's mine. Ah had no right to think you wouldn't mind. Earl helped me when Ah was a newcomer and Ah'd love to do him a favour. But Ah won't if you don't want me to. Now eat your dinner before it gets cold. You've had a hard day.'

Ena stood up. 'I'm sorry I meddled where I shouldn't. I think I'd better go.'

Jack held on to her arm. 'Sit down! Don't be silly, but you should have at least asked me before making a decision.' He played with his fork for a moment, staring at the embroidery on the tablecloth. 'Well . . . as long as it doesn't become a habit.'

Alice kissed him on the cheek. 'No, Jack, Ah wouldn't dream of entering the competition now. You're my husband and you come first.' She held her breath as she waited for him to speak.

'Go on then,' he said. 'You can do it this time. But before making decisions in the future, discuss them with me first.'

Chapter 6

As the day of the dance approached Alice opened her wardrobe and swept back the hangers. She was glad she had kept her old dance dresses and examined them one by one. What about this? She took out a silver lamé gown trimmed with feathers and held it front of her. Oh bloody hell, half the feathers were missing. She put it back and rifled through the rail again, rejecting the pink silk satin and the red chiffon. Then she came across the dress she had worn on the night she met Jack – the one with the diamanté shoulder straps. She slipped it on and was admiring herself in the mirror when he came in. She turned around. 'Do you think it still fits, Jack?'

He felt weak at the knees when he saw her. The dress fitted perfectly. 'Come here,' he said. 'You look good enough to eat.'

She giggled. 'What are ye playing at, ye silly bugger, yer dinner's nearly ready.' He started to slip the straps off her shoulders.

'Be careful!' she said. 'Ah'm wearing this in the competition on Saturday.' He released her and watched as she unfastened the dress herself, allowing it to fall to the floor. He took her in his arms but she pushed him away. 'Let me hang it up first.'

He feasted his eyes on her figure while he undressed. It was hard to believe she had given birth so recently. Alice walked towards him. 'Ah'm ready,' she said. But he had just placed his hands on her breasts when Lizzie started to cry. He grabbed his trousers and buttoned up his shirt but Alice held on to his arm. 'Divvn' be in such a hurry to leave, Jack. She's likely to drop off again in a minute.'

He pulled his arm away. 'No. I'd better take a look and make sure she's all right. I'll be back in a minute – don't get dressed!'

Alice threw on her clothes. 'That's right!' she muttered. 'Put her first. You always do.' And with that she flounced downstairs.

❧

On the morning of the competition Alice checked the contents of Lizzie's little suitcase as the car drew up outside Ena's house. 'Ah hope Ah haven't forgotten owt, Jack, or your sister might think Ah'm a bad mother.'

'Shut the case and hurry up,' he said, 'or she'll think you've changed your mind.'

Ena was already waiting on the doorstep with her arms outstretched. 'Give me the bairn,' she said as they walked up the path towards her. 'You don't want to crease that lovely dress, Alice.'

Ena disappeared with Lizzie while Jack picked up the suitcase and helped Alice inside. Peter stared at Alice as he took her arm and led her into the sitting room. Jack followed behind.

'So, what do you think of my wife, Peter? How do you think she looks?'

Alice twirled around and Peter looked her up and down. 'You should be in the movies, pet. You look like a film star. Isn't that right, Ena?'

'Of course she does,' said Ena, as if there was no doubt about it. She passed her hand through her curls. 'And don't worry about Lizzie – I won't take my eyes off her for a minute. You won't forget about my hospital appointment in the morning, will you, Alice?'

Oh aye, the hospital, Alice thought. All those tests to find out if they could have a bairn. They'd better hurry up – they're not getting any younger.

Jack shook Peter's hand. 'Thank you both. What would we do without you?'

Alice hugged Ena. 'Just wait! You'll get your reward in heaven. And don't worry about the hospital. I'll be round at the crack of dawn.'

ᘐ

The Oxford Galleries were a step up for Alice. It was a feather in her cap to be chosen to compete in such a well-known venue, right in the heart of Newcastle. She stared up at the impressive building with its broad white façade. What an honour, she thought, as she climbed the marble steps that so many champions had climbed before her.

As Jack pulled open one of the heavy doors, she took in the elegant art deco work ingrained in the glass.

He held the door open while Alice stepped inside. A burly, dark-haired man, who looked as though he meant business, stepped forward.

'Come this way, Miss Rooney,' he said, taking hold of Alice's arm, 'they're waiting for you.'

'Excuse me,' Jack protested, 'I'm her husband and her name is Wood now, Mrs Wood.' He glared at the man's hand on his wife's arm.

'Congratulations, sir,' the man said brusquely. 'Wait there and someone will show you to your table, we always keep one or two reserved for family.' Then he whisked Alice away before Jack even had time to wish her good luck.

A tall, thin man in a dinner suit tapped Jack on the shoulder. 'This way, sir,' he said. He led Jack across the large hall, threading his way through the tables until he reached one near the stage. Then he pointed to an empty seat, turned on his heels and hurried away. Several other men were already seated. One of them winked at him. 'Sit down,' he said, 'you're new here, aren't you? Who are you supporting?'

'The lady's professional name is Alice Rooney.'

The man laughed. 'Oh yes!' he said. 'Hot Alice! We all know her.' He lowered his voice. 'She's fantastic if you can get her on the floor.'

'Hey!' said Jack. 'That's my wife you're talking about! I think that deserves an apology.'

'Sorry, mate, didn't mean any harm.' The man looked at him for a moment and then turned away.

Jack was saved a reply as the drums rolled and a large man came on to the stage, out of breath from the effort of climbing the steps to reach it. He was wearing a dinner jacket that was struggling to meet in the middle and a smile that said, *I'd rather not be here.* He stood in front of the microphone. 'Good evening, everyone. My name is Mr Edward Brady and I am honoured to be your MC on this important occasion: the Ballroom Championships for the North East 1934. And now, it gives me great pleasure to introduce the contestants.'

Jack glanced at the programme. Alice and Earl were last on the list. He could tell this was going to be a long night.

The first couple took to the floor and Jack watched as they strutted their stuff. They were all right, he thought, but Alice had nothing to worry about, she'd knock them into a cocked hat.

The next contestants seemed much the same to him and he began to feel bored. He looked around at his fellow supporters – like him, they didn't seem that interested in anyone they didn't know. They were knocking back the drink and their chat was getting louder – it seemed like an eternity before the MC made the announcement he had been waiting for. 'Our final contestants will be Alice Rooney and Earl Dixon.'

Jack was overcome by the sheer elegance of Alice as she floated on to the floor. She looked just as stunning as she did on the night he first met her at the dance in Blaydon. My God, he thought, there isn't a woman on this floor tonight who could hold a candle to Alice. Or a man in this room who wouldn't be proud to be called her husband.

Earl held Alice in his arms and as they glided across the floor Jack felt a twinge of envy. What I wouldn't give to be in Earl's shoes, he thought, but then again he wouldn't be driving her home tonight. Jack couldn't take his eyes off her. Nobody would have believed she'd had a child a year ago; she was as slim as ever.

Too soon, the dance was over, with Alice and Earl standing in a spotlight, acknowledging their applause. The MC came back on stage. 'Ladies and Gentlemen!' he said. 'The results of the competition will be announced in half an hour. While you're waiting, please carry on dancing and enjoy the amenities of the bar.'

Jack joined the queue and ordered a brown ale. He found a quiet corner and sipped his drink while listening to the comments of the punters. From the way they were betting it would be hard to choose a winner. Alice looked more at home here than he'd ever seen her.

He was considering another beer when the MC tapped on the microphone. 'Ladies and Gentlemen!' he called. 'Please return to your seats. The results are about to be announced!'

Jack reached his table as the final six couples returned to the stage. From the way the girls were dressed, it was hard to believe that Tyneside was in deep recession. They looked like they had stepped from a set in a Hollywood musical and the onlookers cheered at the dazzling sight.

The MC tapped the microphone again. 'Ladies and Gentlemen!' he called. 'Can I have your attention? I have the results.' He waited for the room to quieten before continuing. 'In third place . . . '

Jack tried to control his impatience as the MC paused for dramatic effect.

' . . . Number 5! Maud and Alan Snaith!'

The runners up looked disappointed, Jack thought, as they smiled bravely and stepped forward to accept a small cup.

'And in second place . . . No 3! Howard Rutter and Polly James!'

'You were robbed, pet!' a man shouted.

'And in first place . . . ' Jack held his breath. There would only be one fair result to his mind. 'It's No 6 – Earl Dixon and Alice Rooney!'

Jack got to his feet and punched the air. 'That's my wife!' he shouted. The tall, thin man who had guided him to the table earlier handed the MC a large silver cup. 'I'm delighted to present this trophy to our new ballroom champions of the North East, Alice Rooney and Earl Dixon!'

Earl held up the large cup and Alice kissed it. Jack pushed his way through the crowd to the foot of the stage and gave Alice a triumphal wave. She waved back and pointed to the cup.

♂♀

Alice was posing for a picture when Jack came into the dressing room. When she saw him, she smiled at the photographer. 'Go on, hinny, take one of Jack and me with the cup.'

'Of course, Miss Rooney. Where is it?'

'Come here, Earl!' she shouted. 'Bring the cup and get yer picture taken with us.'

Why does Alice want him in the picture, Jack wondered. She had said just the two of us and the cup.

Earl hurried over and stood between them, holding up the trophy. The bulb flashed and immortalised a delighted Alice and Earl, and a rather disgruntled Jack.

Alice rounded up her friends and proudly introduced her husband. Jack hardly knew what to say, especially to the contestants who had lost. They looked as though they'd rather be somewhere else.

A hush came over the room and Jack turned to see a smart man standing in the doorway, puffing on a huge cigar. Alice nudged him. 'That's Mr Davis, the manager.'

He strode through the room and turned to face the onlookers. 'Good evening,' he said, 'I've come to tell you all how proud I am to have seen so much talent on the floor tonight. It must have been hard for the judges to reach a decision. Now, let me congratulate the winners – Alice Rooney and her partner, Earl Dixon. Let's hear it for them!' After a hearty cheer, he went on, 'I would like to thank everyone who took part in the competition tonight. And in appreciation for all your efforts, please join me in the hospitality room for refreshments.'

Alice took Jack's arm. 'Ah'm starvin',' she said. 'Ah haven't had a bite since breakfast. Let's gan in, hinny, before there's nowt left.'

Jack flushed with embarrassment. 'Keep your voice down, Alice, or they'll think I starve you.'

There were two long tables, one covered in a display of sliced cold meats and a selection of salads; the other was packed with plate pies, sausage rolls, Scotch eggs and trays of tiny sandwiches. Alice filled her plate and dug straight in.

When the waiters began to serve the wine, Mr Davis cleared his throat. 'I hope you are all enjoying yourselves. And now please raise your glasses to this year's winners, Alice Rooney and Earl Dixon. Let's drink a toast to our champions of 1934!' He kissed Alice on the cheek and shook Earl's hand. 'Thank you both for keeping up the standard of this most coveted award. Here's to Alice and Earl!'

After raising his glass with the rest of them, Jack put it down and threw his arms around Alice. 'I'm the proudest man in this room tonight.'

Alice took his hand. 'Find me a chair,' she whispered. 'Ah'll have to sit down for a bit, Ah'm worn out.'

'Let me know when you're ready, pet, and I'll take you home.'

'Can we go now?' she said. 'Me feet are killing us and Ah'm that tired Ah can hardly keep me eyes open.'

Jack made her excuses and helped her to the car. She slept all the way home.

❧

Next morning Jack left for work without disturbing Alice. She was sleeping so soundly he didn't have the heart to wake her. Sometime later, the phone rang. She woke up with a jolt, grabbed her dressing gown and hurried downstairs to answer it. It was Peter and he sounded angry. It was only then that she remembered her promise to Ena.

'Why aren't you here?' he said. 'What about Ena's appointment at the hospital? It's already nine o'clock. How could you let her down? I'm disappointed in you, Alice, especially as Ena's been so good to you.'

Oh, my God, she thought, I hope he won't stop her from looking after Lizzie! 'Ah'm sorry, Peter, I'll get dressed and come straight over.'

'Forget it, Alice, it's too late,' he said and banged down the phone.

⚜

Alice stood nervously on Ena's doorstep and rang the bell. 'Ah'm sorry,' she said, almost before Ena had opened the door. 'Did ye get to the hospital after all?'

'No I didn't. I'll have to make an appointment for next week.' Ena looked pale and worn, older than Alice had seen her before.

'Ah'm sorry Ah let you down, Ena. Ah don't know what to say.'

'Stay there,' Ena said shortly, 'and I'll get the bairn.'

'Can Ah come in fer a minute?' Alice pleaded.

'I suppose so. But don't bother sitting down, I won't be long.'

Ena brought Lizzie downstairs and handed her to Alice. 'You don't know how lucky you are to have this bairn. She's as good as gold. I wouldn't mind half a dozen like her.'

Alice put Lizzie straight into her pram.

'Aren't you going to give the bairn a kiss?' asked Ena.

'Of course I am!' She bent over and pecked Lizzie on the cheek. Then she turned back to her sister-in-law, her face concerned. 'Ah'm sorry for the way Ah've behaved, Ena. Ah know Ah should've been there for you this mornin', but Ah'll do anything to make it up. Please don't let's be bad friends. It's thanks to you, Ah won at the Oxford Galleries last night. Who would have thought that? Alice Wood, champion dancer, 1934! If ye could just look after Lizzie until the competitions are finished, Ah'll be forever in yer debt.'

'I don't know, I'll have to think about it, Alice.'

'If only ye knew the difference it would make to Jack, Ena. He loves watching us dance. If you'd seen his face when Ah won last night, ye'd have thought he'd won the pools.'

'You know I love having that bairn, Alice.' Ena gave a long sigh. 'And I'd like to give you another chance, if I could depend on you keeping your word.'

'But Ah would!' Alice protested vehemently. 'Ah promise Ah've learnt me lesson.'

❧

One morning, not long after the competition, Ena sat at the table slowly sipping her tea.

'Eat your breakfast before it goes cold,' said Peter.

She put down her cup. 'I'm sorry but I'm not hungry, dear.'

'What's the matter, pet?'

'I'm just tired. Alice has been asking far too much lately. It was supposed to be three competitions and a bit of rehearsing, but it's been much more than that and I'm feeling the strain. I don't think I can manage much more of it, I'll have to have a word with her.'

'No you won't. I'll do it. I've got an hour to spare before surgery.'

'I'd appreciate that, Peter. I'd rather not see her.'

She held on to the arms of her chair and wearily got to her feet. 'Mind you don't make yourself late, Peter.'

'I won't.' He picked up her shawl from the floor and wrapped it around her shoulders. 'Don't worry,' he said. 'I'll be back before you know it.'

⁊⁊

Alice's door was on the jar. 'Is anybody in?' Peter called. He pushed the door open and put his head inside. 'Are you there, Alice?'

Alice was polishing her dancing shoes. Her ears pricked up when she heard his voice. What the hell's he doing here at this hour, she wondered, and just look at the state of my hair! 'Come in, Peter,' she shouted. 'Gan in the sittin' room, I'll be there in a minute.' She hastily ran a comb through her hair and hurried downstairs. 'Sorry to keep you waitin',' she said, 'but . . . Ah was just seeing to the bairn.'

97

He smiled. That's a change, he thought.

'Anyway,' she went on, 'what fetches you here at this time in the mornin'?'

'I'd like a quiet word with you, Alice. Shall we sit down?'

'Excuse me, Peter,' she said, 'Ah must have left me manners upstairs. Can Ah get you a cup of tea?'

'No thanks, I haven't got much time. I've just come to tell you what Ena hasn't got the heart to tell you herself.'

Alice screwed up her face. 'What d'ye mean? We get on like a house on fire!'

'Ena feels you've been taking advantage of her and I'm putting a stop to it.'

Alice was taken aback. 'What are ye talkin' about, Peter?'

'You've been taking advantage of my wife, Alice, dropping the bairn off whenever you've felt like it and picking her up at all hours.' Peter saw no point in beating about the bush. 'Ena's worn out and I'll have no more of it.'

Her face hardened. 'That's funny,' she said, 'Ena's never let on to me! Why didn' she say something if it was too much?'

'Because she's too kind-hearted, that's why.'

'That's rubbish!' Alice threw up her hands at the idea. 'Truth is, she could never get enough of the bairn – not having one herself.'

'That's below the belt, Alice.' Peter's voice grew harsher. 'Do you think we haven't longed for a bairn?'

'Well it's not my fault the two of you couldn't manage it!'

'And what's that supposed to mean?'

'You should know better than me, Peter. You're the doctor.'

'I've heard enough of this.' He got up and pushed his chair aside.

'And to what do we owe this pleasure?' Peter and Alice both started at the unexpected voice. Jack was standing in the doorway. 'I came back for my wallet,' he said. 'I thought it was you I heard, Peter.'

'I wish it was a pleasure, Jack, but I'm sorry to say I've just had words with Alice.' Peter stood up and headed across the room.

'It's not *my* fault!' Alice said. 'He came in here, shoutin' the odds, tellin' me Ah was takin' advantage of Ena! This is my home – it's not right!'

'What on earth is this all about, Alice?'

'Don't ask her, Jack. I'll tell you,' said Peter. 'It's about your sister. I've never seen Ena so run down. She's worn out from the way Alice has taken advantage of her, dropping the bairn off whenever she feels like it and never bothering to say when she'll be back. Most nights, when I finish practice, I find my wife asleep in an armchair.'

'That's nowt to do with me!' said Alice.

'It is to do with you! I came here to talk about this in a civilised manner. And then you imply we can't have children because I've got some kind of medical problem!'

Jack stared in disbelief. 'Did you say that, Alice?'

'Oh he's just jealous, because they can't have their own bairns,' said Alice dismissively.

'That's enough! I won't have you speaking to Peter like that.'

'Don't waste your time, Jack,' said Peter wearily. 'Anyway, I'll have to go now or I'll be late for surgery. I'm only sorry it had to come to this.'

As Jack walked to the front door with his brother-in-law, he turned and glared at Alice. 'Wait there,' he said, 'we've got some talking to do.'

Alice listened to their muffled voices, hoping to pick up a word or two. It's not fair, she thought. I was doing Ena a favour, letting her have the bairn!

Jack's face was taut when he came back into the room. Alice had never seen him like this before and sat upright in her chair as he slowly walked towards her. The tone of his voice was measured as he spoke. 'You've done some pretty ghastly things, Alice, but speaking to Peter like that – that was unforgivable.'

'Ah didn't . . . '

Jack took a step forward and she cowered. 'Easy on, Alice,' he said. 'What did you think? I've never laid a hand on you before and I never will.'

She stood up.

'Where do you think you're going, Alice?' Jack was forced to step back as she pushed past him. He called up after her as she ran upstairs. 'I haven't finished yet. I can just imagine what's been going on. From now on, don't expect my sister or anyone else to look after our daughter. It's about time you looked after her yourself. And you can tell Earl Dixon, there'll be no more competitions.'

PART 2

Chapter 7

Newcastle upon Tyne, 1938

Lizzie held on tight to Jack's hand as they walked through the big iron gates into the schoolyard. The old Victorian building had undoubtedly seen better days. It had been an almshouse at one time, until the council took it over and converted it into a school. It was sadly in need of repair, but then it wasn't the only building to be neglected due to the recession.

'Look, that's your new school,' Jack said as he patted Lizzie's head with its tousled mop of black curls. She squeezed his hand and looked at him with a smile that never failed to make his heart ache.

The playground was buzzing with mothers and their excited children. Lizzie had never seen so many people in one place. She was wondering where they had all come from and how they would fit into the small schoolhouse, when she noticed a tall, thin woman with red hair coming towards them. 'And who are you?' the woman asked.

Lizzie half hid behind Jack as he held out his hand to greet the teacher. 'I'm Mr Wood and this is my daughter Lizzie.'

'Don't be shy, dear. My name is Miss Birkstrand and I'll be your teacher.' The woman smiled down at her.

Lizzie slowly came from behind Jack and the teacher took her hand. 'Say goodbye to Daddy and come with me. I'll show you to your desk.' Miss Birkstrand gave Jack a knowing look. 'Don't worry, Mr Wood, she'll settle in, in no time.'

He crouched down and leaned forward to give Lizzie a hug. 'Be a good girl,' he said, 'and I'll see you later.'

She waved as Miss Birkstrand led her away and Jack stayed until she was out of sight.

⁂

Lizzie had never been in such a big room. There were rows of desks, with children already sitting at most of them. A giant desk at the front towered over the others and a blackboard like her tiny one at home, but much bigger, stood in a corner.

Miss Birkstrand showed her to a place next to a girl wearing a blue dress. 'This is Molly Brown,' she said. 'You'll be sharing this desk with her. And this is Lizzie Wood, Molly. I'm sure you'll get on together.'

Lizzie thought Molly a pretty girl. Her blonde hair fell to her shoulders in bouncy curls. She had bright blue eyes that matched her dress and cheeks like rosy apples. Lizzie liked the look of her and thought she smelt nice too.

Molly took Lizzie's hand and pressed something into her palm. 'It's a pear drop,' she whispered. 'Suck it, they last for ages.'

'Oh, thank you!' Lizzie said, putting the sweet in her mouth just as the teacher banged on the desk.

'Hush, children! I'm Miss Birkstrand.' She held up a large book. 'This is called a register and all your names are printed in here. Every morning, when I call your name, you will say "Here, Miss." Then I will know that you are present. I shall write a tick for present and a cross for absent. Now, here we go.'

She called out the names and one by one the children did her bidding.

Molly whispered to Lizzie, 'Isn't she tall!'

'Yes, she is! And she's as thin as a drainpipe!'

'Now pay attention,' Miss Birkstrand said, as she stood at the blackboard and began to write. 'I want you to copy these words on to your slates as neatly as you can.'

Jack had already taught Lizzie some of the words and she copied them with ease. Molly leaned over and looked at Lizzie's slate. 'Where did you learn that?' she whispered.

'My dad showed me.'

'Can I copy it, Lizzie? I gave you a pear drop, didn't I?'

Lizzie turned the slate so Molly could see it, but as she did so, she saw Miss Birkstrand frowning at them. 'No talking in class!' she called.

Lizzie pulled a face at Molly and mouthed, 'Sorry!'

Molly put her head down and tried as best she could to copy each letter from the blackboard, but Lizzie could tell she was struggling. In fact, by the time she had finished,

Molly was only halfway through. If only I could have helped her, she thought; I hope she'll still be my best friend. When the bell rang, Lizzie grabbed Molly's hand. 'Come on!' she said. 'Let's go out and play!'

They stood up together and hurried out of the classroom into the busy corridor. Children were spilling into the hall from all directions. Lizzie held hard on to Molly's hand as they rushed through the big school doors and into the playground. 'Look!' said Molly, pulling Lizzie over to one side of the yard. 'Hopscotch!' She pointed at chalk squares on the ground. 'Shall we play?'

'Ooh yes!' said Lizzie. 'Here's a marker!' She picked up a small stone from the ground and threw it carefully into a square. She was just about to hop forwards when two girls marched up to them. They were much bigger than Molly and Lizzie and they were both scowling. One of them had blonde hair and the other was dark. The dark one was really huge; Lizzie didn't want to get on the wrong side of her.

'Get off!' said the scary dark-haired girl. 'This is our hopscotch!'

'All right,' said Molly, 'we're just going.' She pulled Lizzie away and they ran to the far end of the playground. 'Never mind, Lizzie, let's play *I Spy*. You start.'

Lizzie looked around her, trying to find something really difficult for Molly to guess. 'I spy with my little eye, something beginning with, um . . . H!'

But Molly wasn't looking at her; she was looking past Lizzie at something behind her. 'There's a lady waving at you from the gate,' she said.

Lizzie turned to look. 'It's Auntie Peggy! Come on, you'll like her. She's lovely.' She grabbed Molly's hand and they ran over to the gate together.

'What are you doing here, Auntie Peggy?' asked Lizzie, jumping up and down with delight.

'Why shouldn't Ah be?' Peggy laughed at her niece's excitement, while buttoning her own coat against the wind that whipped across the playground. 'It's yer first day at school and Ah wanted to make sure you're all right. And who's yer little friend?'

'Oh I'm sorry, Auntie, this is Molly,' Lizzie said seriously. 'We share a desk together and we're best friends.'

'You're a nice little girl, Molly!' Peggy beamed at the child in the blue dress. 'And what a lovely head of hair you've got. Does yer mother put it in rags? Ah bet she does.'

'Only sometimes, when I'm going somewhere special.'

Happy to see how Auntie Peggy had taken to Molly, Lizzie jumped up and down again.

'Ah can't stop long, Lizzie, but Ah'll be seeing ye later. Your mother's invited Grandma Wood and me fer tea. Oh, and before Ah forget, these are fer you.' She passed Lizzie a packet through the gate. 'Bye fer now, girls, and don't let the teacher see the bag.'

Lizzie waved until she was out of sight, then opened Peggy's packet. An expression of delight crossed her face. 'Oh look, sweeties! We can share them.'

Molly took her hand. This was the best start to the term she could ever have hoped for. 'I think we'll be best friends for ever, Lizzie.'

⚕

Jack came home early that day, eager to hear about Lizzie's first day at school. And he wasn't alone. His mother was already there when he arrived, sitting in the living room with Lizzie and Peggy. They were firing questions at Lizzie when Alice called them into the dining room. 'Tea's ready!' she said. 'Don't let it get cold.'

Mrs Wood went in with Lizzie and sat her at the top of the table.

'Is that one of my best cushions she's sitting on, Mother? Well just mind ye don't spill owt on it, Lizzie.'

'What a lovely spread!' Mrs Wood hastened to say. 'And I see you've made one of your special cakes, Alice. Isn't that lovely, Jack?'

'Very nice,' he said, but he was already turning to Lizzie. 'This is for you, pet.' He handed her a package. She tore off the wrapping paper and screamed with delight when she saw the little red school bag with the shoulder strap. 'Go on!' he said. 'Look inside.'

It contained a notebook, coloured pencils and an envelope. Lizzie tore it open, took out a card and gave it to Peggy. 'Can you read this for me, Auntie?'

'Give it here, pet. It says, "To my clever girl, with love from her Daddy"?

Lizzie passed it to Alice. 'Look, Mam!'

'Can't you see I'm serving the salad? I've already heard what it says.' She glared at Jack. 'Yer ganna spoil that bairn. She only needs to open her mouth to get what she wants. Ah reckon it's a bit of discipline she needs, so for a start, Ah'll be takin' her to mass on Sundays. You won't mind if the dinner's a bit late, will you, Mother?'

'Why on earth would you want to do that?' said Jack. 'You haven't seen the inside of a church since Lizzie was christened.'

'Ah'm a Catholic and ahlways will be,' Alice snapped. 'The bairn was christened a Catholic and it's my job to see she's brought up as one.'

'As far as I can see, you're just trying to control the bairn and get your own way.'

'Ye can say what ye like, Jack. Ah've made me mind up and Ah'm takin' her. So let's hear no more about it.'

Jack turned to his mother. 'What do you think about this carry on, then?'

Mrs Wood knitted her brows. 'Don't drag me into this, son, it's something you'll have to settle between yourselves.'

She looked over at her granddaughter and noticed the worried look on her face – a far cry from the happy glow she'd had when she had opened her father's present. Mrs Wood had coped with Alice for the last five years for Lizzie's sake, but it was hard to watch her coldness towards the bairn today. She hadn't said a kind word to her on her first day home from school.

⚜

Lizzie loved school. She enjoyed her lessons and she had made a good friend. On days when Peggy couldn't pick her up, Mrs Brown would take her home for tea with Molly. They only lived down the road, which was even better. And today was a Mrs Brown day! She couldn't help smiling when she saw her at the school gates in her practical shoes and sensible coat, with her arms just waiting for a cuddle.

Molly's mother always had something tasty for tea and Lizzie loved eating there. It was all so friendly! The house was just like hers, but everything had a homely feel to it and she and Molly were never warned not to spill anything. Mrs Brown never shouted at Molly and when Mr Brown came home from work she didn't shout at him either.

Molly's mother was easy-going. They could do whatever they liked until Molly's bath-time. Sometimes Lizzie stayed to watch as Mrs Brown bathed Molly, wrapped her in a warm towel and dried her in front of the fire. She hoped, should she ever stay the night, Mrs Brown would bath her like she bathed Molly.

It was hard to drag herself away that night. It was cold outside and sitting by the fire at Mrs Brown's was so cosy. Lizzie watched the clock ticking forward and knew she would have to leave soon. What a shame she couldn't live here forever!

Her thoughts were interrupted by a loud knock on the front door. She crept into the hall as Mrs Brown went to answer it. As she had feared, it was her mother. Lizzie cringed when she heard her shouting at Mrs Brown.

'Ah'm Lizzie's mother and Ah'd like to know what the hell yer playin' at, keepin' her here till all hours.'

Lizzie rushed to the door and pushed in front. 'I'm sorry, Mam. It was my fault. Please don't blame Mrs Brown . . . '

'Is that right! So it was your fault, was it? Well just wait till Ah get you home!' Alice grabbed Lizzie's arm and dragged her outside. 'Take a good look,' she shouted, ''cos that's the last time you'll see ma lass in your house.'

Molly, who'd been hanging back in the hallway, started to cry. 'Do you think she means it, Mam?'

'Don't worry, pet,' said Mrs Brown with a heavy sigh, as Alice frogmarched her daughter down the road in the fading light. 'At least she can't stop you seeing each other at school.'

⁂

It was a brisk, cold Sunday morning as Lizzie walked home from her first mass. Alice, smart in a new mac and patterned scarf, pushed at her. 'Hurry up, Ah've got to check the oven.' The rosary beads clattered around Lizzie's neck as she tried to keep up. Alice stopped suddenly. 'Get them off!' she shouted. 'Rosary beads are for prayin', not for wearin'. Now hurry up or the meat'll be a goner.'

The moment they got home, Alice hurried to the kitchen to check the roast. Sunday lunch followed by whist was the highlight of her week. Mrs Wood never failed to praise her cooking and at teatime always complimented her on her home-made cake.

She was basting the meat when she heard the doorbell. 'Mother's here,' Jack called and Alice rushed from the kitchen to greet her. 'Come in,' she said, 'sit down and rest yer feet. Ah won't be long, Ah'm just seein' to the dinner.'

Mrs Wood cuddled Lizzie and asked her what it had been like at church. 'Well, it wasn't like a proper church, Grandma. It was the hall at the Co-op. You know, where they have the dances. The proper church is in Blaydon and it's too far away for the old people who can't manage the bus. And Grandma, you won't believe it! There was a man in a long black dress and a coloured pinny. He was drinking blood from a silver cup and eating the body of Jesus. I didn't know what he was talking about but Mam says I'm going to have lessons.'

Goodness, Mrs Wood thought. What an impression for the child to have of the Eucharist at her first visit to mass!

'And you'll never guess what, Grandma. My friend Molly Brown's a Catholic! She goes to Blaydon mass. Can I go to Blaydon mass, Grandma?'

'You'll have to ask your mother about that.'

'And what's that you've got to ask your Mam about?' Lizzie and Mrs Wood both looked round to see Alice standing in the doorway. 'Whatever it is, be quick about it, the dinner's nearly ready.'

'Did you know Molly Brown's a Catholic, Mam?'

'Divvn' be daft!'

'It seems she is,' said Mrs Wood. 'Lizzie tells me they go to Blaydon church.'

'Well,' said Alice, smiling from ear to ear, 'that makes ahl the difference. If Molly Brown's a Catholic, then there's no reason why the two of you shouldn't play together.'

Lizzie's mouth dropped open. 'But you had a row with Mrs Brown!' she said.

'Never you mind about that. I'll sort it out. Remember, you come from a Catholic family – at least on my side,' she shot a dark look at Mrs Wood, 'and you can always play with Catholic children. What do you think about that?'

Lizzie didn't know what to think. One moment she wasn't allowed to play with Molly and the next moment she could. But she'd been praying for this ever since the night she was dragged from Molly's house. Surely this was a miracle – and she'd only been to mass once!

❧

That night, Lizzie talked to God for the first time. 'Dear loving God,' she said, 'it's Lizzie Wood here. Thank you for your wonderful miracle. All thanks to you, I can play with Molly again. I love her but you are my special friend. Please watch over me. Love from Lizzie.'

Chapter 8

Newcastle upon Tyne, 1939

Lizzie stood at the bedroom window in her new party dress, nervously twisting one of her curls. Where could they be? Had they forgotten? She'd got their cards. She'd remembered because Grandma Wood's had 'Six Today' on it. So what was keeping them?

At last she finally saw Uncle Peter parking his car outside and ran downstairs two at a time, colliding with Aunt Ena in the hall.

'Whoops,' Ena said, 'you nearly knocked me over!' She was holding a parcel wrapped in red, shiny paper. Lizzie's eyes were fixed on it.

'That's pretty,' she said, 'is it for me, Auntie?'

'You'll have to wait and see,' said Uncle Peter as he helped Mrs Wood into the house. 'And look who's here, Lizzie!'

She threw her arms around her grandma. 'I nearly thought you weren't coming! I'm glad you're here, because I want you to meet Molly. She's my best friend and Mam said she could come to the party!'

Jack heard their voices and hurried to the hall. 'Thank goodness! At last you're here! Lizzie's almost worn out the carpet, pacing up and down. Come through and make yourselves at home.'

They were on their way to the sitting room when a booming voice stopped them in their tracks. 'Had on, then! Wait for me! Ah am invited, aren't Ah? Ah brought the bairn a present.'

They all turned to see Mrs Rooney standing in the doorway with Peggy.

'Behave yourself, Mother!' she whispered.

'Divvn' be daft! Ah can say what I like, can't Ah, Jack?' She was dressed all in black, apart from a splash of colour from the gaudy red feather adorning her hat. Most unsuitable for a child's birthday party, thought Ena. Had she been to a funeral, Mrs Wood wondered.

Mrs Rooney smiled at Lizzie, exposing her yellow, stained teeth. 'Ah, there you are,' she said, 'hidin' behind yer Auntie Ena, are ye? Come and give yer Grandma a kiss, then!'

Lizzie crept towards her and, shutting her eyes tight, pecked her on the cheek. Then, latching on to Peggy's hand, led her into the sitting room.

'Let's all go in and make ourselves comfortable,' said Jack.

Mrs Rooney barged in front, making a beeline for one of the comfy chairs while Jack helped his mother on to the sofa next to Ena.

Alice popped her head around the door. 'Excuse the way I look,' she said, 'but Ah've been at it ahl day. Ah hope Jack's bin looking after you?'

'Don't worry about that, pet, we've got everything we want,' said Mrs Wood.

'Sorry we're late!' Annie appeared in the doorway, followed by Joe. 'Look what we found on the doorstep!'

'It's Molly!' Lizzie shouted. 'I thought you'd never get here! Look everybody, this is my very best friend, Molly Brown.'

Molly looked a picture in her pretty pink party dress with matching bows in her hair. 'Happy birthday, Lizzie!' she said, struggling to hide something behind her back.

'Well, so you're Molly Brown,' said Mrs Wood. 'What a pretty little girl! Lizzie's told me all about you.'

'All right,' said Alice impatiently, 'now we're all here, let's get into the dining room.' She held back the door and waved them through.

'Ah thought you'd never ask,' said Mrs Rooney. 'Ah'm that hungry Ah could eat the hind legs off a donkey!' She stood up and, pushing past the others again, made sure she got there first.

Lizzie stared in disbelief when she saw the dining table. It was packed with trifles, fruit jellies and tiny sandwiches her mother had prepared herself. In the centre sat the most wonderful cake – pink and white with silver trim around the edge and six pink candles in the middle. She ran to her mother and impulsively threw her arms around her. 'It's the best cake I've ever seen!'

Alice stiffened. 'I'm glad you like it,' she said. 'It took long enough to make.'

Jack showed them to their seats. 'Come on, party girl! You're at the head of the table.'

'What about Molly, Dad? I want her next to me.'

'You're the boss today!' he said. 'Your wish is my command.'

Mrs Rooney sat down next to Mrs Wood and nudged her forcefully with her elbow. 'There's one thing Ah can say aboot mah lass – she's a bloody good cook.'

Peggy flushed, and kicked her under the table. 'Hush up, Mother,' she whispered, 'there's bairns present.'

Jack could hardly take his eyes off Lizzie in her blue organza dress. His mother had made it specially for the occasion. Alice had put her hair in rags the night before and the dark, shiny curls bounced on her shoulders. He thought his daughter looked a picture and his heart melted again with love for her.

Mrs Rooney sipped her tea. 'Ooh, that's bloody hot!' she cursed, then poured it into the saucer, blew on it and gulped it down. Trust the old bugger to show me up, thought Alice, and the way she eats, you'd think she'd been bloody starved for a week.

Lizzie couldn't take her eyes off the birthday cake. When is Dad going to light the candles, she wondered. I can't wait to make my wish. She clapped her hands when, at last, he held up the matches. 'OK folks,' he said, 'I hope we've all enjoyed the food. Now for the *pièce de résistance*. The birthday cake, made by no other than my wife, Alice Wood! And isn't it a cracker!'

Joe turned out the lights and Jack lit the candles. After they all sang 'Happy Birthday' at the top of their voices, Lizzie took a big breath and blew the candles out in one go. Alice was about to remove them when Lizzie shouted, 'Not yet, Mam! Light them again, Dad. I want Molly to blow them out with me!'

Jack relit the candles and together the girls blew them out.

Alice sighed. 'For God's sake,' she said, 'we'll be here forever.' She glared at Lizzie and stripped the candles from the cake.

Lizzie looked worried. If I say something nice, she thought, maybe Mam won't get cross and spoil the party. 'My mam made this cake, Molly,' she said. 'Isn't she clever?'

'That's as maybe,' said Alice, 'but we can't be here ahl night.'

Jack sensed trouble. 'Time for presents!' he said. 'This way.' They followed him into the sitting room.

Joe helped his brother to serve the drinks, and once the grown-ups had their glasses, Jack raised his hand. 'I'd like to make a toast to the apple of my eye. Here's to you, Lizzie!'

That's right! Don't mention me, Alice thought, brushing a few cake crumbs from her hands as she made her way into the room. I'm just the bloody skivvy in this house!

Lizzie began to open her presents. She picked Molly's first. Jack read out the card. '"To my best friend forever.

Love from Molly. P.S. I hope you like Liquorish Allsorts".'
Lizzie hugged her. 'They're my favourites!' she said as she peeled off the wrapping.

She opened Grandma Wood's present next. The paper was so pretty she tried her hardest not to tear it. Inside was a pink leotard and pink ballet shoes. 'Listen to this!' said Jack. He read out the message. '"To my darling granddaughter. You will need these for your dancing lessons. I have booked a course for you. Happy Birthday, pet. With love from Grandma".'

Lizzie tried on the shoes and danced around the room. Then, climbing on to Mrs Wood's knee, she smothered her with kisses.

'Get down!' said Alice. 'You're too heavy for your grandma. Go on, open the rest of your presents.'

'Come over here, pet,' Aunt Annie called, 'and see what we bought you.'

Alice faced Mrs Wood. 'Why didn't you tell me your plans for Lizzie?' she whispered. 'Did you not think it might interfere with her schoolin'? But then Ah'm just her mother so why should anybody care what Ah think?'

'That's enough, Alice,' Jack said sharply. 'You can settle this later.'

'Don't worry! Ah can see where Ah come in the peckin' order! She's got a cheek, bookin' dancin' lessons without askin' me first!'

'For goodness sake, Alice, it's the bairn's birthday. Make an effort and crack your face.' Jack tried to keep his voice down so Lizzie wouldn't hear but very nearly didn't succeed.

Annie gave Lizzie her present and helped her to open the box. Lizzie looked inside. 'What is it?' she asked.

'It's a game.' Annie took out the instructions. 'Give this to your mother and ask her to read them for you.'

Mrs Rooney glared at Annie and, without warning, snatched the instructions from her hand and tore them up. Joe leapt to his feet. 'What the hell's the matter with you, woman? Just look at my wife's hand!' Everyone was staring at them.

'It's nowt,' she said. 'I hardly touched her.'

Joe examined Annie's hand. There was a nasty scratch on the back of it. 'Just clap your eyes on this!' he said. 'It's more than nowt!'

Mrs Rooney placed her hands on her hips and sneered at Joe. 'Yer making a mountain out of a bloody molehill!' she spluttered.

Joe looked away, distaste written all over his face. 'I think we'll be on our way, Jack. I'd better see to Annie's hand. That woman's nails are filthy and her bad language is disgusting.'

'Did you hear that?' Mrs Rooney screeched. 'He's got a bloody nerve, yer brother! Are ye not ganna say somethin'?'

'That's enough!' said Peggy. 'Ah'll take her home, Jack.'

'Yes, I think you'd better or I won't be responsible for my actions.' Jack didn't trust himself to say anything further. His mother-in-law had been responsible for plenty of scenes over the past six years but this took the biscuit. What did she think she was playing at?

Peggy took her mother by the arm and almost dragged her from the house.

'We'd better go too,' said Peter into the silence that remained after their departure. 'We'll drop Joe and Annie off on the way. Goodbye, Alice, thanks for a lovely party. You did the bairn proud.'

Mrs Wood turned to Lizzie and Molly, who had been sitting silently by. 'Don't let these silly grown-ups spoil your party.' She took out her smelling salts. 'I've got a splitting headache, Jack. Do you think you could run me home?' She kissed Lizzie. 'Grandma's got to go now, pet, but I'll pop by tomorrow.'

Jack took his mother's arm and helped her to the door. 'Wait for me!' called Alice. 'Sorry you're leaving so soon and Ah'm sorry Ah was a bit brash over the bairn's dancin' lessons.'

'No, Alice, it's me who should be sorry. I should have asked you first. Now go back inside, you'd better see to the bairns.'

See to the bairns, Alice thought, as Jack escorted his mother out and the others followed. I'll be glad when Lizzie's in bed. She strode back to the kitchen and was about to start clearing up when there was a knock at the door. Who the hell's that, she thought.

Mrs Brown was standing on the doorstep. 'I've come to collect Molly.'

'Come inside,' said Alice, trying to make an effort. 'Can Ah get ye a cup of tea?'

'Thanks all the same, Mrs Wood, but my husband's waiting for me.' Mrs Brown made no move to step over the threshold.

Molly heard her mother's voice and ran into the hall with Lizzie.

'Can't I stay a bit longer, Mam?' Molly pleaded. 'We've hardly had any time to play together.'

'I'm afraid not, pet. Your dad's outside.'

Lizzie took Mrs Brown's hand. 'Can I come with you?'

'No you can't,' said Alice. 'It's nearly bedtime.'

'Your mother's right, Lizzie, come tomorrow,' said Mrs Brown. 'Hurry up, Molly. Say goodbye and thank Mrs Wood for the party.'

Lizzie followed them to the door. 'I really want to go with them,' she said. 'That was horrible, all that shouting. There's never any shouting at Mrs Brown's house.'

Alice dragged her back inside. 'Ah! Ah hear aboot's Mrs Brown! Why didn' you get her to see to your bloody birthday party!'

Lizzie stamped her foot at the unfairness of her mother's remark. 'I wish I had! Because you and Grandma Rooney never stop rowing! You make me sick!'

'You ungrateful little bitch!'

'I hate you!' said Lizzie. 'You spoil everything!'

Without warning, Alice slapped her across the face. 'Now had away and get ready for bed!' she said. 'And Ah won't tell ye twice.'

Lizzie ran upstairs two at a time and Alice hurried after her. 'Ah haven't finished with ye yet, ye little bugger!' she shouted, but Lizzie got to her bedroom just in time to lock the door behind her. She was all of a tremble as Alice tried to open the door. 'Let me in,' she screeched, 'or ye'll be sorry ye were born!'

Lizzie stood, shaking, with her back to the door, fighting back the tears. Alice started to bang on the door, but stopped abruptly as she heard the car pull up outside. Oh God, she thought, Jack's back.

She ran to the kitchen and pretended to be clearing the table as he came in.

'What's going on, Alice? I could hear the racket from the street!'

'Thank goodness you're back, Ah don't know if Ah'm comin' or goin'. That girl'll be the death of me!'

'What has she done this time, Alice?'

'You should've heard the mouthful of cheek Ah had to listen to. Ah had to send her to bed in the end.' She turned away from her husband, afraid she'd give the game away by the look on her face.

'That doesn't sound like Lizzie. And on her birthday, too! Let me talk to her.'

'Not tonight, Jack. She's sure to be asleep by now.'

'Well I'll just go and see,' he persisted. 'I'm surprised she upset you after you gave her such a lovely party.'

He began to climb the stairs. 'Don't bother, Jack,' Alice shouted, 'let her sleep, she's bound to be sorry in the mornin'.'

'No, I want to hear what she's got to say for herself.'

But when Jack got to Lizzie's room he found the door locked. 'Let me in, Lizzie. It's Dad!'

She half opened the door and after making sure her mother wasn't there, she let him in. He gasped when he saw the red mark on her face. 'And where on earth did this come from?'

The words tumbled from her mouth. 'It was all my fault, Dad. I was really cheeky to Mam in front of Mrs Brown, because she wouldn't let me go home with her to play with Molly.'

Jack shook his head but couldn't give way to what he really felt in front of his daughter. He forced himself to speak calmly, for her sake. 'All right, Lizzie, that's enough for now. Get ready for bed, I'll come back later and tuck you in.' Smiling gently at her, he closed the door once more.

Alice was waiting at the bottom of the stairs. 'Did you see her, Jack?'

'Yes, I did, and I'll bet you wish I hadn't.' His face was like stone. 'I'm warning you, Alice, that's the last time you'll ever lay a finger on Lizzie. The way you go on, it's no wonder the bairn wanted to go with Mrs Brown. With a mother like you, who could blame her?'

He turned his back on her and walked towards the stairs. Alice followed. 'Where're ye goin', Jack?'

'In case you've forgotten, it's still the bairn's birthday. I'm going to tuck her in and tell her a story.' He swung around to meet her eyes. 'That's something I've never heard you do.'

Chapter 9

Jack was in the sitting room with his mother listening to the news when Alice and Lizzie returned from mass.

'Sit down,' he said. 'You'd better hear this, Alice.'

'What is it?' she demanded, taking off her smart new edge-to-edge coat. 'You look like you've lost a pound and found a penny.'

'It's a little more serious than that. We've just heard some terrible news. Hitler's invaded Poland.'

She froze on the spot. 'Get away! You're kiddin'!'

'I'm afraid I'm not. We're at war with Germany now.' He switched off the radio. 'The BBC are repeating Mr Chamberlain's speech at three o'clock and you can hear it for yourself.'

'A fat lot of good Chamberlain did then!' Alice sneered. 'Sucking up to that little man with the 'tache.'

Mrs Wood stood up. 'This is no joke, Alice. I remember the Great War. Thousands of young men were killed.'

'Will this war kill more young men, Grandma?' Lizzie asked, not sure what all of this meant but certain it wasn't good news. She'd picked up on the tone of anxiety in her grandmother's voice.

'Let's hope not, pet. But remember this day, Sunday, 3rd September 1939, for it will go down in history, just like the last war did.'

'Well, if the Prime Minister's declared war, there's nowt we can do about it, is there, Mother?' Alice said dismissively, gathering up her things and preparing to go into the kitchen.

'No Alice, I suppose not and I expect we'll have to get used to rationing again.' Mrs Wood tried to repress a shudder at the idea. She had hoped she'd never see such times again, and wondered if the rest of her family even understood what they could be in for.

'Well, we're not rationed yet, so I'll get on with the dinner. I've got a nice leg of lamb. With roast potatoes and a spot of mint sauce, you'll forget ahl aboot the war.'

'What's rationing, Mam?' Lizzie asked.

'I've got to get on with the dinner. Ask yer grandma. She knows more about it than me. And don't wear her out! Ah know you. Ye'd want to know the far end of a fart.'

Lizzie ran to her grandma and sat on her knee. 'Well now,' Mrs Wood said, 'where to start? A lot of food we eat comes from other countries and some of it is brought here in big ships. Because we need the ships to protect us during the war, we'll have to do without the food they used to deliver, and to make sure the food we already have is shared fairly they'll give us a little book.'

'Will there be stories in it, Grandma?' Lizzie thought it didn't sound too bad so far.

'No, dear, it's a book of coupons you swap for food. You can use them for butter, meat, eggs and even sweeties. But you're only allowed so many. Mind you, some people don't behave fairly. They buy extra ration books and pay lots of money for them. This is called the black market. If people get caught doing this they can be sent to prison.'

'Good job,' said Lizzie. 'They're just greedy.'

'Yes, pet, and there are other people who fill their cupboards with tinned food like salmon, sardines and stewed steak, and those who can afford it buy sacks of sugar, even though they know there's not enough to go round. It's called hoarding.'

'I'd never do that, Grandma.'

'I'm sure you wouldn't, Lizzie.' Her grandmother sighed and stroked the girl's head, trying to reassure her. 'Anyway, we don't have to worry. Grandma will plant her Victory garden so we'll be all right for fresh veg.'

Mrs Wood looked over at Jack. She could tell there was something on his mind. 'A penny for them,' she said.

He paused, not wanting to put his concern into words, but then he came straight out with it. 'I was just thinking, Mother. It won't be long before they call up the lads at the training centre. With no wood and no pupils it'll just be a matter of time before I get my calling-up papers. I can cope with the inevitable, but it's the thought of leaving Lizzie behind that disturbs me.'

Mrs Wood closed her eyes briefly. She couldn't bear to think of her youngest in danger but she didn't want to betray her fear in front of him and especially not in front of her granddaughter. 'Don't worry, son,' she said steadily. 'I'll keep an eye on things.'

'Come and get it!' Alice shouted.

Once they were seated, Mrs Wood put her hands together. 'Dear Lord, thank you for our food this day and let us not take it for granted. We are about to embark on troublesome times, so please show us how to help ourselves and others worse off than us. And please help our leaders to bring us peace once more.'

It was all so different now, Lizzie thought. We used to talk about nice things at Sunday lunch. Grandma would ask about school and what Molly was up to and sometimes they'd talk about recipes or the price of food. Now all they're talking about is war.

⁂

There were many changes for Lizzie as the weeks went by. A strange new building was erected in the school playground. A red-brick house without windows. It was called an air raid shelter. Inside were three long benches, a first aid box and a tin of hard mint sweets called Black Bullets.

One chilly morning, the children were instructed to assemble in the playground for their first air raid practice. The noise of all the different classes together was deafening. 'What's going on?' asked Mollie.

'Be quiet,' Lizzie whispered, 'there's the headmaster.'

Mr Sowerby stood in front of the waiting children. He was a scrawny little man with greasy, see-through hair and bony fingers. 'Now,' he said, peering through his steel-rimmed glasses, 'when I blow this whistle you will march into the shelter in an orderly manner and sit on a bench. Is that clear?' He tapped the side of his leg with his well-worn cane. 'On the left, quick march!'

Lizzie and Molly both knew their right leg from their left, unlike some of the others. They were halfway across the playground when several children bumped into each other.

Mr Sowerby blew hard on his whistle. 'Maybe when this pantomime's over, we can get on with it!'

'But what about my trousers, sir? I've split my pocket,' protested one of the boys from the class above theirs.

'Never mind your trousers, boy!' Mr Sowerby lifted his cane. 'You see this? Well, you'll be feeling it in a minute! Get back into line, the lot of you.'

After several attempts, the children managed to form a line outside the entrance to the shelter. Lizzie and Molly were near the front. They squinted as they went inside. The light was dim. They carefully felt their way to a bench at the far end, a safe distance from the headmaster, who was sitting near the entrance with his scary cane.

When everyone was seated, Mr Sowerby marched up and down with a large tin in his hands. 'Now children,' he said, 'I'll be giving you one black bullet each.'

'Oh Molly, they're my favourite! You can suck them for hours!' said Lizzie.

'Do not place this sweet in your mouth,' he continued, 'until we have finished singing.' But most of them were already sucking it. When he began to sing 'Land of Hope and Glory', there was a sound like hailstones as the Black Bullets were spat on to the stone floor.

'What's that noise!' he said.

A lone voice spoke up. 'It's an air raid, sir!'

Mr Sowerby's eyes narrowed and his face became contorted. 'Whoever said that, come forward or I'll punish the lot of you!'

The culprit was almost thrown into the old man's scrawny grasp. Everyone was afraid of Mr Sowerby and his long, flexible stick.

Lizzie couldn't wait to leave the shelter.

⚜

Jack was standing at the school gates. He had left work early to pick up Lizzie. His calling-up papers could arrive any day now, and the thought of leaving Lizzie alone with Alice worried him. What can I do, he wondered. How can I compensate her for my absence? The poor bairn hadn't even started her dancing lessons yet – no one had dared to raise the subject with Alice after her outburst on Lizzie's birthday and now months had passed. He racked his brains to think of something that Lizzie would like and then inspiration struck him – maybe a pet might help. Something she could look after herself. Something Alice couldn't object to on the grounds it would be too much trouble. He remembered the rabbit his mother had given him when his father died. It had worked for him – it could be the very thing.

At last school was out and children poured out of the building, eagerly seeking their parents.

Lizzie saw her dad waiting at the school gates and ran into his arms. She looked worried. 'Does Mam know you're here, Dad?' She knew how her mother hated it when her dad turned up unexpectedly and it usually meant they'd be in for a big row later.

'Never mind about that,' he said, his eyes shining, 'we're going to the pet shop to look at the animals. Mrs Brown knows you're with me so don't you worry.'

Lizzie looked up at him in amazement. She'd always wanted to go there but Mam had never allowed her, saying it would be a waste of time and money. She couldn't quite believe this was happening now. Well, she wasn't going to object.

When they got to the pet shop, Lizzie let go of Jack's hand and ran straight inside. She hardly knew which way to turn, there were so many adorable animals along each side, most of them behind wire bars, with a few in glass tanks. A fearsome-looking parrot gazed down at her from its perch by the till, and she hastily moved away from it. She was drooling over a cage of puppies when her father tapped her on the shoulder. 'Lovely, aren't they? But they're Alsatians and they grow very big. They need lots of exercise so I don't think your mam would agree to one of those, pet.'

Lizzie lowered her eyes and tried to hide her disappointment as she turned and left the cage behind. She was making her way to the fish tank when she was startled by a screeching voice repeatedly calling, 'Good mornin', Missus!' She turned around and spotted the culprit. It was the big colourful parrot sitting on its high perch, tethered by its leg to a long pole. She laughed. 'Mam wouldn't like one of those, either. He's far too noisy!'

Jack took her hand and led her to the rabbit enclosure. There were three rabbits inside. One was brown with white markings and another was grey all over. They were very lively. The third rabbit was sitting quietly in a corner on its own and was completely black except for a white patch over one eye.

'Look at him, Dad! Do you think he's lonely?' Lizzie breathed.

'Yes, I do. Would you like to take him home with you?'

Her mouth fell open and her eyes almost popped out of her head. 'Can I, Dad?' she asked. 'Can I really?'

'Do I ever make a promise I don't keep?'

Lizzie flung her arms around his neck and almost strangled him with gratitude. Then a worrying thought crossed her mind. She tugged at Jack's sleeve. 'What do you think Mam will say about the rabbit, Dad?'

'Don't worry,' he said. 'Leave it to me. Have you thought of a name for him yet?'

Her face lit up. 'Yes I have – it's Patch!'

Jack paid for the biggest available hutch along with enough hay and sawdust to last for months. It would be delivered that day and they would collect Patch the following morning when the hutch was assembled.

⁕

Lizzie could hardly wait to tell Molly about Patch. As soon as she could get away she hurried to her house. As usual, the door was open. 'Anyone in?' she called.

'Come in!' Molly shouted. 'I'm in the kitchen. Mam's out shopping. She's always shopping nowadays.'

'You'll never guess what I've got,' said Lizzie. 'A rabbit!'

Molly turned in astonishment. 'Does your mother know?'

'Well . . . not yet, but Dad's promised to tell her before we collect him tomorrow. And you can stroke him if you like.'

'Well', said Molly, 'I'll believe it when I see it. Anyway, look what we've got!' Molly opened the larder door and Lizzie's eyes widened. It was stacked floor to ceiling with tins of corned beef and suet puddings. Tinned fruits and packets of biscuits sat on shelves beside boiled sweets and bars of chocolate.

Lizzie gasped. 'I don't believe it! Your mother's in the black market! Grandma said it's against the law to hoard food. Doesn't your mother know there's a war on?'

'Of course she does. Why d'you think she's collecting it?' She noticed Lizzie's accusing glance. 'Anyway it's not your business. And don't you dare tell Mam I've shown it to you.' She banged the larder door shut. 'I thought you were my friend, Lizzie.'

'I am your friend. That's why I'm telling you. Grandma told me about the black market and I don't want your mam to go to prison.'

'Nobody's going to prison,' Molly said. 'Why don't you just go home? And don't dare tell what you've seen.' The atmosphere had turned frosty suddenly and the afternoon was spoilt.

Lizzie wished she had kept her mouth shut. Supposing she'd lost her best friend, just for the sake of a bit of food. She did as Molly had asked and set off sadly for home. Maybe I should go back and say sorry, she thought, but she might still be angry with me. No, I'll make it up with her in the morning.

As her house came into view, she began to wonder about Patch. Had Dad told her mother about him yet? And what if they'd had another row? She decided to go in by the back door and tiptoed into the garden. Jack was there with a hammer knocking a nail in what Lizzie thought to be the fence, until he turned around . . . and there it was! The rabbit hutch!

He looked disappointed when he saw her. 'I wanted to have it up before you got back. Anyway, what do you think?'

Lizzie couldn't think. Her mind was racing. Had he told her mother, she wondered, and if he had, what did she say? It's very quiet around here, maybe he's killed her!

At last she found the courage to ask, 'Does Mam know about Patch?'

'Don't you worry about that,' he said, 'it's all been sorted. Now, let's talk about something more important! What colour shall we paint the hutch?'

⚓

Jack got up early next morning and made his way to the pet shop to pick up the rabbit. It would be in the hutch before Lizzie came down to breakfast. He had not been home long before Lizzie burst into the dining room. 'Today's the day! When can we go and get him, Dad?' She could barely get the words out, she was so excited.

'Well, hadn't you better see if the paint is dry on the hutch first?'

Lizzie ran into the garden. Jack stood at the back door and watched as she tested the paint with her fingers. Then, as she opened the hutch and looked inside, her arm slowly disappeared from view. Jack heard her cry out and his eyes watered as she drew back from the hutch, cradling the rabbit in her arms.

The tender moment was interrupted by Alice's voice. 'Are you comin' in for breakfast or what! Ah didn' cook it to gan cold.'

Jack hurried into the garden. He gently took the rabbit from Lizzie and put him back in the hutch. 'Go along, pet, don't keep yer mam waiting. Tell her I'll be there in a minute.'

By the time he got back, the breakfast was on the table, and his daughter's attention was firmly fixed on her plate.

'Oh look, Daddy,' Lizzie said as she put her fork into her egg, 'there's two yolks! Why's that, Dad? Why's that?'

'That girl never stops asking questions,' Alice muttered. 'Just get on wi' yer breakfast, Lizzie, Ah haven't got ahl day.'

'Why can't you be civil to the bairn, Alice?' Jack sighed, thinking that for once it would be nice to eat their food in peace. 'You can't blame her for asking questions and in any case you never seem to answer any.'

'Ah let her 'ave the rabbit, didn' Ah? Anyway, Ah can't stay. Ah've got to put the washing on.'

Lizzie and Jack finished their breakfast, while Alice banged about in the kitchen.

'Come on, Dad!' said Lizzie. 'Let's go back and see Patch!'

'All right, pet.' But just as he got to his feet, the doorbell rang.

'Molly's here!' Alice shouted. 'I'll bet she's come to see the rabbit, Dad!'

'Well, don't keep her waiting,' said Jack. 'Come on through, Molly.'

Lizzie stood up to hug her. 'Are we still friends?' she asked.

'What do you think?' said Molly. 'What a stupid question! Where's that rabbit, then? I've got a present for him. I hope he likes turnip. I would have brought carrots but Mam cooked them for dinner last night.'

Jack opened the back door. 'Go on, then, you two. What are you waiting for?'

They ran into the garden. Lizzie took Patch from the hutch and put him into Molly's arms.

'He's so soft, Lizzie. Can I stroke him?' Molly had never seen anything like it.

'You can be his auntie if you like.'

'Don't be daft, Lizzie!' Molly held Patch up to her face and examined him. 'He's very pretty, isn't he? I could play with him all day. But I can't stay long. I have to go shopping with Mam. If I come back tonight, can I feed him?'

Lizzie gave her a funny look. 'She's not shopping for food,' said Molly. 'She's buying cloth to make black curtains.'

'Why does she want black curtains?'

'They're for the blackout, silly. When there's an air raid everybody has to have them,' Molly explained. 'It's the law. You have to close the blackout curtains at night when the lights are on in the house. If you don't close them the Germans can look in the windows and bomb you. Be sure to tell your mother 'cos I don't want you to get bombed.'

'Tell you what, Molly, if there's an air raid and Mam doesn't get any curtains, can I come to your house?' Lizzie hadn't heard anything about such plans at home. She couldn't see her mother making ugly curtains.

'You can come to my house any time you like. Anyway, we're all getting Anderson shelters in our road.'

'What's an Anderson shelter?'

'Ask your dad, he'll tell you. I have to go now. Mam's waiting.'

As soon as Molly left, Lizzie hurried back to the dining room and pounced on Jack.

'What's an Anderson shelter, Dad? Molly's going to get one.'

Jack patted his knee. 'Sit here, pet, and we'll solve the mystery of the Anderson shelter.' Lizzie snuggled up to him as he began to explain.

'An Anderson shelter is a little iron house to protect us from enemy bombs. The government are going to give one to every householder with a garden.'

'Why d'you have to have a garden, Dad?'

'Because the shelter has to be dug deep into the ground. It comes in pieces. When I put it together I'll make a concrete floor to stop the damp from getting in. And when it's set I'll cover it with carpet to make it cosy. You'll have bunk beds to sleep on and a strong torch for light.'

'Can I have a little torch of my own, Dad, so I can read in bed?' Lizzie thought it sounded like an adventure.

'Of course you can and if there's an air raid you'll do just like you were taught at school. When you hear the warning siren, leave everything behind and hurry to the shelter. Don't worry, pet, I shouldn't think we'd get many bombs in this part of the country,' he hastened to reassure her.

Lizzie wasn't in the least bit tired as she climbed into bed; it had been such an exciting day. She put her hands together.

'Dear God, it's Lizzie here. Thank you for another miracle. Mam let me have a rabbit! I'll make sure it doesn't bother her and I'll take care of Patch myself. Please don't let Molly's mother get into trouble over hoarding and please don't let the Germans bomb our house. Love from Lizzie.'

Chapter 10

Early next morning Lizzie woke up with a start. Her mother was shouting at the top of her voice. It was very loud and seemed to come from the back garden. She threw on her dressing gown and as she fished under the bed for her slippers she thought about Patch. Had he escaped?

She hurried to the back bedroom and looked out of the window. Her father was in the garden with two strange men. They seemed to be quarrelling over a pile of metal shapes that almost took up the whole garden. Her mother was there too, demanding that they take it away. 'Ah'm not having a bloody Anderson shelter in ma garden!' she shouted. 'Now get it shifted! An' Ah won't tell ye again!'

Lizzie went back to her room, threw on her clothes and ran to the hutch to feed Patch. The shouting seemed to have stopped so she watched him eagerly munching his lettuce, and when she was sure he was safe, hurried inside to join her parents for breakfast.

There was the sound of raised voices as she approached the kitchen. If I wasn't so hungry I wouldn't bother, she thought, but I am so I'll just have to ignore them.

There was a swift silence when she entered the room. 'Where the 'ell 'ave you bin?' asked Alice. 'Yer breakfast's stone cold, but what do you care?'

'I'm sorry, Mam, but I was feeding Patch.' Lizzie looked at her feet.

Jack put down his fork. 'Stop nagging at the bairn, Alice. And, for the last time I'm telling you, whether you like it or not, we're having that shelter. You can risk getting killed if you like but I'll not let you take the bairn with you.'

He kissed Lizzie. 'I'm off to work now, pet. You'd better hurry or you'll be late for school. You don't want to keep Mrs Brown waiting.'

Jack was on his way out when the morning post fell on to the door mat. One letter immediately stood out from the rest. The envelope was brown and marked 'Private and Confidential'. He picked it up, took a deep breath, then tore it open. It was as he had feared. His calling-up papers had arrived with an order to report for his medical in five days. What a time to go to war, he thought, when I'm already fighting a losing battle in my own home.

He decided to keep the news to himself until he had talked things over with Joe. He was bursting to tell him. As soon as he got to work, he went straight to the office and phoned his brother.

'That's lucky,' said Joe, 'you just caught me. I was on my way out to get a haircut. What's up?'

'I got my calling-up papers this morning and I'm due for a medical next week.'

Joe laughed. 'Try limping into the room – you never know, the doctor might exempt you.'

'It's no laughing matter, Joe. It's all right for you, you're over forty so you're too old to get called up anyway but I'm still in my thirties. I'm worried about leaving Lizzie with Alice while I'm gone. I need to talk to you. Can I pop over at the weekend?'

'Of course you can. Have you broken the news to Mother?'

'No, not yet. I wanted to speak to you first.'

'Bring her with you, Jack. We can break the news to her then.'

'Thanks, Joe,' Jack said with a deep sigh. 'I haven't the heart to tell her on my own.'

❧

'If he thinks he's won over that bloody shelter, he's mistaken,' Alice muttered to herself as she cleared the breakfast table. She threw the plates into the sink without scraping off the leftovers and dropped the cutlery in on top, then, taking the kettle from the stove, she poured the boiling water over the greasy dishes while watching the remnants of her cooking floating to the top. She picked up a wooden spoon from the draining board and was stirring the debris when Peggy came in.

'Did ye know yer front door was wide open, Alice?'

'What do they care,' she said. 'Ah'll be done in, one o' these days, then they'll be sorry!'

'What are ye stirrin' in the sink, Alice? It looks like soup to me.'

'Mind yer awn business, Peggy. What ye doin' 'ere anyway?'

'Ah've come to give you the good news!' grinned Peggy. 'Ah'm working for the war effort! Ah've got a job at Vickers Armstrong's ammunition factory. Ah'm doin' shift work and Ah've just dropped by to show you me uniform.' She opened a carrier bag and took out a brown overall, a pair of asbestos gloves and a snood. She proudly held up the snood. 'This is to protect me hair from the machines.'

'Very nice, Peggy, but Ah'm not in the mood for a bloody fashion show after what Ah've been through this mornin'.'

'Are ye not well?'

Alice banged her fist on the table. 'Am Ah not well? Ye wouldn' be well if ye had to listen to the mouthful Ah got from Jack this mornin' – and in front of Lizzie! It's bad enough tryin' to control 'er without him showing me up.'

'What's 'e done this time?'

''E's only forcing me to have a bloody Anderson shelter, and on top of that 'e's bought Lizzie a mangy rabbit!'

'But why wouldn't ye want an Anderson shelter?' asked Peggy in astonishment.

''Cos it messes up the garden, doesn' it? An' nobody asked me about it! Jack just decided to 'ave it without a bloody word!'

'But everybody's got an Anderson shelter around 'ere, Alice,' Peggy pointed out, knowing full well her sister had never shown any interest in the garden before. 'What if there's an air raid? And how would you keep the bairn safe if there was?'

'Don't you start! All ye care about's Lizzie. Never mind about me. Yer just as bad as Jack.'

Peggy picked up her carrier bag and pushed her uniform inside. 'Well, Ah can't stay,' she said, 'or Ah'll be late for me first shift.'

'That's right, desert a sinking ship!'

Peggy made her way to the door. 'You're not fair to that bairn, Alice, an' if ye carry on like this you'll lose Jack. Sometimes Ah wonder how he puts up wi' ye.'

'Well, it's always good to know who yer friends are, isn' it?!'

'I am your friend, Alice. Ah just don' want ye to do somethin' you might regret. Now, shall Ah pop in tomorrow?'

'No! Don't bloody bother!'

⌘

Jack came home early that night to make a start on the shelter. It was more trouble than it was worth to get the workmen back and risk another row with Alice.

He took his spade from the shed and began to dig the foundations.

Lizzie ran into the garden when she saw him. 'Can I help you, Dad? I can't stay in there, Grandma Rooney's here and they're having a row. She called Mam a stuck-up bitch and I thought Mam was going to hit her. She wouldn't hit an old woman would she, Dad?'

With an inward groan Jack put down the spade. 'Why don't you feed Patch while I go inside and see what it's all about,' he suggested.

Raised voices were coming from the kitchen as Jack went inside. A broken cup was lying on the floor and Mrs Rooney's blouse had received the contents.

'Just look at this!' she said as she patted her blouse with a tea towel. 'Ah'm soakin' wet!' She poked Alice with her finger. 'She did that. She's out of 'er bloody mind. She should be put away.'

Alice was about to retaliate but Jack stepped towards them. 'That's enough! You may as well know I got my calling-up papers this morning and if it wasn't for Lizzie I'd be more than happy to leave for war and never come back, the way you two carry on! I think you'd better go now, Mrs Rooney, and I'm warning you both there'll be no more of your antics in this house.'

The older woman turned sharply to face him. 'Don' worry, Ah'm goin'. Ah never thought Ah'd say this aboot me own lass, but she's not fit to bring up a bairn.'

Jack led her to the door. 'That's a bit like the pot calling the kettle black, isn't it, Mrs Rooney? Good night.'

She banged the door behind her as she left.

Jack went back to the kitchen to find Alice on her knees picking up the pieces of broken cup from the floor. She stood up when she saw him and held up one of the larger pieces.

'Just look at this,' she said. 'The auld bugger's ruined me best tea set.'

Jack glared at her. Hadn't she stopped to think how Lizzie would feel after hearing that foul-mouthed carry on, he wondered. And she hasn't even mentioned my calling-up papers. He clenched his teeth. 'God give me patience!'

Alice took in the menacing look on his face. 'Oh never mind about the tea set,' she said, 'ye haven' had yer dinner yet.'

He turned to leave. 'Don't bother, Alice. I'm taking the bairn out for a fish supper.'

Her face became contorted as she struggled for words. 'But it's late,' she said, 'an' she'll never get up for school in the mornin'.'

Jack raised his voice. 'For goodness' sake, woman, tomorrow's Saturday. The bairn doesn't have to get up for school. But then why should you know that when you never take her there yourself.'

As he was leaving, Alice called after him. 'When will ye be back, Jack?'

'When we've had enough, Alice,' he shouted. 'I've had enough of you already.'

⁂

Annie was in the kitchen when she heard the car pull up. She looked out of the window and called to Joe. 'Jack's here with your mother. Let them in. I'm busy making the tea.' She shook her head, knowing what was about to be said, and worried for her mother-in-law.

Joe put down the Sunday paper and hurried to the front door. When he opened it, they were already standing on the doorstep. Joe shook Jack's hand and helped his mother inside.

'Take them into the front room,' Annie called.

Joe hung up his mother's coat and did Annie's bidding. Mrs Wood had just settled herself on the sofa when Annie came in with the tea tray. 'How's this for service?' she said. 'I saw the car draw up.'

Annie poured out the tea and passed her a cup. 'Have you read the paper, Mother? Butter and bacon's going to be on ration from the new year. What do you think about that?'

'Don't worry, Annie, we'll manage. We managed in the last war and we didn't starve.' Mrs Wood nodded resolutely.

Joe caught Jack's eye and gestured towards his mother. Jack cleared his throat and sat beside her on the comfortable old sofa, not really wanting to say what he had to tell her.

'I think it's time you knew. I got my calling-up papers a few days ago.'

Mrs Wood drew in her breath. 'Oh son, I've been dreading the day.'

'I'm not concerned for myself, Mother,' he hastened to add. 'It's the bairn I'm worried about. And that's what I wanted to talk to you about, Joe. Alice's behaviour towards Lizzie is worrying to say the least. She's hardly got a kind word for her. Lizzie's frightened to open her mouth, sometimes even when I'm there, so God knows what it'll be like when I'm not. Alice even resents her having a rabbit. So you can see, I'll be relying on the lot of you to keep an eye on the bairn while I'm gone.'

Mrs Wood held his hand. 'Don't worry, son. Thank goodness I'm still welcome for lunch on a Sunday. I'll bend over backwards to please Alice. I'll even let her win at whist! And by the time I've finished I bet I'll have Alice agreeing that the bairn can have dancing classes.'

Jack hugged her. 'It would be great if you could do that, Mother. It has been such a long time since we promised Lizzie lessons and it would make her really happy.'

'That's decided, then.' Mrs Wood stood up and straightened her skirt. 'We'd better go now, Jack. We don't want to upset Alice by being late for lunch.'

'Heaven forbid,' he said. 'She doesn't know we're here, Annie. She thinks I'm at Mother's mending her trellis. We'll be off now and thanks for everything.'

'Hang on,' said Joe, 'we weren't going to let on, but we're giving you a little send-off. Ena and Peter are coming and if we want to keep Alice sweet we'd better invite Mrs Rooney and Peggy. Is that all right?'

'Invite who you like, Joe. The only person I never want to clap eyes on again is Alice's brother Martin.' Jack shuddered at the thought of the man.

'Don't worry, we wouldn't let him over the doorstep.'

After Joe helped his mother on with her coat, she took Annie aside and spoke in a low voice. 'You know how our Ena can't stand the sight of Alice? So be sure to tell her we'll all be offering the hand of friendship to Alice for Lizzie's sake.'

Jack put down his spade and watched Lizzie as she tenderly stroked her rabbit. Short of a miracle, he realised, the shelter would never be finished by the time he left. That morning he had received a letter addressed to LAC J. W. Wood. Leading Air Craftsman – it was an impressive title for a carpenter. He was being posted to an RAF camp in Wales and to make sure he got there they had even included his train ticket. He would be leaving soon and he still hadn't found a way to break the news to Lizzie. I'm a failure in more ways than one, he thought. If only I could put her in my kit bag and take her with me.

Lizzie noticed the sad look on her father's face. She ran up to him and pointed to her cheek. 'Go on,' she said, 'plant one right there.'

His eyes filled with tears as he kissed her.

'What's the matter, Dad?'

'I have to tell you something, pet, and I don't know where to start.'

She dried his eyes with her Mickey Mouse hanky. 'Don't cry, Dad, just tell me. It can't be that bad.'

'I'm afraid it is, pet. I've been called up to join the Air Force and I'll be leaving soon.' He waited anxiously to see what her reaction would be.

'Molly Brown's uncle's gone already,' she said. 'He's learning to drive a tank! Molly said he loves it! Don't worry, Dad, you're clever. I bet they'll give you something really important to do.'

'You're right,' he said, relieved that she had taken it so well. 'I'm sure they'll give me something important and I know you'll be waiting to hear all about it when I get back. Now come here and give your dad a big, fat cuddle!'

He went back to work on the shelter feeling a little better. But no matter how well Lizzie had taken the news, she would still have Alice's temper to cope with while he was gone.

❧

That night, after dinner, Jack waited until Alice had left to get the coffee and whispered in Lizzie's ear, 'Could you make yourself scarce, pet? I want a quiet word with your mother.'

'I hope it's not trouble, Dad?'

151

He smiled. 'It's anything but. Run along now.' Shooting him an anxious glance, Lizzie did as she was told.

Alice returned with the coffee. 'And where's madam?' she asked.

'I want a private word with you, so I asked her to leave.'

What have I done this time, she thought. 'Go on then, Jack, spit it out.'

'We haven't spent much time together lately,' he began, 'and, what with the war and everything, it's made me think. I'll be going away soon, so why don't we take advantage of the time that's left? Mother's already pulled me over the coals for neglecting you and she's right. She said she'd be happy to look after Lizzie while we spend some time together.'

'Are ye sure that's what she said?' Alice asked suspiciously.

'You know Mother cares about you. And for that matter, so does the rest of the family.'

Well, that's a bit sudden, she thought. All the family likes me now. I wonder what the hell they're after.

She was about to make a tart remark when Lizzie ran into the room. 'I can't get Patch back into the hutch, Dad!'

'Don't interrupt. I'm talking to your mother.'

'But, Dad, what about Patch?'

'You heard 'er, Jack! Go on, run after 'er! Ye always do.'

He put his head in his hands. Getting Alice to change and stop begrudging the little one would be an uphill struggle. Could there be any real hope of making life better for Lizzie before he went off to war?

⚜

Annie moved the sausage rolls and Scotch eggs to make room for the last plate of salmon sandwiches. 'Joe!' she shouted. 'Come here!'

He hurried into the room. 'What is it this time, Annie?'

'Do you think I've made enough sandwiches?'

He scanned the table. 'You've made enough to feed an army, not to mention all those pork pies, cheese flans and cakes.'

'I can't remember, Joe. Is it your Jack that doesn't like salmon?'

'For goodness sake, Annie, there's a war on. By the time it's all over he'll be glad to eat anything.' He glanced out of the window. 'Oh, look what's just landed. It's Mrs Rooney and Peggy. I hope that woman doesn't carry on like she did at our Jack's. You could have been scarred for life, Annie.'

'Let sleeping dogs lie, Joe.' She glanced involuntarily at her hand, which still bore a small scar. 'Today's all about giving Jack a good send-off and making Alice feel wanted. You won't help things by falling out with Mrs Rooney. Now don't keep them waiting.'

Joe did as he was bid and let them in. 'Nice to see you, Peggy. Wow! That's a nice hat you're wearing, Mrs Rooney. Very smart.'

153

'What ye talkin' 'boot, ye silly bugger? Ye've seen it before. Ah wore it to the bairn's birthday party.' She removed the battered hat from her head.

Yes, well, the less said about that the better, he thought. 'Come in,' he said. 'Make yourselves at home. Annie's got the kettle on. Why don't you pop into the dining room, Mrs Rooney, and feast your eyes on the buffet?'

She didn't have to be told twice. 'Come on, Peggy,' she said, 'let's see what they're givin' us.'

What a woman, he thought, and wouldn't she have to turn up first. He didn't fancy making small talk with her. He was saved by the bell as the front door flew open and Lizzie rushed in, dragging a little girl behind her.

'Where's your mam and dad?' asked Joe.

'They're helping Grandma out of the car. They'll be here in a minute. I hope you don't mind me bringing Molly. Daddy said she could come.'

'Of course I don't mind! Nice to meet you, Molly. Why don't you say hello to Grandma Rooney and Peggy, they're in the dining room.'

Lizzie clapped her hands. 'Oh goody! Auntie Peggy's here. We'll have some fun, Molly. Let's go and find her.' They dashed off.

'There you are!' said Joe, as Jack helped his mother up the step into the hall. 'When I saw Lizzie I knew you wouldn't be far behind. Nice to see you too, Alice.'

'Ah hope that girl 'asn't misbehaved 'ersel', Joe. Ah tried to stop 'er, but she took off like a bloody greyhound. Jack's got no idea what Ah have to put up with. Ah tell ye, Ah'll have me 'ands full when 'e's away.'

Joe took his mother's arm. 'Don't worry, Alice, it'll all come out in the wash. Find Mother a comfortable chair, Jack. Her back's playing up again.'

'Now don't fuss, boys,' she said, 'I'll be as right as rain when I've had a little rest.'

Jack glared at Alice. God forgive me, he thought, I could kill her.

Annie bustled up to them. 'Go on, Joe, spend a bit of time with your brother. We can see to Mother. You don't mind, do you, Alice?'

What bloody choice do I have, she thought, damned busybody, but she smiled tightly at Annie. 'Of course not. Go on you two, 'ave a nice natter.'

Joe took Jack by the arm and marched him into the kitchen. 'Sit down,' he said, 'and I'll show you my secret weapon. Keep your eye on the door while I get it out.'

Joe stood on a stool and reached into a high corner cupboard. He swept aside various tins and packets, and carefully brought out a bottle. 'This is it!' he said. 'My best malt whiskey. It's the last bottle and I've been saving it for a special occasion.'

'Why do you hide it, Joe?'

'Well, you see, Annie doesn't hold with strong liquor,' he explained. 'Her father was teetotal until her mother left him. Then he took to drink and ended up an alcoholic.'

'And look at me,' said Jack, 'taking to drink because my wife isn't likely to leave. Make it a big one.'

Joe laughed. 'It's good to see my little brother smiling for a change.' He poured two generous measures. 'Here,' he said, 'get this down you and you'll be a new man. Remember, it's your last day of freedom.'

'To be honest, Joe, I think my freedom ended on the day I met Alice and now I'm living with the consequences.'

'I hope by that remark you're not including Lizzie.'

'Did I hear right, Joe? I hope that's the bloody malt whiskey speaking! Lizzie's the best thing that ever happened to me and I'm depending on the lot of you to see she's all right. Why do you think I'm here?'

'I'm here for the beer!' Jack and Joe turned to see Peter standing in the doorway.

'We didn't hear you come in,' said Joe.

'Annie said I'd find you here. Looks like I'm just in time.' His eyes were fixed on Joe's special malt.

Joe poured him a glass. 'Sit down,' he said, 'we're just drowning our sorrows. Where's Ena?'

'She's drowning hers in a cup of tea, listening to Mrs Rooney's dulcet tones with poor Mother and Alice.'

'Thanks for turning up today,' said Jack, 'especially after the way Alice behaved towards you both.'

'How could you think we wouldn't?' Peter raised his glass in salute. 'We'd do anything for you and the bairn, you know that, and we'll encourage Alice not to be a stranger.'

'Finish your drink,' said Joe, 'we'd better go in before we're reported missing.'

Ena had plucked up courage and joined the women in the dining room. It was a warm and welcoming room, like the rest of Joe and Annie's home. And now the table was groaning from the weight of the most wonderful buffet – she hoped Alice would appreciate it.

'Where are the bairns?' she asked.

Mrs Wood hugged her. 'Peggy's taken them to see the chickens. I was just saying, we don't see half enough of Alice, do we? Let's hope she won't be a stranger when Jack's away.'

'Mother's right,' said Ena dutifully. 'We're family and we're all behind you.'

'Well, thanks,' Alice said awkwardly.

'And what do you think about all this rationing, Alice? They say bread will be next. I hear they're thinking of giving us special bread coupons. "BUs" they're apparently called, short for Bread Units.'

'Ah don' give a damn what they're called, Ena. With the pittance Ah'll get from the government Ah won't be able to buy any bloody bread, coupons or not.'

'Oh but there's good news on that front,' Mrs Wood said hastily, 'Joe read it in the paper. The government has just agreed to an increase for family benefits for servicemen.'

Alice laughed grimly. 'Bloody marvellous,' she said. 'Ah'd better book a holiday before there's a rush.'

How can I offer the hand of friendship to this woman, Ena wondered. Whatever we say she's got some grudging reply. Even when she knows damn well Jack won't keep her short of money while he's away.

'Anyway,' said Alice, 'you'll be all right! Peter doesn't have to leave so Ah don't expect you'll have to go without, Ena.'

Mrs Rooney, who had remained silent throughout the family banter, suddenly came to life. 'An' talkin' aboot goin' without, Alice, reminds me. Ah'm still waitin' for me bloody blackout curtains. Ye said ye'd fetch yer tape to measure the windows.'

'D'ye think Ah've got nowt better to do but run around after you, Mother?'

'Well, what else have you got to do, ye lazy bugger? Wi' a twin tub washin' machine and the bairn at school ahl day.'

'Anyway, what d'ye want wi' blackout curtains, you old bag,' Alice shouted. 'Ye haven' seen the light of day through them windows in years.'

Their raised voices echoed across the room and Annie rushed over. 'Come on,' she said brightly. 'Shall we eat?'

'An' not before time,' said Mrs Rooney. 'Ah'm starvin'.'

'Don't stint yourself,' said Annie. 'There's plenty. Now if you'll excuse me, I'd better get the bairns in – they must be hungry by now.'

'We're already 'ere!' called Peggy from the doorway. 'They were gettin' a bit peckish. Go along, girls,' she said, 'run upstairs and clean yersels up before tea. And hurry up, Lizzie,' she whispered, 'before yer mother sees the state of yer shoes.'

'What's that, Peggy? Ah'm not deaf! What has she done to 'er shoes?'

'It's just a bit of mud, Alice.'

'Let me see! It looks like chicken shit to me!' She strode over to Lizzie. 'So this is the thanks Ah get for buying ye patent leather shoes. Well, ye haven' 'eard the last of this!'

Molly pulled out her hanky, spat on it and began to rub Lizzie's shoes. 'It's just a bit of mud, that's all, Mrs Wood.'

'Is that what ye think, Molly? Well, it's time yer mother taught ye to mind yer ahn business.'

Jack heard the irritable note in Alice's voice and steered her towards the buffet.

'Did ye 'ear that, Jack? The cheek of it! Ah warned Lizzie to keep 'er new shoes clean for mass tomorrow, but d'ye think she listens to me?'

'Stop worrying, Alice.' Jack passed her a plate. 'Come on now, try a sandwich.'

'No thanks. Ah'll 'ave a lump of that pork pie.' She smiled at Annie. 'Ah must say, ye've made a lovely spread.'

Annie thought it politic to return the compliment. 'Well, it's probably not up to your standards, Alice. Mother never stops talking about the wonderful cakes you make for tea on a Sunday.'

Alice's face softened. 'Ye can have the recipe if ye like.'

'And I've heard you're unbeatable at whist,' Annie went on. 'Why don't you bring Mother over one weekend and we can play a few hands.'

'Ooh, that sounds fun,' said Peggy. 'Can Ah come?'

Alice gave her sister a black look. 'Don't be rude, Peggy, go an' see what the bairns are up to.'

'But – '

'There's no buts aboot it. Ye've heard what Ah've said. Do somethin' useful an' make sure ye get ahl the mud off the bairn's shoes.'

Peggy turned away. 'Come on, Lizzie, let's go an' clean 'em up.'

Ena and Annie exchanged looks. 'By the way, Alice, I hear you play the piano,' said Ena. 'I was wondering if you'd like to help us out at the Women's Guild? They're giving one or two sing-songs to collect money for wool. We've started to knit a few warm comforts for the boys at the front.'

Alice was flattered. 'Ah haven' played for ages,' she said, 'but Ah'm a good knitter.'

'I know you've got a lot on your plate, Alice. But whatever you can do to help will be appreciated. Mother's volunteered to knit so Peter could pick you both up and we could all go together.'

'Ah'll think about it, Ena, it sounds like a good cause.' Alice helped herself to a large portion of chocolate cake.

'It's nice with a spot of cream.' Ena passed her the jug.

'Aren't you having any?'

'What? With my figure? We're not all as lucky as you, Alice. You can eat what you like and never seem to put an ounce on.'

'Well, ye've got lovely curly hair, Ena.'

Did I hear right? she thought. Had Alice actually paid her a compliment?

'All done!' Peggy said, reappearing with Lizzie and Molly. ''Er shoes are as good as new. Is it all right for the bairns to finish off the chocolate cake, Alice?'

'Why not? They can only be sick once.' She turned to Jack. 'Where are the other menfolk? Ah expect they'll be legless by now, the way they knock it back.'

Joe tapped her on the shoulder. 'I heard that! We were just coming to find out what you ladies are up to. And you're quite right, we have had a jar or two. We've got to give our Jack a good send-off. Anyway, they'll be rationing booze next. We'll all be teetotal by the end of the war so we might as well fill our tanks up now.'

Peter straightened his tie and laughed. 'My thoughts exactly, old buddy.'

Peggy took Jack aside. 'Can Ah 'ave a quiet word wi' ye?' she said in a hushed voice. 'There's something Ah need to ask ye before ye leave.'

'That sounds intriguing, Peggy. Shall we go out the back and give them something to talk about?'

She put her arm through his and giggled.

Once they were in the garden, Jack urged Peggy to speak. 'You'd better make it quick before Alice wonders where I am.'

'It's aboot ma sister. There's somethin' you ought to know, Jack.'

'Oh really?'

'D'ye remember Lizzie's birthday party, when Mam scratched Annie's hand?'

'Yes I do.' I'm hardly likely to forget it, Jack thought. 'I wondered what that was all about.'

'It was because Annie asked Alice to read the instructions for Lizzie's game.'

'But why was that a problem?'

'Because Alice – well, the thing is, she can't read or write properly.'

Jack stared at Peggy. Half-smiling he asked, 'Is this a joke?'

'No, it's not. Me mother stopped Alice goin' to school when she was seven because she was supposed to 'ave a bad heart.'

'How bad was it, Peggy?'

'How would Ah know?' she said. 'Ah wasn' even born. Anyway, at least she can sign 'er name and play the piano.'

My God, thought Jack. Suddenly things were falling into place. The way Alice shied away from reading to Lizzie, could it have been shame and frustration at her inability to read rather than her impatience with the bairn? He cast his mind back. Now he came to think of it, there'd been quite a number of occasions when Alice had avoided reading. Sometimes he'd been angry with her, thinking she was being deliberately unhelpful. But this could explain it.

'So Ah wondered, while you're away, if you'd like me to read your letters an' write back for Alice, 'cos if you don't, you won't know what's goin' on.'

'That's very kind of you, Peggy.' He smiled at her – Peggy was worth her weight in gold. 'I'd be very grateful.'

'Promise you won't let on what Ah've said, Jack, or Alice'll kill me.'

Jack looked at his watch. 'I'd better put a move on or she'll kill me too. Don't worry, pet, I know how to keep the peace! I won't let on.'

They hurried inside. When they got back, Alice was already helping Lizzie on with her coat. 'Where the hell 'ave ye bin, Jack? Ah promised to have Molly back by six. Mrs Brown'll go sky blue pink if she's not back in time and as usual Ah suppose Ah'll get the blame.'

He put his arm around her. 'No you won't, pet, not this time, because I'll explain the situation. It's my last night at home and I want to make sure it's a good one.'

'That'd make a change, wouldn' it?' she said tartly. 'Now get yer arm in that sleeve, Lizzie. We 'aven't got all night.'

Ena tapped Jack on the shoulder. 'I thought I'd better tell you, Mother's coming home for dinner with us and she's staying the night.'

'That's very kind,' said Jack. 'It'll make the parting much easier. I can't thank you enough for all you've done and when Mother goes to bed tonight, give her a kiss from me.'

Ena looked away hurriedly. 'Stop it, or you'll have me in tears. Don't forget to write. And it goes without saying I'll keep an eye on things while you're away.'

He held her in his arms and whispered, 'You'll always be my big sister, whatever happens, just you remember that.'

'Break it up you two, now, come on,' said Peter, 'your mam's waiting.' He held his hand out to Jack. 'Put it there, friend. And don't you worry, you'll be back before you know it. And don't worry about Lizzie. Ena's determined to win Alice over, whatever it takes.'

Joe took his brother by the shoulders. 'Now stop worrying. It won't be half as bad as you think. We'll all rally round and do our best at this end.' He slipped a coin into Jack's hand. 'This was our dad's lucky penny. He always kept it in his pocket when he operated on an animal. He'd want you to have it now.'

Jack blinked in amazement, a lump forming in his throat. 'I can't take this, Joe, when I know how much it means to you.'

'Go on, Jack, keep it in your pocket just like he did,' Joe insisted. 'You need it more than I do now.'

'What can I say, Joe? Except I'll keep it safe and give it back to you when it's all over.' Hurriedly he tucked it safely away.

'Come on then, folks, let's be off,' said Joe. 'Have you got your coat, Mrs Rooney?'

'It's ahl right, Ah've got it,' said Peggy. 'Just a minute while Ah give Jack a cuddle.' She threw her arms around his neck and kissed him on the cheek. 'Good luck, Jack. Ah'll miss ye. And don't forget wor little secret.'

'I'll miss you too, Peggy, you're a good girl. Don't let your sister be lonely.'

'Ah won't and Ah'll look after Lizzie whenever Ah can.'

'Are we goin' or not?' said Mrs Rooney, as she stuffed her bag with sausage rolls. 'Well, Jack, Ah suppose this is tarrar for now and just make sure ye kill as many bloody Germans as ye can.'

'I'll do my best,' he said. What a shame they hadn't called her up, he thought. She'd wipe out the entire German army in a week.

'Goodbye Mrs Rooney, it was nice of you to come,' said Annie. 'And you've been such a help today, Peggy. Alice is lucky to have you for a sister. Go on, you'd better be off. Take care of your mother.'

Annie had handled the Rooneys so well, Jack thought. Joe had certainly picked a winner when he married her. He hugged Annie. 'Thanks for everything. You're a treasure. Take care of yourselves while I'm away and, for God's sake, keep an eye on Lizzie.'

'As if we wouldn't, Jack. Go on, say goodbye to your mother.'

'I've been dreading the moment, Annie.'

'Well don't let her see you're worried or you'll have her in tears.'

Mrs Wood was sitting alone in an armchair. Jack studied her face as she adjusted the paisley scarf around her neck and nervously fiddled with her beads. He took her hand and kissed it. She smiled. 'I won't wash that hand again until you come home, son. Did you know I'm staying with Ena and Peter tonight?'

'Yes I did, Mother, and I'm glad. It's put my mind at ease. I didn't relish the thought of you being alone tonight of all nights.'

'Now don't go away worrying about me, son,' she said determinedly. 'I'm not one to sit around moping when there's vital work to be done. And there always is in wartime. Did you see that big poster, Jack? Dig for Victory? Well, I've started. I've already planted the cabbages ... ' Tears welled up in her eyes and she threw her arms around him. 'Oh son,' she said, 'come back safe, that's all I ask.'

'I'm only going to Wales for now, Mother. I'll be home before you know it,' Jack said, but he hugged her as though he'd never let her go.

She gently pushed him away. 'You'd better be on your way; Alice is waiting with the bairns. And promise you won't look back, son. I couldn't stand it.'

Chapter 11

Jack got ready in good time to catch the 7.30 train leaving from Newcastle Central Station. He checked the contents of the small suitcase: toothpaste, razor, writing paper and a change of underwear. That's all he would need. Come tomorrow, he'd be one of the boys in blue, with the RAF supplying his entire wardrobe.

Placing his hand in his pocket, he fingered the lucky penny Joe had given him. It had worked for his dad, maybe it would work for him too.

He picked up his case and crept along the landing to Lizzie's room. The door was ajar. He tiptoed inside and stood by her bed. She looked so innocent cuddling her teddy that it made the urge to hold her in his arms unbearable. Why had he listened to Alice? He remembered her persuasive words. 'It's too early to wake her and she'd only be upset to watch ye leave.' If only he hadn't listened, but it was too late now. If he woke her, there'd only be a row and his daughter would pay the price for it in the end.

He took an envelope from his pocket and placed it on a table next to Lizzie's bed. Then, with a lump in his throat, he left the room quietly, closing the door behind him.

The smell of bacon was wafting its way upstairs, but the very thought of food made him feel queasy.

Alice was in the kitchen, standing over the stove in her nightdress and curlers. 'Ye've taken yer time,' she said. 'D'ye want an egg with yer bacon? It's the last one on yer ration book so ye may as well 'ave it. Ah'll have to give the book back tomorrow. Ye won't need it in the Air Force.'

'I'm sorry, dear, but I seem to have lost my appetite.'

'Well, it won't go to waste,' she said, 'Ah'll 'ave it in a sandwich later.'

She filled two cups with coffee and gave one to Jack. 'Get this down ye. It'll warm ye up. It's bloody cold on them trains. Mind you, it won't be that warm 'ere either. I hear they're threatenin' to start rationing coal.'

Jack forced a smile and sipped his coffee.

'And what about the car? If it's left outside it'll be bloody rusty by the time you get back.'

'It's all sorted, Alice,' he assured her. 'Joe's going to see to it – he'll pick it up tomorrow and finish the shelter with Peter at the weekend.'

My God, she thought. Never mind the Germans. I'll be invaded by the bloody in-laws.

Jack finished his coffee and fastened his coat. 'I'd better think about leaving now. And just remember, Alice, there's no need to feel lonely. Ena and Annie are there for the both of you. You only have to pick up the phone.' He put his arms around her and kissed her on the cheek. 'I'll let you know when I'm due for my first leave.'

'Ye'd better not forget. Yer little pet's ahlready countin' the days and you haven't even left yet. Ah suppose she'll have to put up with second best now, won't she?'

He looked out of the window. 'The taxi's outside. I told the driver not to knock in case it woke Lizzie. I hate to leave you both but I'll rest easy once I know the shelter's finished.' He picked up his case. 'Take care of each other. I'll be thinking of you.'

'Ah won't come to the door, Jack, Ah look such a sight in me curlers.'

He gently pulled the door to as he left the house and stood in the street, looking up at Lizzie's window.

'Ye'd better get in,' said the driver, 'the traffic's heavy over Scotswood Bridge at this time of the mornin'.'

❧

Alice poured herself another coffee and began to heat up Jack's discarded breakfast. She cut two slices of bread and plastered them with butter. Bugger rationing, she thought. She took the bacon from the pan and placed it on the bread, then, scooping up the egg, sat it on the bacon and squashed the sandwich together. She took a bite and licked her lips, then wiped her chin with the hem of her nighty, while glancing at the kitchen clock. Is that the bloody time, she wondered. I might as well get back to bed for another forty winks. She finished her sandwich, bolted the front door and made her way upstairs.

❧

Lizzie woke up with a start. Her mother was shouting at the top of her voice. 'Get ready for breakfast or ye'll be late.' She jumped out of bed. It was Daddy's last day! She looked at the clothes she had chosen the night before neatly folded on the chair. Her tartan skirt, red jumper and new knee-length socks. She quickly dressed, brushed her hair and searched for her pretty slides. They were sitting on her bedside table on top of a strange envelope. She brushed the slides aside and picked it up. It said: TO LIZZIE WITH LOVE. READ THIS WHEN I'M GONE. She heard her mother on the landing and quickly put the envelope under her pillow. 'Ah'll expect ye downstairs in five minutes,' she was shouting. When Lizzie was sure she had gone, she took the envelope out again, pushed it down her knickers for safekeeping and ran down to the kitchen.

'Where's Dad, Mam? Has he had his breakfast yet?' She sat at the table and Alice put a plate in front of her.

''E's already gone,' she said. 'He left at the crack of dawn and 'e didn' want to wake ye.'

Lizzie stood up and pushed the plate away, tears filling her eyes. 'Why didn't you wake me? You knew I wanted to say goodbye.'

Alice was beginning to lose her temper. 'Ah won't tell ye agin, Lizzie. Sit down at the table or ye'll feel the back o' mah hand!'

'I don't care! When you said I could wave Dad goodbye, you were lying! I HATE you!'

Lizzie ran into the back garden and hid behind Patch's hutch. She took the envelope from her knickers and tore it open. The letter was written in capital letters, just like on the envelope.

DEAREST LIZZIE

SORRY I LEFT WITHOUT SAYING GOODBYE, BUT YOUR MOTHER SAID IT WAS TOO EARLY TO WAKE YOU. I LEFT AT 5.30 SO I'M SURE SHE WAS RIGHT.

I KNOW YOU'RE A GOOD READER, BUT IF YOU NEED ANY HELP WITH THIS LETTER ASK AUNTIE PEGGY.

I WANT YOU TO KNOW THAT I LOVE YOU AND WILL MISS YOUR PRETTY LITTLE FACE WHILE I'M AWAY.

GO INTO THE SHED AND LOOK IN THE OLD COCOA TIN I KEEP MY NAILS IN AND YOU'LL FIND SOME MONEY. USE IT FOR PATCH'S FOOD AND HAY.

YOU WILL ALWAYS BE IN MY THOUGHTS WHILE I'M AWAY. GOD BLESS YOU, DARLING, AND BE A GOOD GIRL FOR YOUR MOTHER.

LOVE FROM DADDY

Lizzie put the letter safely back in her knickers and took a deep breath. Her father had gone and she had no idea when he would be back, leaving such a gaping hole inside that she couldn't even think about it. At least she had Patch. Adjusting the letter so it wouldn't show, she headed towards the shed. She found the cocoa tin and looked inside. There was a ten shilling note and some loose change. She made sure the lid was on tight before returning the tin to its secret hiding place, then took a large carrot and a cup full of pellets and went to Patch's hutch. The moment she opened the door, he hopped forwards. She stroked him and put his food inside, then she closed the door and knelt down to watch him tucking into his breakfast. 'Don't worry, Patch,' she said, 'we're going to be all right. Dad has left us some money, so you won't have to go hungry. Daddy loves us and he'll come back soon, he promised. Please be a good little rabbit and don't annoy Mummy, then everything will be all right. Don't worry, I'll look after you.'

She almost jumped out of her skin when she heard her mother's angry voice coming from the back door. 'Get inside,' she shouted, 'or we'll be late for church. And Ah won't tell ye agin!'

Lizzie's heart was pounding as she hurried indoors.

⁂

They got back from mass to find Ena and Peter standing outside the house. 'Just look at that,' she said, 'yer dad's only been gone five minutes and they can't wait to get inside, the nosy buggers.'

Ena waved when she saw them and Lizzie ran into her arms.

Alice took out her key. 'Ah suppose you'd better come inside since yer here.' Grimly she opened the door and stepped back.

Ena went in first. 'We were wondering where you were, weren't we, Peter? Mother said you got home from church at about eleven and it's almost twelve o'clock now.'

'Why were you so worried, Ena?' Alice thought it unlikely that her sister-in-law cared one way or the other about her. 'Did ye think Ah'd cocked me hat at another fella? Jack's only bin gone a few hours. Gan inside and ye can put yer minds at rest.'

They followed Alice into the kitchen. 'Go on, Lizzie,' she said, 'put the kettle on and shove some toast under the grill.'

Ena looked concerned. 'Do you think that's all right, Alice? Isn't that a bit dangerous for the bairn?'

'No, she does it all the time! Just as I did for my mam when I was her age. Anyway, Ah'm starvin'. Ah've had Holy Communion this morning and we Catholics have to swallow the body of Christ on an empty stomach.'

Weren't you supposed to take communion in a state of grace? thought Ena. There's certainly no sign of grace in Alice.

'So, what're ye both doing here anyway?'

Ena looked at Peter. 'Do you want to tell her?'

'No, you go ahead, dear.'

'For goodness sake, will somebody tell us what the hell it is?'

'Mother can't come to lunch today, Alice. We ran her home to change her clothes this morning, but she was too tired to get dressed again so she's gone to bed.'

'Bloody hell! The way you two were goin' on, Ah thought there was a bloody death in the family!' exclaimed Alice in exasperation. 'Ah knew she was at your house last night – Ah thought you'd be feedin' her anyway. Is that bloody kettle boiled, Lizzie?'

Ena went to the stove and waved Lizzie aside. 'I'll make the tea, Alice, while you get yourself something to eat. You said you were hungry.'

'Well thanks, Ah'll just make meself an egg on toast.'

Peter called Lizzie over. 'I hear you've got a rabbit, pet. What's its name?'

'It's Patch. Would you like to see him?' She turned to Alice. 'Is that all right, Mam?'

'Go on then, but watch ye don't let the bloody thing out.'

Lizzie held on to Peter's hand and pulled him into the garden. 'Look!' she shouted. 'There's his hutch.' She ran forward and tapped on the mesh window and Patch hopped quickly into view.

'What a beautiful creature, pet. He's the handsomest rabbit I've ever seen.'

'He thinks I've got something for him, Uncle Peter. He's always hungry.' She lowered her voice. 'If I tell you a secret, will you promise not to tell Mam?'

'Scout's honour, you can tell me anything.'

'Then cross your heart and hope to die.'

He did Lizzie's bidding as she led him to the shed. When they were safely inside, she opened the cocoa tin, took out her father's letter and gave it to him. 'Remember you crossed your heart, Uncle Peter. Could you please read it properly for me?'

It was hard for him to hold back the tears as he read Jack's words. When he finished, he swallowed hard. 'Patch is a very lucky rabbit, Lizzie. Just make sure you put the tin back where Daddy left it. Now, we'd better go back or your mother might wonder what we're up to.'

When they got inside, the atmosphere was tense. Alice's face was flushed. 'We've just been talking about that bloody shelter, Peter.'

'Yes,' said Ena, 'and it seems like Alice doesn't want one.'

'"Seems like Alice doesn't want one!" That's right! Because Alice is not bloody having one!'

'It's almost finished,' said Peter, 'the wooden bunk beds are already in. But if the floor's not concreted the whole shelter will flood if it rains.'

Alice grinned. 'Well at least it'll make the bloody frogs happy. And that's an end of it.'

Lizzie felt that funny feeling in her tummy like when she knew things were about to go wrong. 'I've been to Holy Communion class this morning,' she said quickly. 'That's why we're back late. I'm learning how to receive the body of Jesus and I'm going to wear a white dress and a veil, just like a bride, aren't I, Mam?'

'That's right, you'll be a bride of Christ.'

Ena took Lizzie's hand. 'And do you know what that means, pet?'

'Um . . .'

'Well, I'll tell you. It means that you will always try to be a good girl and follow the teachings of your church.'

Alice bristled. 'What do you know about it, Ena? You're not a Catholic – it's none of your bloody business!'

'But does she understand the things she's saying, Alice? Receiving the body of Christ, being the bride of Jesus. I've never heard such a young child talk like that before.'

Peter gave Ena a cautionary glance. 'Now come on,' he said, 'let's not fall out. We all want to do the best for Lizzie.'

Alice rounded on him. 'Why? Do ye think Ah can't take care of her meself?'

'Of course you can, Alice. We just want to help, that's all.'

'Ah yes, that's what you say. Comin' round here, sticking yer oar in: she shouldn't put the kettle on, does she understand what she's sayin'. Well, you'd better understand what Ah'm sayin'. Bugger off and mind yer own business. Yer just like Jack. The only one you're interested in is Lizzie.'

'But she's just a bairn,' said Peter. 'She needs her family while her daddy's away. We're worried about her. And it is dangerous for her to light the gas.'

Ena held her hand to her brow. 'All this arguing has given me a headache, Peter.'

Lizzie ran forward and held her hand. 'Are you all right, Auntie? Would you like a nice brandy? Mam always has one when she has a headache.'

Alice gave Lizzie a black look and she let go of Ena's hand.

'This is getting us nowhere,' said Peter, 'but I beg you Alice, at least do one thing to ease all our minds and allow me to help Joe to finish the shelter. Jack would rest easy if he knew you and Lizzie were safe.'

'Ah've told you once and Ah won't tell you again, keep away from that bloody shelter and keep away from us.'

⁂

Ena was glad to leave her brother's house. She was shaking like a leaf as Peter helped her into the car. 'My God,' she said, 'I can't take my mind off Lizzie, living alone with that excuse for a mother. She talks about religion when it's clear to see she hasn't got a trace of love or understanding in her whole body. What are we going to do, Peter?'

He was lost for words. What could he really do to help Lizzie while her dad was away?

⁂

Lizzie kept out of her mother's way for the rest of the day and to keep out of trouble that night, decided to go to bed early. 'Is it all right if I go upstairs now, Mam?'

'Why, what's the matter with you?' Alice was instantly on the alert at such an unusual request.

'I'd like to start reading my new catechism, if that's all right with you.'

'What did ye say?'

'I thought if I learnt it, the priest would be pleased.'

'What brought this on, then?'

'I know you want me to be a good Catholic, Mam. And I'm going to try my best,' Lizzie said earnestly.

My God, thought Alice, I never thought I'd see the day. 'Of course ye can go to bed, pet. Sleep tight an' mind the fleas don't bite.'

Lizzie kissed her mother on the cheek and went to her room. She undressed and folded her clothes, then, after a pleasant soak in the bath, got into bed and said her prayers. 'Dear loving God, it's me again. I'm sorry, I had to lie to Mam tonight. She thinks I'm reading my catechism, but I'm not. I just wanted to be on my own for a bit. It's been a horrid day. My dad was gone when I got up this morning and I don't know when I'll see him again. My mam has rowed with Auntie Ena and Uncle Peter, and I don't think they'll come to our house any more. Please keep my dad safe and thank you for Patch. Love from Lizzie.'

⁂

Alice burst into Lizzie's room next morning. 'Get up,' she said. 'Ah've got a surprise for you. Hurry up now, you don't want to be late for school.'

Lizzie wondered what the surprise could be. She threw on her clothes and hurried downstairs. Her mother was already dressed and had even brushed her hair. 'Sit down and close yer eyes,' she said, 'and don' open them till Ah tell ye.'

Lizzie did as she was told.

'You can look now,' said Alice, as she proudly presented her with a boiled egg and a plate of bread soldiers. 'This is for bein' a good girl and reading your catechism.'

My goodness, thought Lizzie, if reading my catechism puts her in this mood, I'll read it every night! She couldn't remember the last time her mother had made her an egg for breakfast.

'Well, aren't you going to say something, Lizzie?'

'Yes Mam, what a lovely surprise, thank you. Would you like the top off my egg?'

'Ah wouldn't dream of it, pet,' smiled Alice. 'See what you get when you're a good girl. Now hurry up, you don't want to keep Mrs Brown waiting.'

It was lovely when Mam was so nice to her. From now on, she would do anything to keep her happy. She read her catechism every night and sometimes even struggled to read the easy bits out loud to her. She was never late for breakfast and even began to say grace, just like Grandma Wood did.

And it was true, Alice did seem happier. Sometimes she would play the piano and sing 'We'll Meet Again'. Lizzie once heard a lady sing it on the radio and it had made her cry and wonder when her father would come back.

One morning, not long after that day, Lizzie stood in her bedroom, trembling with excitement. She could hardly believe what was going to happen. Mam had broken the news to her a few days ago.

At last, she heard her mother calling, 'Yer grandma's here, don't keep her waiting.'

She ran down the stairs two at a time. Today was the day it was finally happening! Her mother had agreed she could have dancing lessons! She reached the hallway to hear her mother chatting to Grandma Wood.

'Ah'm surprised to see you on yer own, Mother,' Alice was saying. 'Where's Joe?'

'He's in the car, having a smoke. Thank God I heard they might be rationing cigarettes soon. Filthy things. Annie never stops nagging him to give them up, but he won't listen.'

'Well, if Ah was Annie, Ah wouldn't bother. He's a big lad now and if he wants to smoke himself to death, let him.' Alice thought it was his look-out.

Lizzie ran into the room and flung her arms around her grandma. 'I'm ready! Shall we go now?'

Alice held out a small carrier bag. 'Don't ye wanna see what's in here before ye leave?'

Lizzie gasped when she saw the tap shoes. She took one out and tried it on. 'Look, Mam, it fits me!'

'My goodness,' said Mrs Wood, 'you must have been a good girl to deserve these.'

'Oh but she has, Mother,' said Alice proudly. 'She reads her catechism every night and she's having instructions for her first Holy Communion every Sunday morning. And that reminds me, we'll be eating a bit later tomorrow.'

'That's all right, Alice,' Mrs Wood said kindly, retying her paisley scarf. 'You don't have to hurry back for me. After all, we'll have the whole day together. And who knows, I might even beat you at whist this week! Come on, Lizzie, we'd better go. Uncle Joe's waiting in the car.'

Lizzie hugged her mother. 'Thanks for the tap shoes,' she said, and waved all the way to the door.

Mrs Wood smiled. It was lovely to see her looking so happy, but at the same time, it was odd to see Alice being so kind to Lizzie. She didn't believe for a moment that it would last. What would happen when Alice went back to her old ways? How would the bairn cope with that? But for Lizzie's sake, she would put her worries aside and focus on her grandchild's special day.

She opened the car door and quickly stepped back. 'Don't go in there yet, Lizzie,' she said. 'Open the windows, Joe, or we'll all be gassed.'

Lizzie laughed. 'I'm getting my gas mask next week, Grandma, and I'll be able to wear it in Uncle Joe's car!'

When the smoke had cleared to Mrs Wood's satisfaction, she helped Lizzie into the back seat and they got on their way.

'Are you all right, pet?' asked Joe.

'I'm fine, thank you. Mam's been so nice to me. She even bought me some tap shoes for being a good girl!'

'That's nice.'

Mrs Wood gave him one of her telling looks. He got the message and raised his eyebrows. 'I'm coming round tomorrow with Uncle Peter, Lizzie. We promised your dad we'd finish the shelter.'

'I don't think Uncle Peter is allowed,' Lizzie said, remembering the row. 'Mam said he had to keep away from the shelter and away from us. She said she wants to keep frogs in it.'

'That's enough about shelters, Joe. Keep your eyes open or you might miss the turning. I don't want Lizzie to be late for her first lesson.'

'For goodness sake, Mother, I know the place like the back of my hand. Don't you remember? It used to be Jack's old infant school.' He turned the corner and pulled up outside rusty gates. 'The council use this place for evening classes now.'

'Is that true, Uncle Joe, did Daddy really go to this school when he was a little boy? Do you think they've still got his desk?' Lizzie asked eagerly.

'I shouldn't think so, pet.'

What a shame, she thought, he might have carved his name on it.

The building had seen better days; it was neglected, a shabby-looking place, with big gates that made it look like a prison. But Lizzie didn't care. This was where she would learn to dance!

They got out of the car and Joe pointed to a sign on the wall. MRS MASON'S SCHOOL OF DANCE. 'This is definitely it,' he said.

A woman came along with a little girl in a blue dress and tight plaits and pushed open one of the gates. Seeing Lizzie she asked, 'Are you looking for the dancing class?'

Joe stepped forward. 'Yes, we are.'

'Then you'd better follow us. It's like a warren in there. You'll never find it on your own.'

Mrs Wood introduced herself. 'I'm Mrs Wood. This is my son and my granddaughter, Lizzie.' She nodded proudly as Lizzie eagerly looked up.

'Pleased to meet you, I'm sure,' said the woman, smoothing her wavy hair. 'This is Daisy and I'm her Auntie Joan. We'd better put a step on it. Mrs Mason doesn't take kindly to latecomers.'

Auntie Joan led the way at a pace and the others hurried behind through cold, echoing corridors. They stopped at a door with a frosted glass window. Daisy nudged Lizzie. 'This is it,' she said, 'you'd better go in quietly.'

Lizzie was standing on her tiptoes in an effort to see through the glass when the door opened. Mrs Wood pulled her back and turned to Joe. 'We'll see you in an hour. I don't think you'll be very welcome here.'

'All right, Mother, I'll wait in the car and read the paper.' Joe seemed slightly relieved he wasn't expected to stick around.

Auntie Joan took Daisy's hand and whisked her inside, while Mrs Wood and Lizzie waited for Mrs Mason to speak. She was a tall, thin lady with a shock of carrot-coloured hair and a face covered in freckles. She was wearing black tights and a leotard that accentuated her flat chest. 'You must be Mrs Wood,' she said.

'That's right. I'm Lizzie's grandmother and I'd like to apologise for being late on her first lesson.'

Mrs Mason smiled and took Lizzie's hand. 'Don't worry, it's not the easiest place to find. Come inside and take a seat while I introduce Lizzie to the class.' She led them into a big room, bare apart from a practice barre on the far wall. One of the walls was almost covered in a huge mirror and the floor was a well-worn oak.

What a lovely welcome, Mrs Wood thought. Not at all like Auntie Joan's impression of Mrs Mason. She sat down and looked around her. There were twelve happy children of all shapes and sizes, aged between about five and ten. Yes, Lizzie would fit in here nicely.

'Gather round, children,' said Mrs Mason, 'and welcome Lizzie Wood. What do we say to a new girl?'

'Welcome to Mrs Mason's School of Dance!' the girls said in unison as they clustered around Lizzie.

'I knew her first!' said Daisy, her plaits swinging as she nodded vigorously. 'I met her outside, on the way in.'

Lizzie was surrounded by chattering girls, all wanting to talk to her at the same time. She had never felt so popular. She could see she fitted right in as they all wore leotards with woollen cardies tied across at the front, just like hers, and some even had the same pink knee-high socks in thick wool.

Mrs Mason held up her hand and the noise died down. 'Now children,' she said, waving her arms about, 'we must make a start. I want you to imagine you're a tree. With your branches blowing in the wind. Spread out and Mr Bell will play some windy music. Mr Bell!' she shouted. 'We're ready.'

But there was no sign of music. My goodness, thought Mrs Wood, noticing for the first time that somebody was slumped in the corner of the room, the man's fast asleep!

Mrs Mason called again. Mr Bell almost jumped out of his skin and, as if by habit, automatically began to play. It didn't seem to bother Mrs Mason and she joined in with the children as they wafted their arms through the air.

This is fun, thought Lizzie. And what a big draught we're making. I hope we don't blow Grandma away!

'Now,' said Mrs Mason, 'it's time to divide into two groups. Melanie, it's your turn to take the little ones today and I'd like you to work on posture.'

A slender girl with fair hair and sharp features stepped forward. 'Thank you, Mrs Mason.'

The younger children ran towards the big mirror. Melanie took Lizzie's hand and followed the others, who were already jumping up and down, making faces at themselves in the glass. 'That's enough!' said Melanie. 'That's no way to behave in front of Lizzie on her first day. Get ready and stand in your first position!' She turned to Lizzie. 'Stay where you are and watch.'

Melanie stood in front of the children. 'Now, if we're ready, with hands on hips, point your toes, and: step to-gether, point; step to-gether, point.'

Lizzie kept repeating the words. Step to-gether, point; step to-gether, point. She couldn't wait to have a go.

'Now,' said Melanie, 'with hands above your head, turn daintily around and face the mirror again. And – rest. Would you like to join them now, Lizzie?'

Her face said it all. 'Yes please, Melanie.'

'Come along then and join the line. Now, if we're all ready: step to-gether, point; step to-gether, point.'

Lizzie wanted to look in the mirror but was too afraid to take her eyes off her feet in case she tripped over. Never mind, she thought, I'll be able to look in the mirror next week. I'll practise 'step to-gether, point' at home.

⁓

Lizzie ran into the house as soon as Joe's car drew up and found her mother in the kitchen. 'Uncle Joe's here! Shall I put the kettle on, Mam?'

'You'd better not, Lizzie, or Ah might be reported for cruelty,' Alice said acerbically.

Joe laughed. 'What are you talking about?'

'Ask yer sister and 'er bloody 'usband.' She threw her head back and scornfully stared at him across the table. 'Ah don't want to talk about it in front of the bairn.'

Joe was desperate to laugh out loud. My God, he thought, is there anything Lizzie hasn't heard from that woman's foul mouth?

'Come here, Lizzie,' she said, keeping an eye on Joe. 'Give your mam a cuddle. Did yer enjoy yer dancing class, pet?'

'Yes I did, Mam, and the teacher was pleased I had tap shoes. She said I'd be starting tap in two weeks.'

'That's good,' she said. 'Now run upstairs and get ready for tea. Ah want a private word with yer Uncle Joe. And ye'd better say goodbye 'cos 'e might 'ave left by the time ye come down.'

Lizzie kissed him. 'Thanks for taking me to dancing class, Uncle Joe, and give my love to Auntie Annie.'

Alice took a deep breath and folded her arms. 'Ah won't beat around the bush, Joe. If yer think yer comin' to finish the shelter tomorrow, forget it. Ah've already told Peter, so just get it into yer bloody 'ead, you and your clan are not welcome around here. Lizzie and me can manage on our own. We're gettin' on much better without you lot. The only one Ah can trust is yer mother, so the rest of you can clear off.'

Joe glared at her. 'There's no talking to you when you're in this mood, Alice, but I'm not leaving it like this. You're part of our family, whether you like it or not, and we won't stop trying to build bridges. And if you had a mind, Alice, you could start pouring oil on troubled waters and pray for a way to heal this fractured family when you're at mass tomorrow. I'll be off now. Say good-bye to the bairn for me.'

⁂

Lizzie came down at teatime, having reluctantly changed out of her precious leotard and wraparound cardie. She was surprised to see Aunt Peggy in the kitchen reading a letter out loud to her mother. Peggy stopped when she saw Lizzie. 'The bairn's 'ere,' she said. 'Ah'll read the rest later, Alice.'

Lizzie cuddled Peggy. 'What're you doing here, Auntie? Why aren't you at the factory?'

'Because Ah'm on night shift, pet.'

Alice glared at Lizzie. 'Shut up! Ah wanna 'ear what else yer dad's gotta say for 'imself.'

Lizzie remained silent until Peggy had stopped reading, then she asked, 'Did he mention me, Auntie?'

'Yes he did, pet. He said he misses ye a lot and sends ye a big kiss. And ye'll be gettin' a letter ahl of yer own soon.'

Lizzie looked at her mother. 'Why didn't you read the letter yourself, Mam?'

'Never ye mind!' Alice snapped and turned back to Peggy. 'Are ye sure 'e didn' say owt else?'

'No, Alice, that's it.'

'Just as Ah expected! Not a bloody lovin' word!'

'Ye're never satisfied,' said Peggy, as she stood up to go. 'Jack worries 'imself to death about you. That's why 'e wants

188

ye to 'ave the shelter finished. Anyway, Ah've gotta be off now. Shall Ah read the letter agin before Ah go?'

'Don't bother!' Alice snapped at her sister. 'But ye don' 'ave to worry, Lizzie, oh no! 'E sent you a big kiss. Now put the kettle on, Ah could do wi' a cuppa tea.'

Peggy watched as Lizzie filled the kettle. What a life, she thought. Poor little soul. 'Ah'm off now, Alice, and mind that bairn doesn't scald 'erself.'

Lizzie made the tea and poured it out, making sure not to spill any in the saucer. She opened the biscuit tin and took out the last two biscuits. She put the tea on the kitchen table and passed the biscuits to Alice. 'Look,' she said, 'they're custard creams.'

Alice gave her a begrudging smile. 'Very nice,' she said. 'Now get upstairs and get ready for bed.'

Oh my God, what have I done now, Lizzie wondered. She turned on her heels and ran to her room, closing the door behind her. It was good to savour the peace and quiet of her own space. She took a bath, got ready for bed and thought about Patch. His food was running low and there wasn't much left in the kitty. She sat at the little table in her bedroom and counted the last few coppers in her purse. Would it be enough for Patch's food? If only her mother hadn't fallen out with everyone, Uncle Joe would have lent her some money. Never mind, Dad will be home soon and he's sure to leave more money in the cocoa tin. Then she remembered Grandma Wood's victory garden. At least her mam hadn't fallen out with her yet and Patch would love her juicy carrots.

I wonder why I feel so sad, she thought. Hitler's not dropping bombs on Newcastle and I'm going to Mrs Mason's dancing class. And Grandma was really happy today when Mrs Mason said I was doing well.

She put the money back in her purse and was hiding it under the wardrobe just as her mother came in to the room.

'What are you up to?' said Alice.

'Nothing, Mam.'

'Yes, you are, what have you got there?' Alice pulled the purse out from under the wardrobe and tipped the coins on to the bed. 'And what's this for?'

'It's for feeding Patch, Mam.'

'That bloody rabbit, it'll eat us out of house and home! Yer father should never have given you the bloody thing,' Alice grumbled. 'He spoils you rotten and Ah'm sick of it! Well, it won't go on for much longer, Ah can tell ye. Now get off to bed and don't forget to read yer catechism. Father Kelly might be testing you tomorrow. And when ye've finished readin', don' forget to put the light out. Ah'm not made of money.'

Lizzie got ready for bed and flicked through her catechism before saying her prayers. 'Dear loving God, thank you for this day. And most of all for Mrs Mason's dancing class. There's no pleasing Mam so will you kindly help me not to answer her back. She's cross again now. I miss Uncle

Peter and Auntie Ena, and Uncle Joe and Auntie Annie too. I even miss Grandma Rooney. She's not that bad really. Thank goodness Auntie Peggy still comes to read Dad's letters or I wouldn't know how he is. She makes me laugh. I don't know where she gets the coupons from but she always brings me sweeties. I hope she's not in the black market. Please keep Dad safe and don't let Patch's food run out before he gets back. Thank you for watching over me. Love from Lizzie.'

Chapter 12

Lizzie was leaving the house one Monday morning when Alice called her back. 'I forgot to tell you, you can play with Molly after school today. Ah've got something to see to and Ah won't get back till six.'

'What's that, Mam?'

'Never you mind. You'll find out soon enough. Ah've asked Mrs Brown and she said ye can stay for tea if ye like.'

Lizzie jumped up and down. 'Oh, can I really, Mam? Mrs Brown always has teacakes on Mondays and sometimes she's got apricot jam as well.'

'Ah'm not interested in the bloody menu, Lizzie.' Alice raised her eyebrows. 'Do ye want to go or not?'

'Yes please, Mam.'

'Yes please, Mam,' mimicked Alice, 'I bet ye can't bloody wait to get there. Gan on then, get off to school and behave yerself at Mrs Brown's.'

'I will, Mam, and thanks for letting me go.'

'Just make sure yer back by six. And don't be bloody late.'

Lizzie breathed in deeply as she closed the front door behind her. How lucky I am. And if Mam doesn't fall out with Grandma Wood I can still go to dancing lessons as well.'

She couldn't wait for school to end. The lessons seemed to last for ever. But then, at last, she was running towards the school gates. Mrs Brown was already there, standing in her usual place with a big smile on her round face. She looked plumper than ever in her cosy little hat and well-worn tweed coat. Lizzie had never seen her wearing anything else. It was clear to see she was no follower of fashion. Mrs Brown opened her arms and Lizzie ran into them, wishing she could stay there for ever.

'Come on,' said Molly, 'it's my turn.' She gave her mother a big hug. 'Now let's go, Lizzie! Mam's got your favourite teacakes – I'll race you!' They set off for Molly's house at a gallop.

Lizzie loved Mrs Brown's house. It was cosy, just like she was. When they went inside the table was already laid and, sure enough, there was the jar of apricot jam. It was wearing its little muslin hat, edged with tiny beads, just like the one at Grandma's house. She sat at the table with Molly and it wasn't long before Mrs Brown came in with the toasted teacakes. They were oozing with butter. Just for a moment, Lizzie remembered her pantry and the black market, then, quickly casting the memory aside, picked up a teacake and plastered it with her favourite jam. Licking her lips after the first bite, she asked, 'Is this homemade jam, Mrs Brown?'

'Yes it is. And don't you think it's time you called me Auntie Marion?'

'I'd love to,' she beamed, 'and I'm glad the jam's homemade.'

After tea, Molly took Lizzie into the garden to show off her Anderson shelter. It was sunk into the ground and covered in grass. It's nothing like ours, Lizzie thought. Molly opened the door. 'Have a look inside and see what a good job Dad's made of it.'

'Why isn't your dad in the forces, Molly?'

'Because he's got a fatty heart and flat feet. That's why they didn't pass him. Anyway, do you want to see inside the shelter or not?'

Lizzie reluctantly went inside, afraid it would be like the shelter at school, but when she saw it, she gasped. 'It looks like a proper room, Molly.'

'I know,' she said. 'Dad covered the cement with carpet and do you see these posters? I put them up myself. And do you remember those black bullets in the school shelter?' Lizzie nodded her head. 'Well, we've got some of those as well.'

Lizzie sat on a bunk bed and cast her eyes around the shelter. There was a kettle sitting on top of a paraffin stove and piles of books and magazines were scattered around. 'You'd better be careful, Molly,' she said, 'or you could start a fire in here.'

Molly pulled a face. 'You're only jealous, that's all.' The moment the words had left her lips, she threw her arms around Lizzie. 'I'm sorry,' she said, 'I didn't mean that. Anyway, you're welcome to share our shelter any time.'

When they got back inside, Mrs Brown was sitting by the fire, steeped in a book. Lizzie could tell how many chocolates she'd eaten by the number of wrappings in the fireplace. Mrs Brown often had her face in a book and Lizzie wondered why her mother never read one.

Mrs Brown looked at her watch. 'My goodness, it's nearly six o'clock, pet. You'd better be off home. You don't want to make your mother cross again.'

Lizzie's heart sank at the thought of leaving, but Auntie Marion was right. She couldn't afford to upset her mother.

⊰⊱

Lizzie ran to the back door and shouted, 'I'm back, Mam! I'll just pop in to the garden to feed Patch before I get ready for bed.'

'Don't bother,' Alice shouted back. 'Ah've already fed him. Come in to the kitchen.'

Lizzie hurried inside. 'What about his water, Mam?'

'He's got water! Now let the bloody thing settle down for the night. Anyway, how did ye get on at Mrs Brown's?'

She wondered what she could say that wouldn't upset her mother. If she mentioned the lovely shelter, it would only make her cross and remind her of the row with Uncle Joe.

'Well, Lizzie? How was it?'

'It was lovely, Mam, and Mrs Brown said I could call her Auntie Marion if I want to.'

'And do you want to?'

Lizzie paused. 'Yes, if it's all right with you, Mam.'

'Ah'll have to think about that. Now get upstairs and get ready for bed.'

What a relief, thought Lizzie. It's the only place I want to be. But she wouldn't let her mother know, or she might keep her up all night just for spite.

⚜

She got up early next morning and hurried to the hutch to collect Patch's water bowl. She froze to the spot when she saw the door was wide open. 'Patch! Patch!' she called, as she rummaged through the hay. But there was no sign of him. She ran around the garden, searching under bushes, calling his name, but he was nowhere in sight. Then she thought of the shelter and remembered it had no door – could he have fallen inside? She felt a glimmer of hope, but it vanished when she found he wasn't there either.

Her mother shouted from the back door, 'Come and get yer breakfast, Lizzie, or ye'll be late for school.'

She ran inside. 'Patch has gone!' she screamed. 'You left his door open! It's your fault!'

'Well, Lizzie, that's a nice little mouthful of cheek, Ah must say! Where the hell did ye learn that from? And blamin' me for yer lost rabbit!'

'Well, you fed him last night! You were the last one to see him!'

'Oh, stop yer blathering! Knowing yer dad, he'll get ye another one the minute he gets back. Now eat yer breakfast.'

Lizzie pushed the plate away. 'You're as hard as nails, Mam. You couldn't care less what's happened to Patch! Poor little thing! He'll be frightened all on his own!'

'It's just a bloody rabbit, Lizzie,' Alice snapped. 'There's plenty of victory gardens round here. He won't be short of a lettuce or two.'

'He could have been run over for all you care! You haven't even looked for him! And I wouldn't be surprised if you let him out on purpose!'

'Think what yer like. Ah'm used to gettin' the blame. Yer gettin' more like yer dad every day. Now get yerself off to school.'

'I will! And I wish I didn't have to come back here!'

Lizzie walked out, banging the door behind her. She hadn't gone three steps before the tears came. When she got to the end of the street, she saw Molly and Auntie Marion walking ahead. 'Molly! Molly!' she shouted. Molly turned round.

'What is it?' asked Mrs Brown when she saw Lizzie's grief-stricken face.

'It's Patch, he's gone missing! Mam said she would feed him last night but when I got up this morning the hutch was open and he was gone!'

'Oh that's awful!' said Molly. 'But don't you worry, we'll find him, won't we, Mam?'

'Of course we will,' Mrs Brown told her. 'I'll make some enquiries. He's got a very distinctive mark. I'm sure somebody's seen him.'

'Do you really think we'll find him, Auntie Marion?'

'Don't worry, pet, we'll do our best.'

But Mrs Brown was not as confident as she appeared. She couldn't help wondering, had Lizzie's mother deliberately harmed the rabbit?

Lizzie lay awake that night, thinking of ways to leave home. If I ran away, I'd need money, she realised. Maybe I could get a job and deliver newspapers like that boy in my school. He always had enough to buy comics and sherbet dabs. Dad had advertised his car in that newspaper. That's it, I'll write for a new mother! Somebody must want me.

She collected her notepad and pencil, jumped back into bed and began to write. 'Mother wanted for a girl, seven years old, willing to help in the house, not a fussy eater and a very good dancer. PS. The lady must love animals.'

But Mam mustn't find out. I know! I'll write 'Send to Mrs Wood at The Lilacs, Blaydon, County Durham. And please mark it private for Miss E. Wood.'

She would buy a stamp with the last of poor Patch's food money, and post her letter on the way to school.

She plumped up her pillows and put out the light. What will my new mam look like, she wondered. Maybe I'll have a brother or sister. And maybe my new mother wouldn't have a husband. Then she could meet my dad! I'm sure she would love him and never nag him. I wouldn't mind if he kissed her. I wouldn't be jealous. She put the letter under her pillow and fell asleep, dreaming of her new life.

⁂

A few days later, Peggy came back to read another letter from Jack. She sat at the kitchen table with Alice, while Lizzie hopped up and down, waiting to hear the news.

Peggy began to read. 'Dear Alice, I've got my first leave pass and look forward to coming home on Sunday . . .'

'Is that true, Auntie Peggy, is he really coming?'

'Shut up,' said Alice, 'Ah'm tryin' to listen.'

'The train should arrive about one a.m. on Sunday morning,' Peggy continued. 'I've got my key, so there's no need to wait up for me. Tell the bairn I've got a little case for her. It's filled with sweets and chocolates I managed to exchange for cigarettes. I have a little gift for you too, Alice. I can't wait to see you both. Lots of love Jack/Dad xxxxx.'

⁂

Alice looked in her wardrobe mirror and patted her hair. Thank God the hairdresser fitted me in today. Ah looked a right sight this morning. She put her hands on her hips and pulled in her stomach. Ah hope Ah can still get into

199

that frock he likes. She sighed. Ah well, Ah'd better get on. Jack's steak and kidney pie won't cook by itself.

Lizzie was in the kitchen reading a comic. She jumped up when she saw her mother. 'How many hours till Dad gets back, Mam?'

'How the hell do Ah know? And where did ye get that bloody comic?'

Lizzie's heart sank. 'I got it from Molly. Her mam buys it for her every week.'

'She must have money to burn, buyin' that bloody rubbish!'

'Can I stay up for Dad, Mam?' Lizzie asked hopefully.

'No ye bloody can't. Now get out from under me feet – Ah'm making a pie for 'im.'

Disappointed yet again, Lizzie did as she was told and went upstairs. What's the point of arguing? she asked herself. Mam always wins. I wish I was Molly. She never gets told off and she gets the *Dandy* every week.

She started to read, but it was impossible to concentrate. Her dad was coming home and she could hardly wait to see him. What shall I wear in the morning, she wondered. But just as she was looking through her wardrobe, her mother called her down for tea.

When she got to the kitchen, *Forces Favourites* was playing on the wireless and Vera Lynn was singing 'We'll Meet Again'. Lizzie smiled. That woman's got a lovely voice, she thought, I bet my dad would like her.

She sat at the table and stared at her plate of corned beef and cabbage. She hated corned beef – her mother had said it was made from horses! Remembering Roy Roger's horse, Trigger, from Saturday morning pictures, she pushed the plate away.

'It's no good turning yer nose up at that!' said Alice. 'There's nowt else.' She put an apple on the table. 'Here, take this and get up to bed.'

'Ah'm not tired, Mam, please can't I wait up for Dad?'

'No, Ah've already told ye. Now get to bed.'

Lizzie picked up the apple and trudged upstairs.

It was 2 a.m. when the doorbell rang. Oh bugger, thought Alice, I forgot to take the bloody bolt out. She hurried to the door, hoping the noise hadn't woken Lizzie. But Lizzie had heard the bell and was already running downstairs, in her dressing gown. She tripped on the last stair and Jack caught her in his arms and held her tight.

'My goodness,' he said, 'how my little girl has grown.'

'There's somebody standin' over here in case ye hadn't noticed,' said Alice sharply.

'Come here,' he said, 'you haven't changed a bit!' He put his arms around her and kissed her on the cheek.

Lizzie noticed the little suitcase Dad had mentioned in his letter and smiled. Alice glared at her over Jack's shoulder. 'I see ye've got yer eyes on the case, Lizzie. It's not you she's excited about, Jack, it's the sweets she's been waitin' for. Isn't that right?'

Lizzie's heart sank. 'You know that's not true! Anyway, you can have them, I don't want them now.' She began to cry.

'Never mind the bloody waterworks,' said Alice. 'Get off to bed. Dad and me 'ave grown-up things to talk about. Ye can see 'im in the mornin".'

Jack took Lizzie's hand. 'I'll just tuck her in, Alice.'

She stood with her hands on her hips as they went upstairs. 'Don't be long!' she shouted.

Lizzie climbed in to bed and Jack bent over her. 'I'm sorry about that. But I promise things will be different when the war's over. I've had time to think while I've been away. Trust me, things will get better when I'm home for good.'

Lizzie was still crying. 'No they won't, Dad! Patch has gone and it's Mam's fault! I'm sure she left the hutch open on purpose. I know she did!'

Alice shouted upstairs. 'What's goin' on, Jack? Are you comin' down or what?'

He kissed Lizzie. 'Dry your eyes, pet, I have to go, but don't worry, I'll get to the bottom of this.'

Lizzie looked up at him, wanting to believe his comforting words, like she had always done in the past, but she couldn't pretend to herself that things would really change. 'No you won't, Dad,' she said sadly. 'Mam always gets her own way.'

'Come on, pet, it'll be all right, you'll see.' Her dad sounded like he meant it.

But she doubted it ever would be.

Chapter 13

Lizzie woke to an unusual silence. She had fallen asleep last night to the sound of raised voices and now the peace and quiet worried her. Had her parents worn themselves out with their rowing, she wondered. She went to the dining room and gasped in dismay. There they were, drinking coffee together as though they were the best of friends.

Jack held his arms out when he saw her. 'Come here, pet, and give your dad a cuddle.'

She sat on his knee and kissed him. He hadn't changed a bit since he'd been away. She nuzzled into him. 'Is everything all right now, Dad?'

'What sort of question's that?' said Alice. 'Why shouldn't it be? Anyway, sit at the table and Ah'll fetch yer breakfast. Ye don't want to be late fer school.'

Lizzie jumped from Jack's knee. 'Not today, Mam!' she shouted. 'Dad's just got here and I've hardly seen him!'

Alice banged Lizzie's plate on the table. 'See what Ah have to put up with, Jack? Have ye got nowt to say?'

Lizzie looked up at her dad. Surely he would stick up for her. She hadn't done anything wrong.

'Mam knows best, Lizzie,' he said. 'You don't want to miss school.'

She took a deep breath. 'Have you asked Mam about Patch, Dad? You said you would.'

'For God's sake, Jack! She's not still goin' on about that bloody rabbit, is she? Blamin' me for gettin' rid of the thing.'

'Calm down, Alice.' He turned to Lizzie. 'After discussing Patch's disappearance with your mother last night, I'm convinced it was an accident. She's even happy for me to buy you another one.'

'That's funny, Dad, because that's just what she said you would do.' She raised her voice. 'Well don't bother because I don't trust her.'

She ran from the room. Jack called after her, but it was too late. She had already banged the door behind her.

Mrs Wood was pottering in the garden at The Lilacs when she heard the gate open. She turned to look and the trowel fell from her hand. 'Jack! Thank God you're home!' For a moment she couldn't move, she was so relieved to see he was safe.

He came over to the flower bed and put his arms around her. 'Come on now, Mother, I haven't exactly been in the thick of it.'

'Come inside and I'll put the kettle on, son.' She hastily fought to compose herself. It wouldn't do to let him see how worried she had been, even though, as he said, he hadn't been caught up in any fighting, or at least not yet.

It was lovely being back in his mother's comfortable sitting room, surrounded by all the old familiar knick-knacks. He let his eyes travel across the pictures and souvenirs he knew so well from his boyhood. He sat down with a sigh and, closing his eyes for a minute, listened to the reassuring sounds of her moving around in the kitchen. It wasn't long before she reappeared with a tray of tea and biscuits she must have been saving.

'So tell me, are they treating you all right? I hope there's no sign of you going to the front?'

'Don't worry, Mother. There's plenty of work for us in Wales, keeping those planes in good repair.'

'That's a relief, son. It may not be very patriotic, but I do hope nothing changes.'

Jack stretched out his legs and savoured his mother's special Lipton's tea. He smacked his lips. He'd never get this in the NAAFI.

Mrs Wood put her hand in her pocket and nervously fingered the letter she'd been carrying around for several days. 'I hope you won't mind me giving you this the moment you've come home, but it's been worrying me.' She took out the letter. 'Read this, son, while I pop in to the garden and turn off the hose.'

For a moment, Jack couldn't work out what it was – an envelope written in a child's hand, with 'Return to Sender' clearly added across the top later. There was something very familiar about it. He opened it with a sense of dread, drew out the single piece of paper and read every heart-breaking word.

He was wiping his eyes as his mother came in. 'Don't cry, son,' she said, 'it's better we know than being kept in the dark. They must have known it was from a child. Besides, she didn't include any money for the insertion. We must never let on we know and maybe she'll forget about it.'

Jack put his head in his hands. 'That's not the point, Mother. The point is that she wrote the letter in the first place. Whether she gets a reply or not won't make a difference to how she feels about Alice. I wish this bloody war was over. You've got no idea how it is for Lizzie. And to think I had to stand there listening to Alice screaming at her last night. If I hadn't agreed with her, things could get a lot worse for Lizzie when I'm away.'

He told his mother about the sweets and the rabbit and about how he had allowed Alice to send Lizzie to school on his first day at home. 'How do you think I felt, watching the bairn slowly turning away from me?'

'Don't be hard on yourself, son. Lizzie's a clever girl. She loves you. And I'm sure she'll see through it.'

'I hope you're right, Mother. Anyway, I've made a decision and I've been up half the night trying to persuade Alice to go along with it. If I can bring it off, Lizzie could enjoy a couple of days away from her mother. I told Alice we needed more time on our own. I suggested taking her dancing again and maybe going to Newcastle to see Vivien

Leigh and Clark Gable in that new film, *Gone With the Wind*. I couldn't think of any other way to get her to agree with Lizzie staying at Joe's for the weekend.'

'So, what did she say?'

'The jury's still out, Mother. I think it's just a case of her swallowing her pride after falling out with them. I went out early this morning and rang Joe from a phone box, just in case Alice overheard, and he said they'd be more than happy to have Lizzie. Annie said the Hoppings Fair has come to Blaydon and they've even got Dodgem cars. She said she can't wait to take the bairn.'

'Let me have a word with Alice, Jack, and I'll see what I can do.'

⚓

Alice was all smiles as Jack left with Lizzie for his brother's house. She had never intended to turn his invitation down in the first place, but it had been fun to make him wait for her decision. The thought of spending the weekend alone with Jack was more than she had hoped for.

Lizzie felt confused as she got into the car. Why am I spending the whole weekend with Uncle Joe, she wondered. After all, Dad's going back on Monday – when am I going to spend time with him?

On the way, Jack held on to Lizzie's hand. He prayed his mother was right and that the bairn would understand he was doing this for her.

He felt better when they got to his brother's house. Annie and Joe made a fuss of Lizzie and she seemed more relaxed. By the time he left she was already in her nightdress, with Joe reading her a story while Annie prepared their supper. Jack couldn't help envying his brother's happy marriage.

On his way home, Jack passed the Miner's Social Club. I could do with a drop of Dutch courage, he thought, before spending the weekend with Alice. He parked the car and made for the door. Not being a member, he would need someone to sign him in and he hoped he would see someone he knew. Just as he was thinking that, he felt a tap on his shoulder. 'Well Ah'll go to wor hoose, if it's not Jack Wood!' Recognition spread across Jack's face. 'Ah used to work for ye, before ye had to shut down.'

Jack shook his hand. 'Nice to see you, Tom. How come you're not in the forces?'

The young man laughed. 'Lucky me. Ah failed me eyesight, bonny lad.'

'I'm glad you're not still working for me in that case!' said Jack, relieved to have found a friendly face. 'Any chance of signing me in?'

'Ah'll do better than that! Come and join wor table and meet the family. They're ahl here tonight to hear Bobby Thompson. That's why the place is packed.' Tom clapped him on the back. 'He'll have ye in fits. There's nowt hitty missy about him, lad. He's that good, the club'll find it hard to afford his fees soon.'

Tom took Jack in to the hall, which as he had predicted was full to the gills. Large tables, each one big enough for ten people, packed the room. Pint beer glasses for men and smaller ones for ladies vied for space with packets of nuts and pork scratchings.

Everyone was jolly, anticipating the arrival of Bobby Thompson. It was so crowded, Tom had to squeeze between the chairs with Jack to reach his family's table. He introduced Jack to his grandmother, whose animated expression and bright eyes belied her age. Her face broke into a broad smile, showing her missing teeth. 'Sit down, canny lad,' she said, shifting a little and pulling her woollen shawl a little tighter. 'Any friend of wor Tom's is welcome.'

Tom went around the table naming the rest of his clan. Jack couldn't possibly remember all their names, but he would never forget their warmth or the smile on the grandmother's face.

Tom got to his feet. 'Ah'd better get the drinks in before Bobby Thompson comes on. What's yer poison, lad?'

'Put your money away, Tom, this is on me,' Jack insisted. It was the least he could do. Tom had given him such a friendly welcome, he was tempted to stay for the whole evening.

'Well, cheers, Jack. That's very generous of ye.'

The drinks arrived just in time before the lights dimmed. The small stage lit up and Bobbie Thompson's theme tune, 'Blaydon Races', blasted through the room. A spotlight focused on the side of the stage and, when a slight, anaemic-looking man walked into it, it seemed like the roof would lift from the roar of his devoted fans. He stood quite still as he searched in his pocket and brought out a tired old Woodbine, then, allowing the spotlight to take him a few steps further, stopped again to search for a match. After taking his time trying to light the weed, the spotlight guided him to the centre of the stage, where he struggled to puff on the dog-eared dumper.

He was a pathetic sight in trousers that hung around his shoes like concertinas, an old jumper that engulfed his little body and his famous old army beret that he never worked without. Bobbie Thompson knew his audience and held them in the palm of his hand.

'How's yer debt?' he said, with a big grin on his face. 'Ah'll bet there's a lorra debt in 'ere the neet!'

Jack smiled. Debt was Bobbie's usual subject and it went down well with an audience up to its eyes in it.

Holding the attention of them all, Bobbie went on, 'Eee, last night Ah couldn't sleep fer debt. And there's wor lass, sittin' there.' He pointed to a woman and the crowd loved it. 'She'll pay nobody! There was a knock on the door last Thursdy. It was the tally man. She says, in a posh voice, "Come in and take a seat, hinny." He said, "Don't worry, Missus, Ah'm comin' in to take the bloody lot!"'

The audience roared with laughter. Jack was grateful to be sharing a table with these kind-hearted people, who had welcomed him like one of their own. It was hard to remember the last time he had felt as relaxed as this. He looked at his watch. My God, he thought, I'm already late for Alice. Reluctantly, he said goodbye to his new friends and left with the sound of laughter ringing in his ears. What kind of mood would Alice be in, he wondered.

When Jack opened the front door, he heard music booming from the dining room. It was instantly recognizable: Richard Tauber singing 'You Are My Heart's Delight', the very song Alice had been playing on the night she had tried to hide Lizzie's accident from him. For a moment he froze, but this was no time to revisit old emotions, he had enough on his mind already. He pulled himself together and went inside.

'Hello, Alice,' he said, 'I'm sorry I'm late.'

She was bubbling with excitement, just as she had been on that dreadful day. 'That's all right, Jack,' she said, 'the night's still young. Ah've made us a little snack before we go. Well, how d'ye think Ah look?'

Alice was still a beautiful woman so he didn't have to lie. 'You look lovely.' He looked her up and down as she poured him a drink. She was wearing the gold pendant he had given her on their wedding day. It had belonged to his grandmother. He realised now that he had made a mistake. Alice didn't deserve the necklace and he wished he had saved it for Lizzie.

'Here's to us,' said Alice, as she raised her glass. 'Now, sit down and I'll get yer kippers.'

Jack did as he was told. The kippers were wizened and dry and he almost choked on every bite. Never mind, he thought, I'll get through this weekend as long as I remember I'm doing it for the bairn.

❧

Although she had missed her dad and felt angry about him going off with Mam for the weekend, Lizzie had enjoyed her time with Uncle Joe and Auntie Annie. It had been good to have a break from the constant bickering at home. Now it was time for Dad to come and get her. She wanted to see him, of course she did, but she still couldn't help feeling cross with him.

She was sitting quietly in the living room when the doorbell rang. At any other time, she would have rushed to the door, but this time she held back.

'Come inside,' she heard Uncle Joe saying. 'The bairn's waiting for you. She's been as good as gold.'

Lizzie looked up as her dad came in with her uncle. Her mam was there too. She wasn't expecting her after all the things she'd said about Auntie Annie and Uncle Joe.

Annie got up from her comfy chair. 'How nice to see you, Alice,' she said. 'I hope you enjoyed your weekend. We've had a lovely time with the bairn. You loved the Hoppings, didn't you, pet? Go on,' she said, 'give your mother her present.'

Lizzie kissed Alice and gave her a bag of coloured moth balls, which she'd won at the fair.

'Thanks,' she said, 'just what Ah've always wanted.'

Lizzie could tell she didn't mean it.

'Don't I get a kiss?' asked Jack. Lizzie walked stiffly towards him and pecked him on the cheek.

Alice opened her bag and took out a small box of chocolates. 'Ah'm sorry we got back later than we said, but time flies when yer havin' a good time, doesn' it?' She gave the chocolates to Annie. 'This is for lookin' after Lizzie and Ah wouldn't mind if ye could do it again on Jack's next leave. We've had the time of our lives, thanks to you. It was like a second honeymoon.' Alice began to giggle like a teenager.

'Come on,' Jack said hurriedly, 'we don't want to outstay our welcome. Get your coat, Lizzie.'

She dragged her feet into the hall and picked it up. If only I could stay here, she thought, I'm nothing but trouble at home. Anyway, Dad gets on better with Mam when I'm not there. I wish I could stay with Auntie Annie. I would ask Mrs Brown, except she lives too close to our house. Never mind, I can still pop in after school. It's not as if it's very far away.

'We're going now,' said Jack. 'Say thanks to your aunt and uncle, Lizzie.'

Lizzie ran to Annie and cuddled her. Annie smiled at Alice. 'We're glad you had such a lovely time. We hope we don't have to wait until Jack's next leave before we can have the bairn again, do we, Joe?'

'That's right, we've loved having her.'

'Well, Ah'll have to think about that.' Alice turned on her heels and waved. 'Ta ta for now.'

On the way back, Alice fished around in her bag. 'Oh! Ah must have left me moth balls behind, Lizzie.'

'Don't worry, Mam, I'll win you some more when I stay at Auntie Annie's again.'

'Divvn' be daft. The Hoppin's will have gone by that time. Why d'ye think they call them Hoppin's?'

'I don't know, Mam.'

'It's because they hop all over the bloody place. They'll be gone by next week.'

The car pulled up outside the house and Jack got out first. 'I'd better go inside and pack before dinner, my train leaves from Central Station at 8.45 in the morning.'

Lizzie got out next and watched as he opened the front door and disappeared inside. That's all he ever seems to do now, she thought, only this time he had disappeared for a whole weekend. If only I could disappear. I'm sick of the sight of the two of them. It's clear to see whose side Dad's on.

'What the hell are ye standin' there for, Lizzie?' Alice shouted. 'Didn' ye 'ear what yer dad said?'

'Yes, Mam.'

'Well get inside and give us a hand. Ah don't wanna keep 'im waitin' for 'is dinner.'

My goodness, thought Lizzie, as she followed Alice into the house. Dad must've given her a good time for her to make such a fuss over him.

'Stop daydreamin', Lizzie, and lay the table, while Ah warm up the stew. We'll 'ave it in the kitchen.'

I'd rather have mine in Timbuktu than eat with you, Lizzie thought.

'And when ye've finished that, mash the tatties.' She pushed a large fork into Lizzie's hand. ''Ere, and add a bit o' milk. It'll be a lang time before yer dad gets a bit o' home cookin' again.'

'What's that about home cooking?'

Alice turned to see Jack standing in the doorway. 'Yer dinner won't be lang, pet.'

'It's good to see you helping your mother, Lizzie, you're a good girl,' Jack said warmly.

She forced a smile and carried on mashing.

'Am I not getting a kiss, then?'

She pecked him on the cheek.

'Fancy yer dad havin' to ask ye fer a kiss,' said Alice. 'Take the tatties over, the stew's nearly hot enough.'

Lizzie put the dish on the table and sat down, trying hard not to meet Jack's eyes. She wondered why her mam had to make such a nasty remark when she'd had Dad to herself all weekend. Alice put the stew on the table and ladled some on to Jack's plate.

She was about to serve Lizzie, but she pushed her plate away. 'Not for me,' she said, 'I've lost my appetite.'

Jack put his arm around her. 'I know something that'll give you an appetite, pet. Mam said you don't have to go to school until after I've left tomorrow.'

Lizzie stood up. 'Mam's only trying to please you, Dad. She was right. I shouldn't miss school. I'm not hungry anyway. I'm tired and I'm going to bed.'

She was on her way upstairs when Alice called after her, 'Aren't ye goin' to say goodnight to yer dad?'

She came back and kissed him. 'I'd better say goodbye now in case I miss you in the morning. Well,' she said cheekily, 'like Grandma Rooney says, kill plenty of bloody Germans.' She quickly covered her mouth. 'Whoops, sorry. Anyway, there won't be any Germans in Wales, so I know you'll come back safe, Dad.'

She kissed him again and hurried upstairs. She ran a bath and, using the rest of her bath salts, stirred them around before getting in. The water was just right and it smelt lovely. She lay back.

'Dear God, I hope you don't mind me saying my prayers in the bath tonight. I'm so unhappy, I don't think my dad loves me anymore. I've hardly seen him since he came home. He takes my mother's side all the time and I'm always in trouble. My dad used to be so nice and he even bought me a rabbit, but she soon put an end to that and, please forgive me, but I think she killed Patch. I hope that's not a mortal sin and I'll burn in hell. Anyway, I don't really believe in such a place. My mother acts like a saint when she's in church. I only wish people could see what she's like at home. Grandma Wood doesn't go to church and she's a good woman. Please teach me to be like her. I know my dad still loves me really, but my mam gets on his nerves and he tries to keep the peace. Thank you for my dancing classes and please don't let my mam fall out with Grandma Wood. Thanks for listening. Love from Lizzie.'

ɔʄɛ

The moment Lizzie woke, she knew she couldn't let her Dad go without telling him she loved him. She jumped out of bed and ran downstairs. 'Dad! Dad!' she called. He was in the kitchen, drinking a mug of tea. He put it down and she ran breathlessly into his arms.

He held her tight and swallowed hard to hold back the tears. 'I haven't slept all night, pet, for thinking I might not see you this morning. Oh Lizzie, I was afraid I might have lost you.'

Lizzie snuggled against his shoulder and hugged him as if she would never let him go. 'I love you, Dad,' she said. 'And don't worry, you'll never get rid of me.'

Chapter 14

Newcastle upon Tyne, 1941

Lizzie sat at her desk, chewing her pencil. How could she concentrate on her lesson when she was meeting Aunt Peggy after school? She hadn't seen her since she'd fallen out with her mother and that was ages ago. Now there were three unopened letters from her dad sitting on the sideboard just waiting for Peggy to read them.

The classroom clock seemed to move slower than ever. Lizzie was wondering if they had forgotten to wind it up, when the bell rang for home time. She stuffed her books into her desk and hurried out of the classroom with Molly.

'Supposing your aunt doesn't turn up?' she said as they rushed in to the playground.

Lizzie pushed her. 'Don't be daft. Look! She's already there, talking to your mother.' She ran the rest of the way and threw her arms around Peggy.

'Whoops!' said Mrs Brown. 'You nearly knocked her over.'

Peggy laughed. 'She's just excited, we haven't seen each other for ages. Ah haven't seen you either, Molly. Here, Ah've brought ye a few sweets.'

'Thank you, but I'd rather come on the walk with you and Lizzie.' Molly looked up hopefully at the adults.

'Well you can't,' said Mrs Brown, 'they've got things to talk about. Just make sure you take Lizzie back home in time, Peggy. Your sister thinks she's having tea with us and I don't want her turning up on our doorstep. Don't worry, dear, I'm well aware of your situation.'

Lizzie waved at Molly as she skipped away with Peggy. 'Never mind,' she called, 'you can come next time.'

'Let's walk to the war memorial and sit on a bench,' said Peggy as they wandered along the pavement, 'and you can tell me how's it bin.'

The smile left Lizzie's face. 'Mam's up one minute and down the next. I never know what to expect when I get home from school.'

'Does yer Grandma Wood still take ye to dancin' lessons?'

'Yes she does, and I suppose I should be thankful for that, but why don't you come to read Dad's letters anymore?' Lizzie gazed up at her aunt. 'There's three sitting on the sideboard already.'

Peggy fell silent for a moment as they walked along, a serious look on her face. Finally they drew close to the memorial. It was very peaceful and they could hear the birds singing.

'Here we are,' said Peggy, 'let's sit down.' She led her niece to the nearby bench and took a seat on the cold wood. Clouds were gathering and she hoped they'd make it back before it rained.

Lizzie stared up at the huge statue of a soldier with a bayonet in his hands. 'What's he supposed to be doing, Auntie Peggy?'

'He was defendin' our country, Lizzie. The monument is to honour the local soldiers who fought in the first world war. There were hundreds like him – young lads who never came back. Ahl their names are printed on that stone.'

'Will my dad have a bayonet, Peggy?'

'No, hinny. Now sit down, 'cos there's somethin' Ah have to tell ye.' She held Lizzie's hand and snuggled up to her on the bench. Her heart was heavy with what she had to say. 'Ah can't read the letters anymore.'

Lizzie laughed. 'Stop joking!'

Peggie squeezed her. 'Ah wish Ah was, pet, but Ah'm not.'

'But why can't you, Aunt Peggy?'

Peggy sighed. 'Because yer mother's never satisfied with what yer dad writes and she makes my life a bloomin' misery.'

Lizzie realised that this wasn't a joke after all and her face fell. Although she tried hard not to, she started to cry. 'But what about me? I love my dad and I miss hearing you read his letters! Anyway, why doesn't Mam read them herself?'

'I wish there was some other way to tell ye, sweetheart, but the truth is . . .' Peggy swallowed hard. 'Yer mother never went to school.' She breathed out deeply. There, the secret was out.

Lizzie dried her eyes. 'I don't believe you, Auntie – everybody goes to school.'

'Well yer mother didn't. She had trouble with her heart – at least, that's what Grandma Rooney said – and that's why she can't read the letters.' Peggy paused. 'Are you a good reader, Lizzie?'

'Yes, Auntie, I'm very good. I'm eight now.'

'D'ye think you could read them? Ye never know, there might be somethin' yer dad wants to tell ye. Ah'm sorry to lay this on ye, pet. Ah'm sure things canna be easy for you at home.'

Lizzie sat open-mouthed. It was hard to believe Mam couldn't read. Peggy watched her stricken face. 'Forget it, pet,' she said, inwardly berating herself. 'Ah shouldn't have asked ye. It's not fair.'

'No, it's all right, Auntie. I'd love to read Dad's letters, but do you think Mam'll let me?'

'Ye can only ask her, pet. If she's desperate enough, Ah'm sure she will.' She gave Lizzie a hug. 'Cheer up, pet, it'll be all right. But we'd better get back now – we don't want to get Mrs Brown into trouble.' The clouds were looming now and the sky grew darker by the minute. All the more reason to hurry to get the child home.

As they set off, Lizzie thought about reading the letters. If I tell Mam everything Auntie Peggy said she'll go mad, and if she doesn't like what's in the letters, she'll go even madder. Whatever I say, I can't win, so I'll just have to tell her the truth.

At the end of Lizzie's road, near the Browns' house, Peggy stopped. 'Ah'll leave ye here, pet. We don't want yer mam seein' me and causin' a fuss.' She gave Lizzie one last hug. 'You're a good girl,' she said, 'try not to worry. It'll all work out in the end.'

Lizzie watched her walk away, her coat flapping in the wind, and hoped it wouldn't be too long before she saw her again, then gloomily set off for home. She wondered what mood her mam would be in and decided to slip in quietly through the back door. She was startled to see a bald-headed man standing in the garden by the rabbit hutch. He had a hammer in his hand and was prising the wood apart.

'What're you doing here?' she said. 'That's my rabbit hutch!'

The man came forward and stood so close, she could smell his beery breath when he spoke. 'Ah'm takin' this away for yer mam, hinny.'

'No you're not!' she shouted. 'That hutch belongs to me!'

'Ah'm just doin' me job, pet.'

'Well, you can just stop it! Anyway, why aren't you fighting Hitler?'

'Lizzie!' She turned to see her mother running across the lawn. 'Get inside and stop bothering that man! What's the bloody use of a hutch when the rabbit buggered off months ago!'

'But he might still come back, Mam.'

Alice pushed her. 'Divvn' be daft, get yersel' inside and lay the table!'

The bald-headed man stood with his hands on his hips. 'What d'ye want me to do, Missus?'

'What d'ye think?' stormed Alice. 'Get the bloody thing out of here, Ah want to plant some rhubarb!'

Lizzie left Alice in the garden with the bald-headed man and made her way to the kitchen. She considered her options while she laid the table. If she's in a bad mood, I'll never get to read the letters, so I'd better not mention the rabbit hutch. I know! I'll sacrifice my egg ration and surprise Mam with a lovely treat. That'll put her in a good mood. She pottered around the kitchen, making sure everything was just right. She was just placing the jam on the table, when she looked up and saw Alice standing in the doorway, her eyes focused on the boiled egg and buttered toast sitting on the table on one of her best plates. 'And what's ahl this?' she shouted. 'Who said ye could have a bloody egg, Lizzie?'

' . . . But it's for you, Mam.'

Alice's lips tightened. 'Well, divvn' think ye can get round me with a bloody egg!'

Lizzie passed her the salt. 'Would you like me to cut your toast into soldiers, Mam?'

'No! But ye can get me a cuppa tea. Ah'm parched after ahl that carry on!'

Lizzie put the kettle on. By the time she turned round, Alice had decapitated the egg and was dunking the toast in the yolk. She looked like she was enjoying it. Wonders never cease, thought Lizzie, she might even be pleased with me now – this could be the right time to ask about the letters.

'I see Dad's letters are still on the sideboard, Mam.'

'Well, what about it?'

'Well – it's just . . . I saw Auntie Peggy.'

'Oh, ye did, did ye?'

'Yes – and she said I should read the letters.'

Alice glared at her. 'And why would that be?'

'. . . because she said you never learned to read or write.'

Alice took Lizzie by the shoulders and almost shook the life out of her. 'Are ye sure that's what she said? Are ye tellin' me the truth, ye little bugger?'

'Yes, Mam, and if it's really true, can I read them for you?'

Alice was momentarily speechless.

'Are you all right, Mam?'

'Never you mind! Just get on and read the bloody letter!' Alice swept her hand through her hair in aggravation.

'But there's three, Mam, which one shall I read first?'

'Please yer bloody self!'

Lizzie picked up a letter and tore it open. 'Dear Alice,' she read. 'How are things at home? Is there anything you need and how are you both coping? Have you had the shelter floor cemented yet? Please get someone in – it will be too damp to use otherwise. Keep up your schoolwork,

Lizzie, and stay at the top. And Alice, remember what I said about the shelter. Love Jack/Dad xx.'

Lizzie looked up at her mother. 'Did you like the letter?' she asked eagerly.

'Never you mind if Ah like it – Ah'm off to see me mother and if Peggy's there, God help her!' Alice stood up suddenly, scraping the chair against the floor and slamming down her half-drunk tea. 'And since ye ask, no, Ah didn't like the bloody letter and ye'd better behave yersel' while Ah'm gone.'

'But what about the other letters . . .'

'What aboot them? Mention them again and ye'll wonder what's hit ye.'

Lizzie longed to know what the other letters said, but was too scared to mention them again. She was glad when her mother threw on her coat and stormed out of the house. It was good to be alone. The silence was soothing and she read her father's letter again.

Poor Peggy, she thought, I wouldn't like to be in her shoes when Mam gets her hands on her. I'm not surprised she doesn't come any more.

Her stomach was rumbling and she wondered if there was something to eat. After searching through the kitchen cupboards, she found the remains of the cheese ration. At first, she felt reluctant to take it, but hunger won. She sliced it thinly, spread two slices of bread with the last of the pickle, and made herself a sandwich. Not bad, she thought, as she hungrily took a bite. She helped herself to a glass of milk and sat at the table to start her homework. The class had been asked to write a story with a happy ending and Lizzie decided hers would be about a lost rabbit who had found his way home.

She was so engrossed in her work that by the time she looked at the clock, it was already 9.30 and her mother still hadn't returned. Well, there's no point in sitting in the cold kitchen now that the fire's gone out, she decided. I think I'll get ready for bed and wait for Mam.

It was 10.15 when Lizzie went back downstairs and there was still no sign of Alice. She returned to her room and lay on the bed. It was hard to keep her eyes open and in no time she had drifted off to sleep.

She woke with a start as her bedroom door burst open. Alice was standing in the doorway. 'And what have Ah told ye about leavin' the bloody lights on!' she shouted. 'Ah saw them from the bloody street, girl! You know you're meant to check the blackout curtains!'

Lizzie rubbed her eyes and looked at the clock. 'It's half-past eleven, Mam, where have you been?'

'It's none o' your business. Just don't let me catch ye leavin' them on agin!'

Alice switched the light out and left the room, almost removing the door from its hinges.

Lizzie lay in the dark, wondering what her mother would do next. Nothing seems to please her – she moans when she doesn't get a letter from Dad and she moans when she does. It's not my fault he doesn't say what she wants to hear. Maybe if I added a few nice words in his next letter, it might put her in a better mood. She joined her hands together.

'Dear God,' she said, 'I know you won't mind if I tell a few white lies to please my mother by changing Dad's words just a little bit. I'm sorry to say I don't like living with Mam, but I've got nowhere else to go – my dad is fighting Hitler. Nobody answered my letter when I tried to find a new mother so that didn't work. Please let the war be over soon, so he can come home. I know you must be busy, but if you can make my mam friends with my dad's family again, it would truly be your miracle. Please watch over me and keep me safe. Love from Lizzie. PS, I miss Patch. I hope he's with you in heaven.'

Lizzie opened the garden gate. For once she was glad to be home from school. She had been on edge all day. That morning, an envelope with her father's handwriting had dropped through the letterbox and she'd snatched it up almost before it hit the floor. She had hidden it in her knickers and taken it to school to read it first.

She read the letter at playtime – it was a treat to read her father's words before anyone else did. She found a quiet corner of the playground, hidden behind the shed so that not even Molly would find her, and brushing away the dirt she sat down and thought about what her mam might like to hear. Something loving would be nice – she'd like that. And a bit of flattery wouldn't go amiss. She conjured up a few choice remarks, hoping she would remember them by the time she got home. I'll just do my best and keep my fingers crossed.

When she got home, she rattled the letterbox before going inside. 'The second post's here,' she called, 'and there's a letter from Dad!'

'Then hurry up and fetch it, girl, Ah'm in the kitchen!' Alice had her back to the door, busy at the sink. Water splashed noisily from the tap.

Lizzie hastily pulled the crumpled letter from her pocket, straightened it out and hid the envelope in her school bag.

'Go on then, girl, what're ye waitin' for?'

Lizzie was all of a tremble and held the letter high to cover her face. 'Shall I start now, Mam?'

Alice turned to face her daughter, dried her hands on the tea towel and nodded her head.

'Dearest wife,' she said, 'I miss you every day. I can't wait to come home on leave. Have you seen to the shelter floor? I bet you have because you are so clever. I will bring you a nice present when I come home. I hope Lizzie is a good girl and does not worry you or she will be in trouble. I have to go now. Love to Lizzie and lots of love to you. From your ever-loving husband, Jack.'

When Lizzie dared to look up, Alice was grinning like a Cheshire cat.

꣼

Lizzie stood in Molly's garden, clutching a letter Miss Birkstrand had told her to give to her mother. Whatever it is, she thought, it can't be good news.

Since she'd been altering her dad's letters, her life had become so much better. She was allowed to play with Molly at weekends and sometimes they even went to Saturday morning pictures together. Although the cinema was a flea-pit and they had to go down a gloomy, dark street to get there, they never minded. But there was a condition. Now she had to reply to Jack's letters. This was more difficult than reading them. Sometimes there would be words she couldn't spell, but it didn't seem to matter so much because her mother was always happy with her efforts.

But composing the letters, writing back, and working hard to keep Mam in a good mood was taking its toll. She'd been finding it hard to concentrate at school and once she had fallen asleep right in the middle of maths.

'I'm a bit worried, Molly,' she said. 'Can I show you something in private?'

'That sounds exciting, Lizzie, we'd better go into the shelter. Like the poster warns, careless talk costs lives.'

Molly opened the metal door and led the way inside. She lit the paraffin stove and passed Lizzie a torch. 'Go on, then!' she said. 'Keep calm and carry on!'

'This is serious, Molly.' Lizzie was struggling to make her friend understand. Molly's life was so easy by comparison. 'Miss Birkstrand gave me this letter to give to Mam. I haven't opened it yet. So promise to cross your heart and hope to die if you dare to tell what's inside.'

'For goodness sake, get on and read it or I'll die from suspense.' Molly rubbed her hands together, partly because it was cold in the underground shelter, partly from anticipation.

Lizzie opened the letter, switched on the torch and began to read. 'Dear Mrs Wood, I have to inform you that I am less than satisfied with Lizzie's work of late. It distresses me to watch a girl with so much potential slide back so far in such a short time. I have always considered Lizzie to be a bright and outgoing child. Please inform me of any underlying problem, medical or otherwise, that could be causing this state of apathy. The school has a reputation for its care and concern for its pupils, so please get in touch with me and we can discuss the matter further. Best regards, Miss Birkstrand.'

Lizzie looked up at Molly. 'Well!' she said. 'What do you think of that?'

Molly screwed up her face. 'I didn't understand all those big words, but it seems to me Miss Birkstrand thinks you're a dunce.'

Lizzie pushed her. 'I meant, should I give the letter to Mam?'

'Don't be daft! Unless you want another clip around the ears.' Molly reached under a bunk and pulled out a tin of sweets. 'Here,' she said, 'tear up the letter and have a black bullet.'

'I don't mind if I do.' Lizzie took a sweet and was sucking it thoughtfully when there was a knock at the shelter door.

'Come on, you two, I know you're in there.' Mrs Brown put her head around the door. 'Your tea's ready. And make sure you put that smelly stove out, Molly.'

Lizzie took a deep breath and made her decision – she tore the letter up into tiny pieces. 'What'll I do with this, Molly?'

'Come with me,' she said, 'I've got the very place.' She led Lizzie to the bottom of the garden. 'This'll do nicely.'

'But it's a gooseberry bush!'

Molly laughed. 'My mam said I was born under one o' these. Let's dig a hole here. Hang on, while I get the shovel from the shed.'

Lizzie and Molly took turns to dig, as the shovel was big and heavy, almost too much for them to manage. Luckily the soil was loose under the bush and it didn't take long. Lizzie put the letter into the hole, filled it with earth, then stamped it down thoroughly. That's it, she thought, that letter will never be found! And now it's time for tea! She put down the spade and ran into the house with Molly. She was supposed to go home in case there was a letter from

Dad, but she couldn't resist Mrs Brown's homemade fruit cake. What the heck, she thought, I'm already in trouble, so I might as well enjoy the cake.

She was finishing the last crumbs when she heard the short, sharp shriek of her mother's voice.

Mrs Brown popped her head around the dining room door. 'Come on, Lizzie,' she said, 'your mother's here.'

Lizzie walked straight into a slap across the head from Alice. 'Didn't Ah tell ye to hurry home?'

Mrs Brown fought hard to contain herself. What can I do? she thought. If I interfere, it will only make matters worse. I'd like to know what goes on in that woman's head.

'It was my fault,' said Molly, 'I wanted to show her my new comic.'

Alice dragged Lizzie to the door and pushed her outside. 'This had better not happen again!' she said. 'Ah'll say whether Lizzie can stay or not.'

'Of course, I'm sorry. I'll make sure she has your permission next time.' Mrs Brown stood there helpless as she watched Alice repeatedly push Lizzie until they were out of sight.

'Lizzie's mam goes to church every Sunday,' said Molly. 'Do you think she'll go to heaven?'

'No pet, I don't think they'll let her in.'

᚛᚜

Lizzie didn't have to guess what would happen when she got home. The scene had been played so many times, she almost knew the words inside out.

'Well, Ah hope yer proud of yersel', defyin' me like that! Ah don't know what Mrs Brown must think of me!' Alice shouted.

Well I do, thought Lizzie, and so do a lot of other people.

'Anyway, get off to bed, Ah'm sick of the sight of ye.'

'I'm sorry I'm such a nuisance, Mam. Can I take one of Dad's storybooks with me?'

When she saw the look on her mother's face, she already knew the answer.

'No ye bloody can't.'

She climbed upstairs, defeated. Her head was aching and her back was sore from the constant pushing on the way home. I've only got myself to blame, she thought, Mam did say to come straight home from school.

It was good to get into bed. Thank goodness she'd had Mrs Brown's fruit cake, as her mother hadn't thought to give her anything else to eat. She plumped up her pillows and sat up straight to say her prayers.

'Dear God, I want to confess things that might be sins. I tore up the teacher's letter to my mother today and I stayed at Molly's house when my mam said to come straight home. I think I get on her nerves and I wish I didn't live here any more. No matter what I do, there's no pleasing her, so I won't try any more. I'll just do what I'm told and keep my thoughts to myself. I'm not a nasty girl, but I'm tired of being pushed around. Please let the war be over soon and bring my dad home. Love from Lizzie.'

She looked up at the main light to be sure it was off, turned out her beside lamp and snuggled down to sleep.

༺

Next morning, Lizzie woke up late. She was pulling on her cold schoolclothes when she heard the letterbox rattle and ran downstairs, socks still around her ankles, but she was too late. Alice was standing in the hall with a letter in her hand. 'It's from yer dad,' she said. 'Hurry up and read it before you go.'

Lizzie shuddered at the thought. How can I change it without knowing what it says – and what if Mam doesn't like it?

Alice ripped open the envelope and took out the letter. 'Go on then, girl, what the hell are ye waiting for?' She strode into the kitchen and began slamming down the breakfast things on the table.

Lizzie had no choice. She would have to read it. She bought herself a few extra moments by sitting down at the table, carefully pulling in her chair.

As she unfolded the page, she noticed how short it was.

'Dear Alice, It's bad news I'm afraid. All leave has been cancelled until further notice. I can't say any more at the moment because it's top secret. Please be patient and know that I am thinking of you both. Let's hope that the war will be over soon. Lots of love Jack/Dad. PS Please send me a picture of you both so I can remind myself how lucky I am.'

Lizzie waited for her mother's reaction, but there was none. 'Can I go to school now, Mam?'

Alice was staring at the cupboards, with a face like thunder. 'Ye can go where the hell ye like. And don't expect yer dad back! He's probably shacked up with some floozy in Wales.'

'What's a floozy, Mam?'

'Never you mind. You'll know soon enough, when Ah get me hands on her! Now, get off to school before Ah lose me temper!' She stepped forward sharply and took hold of Lizzie's chair. 'Did ye hear me? Get off to school!' She pulled the chair backwards causing Lizzie to slide, face upwards, under the table, grazing her brow on its edge.

'Well, what are yer waitin' for?' Alice shouted.

Lizzie crawled from under the table and rushed upstairs to the bathroom. She looked in the mirror. There was blood on her brow. She soaked her flannel in warm water, wrung it out and dabbed the sore skin. Then she brushed her hair, pulling down the shorter lengths in an attempt to cover the tell-tale mark, and tip-toed downstairs, leaving for school by the back door.

'I can't understand this sum,' said Molly. It was a few days later and they were in the classroom at school. The mark on Lizzie's forehead had faded from angry red to a barely noticeable scratch, but Molly couldn't help staring at it every time she looked at her friend. 'Can I have a look at your answer?'

Lizzie covered her book with her hands. 'I think that'd be cheating, Molly.'

Molly scowled at her. 'You're my best friend, Lizzie, *I'd* cheat for *you.*'

Lizzie chewed the inside of her lip, not sure what to do. She was trying to decide when a high-pitched wailing noise filled the room. It was so strange and so shrill she was forced to cover her ears.

Miss Birkstrand stood up and blew her whistle. 'This is a real air raid warning, children. Please keep calm and do as you've been taught. Leave everything behind and march into the hall with me.'

The children stood up and the sound of scraping chairs filled the room. Susie Brigshaw opened her desk and started to rummage around inside. 'She's looking for her sweets,' Molly whispered, 'the greedy little cat! She'd rather get bombed than leave her sweets behind.'

'Come along now, no dilly dallying,' Miss Birkstrand said as she walked to the door. The children lined up in pairs behind her and she led them into the corridor. They walked briskly to the assembly hall and filed in.

The noise was deafening. Mr Sowerby was standing on the rostrum. 'All right,' he shouted, 'there's no need to panic. We've practised for this moment many times before and you all know the drill. You will remain silent as you walk in an orderly manner across the yard to the shelter. And let me warn all those comedians who decide to do otherwise, you will be invited to my office for six of the best when the all-clear goes. Right! On the left, quick, march!'

The children turned and trouped back out of the room, down the corridor and across the playground. Molly grabbed Lizzie's arm. 'If Mr Sowerby had gone on any longer, we'd have all been bombed before we got to the shelter.'

'Shh!' said Lizzie. 'I don't want six of the best.'

Mr Sowerby reached the shelter first. He unlocked the door and held it open as the children filed inside.

'Make your way to the end,' he said, 'and make room for the rest.'

They sat down on the benches, squeezing together as close as they could. They were much quieter than they had been on the practice drill. Even the most boisterous boys seemed withdrawn. Then, one foolhardy lad piped up, 'When do we get the black bullets, sir?'

Mr Sowerby stiffened and glared at him. 'Haven't you noticed there's a war on?!' he shouted. 'Our brave lads out there in the thick of it will get bullets all right, but they won't be the kind they can suck, you greedy boy!'

Lizzie nudged Molly. 'Do you think we'll have to stay here long?'

'It depends if the Germans have dropped their bombs yet. Maybe they'll drop one on your house, then you could move in with us,' Molly suggested cheerfully.

'But what about Mam, Molly?'

'Don't worry, she'll be safe. She's probably taking a swim in your waterlogged air raid shelter.'

'Now,' said Mr Sowerby, 'to keep our spirits up, we'll start with some patriotic songs followed by a spelling bee.' Several children groaned. 'And you'll be pleased to know,' he continued, 'there'll be a break for milk and biscuits after the singing. We'll start with "Land of Hope and Glory" to get us in the mood.'

Lizzie quite enjoyed the first few songs and sang them with gusto. But by the time they got to song number six, she felt quite exhausted. How could she concentrate on a spelling bee if this went on much longer – and she was good at spelling. They were halfway through 'There'll Always Be an England' when a long, flat wailing sound drowned them out.

'Right, children, that's the All Clear,' Mr Sowerby said. 'And the good news is it's already home time.'

'That's a short air raid, sir,' said a fat spotty boy.

'What about the milk and biscuits?' shouted another.

Molly nudged Lizzie. 'Do you want to stay for milk and biscuits?'

'No, let's see if Auntie Marion's here yet.' She put up her hand. 'Please can we leave now, Mr Sowerby?'

'All right, girls, but make sure your parents are at the gate before you go into the street.'

They clambered across the benches and went out into the yard. 'Phew,' said Molly, 'I'm glad to get out of there. I was sitting next to that pongy Perkins! I swear his mother never washes his sweaty clothes.'

'Look,' said Lizzie, 'there's your mother!'

Mrs Brown was at the gate with her gas mask slung over her shoulder. Molly and Lizzie ran towards her and she held out her arms. 'Give me a cuddle, girls, thank God you're safe and sound.'

'Can we go straight home?' said Molly. 'It was freezing in that shelter!'

'Have you seen Mam, Auntie Marion? I hope she's all right.' Lizzie gazed anxiously at Mrs Brown's kind face.

'I'm sure she is, pet,' Mrs Brown reassured her. 'Let's get you home. She'll be worried sick about you.' She opened her bag and took out two sherbet dabs. 'Here we are,' she said, 'at least Hitler hasn't bombed the sweet shop yet. Now come along.'

As they set off down the street, Molly opened her sherbet dab, wet her finger and dipped it inside. 'Aren't you going to start yours, Lizzie?'

'No, I'm saving mine until I get home.'

'Well,' she said, scooping up a big bit of sherbet, 'please yourself. Aren't you coming to our house then?'

'Not this time, Molly,' said Mrs Brown. 'Her mam's bound to be worrying about her. It's best to go straight home after that air raid, Lizzie.'

❧

Lizzie pushed open the front door and her heart lifted. Aunt Peggy's old grey tweed coat with the astrakhan collar was hanging from a peg in the hall. She dropped her school bag and ran into the kitchen.

'Hello, Mam! Hello, Auntie Peggy!'

'And what am I, the cat's mother?'

Lizzie turned to find her Grandma Rooney perched on a chair near the sink. 'Hello, Grandma!' she said. 'I didn't see you there, sitting in the corner.'

Alice was pouring out the tea. 'Your Auntie Peggy's had an accident, Lizzie. The bloody Germans dropped a bomb at the back of Vickers-Armstrongs factory. Peggy's lucky to be alive.'

'It's only a scratch,' said Mrs Rooney, 'don't bloody exaggerate, Alice.'

Peggy held out her bandaged arm. 'And how would you know, Mother, when ye haven't even seen it? Anyway, the both of ye haven't even asked about the bairn.' She put her good arm around Lizzie. 'How was it in the shelter, pet, were ye frightened?'

'No, Auntie Peggy. Mr Sowerby kept us busy singing songs and we were supposed to have a spelling bee, but the all-clear went. Is your arm all right?'

'It's not too bad, pet. Ah was hit by some flying shrapnel, but the Red Cross man managed to get it out.'

'What's shrapnel, Auntie?' Lizzie was curious.

'It's tiny bits of metal that fly from a bomb when it explodes.'

'Is the factory all right?' asked Alice. 'Have ye still got yer job?'

'The back rooms are all gone – there's just a pile of bricks and rubble left. We don't know what's goin' on, but we could be laid off till further notice.'

Mrs Rooney sat up swiftly. 'Ah hope not,' she said. 'With nowt comin' in, Ah can't afford to keep ye.'

Lizzie had a wonderful idea. 'Can't Auntie Peggy stay with us, Mam?'

Alice gave her one of her black looks. 'Ah don't know,' she said. 'Ah'll have to ask yer dad.'

'Don't bother,' said Peggy. She winced as she sat up straighter. 'Ah've got plans of me own. Ah've decided to join the Land Army. Some of the girls in the factory have already joined and they love it.'

'What would you have to do, Auntie Peggy?'

'Just like the other girls do, Lizzie,' Peggy explained, her face brightening as she warmed to her theme. 'Take the place of the men who used to do the job before they were called up. Some of the girls drive tractors and some plough fields. Others look after the farm animals and see to the sheep.'

Mrs Rooney burst out laughing. 'And what makes ye think they'd have ye in the Land Army, when ye can't even ride a bloody bike, never mind drive a bloody tractor!'

'Don't listen to her, Auntie! You'll be a good driver when you've had lessons.'

'Mind your own business,' said Alice, 'and don't be cheeky to yer grandma.' She refilled her own cup, leaving the pot just out of Peggy's reach.

If only I was a bit taller, thought Lizzie, I could join the Land Army with Auntie Peggy. I'm very fond of her and I'm sure her life's not much better than mine either. Wouldn't it be nice if we could spend the war together, taking care of the animals.

Grandma Rooney invaded Lizzie's thoughts. 'Did ye hear what happened to Mrs Snaith the other night, Alice?'

'What the hell do Ah care, Mother?'

'Ye'd care if it was you! They were asleep in their beds when a bloody burglar came through the window and cleaned them out!'

'Shut up, Mother,' said Peggy, 'ye'll frighten the bairn!'

'Never mind the bairn,' said Alice, 'Ah know you're bloody frightenin' me! It's all right for you two. If anybody got through your window wor Martin would bloody kill 'em!'

Peggy put her arm around Lizzie. 'Don't listen to them, pet. It's safe enough around here.' She gave the girl a squeeze.

Mrs Rooney stood up. 'Come on, Peggy,' she said, 'wor Martin'll be back from work in an hour and Ah'm not keepin' him waitin' for his dinner. He works hard and at least he pays his way!'

'Don't rub it in, Mam.' Peggy stood up carefully.

Lizzie noticed Auntie Peggy looked pale and she was rubbing the bandage on her arm.

'This is giving me gyp,' she said. 'Ah could do with a lie down.'

'What about wor Martin's dinner, Peggy?' Grandma Rooney demanded.

'What about it, Mother?' Peggy fired back, her patience exhausted. 'The way Ah'm placed, Ah can't cook. He'll just have to have fish and chips, and lump it.'

Lizzie put her arms around Peggy. 'You don't look well, Auntie. Would you like to share my sherbet dab?'

'No thank you, pet, but ye can give me a hand to put me coat on.'

Alice took her mother's arm and led her into the hall. 'Say goodbye to your grandma,' she said.

Lizzie pecked Mrs Rooney on the cheek, then hugged Peggy tightly. 'Good luck in the Land Army,' she whispered. 'And please don't fall out with Mam again. I miss you when you don't come.' She stood in the doorway and waved at Peggy until she was out of sight.

When she got back to the kitchen, there was no sign of Alice, but there was a strange banging noise coming from the living room. Lizzie put her head around the door. Alice was standing on a chair with her skirt tucked into her knickers, holding a hammer in her hand. 'Keep this bloody chair steady,' she said, 'while Ah see to the lock on this bloody window. Ah don't want those thievin' Quislin's gettin' in, nabbin' me valuables.'

'But Quislings aren't thieves, Mam. The teacher told us that Quislings are traitors, who sell our secrets to the enemy and we don't have any secrets they'd want, have we?'

Alice leaned over and slapped her hard around the head. 'That'll teach ye not to be so bloody clever! Now hold this chair, girl, and keep it steady when Ah get down.'

Lizzie's ear was throbbing. Never mind, she thought, I won't let Mam see me cry. Maybe one day she'll be sorry she did this. She held on to the chair, while Alice repeatedly checked the lock until she was satisfied it was safe.

Lizzie looked at the clock. It was already 5.30 and she hadn't eaten since breakfast. 'Can we have something to eat now, Mam?'

'No. Ye'll have to wait till we've checked ahl the windows. And put a bloody move on or we'll be here till midnight.'

At last, when the windows were finally finished, Alice put down the hammer and headed for the kitchen. Lizzie watched as she cut the remainder of a loaf into doorsteps.

'D'ye' want fish paste or potted meat in yer sandwich?'

Lizzie was tired and her ear was still throbbing. 'Whatever you like, Mam. And is it all right if I eat it in bed? I can hardly keep my eyes open.'

Alice pressed the palm of her hand on the sandwich in an attempt to flatten it. 'Go on then,' she said, 'get ready for bed and Ah'll fetch it up.'

But when Alice pushed open Lizzie's door, she was already asleep. Oh well, waste not, want not, she thought as she turned out the light and left, taking Lizzie's supper with her.

Chapter 15

Alice put her mending on the kitchen table, next to her sewing box and turned the radio on low. She sighed wearily. Jack's got no idea what Ah have to put up with from that little madam. She's never satisfied with what Ah give her. Ah blame Mrs Brown for spoilin' her.

Now she could settle down and enjoy a bit of time to herself. She went to the dresser and unlocked a drawer marked PRYVAT. Why shouldn't she spoil herself, she thought, nobody else did. The drawer was filled with bars of chocolate, packets of sweets and a selection of different flavoured fudge that she'd been hoarding for herself. She took out a bar of Cadbury's Fruit and Nut, broke off a square and sucked it slowly as she picked up her last pair of nylons and searched for the right thread to repair the ladders. As she enjoyed her chocolate, she forgot about burglars, Quislings and threats from outside. Henry Hall's Dance Band was playing on the radio and she tapped her feet to the rhythm.

She was about to thread the needle when she heard a loud knock on the front door. She stood up, dropping her laddered nylons on to the floor and, as quietly as she could, slipped out into the hall to check the time on the grandfather clock. It was half-past eight. Who the hell could this be?

Her heart was pounding as she tip-toed to the front door. She hesitated, then pushed back the letterbox and peeped outside. It was pitch dark, except for a single, moving beam of light. There was someone out there with a torch.

She jumped at the sound of a hoarse voice. 'Open up! Ah know somebody's in there!'

'Who the hell's that?' she shouted.

'It's Mr Jones, your local ARP man. Now hurry up and open this door or there'll be trouble.'

Reluctantly, she released the bolt, turned the key in the lock and opened the door slightly. Placing her foot in the gap, she caught a glimpse of a short man in a tin hat before being momentarily blinded by his torch shining directly on to her face.

'What the hell d'ye think ye're doin'?' She leaned forward, opened the door a little wider, and caught hold of his hand. She pushed it upwards, to get rid of the glare, and the torch flashed back towards him, briefly revealing the letters ARP on his tin hat.

'What do you want at this hour?' she yelled. 'Keepin' folks out of their beds.'

'Ye'll have no bloomin' bed to sleep in, Missus, if ye carry on like this. Ye'd better let me in.' He pushed at the door. 'Ye've got a two-inch gap in yer blackout curtains.

Ah can see the light from across the road. This house is a sitting target for a flyin' bomb.'

Alice opened the door and he marched inside. 'Now, Ah need to check the curtains. It looks like the ground floor front to me.' He strode towards the living room and she followed him in. 'This is the culprit, Missus,' he said, as he pulled the curtains tightly together. 'Ah'll let ye off with a warnin' this time, but there'll be a hefty fine if it happens again.'

Silly auld bugger, she thought, he should be shot with his own shit. 'Thanks for your advice,' she said, 'Ah'll show ye out.'

'All right, Missus,' he said as she led the way into the hall. 'And don't forget to check the sticky tape on yer windows.'

Alice shut the door firmly behind him. Ah know his bloody type, she cursed, as she went back to the kitchen. He's just a hen-pecked little man with his first taste of power. Ah can just imagine what his wife looks like. She sat down at the table, broke off a big chunk of chocolate and returned to her laddered stockings.

That night, even though she was tired, sleep didn't come easily. 'That creepy little man,' she said to herself, 'frightenin' the life out o' me with his bloomin' flyin' bombs! What the hell does he think he's playing at? As if Ah don't have enough to worry about. Ah wonder, did Ah check the lock on the bedroom window? Oh bugger, Ah cannat check it now, canna, when Ah'd have to leave the light on to see the bloody thing and Ah'm not allowed to open the damn blackout curtain either! What a bloody life. Being dictated to by that cocky little man, who, for all Ah know, could be a bloody burglar!

'What the hell's that?' She sat bolt upright. She was sure she could hear a high-pitched wail. Could it be the siren at the pithead? Was this the time the men changed their shift? She looked at the clock. No, that was the bloody air raid siren!

She jumped out of bed and ran to Lizzie's room. 'Get up!' she said, as she switched on the light. 'Put a move on! Ah've just heard the bloody air raid siren. We're gannin' in the shelter.'

Lizzie sat up, shielding her eyes with her blanket. 'Are you sure, Mam? I didn't hear it.'

Alice pulled back her bedclothes. 'Hurry up,' she said, 'get dressed while Ah find a bloody torch.'

Lizzie sat on the bed as Alice ran downstairs and wondered if she'd heard right. Surely she wasn't expected to go in the damp shelter with no light or heating. It smelt of rust and the floor was muddy.

'Hurry up!' Alice shouted and Lizzie knew she had no choice. She kept her pyjamas on and pulled her warm bed socks over the legs. Her grandma had knitted the socks on four needles and had said they would keep the life in her. She took her tartan skirt and Aran jumper from the wardrobe. These should keep the life in her too. She finished dressing and sat back on the bed. As she was trying to squeeze her feet into her shoes, she caught sight of her father's picture. How could she leave him behind? Taking him from the frame, she hid him in her overcoat and hurried downstairs.

Lizzie was surprised to see her mother wearing her Sunday coat and her best hat with the diamanté buckle. 'Why are you all dressed up, Mam?'

'Because Ah want to look decent if Ah pop me clogs in that bloody shelter!' Alice exclaimed, buttoning the coat all the way down.

'Why can't we go into the public shelter, Mam? I've heard they've got lights and sometimes they have a sing-song.'

Alice tossed back her head and straightened her coat. 'We're not mixing with the likes of them, they're not our class! Here, Ah've got the torch. Hold this bag and follow me.'

She marched through the kitchen and flung the back door open. It was pitch black outside. She switched on the torch and stood outside to get her bearings. 'Hurry up, Lizzie!' she said as she set off across the grass. 'Follow me. Ah can see the shelter.' Lizzie struggled behind with the heavy bag, hoping her mother had packed some food and a flask with something hot to drink. Even wearing her thick jumper and coat, she still felt the chill. When they got to the shelter, Alice stopped and shone the torch inside. It was a big drop and there were no steps. 'Well it's now or never,' she said grimly. 'Ah've got no choice, unless Ah want to be blown to bloody smithereens.' She took a deep breath and jumped inside. 'Come on, Lizzie,' she yelled, 'give me that bag and jump!'

Lizzie passed the bag and stared inside. Her mother's torch barely lit the damp space. 'But it's all muddy, Mam!'

'Divvn' be daft,' she said, 'a few clarts never hurt anybody. Now bloody jump!'

Lizzie hesitated. The drop was too forbidding. 'Oh bloody hell!' said Alice. 'Wait a minute then.' She put the bag down on one of the wooden bunks and held out her arms. 'Ah'll catch ye. Now jump, ye bugger, jump!'

Lizzie held her breath and jumped. But as soon as her feet had left the floor, she realised she hadn't quite made it. Alice didn't move forward to catch her in time and she landed on her backside in the mud. 'Ye daft bugger,' said Alice as she took hold of her hand and pulled her to her feet. 'Just look what ye've done to yer best skirt! It's covered in bloody mud! Buck up and get yersel' sorted.'

Lizzie wrapped her coat tightly around her and climbed on to the lower bunk.

'Divvn' look so damned miserable,' Alice shrieked as she picked up her bag and rummaged inside, passing the torch to Lizzie. 'Take this in case ye have to do a pee.' She pointed to a corner. 'Do it over there if ye have to and watch out for the bloody frogs.'

Shivering, Lizzie pulled her coat over her ears and curled up on the bunk, praying for the night to end. It was so cold and the bench so hard, it was impossible to sleep, but it didn't seem to bother her mother. She had already begun to snore. Lizzie took out her torch and shone it on her father's picture. He looked so handsome in his Air Force uniform. She was struggling to remember the smell of him when her mother stirred. 'Are ye still awake?' she called. Lizzie hastily turned off the torch, hid the picture in her pocket and pretended to be asleep. Despite the discomfort and the bitter cold, she didn't have to pretend all night. Exhaustion overcame her and she eventually dropped off to sleep.

৵

Alice woke to the sound of bottles rattling on the milk cart. She jumped down from her bunk and shook Lizzie. 'Get up,' she said, 'Ah've just heard the all-clear.'

Lizzie shielded her eyes as daylight streamed through the doorless shelter. She was freezing cold. The mud had caked on her skirt and bed socks, and she was covered in bites from the midges.

Alice climbed out of the shelter. 'Come on!' she said. 'Get yer skates on. We haven't got ahl day.'

Lizzie stepped down from her bunk. She had forgotten the mud and it stuck to her shoes as she plodded to the doorway. She was so tired she wasn't sure if she could climb out, but once she got her knee up on to the grass, she managed to haul herself up.

'Come on,' said Alice. 'Stop bloody daydreaming. Get indoors and put the kettle on.'

Lizzie hurried inside. 'Can I have a bath first, please Mam?'

'No ye can't. Ye'll have to wait till Ah've stoked the fire up. The boiler's stone cold. Now get a move on and make the tea while Ah fetch some bloody coal.'

Chapter 16

1942

Lizzie put down Molly's *Beano* and laughed out loud. 'Pansy Potter's good this week. Have you finished with the *Dandy*?'

Molly passed her comic across the dining table. 'Come on then, I'll swap with you.'

Mrs Brown smiled at Lizzie as she set down the tea tray. It was good to see her looking better after spending time with Molly. When she'd picked her up from school that day, she had looked quite pale and was it any wonder if those dreadful rumours were really true? For some time now, according to various neighbours, Lizzie and her mother had been spending most nights in that dreadful excuse for an air raid shelter. She could hardly bear the thought of it.

Mrs Brown looked out of the window. 'Just look at that! It's raining cats and dogs! It's a good job I brought the washing in earlier or I would have had to put it through the mangle again. Here, girls, help yourselves.'

She couldn't help noticing Lizzie's eyes light up as she looked at the apricot jam. 'Make the most of it,' she said. 'It's the last jar. Here, have a teacake while it's still hot.'

Lizzie didn't need to be told twice. She spread the tea-cake with butter and, mindful that it was the last jar, spread the jam on sparingly.

'I hear you're spending a lot of time in that shelter, Lizzie,' Mrs Brown commented, taking a teacake for herself. 'What do you find to do, dear?'

'We go in at night time, Auntie Marion, so I just go to sleep.'

'Are you warm enough in there?' Mrs Brown asked anxiously. 'The shelter isn't finished, is it? I'm surprised you haven't caught your death.'

'It is cold, but I wear my warm coat.'

'And do you get enough sleep, pet?'

'Well, it's not too bad.' Lizzie had to look away, unable to meet Mrs Brown's kind eyes.

'It is bad!' Molly said. 'Tell the truth! You're late for school half the time and I've seen you fall asleep in class!'

'I'm all right, really.'

'Well, I wouldn't like to be in your shoes. Have another teacake,' Mrs Brown insisted. 'And, go on, have another bit of jam.'

'Are you sure? Is that all right, Auntie Marion?'

'Go right ahead, pet. You look as though you could do with putting a bit of weight on.'

Lizzie ate the teacake as slowly as she could, but she couldn't put off the inevitable. It seemed only moments before Auntie Marion pointed to the window again. 'Just look at that rain. It's coming down in buckets. We'd better get you home, Lizzie. Have you got a raincoat with you?'

'No. It wasn't raining when I left.'

Mrs Brown thought quickly. 'All right, then. Come with me.' She led the way into the hall and took a large, heavy coat from a hook. 'This is Mr Brown's,' she said, 'it'll keep you dry. Now, you'd really better be off. We don't want to upset your mother. Put this over your head and run all the way.'

Like always, Lizzie wanted to stay, but she put on a brave smile, kissed Auntie Marion and set out into the rain. I wonder if I should have told Auntie Marion what it's really like in that shelter, she thought. Maybe I should tell Grandma Wood, but she's the only one who stays friends with Mam, so I can't risk it. If Mam falls out with Grandma, there'll be no more Sunday lunch or dancing classes and maybe I won't even get to see her at all! If only Dad could come home on leave, I'd tell him what's been going on. Then maybe, at last, he would do something. But now they've sent Dad abroad, we hardly ever hear from him. And, to make things worse, Mam still suspects he has a floozy in Wales and she never stops going on about it – sometimes she gives me a headache. I miss Aunt Peggy too. She's been in the Land Army for almost a year and she's only been home twice. Even though I'm nine now, I'm still not tall enough to join.

By the time she reached the house, she was soaking wet, despite Mr Brown's heavy coat. She pushed the door open and went inside. It was good to be out of the rain. She hung the coat in the hall and slowly made her way to the kitchen. Alice was sitting by the fireside, making toast. 'So you're back at last,' she said. 'You took yer bloody time. There's a card from Auntie Peggy. Go on, read it, Ah want to hear what she's got to say.' Alice put her toast on the table and buttered it.

Lizzie picked up the card. 'It's addressed to me, Mam. Can I just dry myself first before I read it?'

Alice plastered the toast with jam. 'Didn't yer hear what Ah said? Take those bloody wet shoes off and read it now.'

Her shoes were soaked through so it was a relief to unlace them and kick them off. She sat down by the fire to warm her toes.

'Go on then, what're ye waitin' for? Ah wouldn't have to tell ye twice if it was yer dad's letter, would Ah?'

That's for sure, thought Lizzie, if only it was. She began to read.

'Dear Lizzie, just a line to let you know I'm thinking of you. I'm stationed in Norfolk now and I wish you were here. You'd love the animals. I look after the chickens and they all know me now. I call one Lizzie, because you're my little chicken. The food is good and there's a social in the village hall every Saturday. I'll let you know when I'm com-ing home on leave. Lots of love, Auntie Peggy. PS tell your mam I'll get in touch later.'

'Get in touch later!' Alice was incensed. 'See what she thinks o' me? Ah'm just a bloody afterthought. Well, don't just stand there, little chicken, bugger off and get ready for bed. And if ye want owt to eat, put yer skates on.'

Lizzie picked up her shoes and hurried upstairs. She quickly undressed, put on her dressing gown and tested the water in the bathroom. Thank God it's hot, she thought. I'll just gather up my wet things before I have a soak.

She lay in the bath and thought about Molly. I'm really not jealous of her, but I do wish the stork had dropped me down Auntie Marion's chimney. She was imagining a lovely life sitting by the fire at Molly's and eating endless teacakes when she was overtaken by a violent sneeze. Oh dear – she remembered Mam telling her about a neighbour who died from sneezing. It had worried her ever since, especially as the woman had died in the bath. She tried hard not to sneeze again, but she couldn't stop. Afraid to take a chance, she got out of the bath, threw her dressing gown back on and dashed to the bedroom.

There was no fire in her room and she began to shiver. Then she remembered the Donald Duck hot water bottle Auntie Peggy had given her one Christmas. Now, where could it be? She opened the lid of her old wooden toy box and began to rummage inside. Here was the old rag doll she had loved for years but had completely forgotten about, and the puppets Grandma Wood had bought her. Their strings were all tangled up around a soft toy rabbit that reminded her, for a melancholy moment, of Patch. Then, at last, she saw the yellow rubber beak of Donald Duck and pulled him out gratefully.

She hadn't wanted to go back to the kitchen tonight, but now she had no choice. It was either fill Donald Duck or freeze to death. Hastily pushing her toys back into the box, she closed the lid, then, clutching Donald to her chest, tiptoed downstairs and hurried to the kitchen.

Alice was dozing in front of the fire. Lizzie hovered in the doorway, wondering what to do. She crept over to the stove, then, as quietly as she could, picked up the kettle and filled it. But as she replaced the lid, it slipped from her fingers and fell into the sink.

Alice leapt from her chair. 'What the hell's going on?' she shouted.

Lizzie replaced the lid and put the kettle on the stove. 'Don't worry, Mam, I don't want any supper. I just came down to fill my hot water bottle. Sorry if I woke you, but it's freezing cold in my bedroom and I've got a sore throat.'

'Well be quick about it then. Ah'm off to check the locks and Ah'll expect you in bed before Ah've finished.' Alice got to her feet.

It'll be my pleasure, Lizzie thought. I'll be glad to see the back of you. I wish the kettle would hurry up and boil, but then Grandma always said it never boils while you're waiting. She glanced at the drawer in the kitchen dresser, the one with PRYVAT written on it in a shaky scrawl. She had always wondered what was inside. She tried the drawer and laughed. Good old Mam, she never forgets to lock that, at least.

At last, the kettle boiled. She filled Donald Duck almost up to the brim, then, just like Grandma Wood did, squashed out the spare air before screwing in the plug. She tucked him under her dressing gown, hurried back upstairs and climbed quickly into bed. It was too cold to sit up and say her prayers, so she snuggled under the blankets and cuddled Donald.

'Dear God, I'm trying to think of something I can be grateful for today, but the only thing that springs to mind is Dad. Please let him come home soon. My mother's impossible and in her eyes, I'm just a nuisance. I wish I could be a Land Girl with Auntie Peggy and look after the chickens. I thank you for Grandma Wood and friends like Auntie Peggy, Auntie Marion and Molly. There we are! I've found something to be grateful for. And for you too. For always being there for me. Love from Lizzie.'

She lay awake listening to the rain as it lashed against the windows, making them rattle. Her feet were cold. She took Donald Duck from inside her dressing gown and pushed him to the bottom of the bed. He wasn't as hot as he had been, but at least her toes appreciated the warmth.

She was settling down to sleep when the door flew open. The light was on in the hall and Lizzie's stomach sank at the sight of her mother's silhouette framed in the doorway. She was wearing what looked like her old hat and raincoat. As far as Lizzie was concerned, that could only mean one thing. She sat up in bed and prepared herself for the worst.

Alice stood at the bottom of the bed, her face flushed. 'The bloody Germans are flying over Newcastle on their way to London – Ah've just heard it on the news! And the man said casualties are expected.'

Lizzie held her chest and coughed. 'I don't believe it, Mam. We've got nothing worth bombing around here and in any case, before you ask, I'm too poorly to go into the shelter. I think I've got the flu.'

Alice shook the bed. 'The flu, my arse!' she yelled. 'Now get up and get dressed or ye'll feel the back of my hand!'

Lizzie slid down the bed and pulled the blankets up under her chin. 'If you want me in that disgusting shelter, you'll have to carry me in!'

'And don't think Ah wouldn't, ye cheeky little bugger! Ah'm off to fill the flask up and if you're not out of bed by the time Ah get back, Ah'll bloody haul ye out.'

Lizzie listened to her mother muttering on the way downstairs. Her pyjamas were wet with sweat and they clung to her body. Donald Duck was cold now and there was no chance of filling him again. She fought hard to hold back the tears. Never mind, she thought, I won't let her see me cry.

At that moment, the door opened. Alice marched back inside. 'Are you not up yet? Ye'd soon get up if ye could see the bloody searchlights! The sky's lit up!' She picked up an armful of clothes and flung them on to the bed. 'Now get dressed! Ah'll not tell ye agin.'

Lizzie clung to the blankets. 'Get out!' she said. 'You can't make me!'

Alice gripped her arm and pulled her out of bed. She undid her pyjama jacket and tugged at the sleeve. Lizzie pushed her away. 'All right,' she said, 'you've won. You're stronger than me. Leave me alone and I'll dress myself.'

'Well, see that you do and hurry up.'

Lizzie knew what was in store for her. She took off her wet pyjamas and put on her warm vest and fleecy knickers. Then she remembered her Christmas jumper, with Santa Claus embroidered on the front. She opened the drawer at the bottom of the wardrobe and looked inside. Yes! It was still there, along with her thick red scarf and leggings. She had grown since the last time she had worn her winter woollies, but never mind, they would keep the life in her, just like Grandma's bed socks had done.

She got dressed and went on to the landing, but as she stood at the top of the stairs, she began to feel dizzy. It looked a long way down. Holding on to the banister for fear of falling, she tentatively took the first few steps.

'For God's sake, hurry up!' Alice shouted from the bottom of the stairs. 'We'll be buried alive if ye carry on like this!'

Lizzie stumbled down into the hall and followed her mother into the kitchen. The back door was already open and the rain was wafting inside. Alice pointed into the darkness. 'Get out there! And take the torch, while Ah lock up.'

She pressed the torch into Lizzie's hand and pushed her into the garden. It was pitch dark. What was Mam thinking about? she thought. I can't see any searchlights. She fumbled with the torch. Her instinct told her to run back inside and suffer the consequences, but it was too late. Alice had locked the back door and was already standing behind her. 'Switch that torch on!' she shouted. 'Do ye want me to break me bloody neck?'

At last Lizzie managed to find the switch. She pointed the torch towards the shelter and made her way across the wet grass.

'Had on there a minute!' Alice called. 'Ah can't see a bloody thing! Shine the torch over here.'

The grass squelched under Lizzie's feet as she turned and shone the torch in her mother's direction. Alice grabbed it and as she pulled the torch from her grasp, Lizzie slipped backwards. She staggered a couple of steps and gasped as she felt the ground disappearing under her feet. Helplessly, she tumbled into the waterlogged shelter.

After the downpour that day, the floor was like a paddling pool. Lizzie screamed as she landed in the freezing water. Her foot had caught the side of the lower bunk and the pain was excruciating.

Alice shone the torch inside the shelter. Lizzie was sitting on the floor with water up to her waist, trying to dislodge herself from the bunk. 'Get up,' said Alice, 'd'ye want to catch yer death?'

'I can't move, Mam,' Lizzie sobbed. 'You'll have to help me.'

'Well just wait till Ah get this bloody bag inside,' Alice snapped. 'Ah'll try an' chuck it on the top bunk.'

Lizzie winced as she heard the splash.

'That's all Ah bloody needed!' Alice yelled. 'Ye can wave goodbye to the tea an' sandwiches.'

'Never mind the sandwiches, Mam, I'm soaking wet and I can't move.' Lizzie could barely get the words out, she was so cold and shivering hard from the shock.

'Shut up, Lizzie, Ah'm doin' me best. Ah'm not bloody Houdini.'

Alice tucked her skirt inside her knickers, held the torch between her teeth and lowered herself inside. 'Bloody hell, this water's cold enough to freeze the balls off a brass monkey and it's nearly up to me knees!'

Alice waded towards Lizzie. 'Give us yer hand, then.'

Lizzie screamed as Alice tried to drag her from the rotting base of the bunk. 'Stop it, Mam!' she shouted. 'My woollen leggings are caught on a big nail.'

'Shh! Keep yer bloody voice down, Ah thought Ah heard somebody!' She tore the leggings from the nail and tried to help Lizzie on to her feet. 'And don't think Ah'm hearing things either! Ah'm sure there's some bugger out there.'

'Stop, Mam, I don't care who's out there. It hurts too much to stand up!'

'Well ye can't sit in that bloody water all night!' Alice lifted Lizzie fully on to the bunk and the water dripped from her clothes like a leaking tap.

'Leave me alone, Mam,' she cried. 'I want to go home.'

Alice put her hand over Lizzie's mouth. 'Keep yer voice down! There's a torch flashing out there! Ah think it's that bloody ARP man.'

Please God it is, thought Lizzie. She pushed her mother's hand away and started to cough.

Alice took her by the shoulders and pinned her down on to the bunk. 'Keep quiet,' she said, "cos we're not leavin' this bloody shelter till Ah've heard the all-clear.'

And when will that be, Lizzie wondered. I'll bet we're the only ones hiding underground like moles for no reason. She watched Alice climb on to the top bunk. If only I had a bomb, she thought. I'd know where to drop it.

'It's ganna be a lang night, Lizzie, so Ah'm gonna try an' get forty winks. And divvn' wake us up with yer snivellin'. D'ye hear?'

I've no intention of going to sleep, thought Lizzie. She needn't think I'm going to stay here for the night either. I'll get out of here if it kills me. I'm sure Mam'll kill me herself if she catches me, but never mind, I'd rather be dead than live with her! She listened as her mother's breathing got slower and deeper, and waited until she began to snore, then she drew in her breath and slowly let it out again.

'Dear God,' she whispered, 'please keep my mam asleep and help me get out of this shelter.' She eased herself up from the bunk, swivelled her legs around to the side and slipped her feet into the water. Holding on to the end of the bunk with one arm, she stretched out the other and carefully felt around for the entrance. When at last she found it, she fumbled her way towards it and, grasping the side of the doorless shelter, made her bid to escape.

She hauled herself upwards as quietly as she could, but a loose stone came away in her hand and fell into the water with a loud splash.

Alice sat bolt upright. 'What the hell d'ye think ye're doin', ye little bugger!' She lowered herself into the water and waded across to her. Lizzie's legs were dangling from the doorway. Alice threw down the torch and tried to grab them, but Lizzie held fast, clinging to a bush near the edge of the shelter. Alice tried to grab her leg again and Lizzie lashed out with her foot. Alice screamed as she fell backwards into the water, while Lizzie tumbled out on to the soggy grass. She struggled to her feet and peered back into the shelter. Alice was splashing around, searching for the torch. Thank God, thought Lizzie, I didn't kill her. But what am I going to do now? Mam's locked the back door so I can't get inside from the cold. She hobbled over the grass towards the house and huddled in the doorway. Never mind, she thought, at least I'm not sitting in that freezing water.

Alice's voice rang out from the dark. 'Just wait until Ah get me hands on you!'

Lizzie shrugged her shoulders. What do I care, she thought. What else can you do to me?

She didn't have to wait long to find out. Alice emerged from the gloom and glared at her. She pushed her aside to unlock the door. 'Get into the bloody house,' she said, 'and explain yersel'. Just what the hell d'ye think we're playin' at?'

'I don't want to play at anything with you, Mam.'

Alice lifted her arm. Lizzie flinched and moved away. 'Don't dare lay your hands on me! And don't ever try to drag me into that shelter again!'

Desperate for the safety of her own room, Lizzie hobbled to the bottom of the stairs. She switched on the light and reached for the banister.

Alice hurried after her, ready to lay down the law, but she froze when she saw Lizzie's face under the bright light. She looked feverish, and although she was shivering, her face was dripping with sweat. Bloody hell, she thought, I suppose I'll get the blame fer this. 'Can Ah help ye upstairs?' she said, but Lizzie didn't reply. Oh well, thought Alice, at least she can't say I didn't ask.

ᕙ᙭

Alice stormed into Lizzie's bedroom. 'Have ye not finished yer bloody breakfast yet?'

'I've had enough, Mam. Are you sure Molly knows I'm poorly? I've been in bed for three days and she's not been near.'

'Didn't Ah tell ye Ah told her?'

'Then why hasn't she come?' Lizzie was desperate to see her friend.

'How the hell should Ah know? Ah'm not a bloody fortune teller!'

'Do you think you could ask her to lend me her comic, Mam?'

'No! Ah'm busy enough, runnin' around after you. Oh and there's the bloody doorbell.'

Alice slammed the breakfast tray back down on Lizzie's bed and hurried from the room. 'Will you tell me who it is, Mam?' Lizzie called after her.

'No, Ah bloody won't,' Alice muttered to herself as she ran down the stairs and threw open the door. 'What're you doin' 'ere?'

Mrs Wood smiled at her. 'I'm doing what I always do on a Saturday,' she said. 'I've come to take the bairn to her dancing classes. Fancy forgetting that!'

'Ye'd better come in, then. Sorry, Ah'm not meself today. Lizzie's in bed with a bad cold so Ah'm afraid ye've wasted yer time.'

'Oh, the poor bairn! I'll just pop up and see her, Alice.'

'No, Mother, ye'd better not or ye might catch what she's got.'

'At my age, Alice, they haven't invented anything I haven't caught already.' She squeezed past Alice and into the hall. 'I'll just make my way up then.'

Alice fidgeted with her pinny as she watched her walk towards the stairs. 'Ah'll come with you,' she said. 'Lizzie might want her hot water bottle seen to.'

On the landing, she pushed past Mrs Wood and opened Lizzie's door. 'Ye'll never guess who's here,' she said.

Mrs Wood popped her head inside and smiled, but the smile soon faded when she saw her granddaughter looking so pale and drawn. She sat down on the bed and held her hand. 'I hear you've not been well, pet? Tell Grandma what's the matter.'

'She got soaked on her way home from Molly's the other night, didn't you? Tell Grandma how wet you got, pet.'

Lizzie lowered her eyes. 'I would have got wetter, but I borrowed Mr Brown's coat, Grandma.'

'Well that was kind of him.'

If only I dared tell Grandma the truth, she thought, maybe she would take me home with her.

'She sounds a bit chesty,' said Mrs Wood. 'Have you had the doctor in, Alice?'

'No Ah haven't, but Ah think she's on the mend now.' Alice looked at Lizzie and smiled. 'Show yer grandma the nice new nighty Ah bought ye.'

But before she could do so the doorbell rang again. Alice jumped. Oh bugger, she thought, who the hell is it this time? 'Ah won't be long, Mother, Ah'll just see who it is.' She smiled at Lizzie again. 'Give us ye' hot water bottle, pet, and Ah'll fill it for ye.'

She hurried downstairs and threw the hot water bottle on the kitchen table. No bloody peace for the wicked, she grumbled as she opened the front door. Mrs Rooney burst in like a rocket and their eyes met like daggers drawn.

'What the hell do you want?' said Alice. 'Ah'm busy with the bairn.'

'Ah've already heard how busy you've been!' her mother exploded. 'Folk've seen ye, draggin' Lizzie into that shelter at all bloody hours! With a mother like you, she'll be lucky to see the bloody war finished!'

'And what kind of mother are you?' Alice shouted. 'What about me? Ah can't read an' write because o' ye, ye auld ratbag! Ah'm just doin' my best!'

'Ye' not draggin' that up agin, are ye?'

Before Alice could reply, she heard a noise behind her and spun around. Mrs Wood was standing in the hall. 'Keep your voices down, ladies,' she said. 'Lizzie's just dropping off to sleep.'

'Tell her!' said Mrs Rooney. 'Tell her it's you what's makin' the bloody noise, Alice!'

Mrs Wood reached for her coat. 'I think I'd better be off now. I'll be back in the morning to see how the bairn is.'

'Not before ye hear what she's bin up to!' said Mrs Rooney, pointing her finger at Alice.

'Divvn' listen to her, Mother! She's just jealous because we get on so well!' Alice wiped her hands on her pinny in agitation.

'That's because she doesn't bloody know ye, Alice!'

They all jumped as the doorbell rang again. Hell, Alice thought, it's as bad as Newcastle Central Station! She turned on a smile for Mrs Wood. 'What a nuisance,' she said, and she pushed past Mrs Rooney to open the door.

Mrs Brown was standing on the doorstep, holding a bunch of flowers. She held them out to Alice. 'These are from Molly and me,' she said. 'Lizzie hasn't been to school for the last few days and we've heard she's not well.'

Alice glowered at her. 'Ye shouldn't listen to gossip! There's nowt the matter with her, so we won't be needin' the flowers. Now ye'll have to excuse me,' she said, shutting the door abruptly in Mrs Brown's face.

'Who was that?' asked Mrs Wood.

'It's just a busybody neighbour, Mother. Ah don't want to talk about it.'

'Of course she doesn't!' Mrs Rooney said. 'Ah know that voice, Alice. It was Mrs Brown, wasn't it? If it wasn't fer her, Lizzie would bloody starve to death.'

'It's time you left,' said Alice, pointedly holding open the kitchen door.

'Don't worry, Ah'm leavin'. But before Ah do . . .' she turned to Mrs Wood. 'Ah can see ma lass has got ye tied round her little finger, but just you mark ma words, one o' these days ye'll see her in her true colours!' She yanked the front door open and slammed it behind her as she left.

Mrs Wood's fingers shook as she tried to do up her coat. And to think the bairn had to listen to this sort of thing! But this was no time for questions or accusations. Her access to Lizzie was paramount. She'd have to steer clear from giving Alice an excuse to fall out with her.

'I'll be off now, Alice,' she said. 'You look tired and I'm not surprised. I've had bairns of my own and I know the strain of nursing them when they're not well.'

Alice's face lit up. 'Do you know, Mother, you're the only one who understands me, the only one who knows what a kind word can do.'

Mrs Wood swallowed hard and kissed her. 'I'll be off now, pet. Try and have a rest. It'll do you good.'

As she walked home, Mrs Wood recalled Alice's words. *You're the only one who knows what a kind word can do.* If only she knew what a kind word could do for that bairn, she thought, I would die a happy woman.

PART 3

Chapter 17

Newcastle upon Tyne, 1945

Molly stared at the clock in the school hall. 'I wonder what it's all about this time. I hope it's not another blooming air raid practice.'

'Hush up!' said Lizzie. 'The headmaster's about to speak.' She wriggled uneasily in her cotton dress. She had worn it last summer but she'd grown much taller since then and it didn't fit properly. Mam had said it was a waste to buy her a new one as it was almost impossible to get anything decent anyway.

Mr Sowerby squinted through his steel-rimmed glasses and stretched his small frame to its limits. He surveyed the school hall and the mass of children and teachers for a moment, then brought his gavel down hard on the rostrum. 'Silence!' he shouted. 'I'm about to deliver the news we have all been waiting for.'

Lizzie held her breath – could this be what she had been hoping for, ever since her daddy had left?

Mr Sowerby stood to attention and stuck out his chest. 'Never forget this day,' he said, 'eigth May 1945.' He cleared his throat. 'At 3 p.m. today, our great Prime Minister, Winston

275

Churchill, broadcast to the nation that the war will officially be over at midnight!'

Lizzie's heart was beating so fast it almost stopped as Mr Sowerby brought his gavel down on the rostrum again.

'Now, children,' he said, 'let us give three cheers for our brave forces, who can at last be reunited with their families.'

The children jumped up and down, shouting at the top of their voices.

'All right, all right! Now control yourselves and remember, it was discipline that won the war.' Mr Sowerby puffed out his chest again. 'Long live the cause of freedom! And God save the King.'

Lizzie reached out and took Molly's hand. 'Molly!' she said. 'The war's finished! At last my dad will be coming home!' She threw her arms around her friend and squeezed her tightly, but then a thought struck her. 'It's so long since I've seen him, though, and I've grown so tall – do you think he'll still know me when he gets back?'

'Of course he will. Don't be silly, he's daft about you! Now pull yourself together, you're shaking like a leaf.' Molly dug her in the ribs.

Mr Sowerby closed his eyes and lowered his head. 'Now children, with thanks to Mr Churchill, you are all free to go home.'

The children made a beeline for the door.

'Not just yet!' Mr Sowerby shouted. 'Miss Gorley will play you out with "Land of Hope and Glory"!'

Miss Gorley struck up the opening bars and the teachers lined up the children, ready to march them outside. They were singing at the top of their voices and some of the teachers could hardly hold back their tears.

A crowd of parents had gathered outside the doors and as Miss Birkstrand threw them open, Molly and Lizzie pushed their way through and ran straight into the schoolyard. The noise was deafening. Pit sirens were screaming at full blast, along with car hooters, church bells and parents shouting as they tried to locate their children. The girls covered their ears as they searched for Mrs Brown.

'Look,' said Lizzie, 'there's your mother up by the railings!'

Mrs Brown was waving a Union Jack and shouting at the top of her voice. 'Let's get out of here, girls, before we're killed in the crush.'

Lizzie lingered behind.

'Come on,' said Molly, 'what are you waiting for?'

'I'm looking for Mam – I thought she'd be here today.'

Mrs Brown took Lizzie's hand. 'I'm sure she meant to come, but on the way here, I saw your Grandma Wood going into your house. Now, I'm sure your mother wouldn't want to leave her on her own, would she?'

Lizzie's spirits lifted. 'Then I'd better run home – Grandma should be waiting for me.'

⚜

Lizzie was breathless as she pushed open the back door and burst into the kitchen. Alice was busy at the stove, furiously stirring something, while Mrs Wood was listening to Mr Churchill's speech. She held out her arms and Lizzie ran into them. 'Well it's all over now, pet, it won't be long before your dad's back and it'll be like old times again.'

Oh yes, I bet that'll please her, thought Alice as she abruptly switched off the wireless.

Mrs Wood stiffened. 'Why did you do that, Alice? I wanted the bairn to hear Churchill's speech.'

'For God's sake, Mother, the BBC must've played the bloody thing half a dozen times. Ah know the bloomin' thing off by heart.'

'It's all right, Grandma, Mr Sowerby read some of it in assembly,' Lizzie told her, too excited to be cross with her mother for once. 'And anyway, it doesn't matter. All that matters is that Daddy's coming home!'

⚜

Peter stood outside Alice's front door, wondering if he should take his courage in both hands and knock or take the coward's way out and leave while he still had the chance. But who knows, he reasoned, I haven't seen Alice for over three years. Maybe she's changed and, in any case, Jack's message is not just for Alice, it's for Lizzie too. He took a deep breath and knocked. When the door opened, he sighed with relief to see Lizzie. Mrs Wood came up behind her.

'My God, Peter,' she said, 'what are you doing here?'

'I've come with a message for Alice. Will you ask if I can come in?'

Lizzie jumped up and down. 'I'll ask her, Grandma.'

'No,' she said, 'you wait there till I come back.'

'And remember, tell her I've got a message!' Peter shouted as she disappeared inside. He leaned down and hugged Lizzie. 'We've really missed you, pet, and Aunt Ena can't wait to see you again. Just look at the way you've grown! She'll hardly know you!'

'Do you think Dad will know me, Uncle Peter?'

'Of course he will! It'll be like looking at himself! You're the image of him, Lizzie.' He looked up and smiled as Mrs Wood returned. 'It's all right,' she said, 'you can come in. I've told her you've got a message.'

Lizzie took hold of her uncle's hand and excitedly pulled him inside. Alice was waiting in the kitchen. Her arms were folded and Peter felt the chill as she looked him up and down. 'So! Who's this message from?' she demanded.

'Nice to see you again,' said Peter, 'and on such a wonderful day. The message is from Jack.'

'Oh aye, so how did you get it? Ah haven't heard from him in ages!' Alice was in no mood to build bridges.

'One of Jack's comrades rang me at the surgery, Alice. He said Jack said to tell you he loves you and can't wait to come home, and in the meantime he'd be happy if you celebrated victory with the family at our house tomorrow.'

Mrs Wood put her arm around Alice. 'What a lovely, thoughtful message from your husband, pet.'

Alice glared at Peter. He'd aged since the last time she'd seen him – his hair was thinner and his forehead was lined. 'Why should Ah come when the lot o' ye hate the sight of us?'

'That's rubbish,' he said, 'it's all in your mind. But at least you could come just to stop Jack from worrying about you. It would make us all happy to see you and the bairn again.' He turned to Mrs Wood. 'You're very quiet, Mother, let's hear what you think. After all, you're Jack's mother. Go on, speak your mind.'

'That's easy,' she said. 'We've seen enough fighting these last few years and I don't want my son to come home to another war. I think it's time to bury the hatchet and get on as a family – just think of those who might never have that chance and the poor mothers with sons scarred for life.'

Lizzie whispered in her grandma's ear. 'Do you think Mam will let us go to Auntie Ena's?'

Mrs Wood squeezed her hand and winked as she turned to Alice. 'Now, far be it from me to try and persuade you to do anything you don't agree with, dear. You're an independent woman with a mind of your own, but for goodness sake, at a time like this, think of your husband.'

'Why should Ah, when Ah haven't had a letter in bloody weeks!' Alice snapped. 'The only reason he wants me at the party is so that they can all get their hands on Lizzie again. They couldn't care less about me!'

Mrs Wood took Alice's hand and held it in hers. 'I care about you, Alice, and I can't bear to see you in such turmoil.

If you can't go to the party for Jack's sake, then go for mine. You're a member of my family and always will be.'

Alice looked up to the ceiling and sighed. She didn't want to give in, but she couldn't help softening at her mother-in-law's words – she was the only woman ever to have shown her kindness. 'All right then,' she said begrudgingly, 'Ah'll do it for your sake, Mother.'

'Thanks,' said Peter, 'you'll make more than one person happy tomorrow. I'll pick you up at 3.30. Do you need a lift home, Mother?'

'No thanks, pet, Alice has kindly asked me to stay for dinner.' She nodded towards the stove, where a large pan simmered. 'It's hotpot, my favourite. I wouldn't miss it for the world.'

'All right, we'll be off now,' he said, 'and by the way, Ena said to be sure to tell you, your mother and sister are more than welcome tomorrow.'

'Well, ye can tell her she won't have to bother,' Alice responded tartly, "cos Peggy's not demobbed yet and me mother's helpin' out at a street party.'

❧

Lizzie found it hard to sleep that night – the thought of seeing her father's family again was more than she had hoped for. What shall I wear, she wondered. I know! What about the dress with the lace collar Grandma made for me last year? I've grown a lot since then, but I'm sure she could let down the hem. Anyway, Auntie Ena won't mind what I wear. She would love me just as much if I turned up in a sack!

She snuggled down, pulled the quilt up under her chin and put her hands together.

'Dear loving God, thank you for letting us win the war. And thank you for keeping Dad safe all these years. And a big thanks for Grandma Wood – I couldn't have survived without her. As I grow up, I can understand now why she gave in to my mother so much – it was for my sake so I wouldn't miss dancing lessons and to make sure she'd always be welcome at our house for Sunday lunch. And all that, just to keep an eye on me. Dear God, my grandma should be a saint for putting up with my mother. Oh, and thanks for keeping Auntie Peggy safe, I've really missed her. In spite of my mother, I've managed to come out of this war in one piece. All thanks to you, dear God. Love from Lizzie.'

After breakfast next morning, Lizzie slipped out of the house and ran to Auntie Marion's. Laughter was coming from the back garden and she hurried to investigate. There was a long trestle table in the middle of the lawn and the bushes were decorated with streamers in red, white and blue. Molly ran towards her holding a large bag in her hands. 'What on earth's going on?' said Lizzie.

Molly carefully put down the bag. 'We're having a victory party this afternoon. Do you want to help to decorate the garden? I've got all of this still to do.' She indicated the contents of the bag. 'Fingers crossed it doesn't rain. I've invited half of our class and our teacher promised to pop in if she can.'

'Oh bother,' said Lizzie, 'I have to go to a grown-up party at Auntie Ena's. It's a sort of reunion to end my mother's war with her in-laws.'

'That's a pity,' said Molly, then she looked past Lizzie and gasped. 'Oh boy,' she exclaimed, 'look what Mam's got!' Lizzie turned to see Mrs Brown walking across the lawn towards them with a jug of orange squash and a plate of delicious-looking biscuits. She put the tray down and poured out the drinks, and Lizzie threw her arms around her. 'What a shame I can't come to the party! I'm leaving for Auntie Ena's at half-past three.'

'Never mind, pet, our party's not starting till five, we've got a whole crowd coming. I expect it'll still be going on when you get back. Now have a glass of squash and a few biscuits and you can help us get things ready. I'll bring out the rest of the stuff.'

Lizzie smiled as Auntie Marion sang 'There'll Always Be an England' at the top of her voice as she marched back to the house. I wonder, she thought, does Molly really know how lucky she is?

The girls sat together, sipping their squash through a straw. 'You know that new boy in our class, Lizzie? Well, I've invited him to the party! He's got lovely blue eyes and long eyelashes. His name's Harry Murphy and he's a Catholic.'

Lizzie pulled a face. 'So when are you getting married?'

'You're in a right mood!' Molly observed, absent-mindedly plaiting some red ribbon from the bag. 'What's the matter with you? You should be happy now you know your dad's coming home. When are you expecting him?'

Lizzie bit her lip. She was happy, of course she was, but she didn't want to get her hopes up too high just in case it didn't happen. 'It's supposed to be in two weeks,' she answered, 'but as Grandma Wood always says, there's many a slip 'twixt cup and lip.'

Mrs Brown had brought another box into the garden and held it out towards them. 'Here we are, girls, see what you can do with this lot!' she said. 'Put a bit of glitter on the air raid shelter and to hell with Hitler, that's what I say!'

This was the first time Lizzie had heard Auntie Marion swear, but somehow it didn't sound so bad coming from her lips. She decided she liked the idea of glitter on the old shelter – heaven only knew it could do with something to cheer it up.

Lizzie and Molly got on with their tasks and by the time they'd finished, the garden looked like fairyland. They sat down together and poured themselves another drink.

'D'you think we've overdone it?' Molly asked.

'No I don't. Grandma Wood says we can never have enough of a good thing. You're lucky, Molly, because I've never seen anything exciting happen in my garden.'

Molly remembered Lizzie's rabbit and the soggy shelter. 'Never mind,' she said, 'you're always welcome in my garden.'

'I know, Molly. Don't listen to me, I'm just feeling sorry for myself.' She sucked up the last of her orange squash and reluctantly stood up. 'I'd better go home and change now, I don't want to keep Uncle Peter waiting.'

ᕼᕼ

Lizzie tiptoed in through the back door in an effort to reach her room undetected and was halfway upstairs when she heard her mother shouting.

'Come down! Grandma Wood's in the kitchen and she's got something for ye.'

Lizzie ran down to the kitchen and almost skidded to a halt. There, hanging from a knob on the cupboard door, was the dress with the lace collar she'd asked Grandma to alter. She'd loved it ever since she first was given it, but she hadn't dared to hope that it would be ready for today. 'Oh Grandma, how did you find the time to do it?'

'I've always got time for you, pet,' Mrs Wood assured her, delighted that her hard work had been appreciated. 'Now why don't you try it on and see if it's the right length.'

Lizzie hugged her, picked up the dress and hurried upstairs.

'Will ye never stop spoiling that girl!' said Alice as she gave Mrs Wood a look that could turn milk sour.

She was filling the kettle when the door flew open and Mrs Rooney staggered in. Mrs Wood gasped at the sight of her in her old black dress with a large Union Jack tied around her middle like an apron.

'Ah'm knackered!' she said, as she plonked herself down at the kitchen table, pulled a raggedy hanky from up her sleeve and blew her nose.

Alice glared at her. 'What the hell are you doin' here?'

Mrs Rooney looked at Mrs Wood. 'Did ye hear that? And after Ah've run ahl the way here to ask her to the street party, the ungrateful bugger!'

'Well ye've wasted yer time, ''cos we're ahl gannin' to Ena's to celebrate,' Alice told her with satisfaction, banging the kettle onto the hob.

'We didn't leave you out on purpose, I can assure you,' Mrs Wood hurried to say. 'In fact, Peter had already invited you, but Alice said you were helping at a street party.'

'Well Ah've changed me mind, Ah'm gannin' to Ena's!'

Alice swung around. 'How d'ye know if Peter still wants ye?'

'Well, talk of the devil,' said Mrs Rooney, 'ye can ask him yersel.'

Alice turned to see Peter standing in the doorway. 'How nice to see you again, Mrs Rooney,' he said, 'and how is Peggy?'

'Never mind aboot Peggy! What Ah want to know is, did ye invite me to your house today, or not?'

'You're welcome any time, Mrs Rooney.' Peter didn't bat an eyelid at the sudden change of plan.

'Uncle Peter!' Lizzie burst into the room and twirled around. 'What do you think of my dress? Grandma altered it for me!' She ran over and kissed Mrs Wood. 'Thank you, Grandma! It's just the right length!' She caught sight of Mrs Rooney. 'Are you coming to the party too?'

'Just try an' stop us, pet, Ah wouldn't miss it for the world.'

'We'd better be on our way,' said Peter, keen to diffuse the tension that he could tell was building.

Mrs Rooney got up from her chair and hurried outside. Peter followed behind with Mrs Wood. He unlocked the car and guided her into the front seat. 'Well,' Mrs Rooney shouted, 'that's that then! Ah suppose Ah'll have to get in the bloody back as usual.'

'Stop moaning, Mother!' Alice snapped, as she locked the front door and pulled Lizzie towards the car.

'Ye know bloody well Ah get sick in the back of a bloody car!'

'Shut up!' said Alice. 'The last time you were in a car was at me poor dad's funeral and that was bloody years ago!' She shoved her mother into the back and climbed in after her.

Lizzie squeezed in beside them. 'Why are you two fighting when we've just won the war?'

Peter raised his eyebrows and glanced knowingly at Mrs Wood. She placed her hand on his knee. 'Don't worry,' she whispered, 'it'll be all right.'

An ominous silence spread through the car as Peter drove them through the crowded streets. All around them people celebrated, hugging each other, cheering and singing, spilling out into the road. Lizzie wished the atmosphere in the car was as cheerful as that outside it.

Mrs Rooney rummaged through her bag, brought out her snuff box and took a pinch. Then, without warning, she sneezed loudly.

'Ye bloody auld cow!' Alice screamed. 'That went ahl over me!' She turned away to wipe her face. 'What the hell d'ye think ye're playin' at! Just look at me best blouse!'

Lizzie nudged Mrs Rooney as Peter drew to a halt at the kerb. 'See that house? That's where Auntie Ena lives!'

Mrs Rooney wound down the window and stuck her head out. 'Oh my God,' she said, 'just look at the size of the bloody place! Ye could fit half a dozen families in there!'

Peter helped Mrs Wood from the car, giving her a look that needed no explaining. She nodded her head and went inside.

Mrs Rooney got out of the car and stared at the house while Alice pushed past her with Lizzie. Peter sidled up to her. 'Quite a pile, isn't it?'

'You can say that again! It makes ma place look like a bloody matchbox!'

'Well it's not what it seems, Mrs Rooney,' Peter hurried to assure her. 'My father helped us to buy this place when it was badly in need of renovation. I'm afraid to say we still haven't finished it yet. But at least I can run my practice from here, so I don't need to pay rent for a surgery. Come on! We'd better show our faces or they might think we've eloped.'

Mrs Rooney almost smiled. He held the door open and helped her in to a large hall, with a high ceiling and a parquet floor. The walls were decorated with family portraits in heavy frames against faded William Morris paper.

Mrs Rooney pulled a face.

'It's a bit gloomy,' said Peter, 'I know, but it's the next job on my list – as soon as I can get my hands on some wallpaper.'

'Who are ahl these auld folk?' she demanded, going up to one of the pictures and staring at it intently.

'They're my ancestors.' He pointed to one of them. 'That's my great-granddad. Now, let's go through, shall we?'

He took Mrs Rooney's arm and led her through the French windows into the garden. She gasped. 'It's like a bloody park! And what are ahl them fairy lights doin' in the trees? They'll start a bloody fire if ye're not careful!'

Ena hurried forward to welcome her. 'We're so glad you could come, Mrs Rooney. Can I get you a drink? Annie and Joe are here already.' She turned away to call them. 'Annie! Joe! Come and say hello to Mrs Rooney!'

They looked up in response to Ena's call and made their way across the lawn towards them. 'It's so good to see you again,' said Annie, 'isn't it, Joe?'

Joe forced a smile. 'It certainly is,' he said graciously, 'it's been such a long time, we've got a lot of catching up to do.'

Peter appreciated the effort his brother-in-law was making. 'Let's have a glass of my special punch,' he said. 'It's got quite a kick in it. Come on, Joe, give me a hand.'

Annie gave him a disapproving glance. 'Do you think that's a good idea? It might be too strong for Mrs Rooney.'

'Divvn' worry aboot that, Annie, the stronger the better after what Ah've bin through the day!'

From across the garden, Alice watched sourly as Annie and Ena fawned over her mother. I wonder why they're making such a fuss over the auld bugger, when they can't stand the bloody sight of her, she thought.

'Come and sit by me, Alice,' said Mrs Wood, noticing the younger woman's expression, and patting the bench beside her. 'The bairn's just been telling me how happy she is to be seeing all the family again.'

Alice glared at Lizzie. 'Isn't that nice, now?' she said in a sarcastic voice.

Lizzie, who'd been observing everything while talking to her grandmother, smiled at her. 'It is all right if I talk to Auntie Ena, Mam?'

'I'm sure you can,' said Mrs Wood. 'You don't mind, do you Alice?'

'Gan on then,' she said begrudgingly, 'but divvn' be lang.'

Lizzie ran across the lawn to look for Ena and was so excited she almost bumped into Peter, with a tray of drinks in his hands. 'Careful!' he called. 'I don't want to be spilling the punch!'

Alice put her hands over her ears. 'What's that bloody racket, Peter?'

'It's the neighbours. Just like us, they're taking advantage of the weather.' He passed Alice a glass. 'Drink this, it'll get you in the mood.'

Mrs Wood held up her hand. 'Not for me, Peter, I'll have a glass of Ena's special lemonade.' For a moment they gazed at the gathered members of the family and it was almost as if everybody was getting along at last.

Annie came running down the garden, with Mrs Rooney close behind. 'You won't believe it!' she said. 'The folks next door have moved the piano into the garden and they've even got fireworks!'

Mrs Rooney gulped down the last of her punch, smacked her lips and wiped her mouth with the back of her hand. 'Bloody hell!' she said. 'What with bloody fairy lights and fireworks, this place'll gan up like a bloody rocket!' She passed her empty glass to Peter. 'That punch was just the job, hinny. Ah wouldn't say no to another.'

Alice got up from the bench. 'Ah winnit be lang,' she said, 'Ah'm just ganna see if Lizzie's behavin' hersel'.'

'Don't worry,' said Annie, 'she's having a lovely time helping Ena make the sandwiches. I'll come with you, Alice, and show you to the kitchen.' Alice looked askance at her sister-in-law but couldn't think of a reason to turn down her offer, so they set off back across the lawn together.

Mrs Wood sat alone on the bench, twisting her beads, and Joe moved to sit beside her. 'You look miles away, Mother, can I get you another drink?'

Peter smiled at Mrs Wood. 'Leave it to me, I'll see to it,' he said.

At that Mrs Rooney held up her empty glass and Peter smiled and gave her a wink. 'You didn't think I'd forget you, did you?'

She grinned and passed him her glass. 'Ah just wanted to make sure, hinny. Make it a stiff one!'

He laughed. 'You can come and choose a bigger glass if you like!'

Mrs Rooney's grin grew wider. 'Ah wouldn't say no to that!' She struggled to her feet, took his arm in a firm grip and accompanied him across the lawn.

Joe noticed the crestfallen look on his mother's face. 'Cheer up,' he said.

'I'm worried, son. I had such hopes for this family reunion, but from the way Alice is behaving, I can see her heart's not in it. And the way she treats that bairn! She even begrudges her talking to her own auntie.'

Joe put his arm around her. 'Listen, Mother, somebody's playing "Roll out the Barrel" on the piano. Buck up, things will be a lot different when Jack comes home.'

He's right, she thought, and I'll make sure they are. I won't mince my words when I tell him what's been going on and together I'm sure we'll find a way to make life better for Lizzie. She looked up and smiled to see Peter walking back towards them in his old Panama hat.

'This is my official practitioner's hat,' he said, 'and this is your prescription, Mother. It's brandy – now drink it down.'

She took a sip and looked around the garden. 'And what have you done with Mrs Rooney?'

He was about to reply when Annie came running across the lawn. She was out of breath as she grabbed the bench and lowered herself down beside Mrs Wood. 'For goodness sake, Annie,' she said, 'you look like you've seen a ghost. Here, have this brandy. You need it more than I do.'

Annie gulped it down. 'You won't believe it, Mother, but there are ructions going on in Ena's kitchen. Mrs Rooney and Alice are at it hammer and tongs!'

At once Mrs Wood stood up.

'Sit down,' said Joe, 'I'll sort it.'

Peter laughed. 'Leave it to me. This is a job for a doctor. There could be casualties.' He strutted off to the house and went straight to the kitchen. The door was slightly open and he peeked inside. Ena and Lizzie were determinedly piling plates of food on to a trolley, while Alice shouted at her mother. 'We ahl know Lizzie misses her dad,' she was saying, 'but at least he'll be coming back in one piece! Not like my poor dad did in the last war!'

Peter coughed before going inside. Ena's face said it all as she endeavoured to smile at him. What was I thinking about, he thought. How could I expect my wife to cope with these two on a day like this.

'Look, Uncle Peter!' Lizzie shouted, pointing to the trolley. 'I helped Auntie Ena to make the sandwiches!'

He kissed her. 'Now why don't you help her to push it into the garden? Grandma wants to see you anyway.' The sooner she was out of earshot of this pair the better, he thought grimly.

'Gan on,' said Alice, 'ye'd better not keep her waitin'.'

Peter gallantly turned to Mrs Rooney. 'I hope you don't mind me asking, but did I hear right? Was your husband really wounded in the Great War?'

'Wounded?!' she shouted. 'Ah'll say he was! He nearly had his bloody head blown off! They had to put a silver plate where his brains used to be!'

'Ye've got a lot to answer for!' said Alice. 'You as good as murdered ma dad the day ye let them take him to a mental hospital, ye bloody auld cow!' She grabbed her mother in a vice-like grip. 'Ye couldn't wait to get rid of him, could ye? You and yer bloody fancy man!'

Peter leaned across and took hold of Alice's arm, trying to pull her off, but she held on to her mother's hair. 'We ahl know who Peggy's dad is!' she went on. 'And it wasn't ma poor father, was it?'

When at last Peter managed to pull them apart, Alice was still clutching a fistful of hair.

'Ye made me wet mesel',' Mrs Rooney whimpered.

'I hope you're ashamed, Alice,' said Peter, helping Mrs Rooney on to her feet. 'I'm just glad Ena and Lizzie weren't here to witness your unforgivable behaviour.' He sat Mrs Rooney on a chair and felt her pulse.

'Ye're feelin' sorry for the wrang one!' Alice shouted. 'She never stops showin' me up! She asks for ahl she gets!'

Peter ignored this outburst and instead poured Mrs Rooney a brandy.

'Thanks, hinny, that's just what the doctor ordered,' she said, gulping it down and smacking her lips, none the worse for the disagreement with her daughter.

'So that's where you are! We were wondering where you'd all got to.' Peter turned to see Joe in the doorway. 'You're missing the entertainment. Next door's party's in full swing – the piano's rattling out all the old songs and even Mother's joined in.'

Mrs Rooney got up from the chair, straightened her dress and tightened the Union Jack around her waist. 'Ah like a bit of a singsong,' she said. 'Will ye help us into the garden, Peter?'

He offered his arm. 'I'm surprised you've recovered so soon,' he said, 'but I suppose it's all to the good. Come along then.'

'Ye needn't wait for me, Joe, you go right back and join 'em,' Alice snapped. 'Ah'm gonna tidy mesel' up before Ah show me face.'

Thank God for small mercies, he thought, as he followed Mrs Rooney and Peter into the garden. The neighbours next door were singing 'It's a Long Way to Tipperary' at the top of their voices and Joe joined in with Ena and Annie. They could all carry a tune and in the relief of the war finally being over they gave it all they had. Ena's eyes were shining as she hit the last note and held it, safe in the knowledge that her brother would be home soon, back where he belonged. She felt as if she never wanted the singing to end, but eventually even the most enthusiastic of their neighbours grew quiet.

Ena sighed and turned her attention back to the garden. Tasty snacks and a selection of cakes and trifles were displayed on small tables scattered around the lawn, with an extra table for plates and napkins. Mrs Rooney was loitering by a table and Ena went over to assist her. She handed her a plate and a napkin, but Mrs Rooney had already grabbed a handful of sausage rolls and was on her way to the drinks trolley. She shouted when she saw Peter. 'Give us another glass of that punch, lad, it'll buck me up!'

Alice sauntered up to them.

'We were wondering where you were,' said Peter. 'What can we get you?'

'Ah'm surprised ye've got owt left, the way me mother knocks it back.'

'Well, well,' said Mrs Rooney, 'as if it isn't the kettle callin' the bloody pot black!'

'Come on,' said Joe, 'I thought we were celebrating!'

'And so we are, pet!' Mrs Rooney grabbed his hand and pulled him on to the lawn, just as the piano struck up once more with 'Hands, Knees and Boomps a Daisy'. She clapped her hands and was about to bump Joe on the behind when she lost her balance. She fell backwards with a thump, her legs waving in the air. Joe averted his eyes, but not soon enough to avoid the embarrassing sight of Mrs Rooney's faded black dress rucking up to display her soggy old grey knickers. Trying to look anywhere but at her, he leaned over, took her arm and helped her to her feet.

Peter ran forward. 'It's all right, Joe, leave it to me, I'll take her inside.' He wrapped Mrs Rooney's arm around his neck, held her tightly around the waist and supported her across the lawn. Then, just as he thought she couldn't get any worse, she opened her mouth and began to sing.

'She's a big lass and a bonnie lass and she likes her beeeer!

'And they cahl her Cushy Butterfield and Ah wish she was heeeeere!'

'Hush!' said Peter, his eardrums ringing, but she carried on.

'Ye should see her in the mornin' when the fresh herrin' comes in!

'She's like a bag full of sahwdust tied roond wi' the string!'

As he guided her into the house, the neighbours began to applaud. Alice wished the ground would open up and swallow her.

'Is Grandma all right?' asked Lizzie from her position by the drinks trolley. 'She's an old woman and that was a nasty fall.'

'She'll be safe with Uncle Peter,' said Joe. 'Listen, the piano's started up again. May I have the pleasure of this dance, young lady?'

Lizzie curtseyed low. 'Why of course, kind sir!'

Joe swung her away across the lawn. He was a good dancer but he was outclassed by Lizzie – everyone could see how light she was on her feet, how well she moved to the rhythm of the old song.

Ena and Annie had just parked themselves on a bench when they saw Alice standing on her own with a face like thunder. Ena moved up the bench, leaving a space between her and Annie, and patted the seat. 'Sit down, Alice,' she said, 'we've hardly had time for a word. Don't worry about your mother, Peter will look after her.'

Alice sat down. My God, she thought, if Ena thinks I'm playin' happy families, just because Jack's comin' back, she's barking up the wrong bloody tree!

Annie pulled up a chair as she watched Mrs Wood walking across the lawn towards them. 'I did enjoy that singsong,' she said, as Annie helped her to sit down, 'but what's the matter with your mother, Alice? I saw Peter taking her into the house.'

'It's nowt she canna sleep off – the auld bugger's drunk.'

'I did enjoy those little vol-au-vents, Ena,' said Mrs Wood hastily, 'did you try one, Alice?'

'No, Ah've lost me appetite.'

Mrs Wood gave her a sympathetic look. 'I hope you're not sickening for something, Alice, especially now that Jack's coming home.'

'He'll be so pleased when he knows you came to our victory party,' said Ena. 'Won't he, Annie?'

'Of course he will! He'll be over the moon when he hears you're making it up with the family again.'

Ena gave Annie a look that could not be misconstrued. 'We're just happy to see you again, Alice, it's been far too long. After all, we are family – no matter what you think.'

'Now that's enough,' said Mrs Wood. 'Stop pressurising Alice into something she might not want to do. She's a sensible girl and she loves our Jack – I'm sure she'll decide the right thing without your help.'

Alice glared at Ena. 'Yer mother's the only one that's ever understood me!'

Peter walked over the lawn towards them and took a deep gulp from the glass in his hand. 'Phew! That was hard work,' he said. 'Your mother's heavier than I thought. Don't look so worried, Alice, she's all right – she's sleeping now in the spare bedroom. I took her shoes off and tucked her in and she's snoring her head off.'

'Ah wish it'd bloody drop off! Ye've got no idea what a life Ah've got with her,' Alice complained. 'Can ye run us home, Peter? Ah feel ahl in.'

'Of course, Alice, I'll run you back just as soon as we've made a toast to a lasting peace.' He turned to the others.

'Wait there, ladies, the champagne's already on ice. I'll be back in a minute.'

'We'll give Peter a hand,' said Ena and she and Annie hurried after him.

Mrs Wood put her arm around Alice. 'Don't fret, pet,' she said. 'I can understand the pressure you've been under today, but the girls meant well, they just went about it the wrong way, that's all. Don't think badly of them – they didn't mean any harm. They just don't understand you like I do.'

'Nobody does, Mother, you're the only one.' She looked up and scowled as Joe approached, holding Lizzie by the hand.

Poor Joe, thought Mrs Wood, he looks fit to drop.

Lizzie was bouncing up and down like a yo-yo. 'We've had a lovely time! Uncle Joe's a great dancer! And guess what, Mam?'

'Gan on then,' said Alice, 'be quick an' tell us.'

'He said he had always wanted to have a dance with you!'

'Is that right, Lizzie? Well why didn't he bloody ask?' Alice wasn't sure whether to be flattered or annoyed and managed to be both.

'Here comes the champagne,' said Mrs Wood, waving at Ena and Peter, as they pushed a loaded trolley across the grass.

'This is it!' said Peter as he uncorked the bottle. 'The moment we've all been waiting for.' He filled the glasses and Ena passed them around. 'And I haven't forgotten my best girl!' he said, as he presented Lizzie with a glass of pink lemonade. He held up his glass. 'The toast is "Peace!"'

'Yes,' said Mrs Wood, 'and thank God we've had no casualties in this family.'

After the toast they instinctively held hands. Joe smiled at his mother and began the familiar song. 'Should old acquaintance be forgot . . .'

The whole family began to sing and Mrs Wood's eyes filled with tears when she heard the next-door neighbours join in with them.

When the music stopped, a soulful voice could be heard singing 'Keep the Home Fires Burning'.

'That's Mr Hill,' said Peter. 'He lost his only son in the Great War, he was just eighteen years old.'

For a moment nobody spoke. But before long Alice was fidgeting with her handbag. She took out her keys.

'I can take you home now if you like,' said Peter.

'Thanks, but what aboot me mother?'

'Don't worry, Alice, she's in safe hands,' he said kindly. 'I'll run her home when she wakes up.'

'That's very kind of ye. Ye're not as bad as Ah thought.'

Praise indeed, thought Peter.

'Come here, Lizzie,' Alice shouted. 'Give yer grandma a kiss, we're leavin' now.'

Mrs Wood held out her arms and Lizzie ran into them. 'See you on Saturday, Grandma, I've got new tap shoes.'

Ena and Annie held their arms out. 'What about us?' said Annie.

Lizzie kissed them, delighted to be back with her beloved aunties again, and turned to Joe. 'You're as good as Fred Astaire any day,' she whispered.

Alice forced a smile and said her goodbyes, then taking Lizzie's hand, followed Peter to the car.

Mrs Wood waved until they were out of sight. There was a smile on her face as she looked at Ena. 'I think things have taken a turn for the better.'

'Don't get your hopes up, Mother.' Ena raised an eyebrow. 'You never hear of a leopard changing its spots.'

Chapter 18

Lizzie squeezed out the shammy leather, poured the dirty water down the drain and took the bucket back to the kitchen. Alice was busy rolling out pastry. 'Have ye finished them windows ahlready, Lizzie? Ah hope ye haven't missed any corners. Ah want everythin' spick and span for when yer dad gets here, so put that bloody bucket in the cupboard under the sink.'

Lizzie put it away and sat at the table. 'What are you making, Mam?'

'Steak an' kidney pie – yer dad's favourite.'

'Do you think he'll still remember it? He's been away such a long time.'

'Divvn' be cheeky. Ah'll put it in the oven when Ah get back from the hairdressers – and divvn' touch it!'

'What time will Dad get here, Mam?'

'He didn' say, so expect him when ye see him. Ah'll be off now. Make yersel' useful and peel a few tatties while I'm gone.'

⁓

After finishing the potatoes, Lizzie put the kettle on and thought of her dad. *Fancy coming back of his own free will to serve a life sentence with my mother – he must be a glutton* for punishment, unless after all this time he's forgotten what it was like. I know I never will. She switched on the wireless, just in time to hear one of her dad's favourite songs and began to sing:

'They were summoned from the hillside, they were called in from the glen,

And the country found them ready at the stirring call for men.'

She was startled when another voice joined in.

'Let no tears add to their hardships, as the soldiers pass along,

'And although your heart is breaking, make it sing this cheery song.'

'She turned to find a familiar figure in the doorway – someone she hadn't seen for far too long. It was Peggy, grinning all over. They both burst into laughter and finished the song together.

'Keep the home fires burning, while your hearts are yearning,

'Though your lads are far away, they dream of home.

'There's a silver lining, through the dark clouds shining

'Turn the dark cloud inside out, till the boys come home.'

❧

Peggy held out her arms. 'Sorry if Ah frightened ye. Come here an' give us a cuddle.'

'I hope you didn't bump into Mam.' Lizzie gave her a big, heartfelt hug and then took a step back to look at her aunt. She was still the same old Peggy but somehow she had changed, too. She seemed more grown-up and confident – and happier as well.

'Don't worry, Lizzie, Ah waited till Ah saw her leave before Ah came in.'

'She's gone to the hairdresser to get glamorised up for Dad. When did you get back, Peggy? Have you got your discharge?'

Peggy smiled at her. 'That kettle's burnin' its backside out, pet. Turn the gas off and mash the tea, then we can have a good natter.' She stood on a chair and reached into a high cupboard. 'Ah see your mam still hides the biscuits in the same place.'

'Bring the tin down,' said Lizzie, 'who cares?'

She mashed the tea while Peggy opened the biscuit tin. 'Look, custard creams and figgy rolls!'

'Don't take too many, Mam has probably counted them.'

'To hell with her, pet, it's time you stood up for yersel'. Tell her the mice've been at them, Ah'll leave the lid off the tin when Ah put it back.'

Lizzie poured out the tea. 'Are you glad to be home for good now, Peggy?'

'Divvn' be daft! Ah had such a wonderful time, Ah never wanted to come back! Wor Martin still rules the roost in wor house. Just because he pays the rent, me mother spoils him, waitin' on him hand and foot. She even runs his bath! Anyway, Ah want to hear ahl about the victory party at yer Auntie Ena's. Me mother said she had the time of her life.'

She certainly did, thought Lizzie, but I bet she didn't mention what she got up to. 'I wish you could have been there, Peggy,' she sighed. 'We had balloons and fairy lights in the trees. They had a piano in the next door garden and we had a sing-song.'

'Sound likes you had a good time.' For one second neither of them moved. Then they both spun around at the sound of the unexpected voice. There was Jack standing in the doorway. Lizzie stared at him, her mouth wide open. He looked old and tired, but he was here! She couldn't move a muscle. He came inside, put down his case and held out his arms. 'Come here, bonnie lass, let's have a good look at you.'

She stood frozen to the spot.

'Gan on,' said Peggy, finding her voice first. 'Give yer dad a cuddle, ye've bin waitin' lang enough.'

Tears were streaming down Lizzie's cheeks as she fell into her father's arms. She hugged him tight. Now that the moment she had so longed for had finally come she couldn't say a word. 'Just look at you,' he said. 'Where's the little girl I left behind?'

'She's still yer little girl,' said Peggy. She pulled on her coat, keen not to get in the way of the father and child reunion. 'Ah'd better go now,' she said, 'ye'll have a lot to talk about and Alice'll be back from the hairdressers in a minute.'

Jack gave her a big smile, knelt down and opened his suitcase. 'You can't go without your present, Peggy. It's not much – I hope you like dates.'

'Dates!' she shouted. 'Ah haven't had any for years!'

'Neither have I.' Alice sauntered into the kitchen. She looked quizzically at Jack, still kneeling on the floor. 'Well,' she said, 'whatever ye're prayin' for Ah hope ye get it.'

He got up and threw his arms around Alice. 'Now that I'm home, I've got everything I want.' He pulled back from his wife and took a good, long look at her. 'You look a picture, pet,' he said. 'You'll never know how much I've missed my girls.'

'Ah'm pleased to hear that, Jack.' But Alice looked anything but pleased as she turned away from him and glared at Peggy. 'What the hell's she doin' here, I'd like to know?'

Peggy cringed. My God, she thought, she's in one of her moods, I'd better make myself scarce. She opened her bag and hurriedly stuffed the dates inside. 'Ah'll be off now, Alice, Ah only popped in to let ye know Ah'm demobbed. Welcome home, Jack, it's good to see ye agin.'

She made her way to the front door and Lizzie followed. She was on her way out when Lizzie caught hold of her arm. 'Don't let Mam see you're upset,' she said, 'or she'll treat you like a doormat – I should know, I've been one for years. But cheer up, Peggy, Dad's home now and things should be different, just wait and see.'

'Don't hold yer breath, Lizzie. Ah'm off now – she'll gan mad if she thinks Ah'm talkin' aboot her behind her back.'

Lizzie watched as she wearily walked away. Why does she let Mam boss her around, she wondered, as she made her way back to the kitchen. The mood was surprisingly jolly as she went inside – Jack and Alice were sitting at the table drinking tea. A smile spread across Alice's face as she held up a pretty silk shawl. 'Just look what yer dad's given us, Lizzie.' She stood up and draped it around her shoulders. 'What d'ye think? Isn't it lovely?'

The shawl was pale pink, patterned with multi-coloured butterflies and had a deep pink fringe around the edge. 'It really suits you,' said Lizzie, 'I've never seen anything like it. Dad's got good taste.'

Has he brought anything for me, she wondered, and as if he had read her mind he said, 'Close your eyes, Lizzie, and hold out your hands.'

She was all of a tremble – what could it be? Jack placed the gift in her hands. 'You can look now,' he said.

She opened her eyes to see a pretty embroidered box with a tassel on the lid. 'What is it, Dad?'

'You'll never find out until you've opened it, will you?' said Alice.

Lizzie held the tassel, lifted the lid and looked inside. There were rows of coloured bobbins, a small pair of scissors and a thimble. The inside of the lid was padded with red silk and displayed a selection of sewing needles of different sizes. 'Look!' she said. 'There's even a tape measure and a needle threader.' She closed the lid and threw her arms around Jack. 'It's just like Grandma Wood's sewing box, only better. I can't wait to sew your buttons on, Dad!'

A storm was brewing behind Alice's eyes. 'That's not your job, Lizzie. Ah'll see to yer dad's buttons, so if ye want to make yersel' useful, clear the table and lay up for dinner, it's nearly ready.' She smiled at Jack. 'It's yer favourite – steak an' kidney pie.'

He noticed how quickly Lizzie jumped up to clear the table. 'Let me give you a hand, pet. It's nice to see you helping your mother.'

'I do it all the time, Dad,' she grinned, 'but I do get my reward.'

'What's that, Lizzie?'

'Mam lets me go to dancing class with Grandma every Saturday.'

Alice turned round from the stove. 'That's ahl Lizzie thinks aboot, Jack, and yer mother's just as bad. The way she eggs her on, ye'd think she was bloody Shirley Temple! Ah just give in to keep the peace!'

Jack put the dirty dishes in the sink while Lizzie laid the table. When everything was ready, they all sat down and Alice dished out the dinner. 'How's little Molly Brown?' asked Jack. 'Do you still play with her, Lizzie?'

'She's not so little now, Dad. You wouldn't know her! She's taller than me. She's still my best friend, you know.'

Alice nudged Jack. 'Never mind aboot Molly Brown, ye haven' tried yer steak an' kidney pie yet.'

He picked up his fork and took a mouthful, smacked his lips and said the words he knew she was waiting to hear. 'This is what I've missed, Alice, good home cooking, and I can't think of anything better than your steak and kidney pie.'

Alice stood up and grinned. 'There! What did Ah tell ye, Lizzie?' She turned to Jack. 'She said ye wouldn't remember me pie!'

'What does it matter, Alice. I'm sure she was only joking.'

'That's right! Take her side, ye always did. Ye've no idea what Ah've had to put up with from her since ye've bin gone.'

'I'm sure you'll get round to telling me, but in the meantime, let's enjoy the dinner.'

Lizzie lowered her eyes and stared at her plate as she struggled to force the troublesome pie down her throat. She didn't want this to be happening; she'd waited so long to see her dad back home, safe and sound. But it was no good, she couldn't do it. She feigned a coughing bout, spluttering loudly and batting her chest. 'I'm sorry,' she said, 'something's stuck in my throat, I'd better go upstairs.' She stood up and left the room, before Alice had time to object.

'Well! That's a fine how d'ye do! What d'ye think aboot that, Jack?'

He got up from the table. 'I'll just make sure she's all right, Alice.'

'Well, divvn' be lang, then, Ah'll put yer dinner in the oven.' She got up and reached for his plate.

Jack hurried upstairs to Lizzie's room. The door was open. He went inside to find her sitting at the dressing table, brushing her hair. 'Are you all right, pet? I thought you had something stuck in your throat.'

'I have, Dad, but it's not food.'

'Then what is it, Lizzie?'

She shook her head. If she started now she'd never stop and besides, what good would it do? 'I'll tell you one day, but not now. You'd better go back and finish your dinner or I'll get the blame if it goes cold.'

'It won't go cold, dear. Your mother's put it in the oven. If you're feeling all right, why don't you come back downstairs with me?'

'No thanks, Dad, Mam'll want you all to herself, just like she always did. You've been away so long you've forgotten what she's like.' She got up from the dressing table and hugged him. 'It's good to have you home, Dad, but I'm tired so I'll have an early night and see you in the morning before I go to school. And you might as well know, it wasn't the pie that choked me.'

Jack left the room with a heavy heart and leaned against the landing wall, mulling over what Lizzie had said. Could she be right, he wondered. Have I really forgotten what it was like living day after day with Alice or have I pushed the memory to the back of my mind for the sake of peace? I seem to recall that peace was at a premium at our house. And why did I choose to ignore the hurtful jibes Alice threw at Lizzie? She seemed to latch on at every given opportunity. He banged his head against the wall. What was I thinking when it was clear to see Lizzie's time alone with Alice must have been grim. Mother's bound to know what's been going on – after all, she was the only one Alice trusted with Lizzie. He straightened his back. I'll waste no time – I'll be waiting at her door first thing in the morning.

ᴥ

Nostalgia swept over Jack as he made his way down the familiar drive to the house he had once called home. The paint was a little more flaky and faded, the garden not as lush as he remembered, but it was still the same fine house, with its beautiful lilac trees standing proudly by the gate.

His arms were weighed down with flowers and he struggled not to drop them as he reached out to ring the bell. But before he could do so, the door swung open. Mrs Wood, with arms outstretched, was waiting to welcome her son. The first thing she noticed was that he'd lost weight – his face was thin and more lined than she remembered; his best suit hung loosely from his shoulders. But all that mattered was that her precious youngest child was home. This was a sight that in her darkest moments she had feared she would never see.

'I spotted you from the window, Jack. Come here, bonny lad, and give your mother a cuddle.'

When at last she let go, he rescued the flowers and placed them in her arms. 'I hope we haven't squeezed the life out of them, Mother.'

She sniffed the bouquet and kissed him. 'They are lovely, Jack, but they must have cost a fortune.'

He patted his pocket. 'Don't worry, Mother, I'm the last of the big spenders.'

'There's no need to spend your money on me, Jack, I got everything I ever wanted when the good Lord answered my prayers and brought you home in one piece.' She drank in the sight of him, her boy home at last. 'Now let's go to the kitchen. You can put the kettle on while I put these lovely flowers in water. And don't look so worried, I know we've got plenty to talk about, son.'

I was right, he thought as he filled the kettle, it's obvious Mother knows what's been going on and I wouldn't put it past her to have something up her sleeve. He set the cups and saucers on the table and filled the milk jug while his mother mashed the tea.

'Have you had your breakfast?' she asked, as she put the big brown teapot on the table.

Jack looked downcast. 'Yes I did – and it's still sticking in my throat.'

'Sit down,' she said, 'and I'll pour the tea.'

He slumped into a chair, leaned on the table and held his head in his hands. She passed him a cup. 'Here, drink your tea. You can start by giving me an idea of what you've been up to since we last saw you. Oh, I know you've sent letters but what with all the censorship it's hard to make sense of them.'

He looked up and smiled at her. 'Oh, Mother, the last thing I want to do is talk about the war. It's done and dusted. I'm back home now and there's plenty to sort out here without raking over the past.'

Mrs Wood looked at him with loving concern. 'All right, son, we won't say another word about it.' She leaned forward and patted his hand. 'Now it's clear you've got something on your mind – why don't you tell me what it is.'

Jack sat up and faced his mother. 'I've been away so long and with me out of the way, I'd hoped things between my wife and daughter would have improved, but nothing's changed. I wish you could have heard the way Alice went on at dinner last night. She goaded Lizzie until the bairn could take no more, then she pretended to choke on her dinner, faked a coughing bout and went to bed.'

'And did you say something, Jack?'

'No, I didn't. And I didn't say anything when Alice went for Peggy either. I'm surprised the poor girl comes anywhere near the house. I should have said something, knowing how good she is to Lizzie.' He banged a fist on the table. 'I'm just a bloomin' coward!'

'That's enough,' said Mrs Wood. 'Pull yourself together. A lot of water's gone under the bridge since you left and it's time you knew what's been going on. But don't expect a list of everything that Lizzie's been through or we'll be here till Christmas.'

'I hear all the family were kept away, apart from you, Mother. I had quite a few letters from Joe and Ena expressing their concerns, but I'm sure they didn't tell me the half of it.'

Mrs Wood laughed. 'I'm sure they didn't! And as for me, it was like walking over hot coals with that wife of yours. But I stood the heat and bent over backwards to please her. I was even allowed to take the bairn to dancing classes every Saturday. I'm sure that's what helped to keep her spirits up. She has done well, Jack – she's a lovely little dancer!' She leaned forward and tapped his arm. 'I've had an idea,' she continued, 'and I'd like to know what you think. I've got a friend whose daughter goes to Madame Bella's Academy for the Performing Arts.'

'What on earth's that, Mother?

'Be patient and let me explain. Madame Bella teaches elocution, drama and dancing. She likes children with dancing experience, so I'm sure she would consider Lizzie. We would have to enrol her for a year and she would attend from 4.30 to 6.30 three nights a week. On top of that, she would have to turn up on Saturdays to rehearse for the annual showcase. Now wouldn't that be a wonderful way to give Lizzie more independence?'

Jack hugged his mother. 'I had an idea you might have something planned. But what about Alice?'

'Leave her to me, Jack. Take me home with you and I'll try to persuade her it's for her benefit. Of course, in a way it could be, and why not? Whatever we think of Alice, she's been alone such a long time I'm sure she would appreciate a bit of attention. And just remember, you'd be helping Lizzie. Come on, son, we can talk it over on the way.'

Jack's spirits lifted as he heard singing coming from the sitting room. He popped his head around the door. 'You'll never guess who I've brought home with me, Alice!'

Mrs Wood followed him inside. 'I hope you don't mind me popping in like this, Alice.'

Hasn't he seen enough of his mother for one day, she thought, as she struggled to conceal her annoyance. She pecked Mrs Wood on the cheek. 'Ye know yer always welcome, Mother.'

'I came because I was worried about you, pet. Jack told me about the trouble you're having with Lizzie. It can't be easy for you.'

Alice sat on the sofa and held her chest. 'Ma heart's bin ahl over the place with palpitations. Isn't that right, Jack?'

He nodded and caught his mother's eye. 'I was surprised to hear the way Lizzie spoke to Alice last night – it certainly put a dampener on my homecoming.'

Mrs Wood sat on the sofa next to her. 'I'm sorry to hear this, dear, especially as you and Jack have been apart for so long. I know it's not in your nature, but please try to think of yourself for a change. It's time the two of you had some proper time together.' Mrs Wood moved closer to Alice and held her hand. 'And quite by chance, I might have found the very way. There's what I took to be an old vicarage at the end of the village and as it turns out, it happens to be a dance academy! I made some enquiries and it seems to have a good reputation. It's run by a lady who calls herself Madame Bella, but I've heard she's very strict. Some of the girls can't cope with the discipline and drop out halfway through the term, but the ones who stay seem to do well. Madame Bella requires good manners and punctuality.'

'It seems just the thing to me,' said Alice, persuaded by the idea of having time alone with Jack, after so many years of separation. 'Lizzie could do with learning a few manners. Ye should hear the way she talks to me.'

'She'd have to attend three evenings a week and rehearse for the annual showcase on Saturdays,' Mrs Wood explained.

'And what the hell does ahl that cost? It sounds bloody expensive to me, Mother.'

'Don't worry, Alice. It could be my Christmas present to Lizzie.'

Jack pushed in beside Alice and slipped his arm around her shoulder. 'It's a wonderful idea, don't you think, dear?' He turned to his mother. 'And maybe sometimes, when we fancy a trip to the Oxford Galleries, Lizzie could stay the night with you, after class.'

'It goes without saying, son, and it would give you both a chance to make up for lost time. What do you think, Alice?'

'Ah suppose there's no harm in giving it a try, Mother.' Alice was beginning to see more and more benefits to all this. 'But if yer giving her the course for Christmas, make sure ye don't give her anything else. The last thing we want to do is spoil her.'

'Don't worry about that, Alice. You're her mother and you know best. Well, you two, I don't want to outstay my welcome. I'll be in touch with Madame Bella in the morning. I'll be off now.'

Alice glared at Jack as he picked up the car keys.

Mrs Wood buttoned up her coat. 'I don't need a lift, son, the walk'll do me good.'

'Are you sure, Mother?'

Alice frowned. 'Didn't ye hear what she said?'

He walked his mother to the front door and helped her outside. 'Don't you think we handled the situation well?'

Mrs Wood stood on the threshold and gave a small sigh. 'Yes, Jack, but what a shame we had to stoop to such lengths to give the bairn a bit of freedom.'

Chapter 19

Lizzie was so excited she could hardly sleep. On the floor beside her chair were two pairs of shoes; but they weren't ordinary shoes. One was a pair of pink satin ballet shoes with ribbons and the other was a pair of shiny black tap shoes with a metal heel. Grandma had said she was sorry they were second hand, because she didn't have enough points in her ration book to buy new ones – but she had managed to find the right size in a fair condition by advertising in the *Evening Chronicle*. To Lizzie, they looked perfect and tomorrow – if she ever managed to fall asleep so that tomorrow could come – she would have the chance to wear them at the audition for a place at Madame Bella's Academy. Which reminded her, she'd better say an extra prayer to make sure her mam didn't change her mind in the morning. It was nothing short of a miracle that she had agreed to let her go in the first place.

৵৵

Mrs Wood arrived at Lizzie's house early next morning and was welcomed by Alice in her nightdress and curlers. 'Ah hope Ah'm doin' the right thing, lettin' her go to that place,' she said.

'I'm sure you are, Alice. Is the bairn nearly ready?'

'She should be! She's been messing around up there since the crack o' dawn!'

Lizzie heard her grandma's voice and ran downstairs as though chased by a banshee. She threw her arms around her. 'I'm ready to go, Grandma, I'll just find a carrier bag to pack my things in.'

'You'd better open this first, Lizzie.' Mrs Wood handed her a parcel.

Lizzie tore off the brown paper wrapping. Inside was a pale blue, silk drawstring bag with the initials LW embroidered in navy satin stitch. Lizzie screamed with delight. 'It's lovely, Grandma! Just what I needed!'

'I made it from an old silk blouse of mine, but I reckoned it would serve the purpose nicely.'

'You think of everything, Grandma! What would I do without you?'

Lizzie carefully folded the brown paper to keep for later and then held the bag against her face. 'It's so soft!' she said. She put her tap and ballet shoes in first, then placed her practice clothes on top.

Alice was wearing one of her disapproving looks. 'Ah wish you'd stop spoiling her, she already acts like the Queen of Sheba.'

Mrs Wood recognised the danger sign in the envious tone of her voice and turned to Lizzie. 'Come on, we'd better go – we don't want to be late on your first day. Say goodbye to your mother and thank her for the wonderful opportunity she's given you.'

Lizzie kissed her and, mirroring her grandma's diplomacy, said, 'Thank you, Mother, I only hope I can be half as good a dancer as you.'

Alice almost smiled. 'Had away,' she said, 'before Ah change me mind.'

⚜

'Here we are!' Mrs Wood said, puffing a little as they neared the large iron gates. A polished brass sign engraved in curly copperplate writing shone in the morning sunlight: MADAME BELLA'S ACADEMY FOR THE PERFORMING ARTS.

Lizzie pointed to the sign. 'Look at that, Grandma! Performing Arts!'

Mrs Wood pushed open the gate and ushered Lizzie through onto a short gravel drive. At the end of it, stood an old grey stone house that reminded Lizzie of the vicarage near her school. Wide steps led up to the front door where two large urns stood on either side, proudly displaying thick rhododendron bushes with large yellow blooms. 'Aren't they lovely!' Mrs Wood remarked. 'And what a beautiful colour!'

She looked up at the heavy oak door with its knocker in the shape of a lion's head with a brass ring in its mouth. 'Go on,' said Mrs Wood, 'knock. Or they might think we've changed our minds.'

Lizzie knocked twice with the brass ring and after a minute a girl, who must have been one of the students, answered the door and stood aside to let them in. Her hair was coiled in a neat bun and she was wearing tap shoes. She looked the same age as Lizzie, about twelve.

The hall was very impressive, with a highly polished parquet floor and crisp white paintwork. Lizzie stared at the pictures of famous dancers displayed on the walls and imagined her own picture up there one day.

A vase of white lilies stood on a small console table and murmuring could be heard from behind closed doors. 'Listen,' said Mrs Wood, 'we must be close to the classrooms.'

The girl pointed to the corridor. 'Madame Bella's office is down there, second on the left. You can't miss it.'

'Thank you, dear,' said Mrs Wood. She put her arm around Lizzie and gently steered her to Bella's office. Mrs Wood nodded and Lizzie tapped on the door.

A loud, well-articulated voice called from inside. 'Come in, darling!'

Lizzie opened the door and holding on to her grandma's hand, pulled her inside with her.

Madame Bella was a lady of ample proportions, with red hair, bright red lipstick and a smile that lit up her heavily made-up face. She stood up from behind a large walnut desk and came round with her arm outstretched. 'Nice to see you again, Mrs Wood. And this must be Lizzie. Come here, dear, don't be shy.'

Bella offered a hand weighed down with heavy rings. As she leaned forward to kiss her on the cheek, Lizzie dodged the chunky amber beads dangling from her neck. She had never met anyone quite like Bella before, but she had already made up her mind – she liked her!

Bella cleared her throat. 'I am Madame Bella and while we are in the Academy, you will call me Madame.'

'All right, I will,' said Lizzie.

'Your grandmother has great confidence in you – she tells me you're a talented little dancer with ambition to become an actress, and believes the Academy could enable you to fulfil your potential. I'll give you my opinion when I've seen what you can do.'

Lizzie nodded, a little dazzled by Madame Bella. Oh my God, she thought, I wish Grandma hadn't sung my praises. She put it on a bit thick – what if I'm not good enough?

'We work hard here,' Madame Bella continued, 'and if you pass muster, you will be trained for the theatre and, depending on your ability, will have opportunity to perform. Every year, we showcase what our students have learned and invite their families and friends along to show them the results of their hard work.'

Lizzie nodded.

'Now you may change into your leotard and ballet shoes. The changing room is just opposite my office – you can't miss it. I'll call for you when I'm ready. Bring your tap shoes with you too.'

Lizzie nodded again.

'What do you say?' asked Madame Bella.

'Uh – thank you?'

'No, that's not quite right. We say, Thank you, Madame. Let's start as we mean to carry on. Now say goodbye to your grandma and run along.'

'Thank you, Madame,' Lizzie said, desperate to make the right impression and Bella rewarded her with one of her infectious smiles, which made her eyes scrunch up and twinkle.

Mrs Wood reached out and gave Lizzie's hand a little squeeze for good luck as she left for the changing room. In contrast to the colourful, chaotic office she'd just come from, it was bare and cold, the benches worn thin.

She was just tying the ribbons on her ballet shoes, when Madame Bella poked her head around the door. 'Come along, darling, this way!'

She followed Madame Bella down the hall to the practice room. It was just like the one at her old dance class, except it was much bigger, with the same wall-to-wall mirror and practice barre at the end of the room. A pianist in a baggy grey jumper sat hunched on a stool at an upright piano, reading a folded-up newspaper. When Bella called out, 'We're ready for you, Mr Watkins,' he put the newspaper down and looked up over his spectacles. He was younger than Lizzie had first thought, and now it was his turn to do something, he livened up considerably. 'We shall have the Grade Three pieces I believe Lizzie has prepared. Play something suitable, Mr Watkins.'

He bowed his head in Bella's direction and nodded at Lizzie, who had already taken up her position. With her head held high and her back straight, she waited for her cue.

Lizzie was nervous and took a few false steps before she finally found her rhythm. She was confused at the way Madame Bella called over the music, telling her which moves she wanted to see, without waiting for the music to reach a natural pause. It meant she had to try to remember what to do next before she had finished the step she was already on. After her *demi-pliés*, Lizzie bit her lip. She had forgotten what Madame had asked for a few moments ago. Feeling helpless, she waited a few beats while the piano carried on regardless. Finally, she turned to Madame Bella and shrugged – she was lost.

The formidable lady raised an eyebrow. 'I wanted a *battement tendu*, dear,' she shouted. Lizzie raised her leg in front and pointed her toe, trying to use her arms as gracefully as she could. She mustn't let her nerves ruin this audition when all her hopes depended on the outcome. She had got off to a bad start and she knew it. She returned her feet to third position and brought her hands back down to rest in her lap. Then the piano stopped playing and there was silence.

Lizzie struggled to keep her face from betraying her emotions. She expected some acknowledgement or criticism, but there was none.

'What are we waiting for?' Bella called. 'Take the centre of the floor, dear.'

Lizzie did as she was told. She stood with a natural turn-out, Madame Bella noted approvingly, and she had the right physique for a dancer, with her long legs and arms, a willowy figure and such a pretty face too, with its delicate bone structure, high cheekbones and green eyes. A pity about the nerves, she thought, she'd have to buck her ideas up if she wanted a place in the Academy. A pretty face and the right physique weren't enough.

'Now Mr Watkins will play a happy piece of music that will help you imagine you've been given a wonderful present or a piece of good news – something that would make you feel like dancing with joy. We're using one of your Grade Three pieces, but I want you to bring as much life to it as you can. Use as much of the room as you like, darling, it's all yours.'

Lizzie forced a smile. Nothing had gone right so far, so how on earth could she be expected to dance with joy, when inside she felt desperate. But when the piano began to play, Lizzie felt a fresh surge of energy. She knew this music like the back of her hand and had rehearsed the steps again and again. She would not let nerves beat her this time.

Almost as soon as Lizzie's feet touched the ground, Bella could see the difference in her attitude – the stilted quality had gone and been replaced with something much more interesting and expressive. She was throwing herself at her performance. Her technique could be worked on, but was there enough raw talent for her to shape up at the

Academy? Bella watched as Lizzie *jeté*d back to the centre of the floor, then successfully completed a pirouette of two perfect turns, coming to a halt with one hand on her hip and the other above her head.

Lizzie hoped she had impressed the fiery-headed Bella. She stood still, breathing fast from the effort, and studied Bella's mask-like face, that told her absolutely nothing. Hungry for the woman's approval, she waited impatiently, for what seemed like for ever, until at last she spoke.

'Now pop your tap shoes on.' Bella turned to the pianist. 'When you're ready, Mr Watkins, something jazzy for this young lady.'

Was that all she was going to say? It looked like it was. Oh well, I'll just have to knock her out with my tap dancing, Lizzie decided. She laced up her tap shoes and listened as Mr Watkins started playing the opening notes. Oh great, she thought, 'Bye Bye Blues' – I know it! She picked up the beat and began to dance. For the first time in the audition, she felt confident. Now she was in her element, like a bird in flight. Her feet flew through the steps – the times step, the stomp and the rapid ball-and-heel moves, which made a satisfying clickety click noise along with the music. Her heart raced as she moved faster and faster, then suddenly Bella clapped her hands. 'That's enough!' she called. 'You may get changed and come to my office.'

Lizzie's emotions yo-yoed up and down. Is that it? she asked herself. Just when I was dancing my heart out, really showing her what I can do. At least she could have let me finish!

Bella clapped her hands again. 'Thank you, Mr Watkins, that will be all.'

He bowed his head, pushed his spectacles over the bridge of his nose and picked his newspaper up again.

Lizzie went back to the chilly changing room and as she undid the laces on her tap shoes, began to think about all the trouble her grandma had gone to. I hope I didn't let her down, she thought as she slipped the shoes into her embroidered bag and changed her clothes with trembling fingers.

Her heart was in her mouth as she made her way to Madame Bella's office. She stood outside and took a deep breath before knocking – this was one of the most important moments in her life and on the other side of that door, she would know her fate.

Madame Bella summoned her inside. 'Sit down,' she said.

Lizzie perched nervously on the edge of her chair as she waited to hear the verdict. Madame Bella looked deadly serious. 'There's only one thing I want to say to you, young lady.' She paused for what seemed a lifetime while Lizzie held her breath. 'And that is – welcome to the Academy!'

Lizzie leapt to her feet and nervously asked, 'What does that mean?'

'It means you've passed muster and I'm happy to welcome you into the ranks.' Bella was now beaming.

Lizzie could hardly believe her ears. She looked at Madame Bella's face to see if she meant it – and yes, there was the warm, generous smile. It must be true. She had done it! She had really done it! Lizzie Wood had won a place at Madame Bella's Academy for the Performing Arts!

She was still gasping for breath as Bella picked something up from her desk. 'There! Wear it with pride, my dear. You deserve it.'

Lizzie looked down. Madame Bella had pinned on to her blouse a small brooch in the shape of a shield.

'This is the Academy's official badge,' Bella said. 'I consider it to be a badge of honour. Now, don't forget, the early bird catches the worm and I expect all my students to be prompt for lessons. I'll expect you here, bright and early, next term.'

For the first time since her audition, Lizzie found her voice and her words tumbled out in gratitude. 'Thank you, Madame Bella, I'll be here before I get up.'

Chapter 20

Newcastle upon Tyne, 1946

Mrs Wood tried to contain her excitement as she rang the doorbell. Who would have thought it, just nine months at the Academy and Lizzie already performing in Madame Bella's Showcase. The door suddenly swung open and her heart sank to see Alice standing there with her arms folded across her pinny and a face like thunder.

'What're ye doin' here at this hour, Mother? It's only one o'clock and the bloomin' showcase doesn't start till six. Anyway, ye'd better come in – we're just ganna have a bite to eat before Jack runs Lizzie to the Academy to practise.'

Hastily untying her scarf, Mrs Wood followed Alice into the kitchen. 'Don't worry about me,' she said, 'I've already had something. I thought I'd just pop in to wish Lizzie good luck for tonight. Where is she?'

'Wearin' the mirror out, Ah shouldn't wonder. She's that vain, Ah've told her, one o' these days, she'll see auld Nick in there. Give Jack a shout, Mother.'

Mrs Wood turned to call him but he was already standing in the doorway. 'No need,' she said, 'he's here already – he must have smelt the sausages!'

'You're right, Mother,' he said, 'I can smell them a mile off!' He hugged her. 'Lizzie's just on her way down – she's dancing on air, so don't be surprised if she floats in.'

Alice put the sausages on the table with the dish of jacket potatoes. 'Ah'll fetch the butter, Jack, and d'you fancy a bit o' brown sauce?'

'No thanks, I'll just have mustard.' He pulled out a chair. 'Sit down and help yourself, Mother.'

Alice put the butter on the table and gave Jack a sour look as she banged down the mustard. 'Yer mother doesn't want owt. She's just here to wish Lizzie good luck.'

'And here she is,' said Jack. 'Look who's come to wish you good luck, pet.'

Lizzie bounced into the room and threw her arms around Mrs Wood. 'Grandma! I hope you're still coming tonight?'

Mrs Wood had a tear in her eye as she kissed her. 'What a question, bonnie lass! I'd come even if I had to use crutches.'

Alice pulled a face. 'Divvn' talk daft, Mother, and eat up, Lizzie, your dad hasn't got ahl day.'

Mrs Wood could feel the tension and changed the subject. 'How many of the family will be there tonight?' she asked.

Alice folded her arms and tutted. 'The whole bloody lot, Ah shouldn't wonder.' She scowled at Jack. 'He's even invited me mother and that means poor Peggy'll have to keep an eye on her.'

Lizzie pushed her plate away. 'I've had enough, Dad. I'll just get my things, then we'd better be off.'

Jack cringed. Why did Alice have to put a dampener on Lizzie's big night? Just for once, why couldn't she keep her mouth shut?

Alice pointed at Lizzie's plate as she began to clear the table. 'Just look at that, Jack! She's left her sausages!'

He scraped his chair back noisily and glared at her. 'I'm sure you won't let them go to waste, Alice, you've always had a good appetite.'

Lizzie felt the hostility as she came back into the kitchen and was relieved at the thought she'd now be out for the rest of the day. 'I'm ready when you are, Dad.'

Mrs Wood was fidgeting with her beads. 'So am I,' she said.

Lizzie pecked Alice on the cheek and took Mrs Wood's arm. 'Isn't it exciting, Grandma? I can't wait for you to see me tonight.'

Jack couldn't wait to leave.

✿

Alice and Jack arrived at the Academy in plenty of time that evening. They'd both taken the trouble to look smart, Jack because he wanted Lizzie to feel proud of her parents and Alice because she knew she could still turn a head or two. Jack's best suit now fitted him again and Alice had saved enough clothing coupons for a stylish new coat with a turned-up collar, figuring there was no sense wasting the coupons on Lizzie – she would only outgrow everything.

'Don't you think it looks grand, Alice? Just look at the trouble they've taken!'

She remained silent, but Jack couldn't help noticing her gazing up at the balloons in the trees, trying not to smile. He nodded towards the huge welcome sign above the open door. 'Looks like they're ready for us.'

They stepped through into the hall, to be greeted by a tall girl dressed as a clown. She smiled at them and held out a programme. 'The theatre's at the end of the corridor,' she said, lisping a little through prominent braces. 'You can't miss it – it's got fairy lights around the entrance.'

Alice pushed Jack aside and set off down the corridor towards the illuminated door. He hurried behind and watched as she pushed it open and glared inside. 'My God! Your lot are here ahlready. Trust them to take ahl the best seats!'

'Keep your voice down, Alice, you're making a spectacle of yourself.' Jack glanced around warily.

'And just look, Jack, there's wor Peggy sittin' near the front with me mother.'

Peggy waved when she saw her sister and pointed to two empty chairs.

'Ah'm not sittin' there to let me mother show us up, Jack. Have you seen what she's wearin'? That bloody fox collar's riddled with God knows what. She'll be scratching herself ahl bloody night.'

Jack took her arm and practically frog-marched her to the seats. He sat next to Peggy, with Mrs Rooney on her other side, leaving Alice sulking at the end of the row.

'Cheer up,' said Peggy, 'at least you're not sittin' next to me mother.' She waved her programme at Jack. 'Look at page six,' she said, 'Lizzie's in a little playlet!'

Mrs Rooney leaned over. 'What the hell's that, Jack?'

'It means she'll have words to say. And look! On page five, she's tap dancing on her own!'

Jack stood up. 'Have you seen Mother, Peggy?' He was looking around the room in an effort to locate her, when he caught her eye and waved. She was sitting further back with Peter and Ena.

'Sit down,' said Alice, 'it's gonna start in a minute. And look what's just walked in! Trust Joe and Annie to be late – they'll be bloody lucky to find a seat.'

Jack struggled to control his temper as the lights went down. Madame Bella walked on to the stage, engulfed in a spotlight that lit up her colourful, sequinned kaftan and her red hair that twinkled from the generous application of glitter dust. She reminded Jack of a butterfly as she held out her arms. 'What a sight!' said Mrs Rooney. 'She looks like a bloody Christmas tree!'

'Be quiet!' Jack whispered. 'That's enough.'

Mrs Rooney responded with a mocking smile. Jack turned his back on her as Madame Bella began to speak.

'Welcome to the Academy Showcase. You will not be disappointed with the talent on this stage tonight. But before we commence, let me give you the good news. Mr Mark Chapman has honoured us with his presence again tonight.'

Whispering spread through the room. Mrs Rooney nudged Jack. 'Is she gannin' on ahl bloody night?'

'He has decided to put on his pantomime at the Theatre Royal again this year,' Madame Bella went on, 'and will once more consider some of our girls for parts. With the talent appearing on this stage tonight, I'm sure he'll be spoiled for choice.'

Alice nudged Peggy. 'Did ye hear that? He winnit have to look far when he sees wor Lizzie! If she takes after me, she's as good as got a part ahlready!'

Jack gave Alice a fierce look. She scowled back at him. Divvn't worry, she thought, he'll not stop Lizzie's chances like he did mine. She straightened her back, lifted her head and, with a defiant gesture, turned away.

'And now,' said Madame Bella, 'it is time to relax and enjoy the show.'

The music struck up, the lights dimmed and Madame Bella made her exit as the curtains opened. The Academy students were lined up on stage in rows according to their height. Lizzie's line was second from the front.

The room burst into applause as the pianist played the introduction to the Academy Showcase song.

'Bloody hell!' said Mrs Rooney. 'We've heard nowt but bloody clappin' – we haven't seen a bloody thing yet!'

Jack held his temper as the children began to sing.

'Here we are with another show!

'You won't be disappointed when it's time to go!

'For we've planned a show . . .'

Alice turned to Peggy. 'What d'ye think of wor Lizzie's singin'?'

'Shut up, Alice, Ah can't hear her. Anyway, it's a choir.'

'Ah divvn' care what it is, Peggy! Ah just hope that man's here. What's his name, anyway?'

'Mr Chapman. Now be quiet, Alice, Jack's looking this way.'

'Let him look, Peggy, Ah'm past carin' what he thinks! Ah'll do whatever it takes to give Lizzie her chance – that's more than Jack ever did for me!'

'Be quiet,' said Peggy, 'folk're lookin'.'

Alice sat back with her arms folded as the opening song came to a close. The children took their curtain call and Madame Bella came back to the stage.

'And now I'd like to introduce Sara Hobson, one of our older students, who will perform a piece from the ballet, *Swan Lake*.'

The lights dimmed and a follow spot guided a slender young woman on to the stage. She looked elegant and poised in her white tutu and pink ballet shoes. A diamanté tiara was fixed to the little bun on top of her head and as she took up her position the audience applauded.

'Isn't she lovely?' said Peggy.

Alice glared at her. 'Keep your bloody flattery for wor Lizzie. You haven't seen her yet.'

Where's all this bloomin' praise for Lizzie coming from, Peggy wondered. She's never had a kind word to say for the bairn. And didn't poor old Mrs Wood have to bend over backwards to let Lizzie come here in the first place? I'd like to know what my sister's up to.

Alice nudged her. 'So when's it Lizzie's turn, then?'

'How should Ah know, Alice? Ah'm tryin' to watch the ballet!'

'So am I!' said an irate woman from the row behind. 'Ask your mother to keep her voice down, hinny.'

Alice spun round and glared at the woman. 'If you think she's me daughter you need your bloody eyes tested!'

'That's enough!' said Peggy. 'You're nothin' but an embarrassment. Behave yersel' or they'll ask you to leave.'

Alice folded her arms, leaned back in her seat and sulked.

Peggy glanced over at her mother. With her head bent and her chin resting on her chest, she was sleeping like a baby. God is good, she thought, I can settle down at last and enjoy the show.

She watched as a young girl cartwheeled on to the stage and bowed, before commencing a series of acrobatics. It all looked so dangerous – she hadn't seen anything like it before. Time just flew by and her troubles seemed to melt away at the sight of the clever mime and the beautiful dancing.

She came back to earth with a bump when the curtain came down and Alice poked her with the programme. 'It's wor Lizzie's turn now!'

Madame Bella made her entrance through the curtains and raised her arms to acknowledge the applause. 'Thank you!' she said. 'And now, please welcome one of our first year pupils making her debut performance. Please put your hands together for Lizzie Wood!'

The curtain opened to a round of applause, with Lizzie framed in a spotlight. Peggy gasped at the sight of her, in a black sequinned leotard and her black tap shoes with the red satin bows.

Lizzie began by dancing on the tap mat, performing all the on-the-spot steps she had learned.

'What's that bloody thing she's standin' on?' asked Mrs Rooney.

Peggy prodded her with her elbow and Jack, determined not to miss Lizzie's performance, turned away.

The audience gasped as one as Lizzie leapt off her mat and spun across the floor, using every inch of the stage. They burst into applause when she finished with a somersault, ending in the splits.

Alice, who for once had remained silent throughout Lizzie's performance, was as proud as a peacock. She stood up. 'That's the way, my girl!' she shouted. 'Show them how to do it!'

Peggy grabbed her jacket and pulled her back into her seat.

Lizzie blushed as she took her curtain call and hurried from the stage. Bella was waiting in the wings and caught her by the arm. 'They haven't finished with you yet,' she said. 'Go back and take another call.'

Lizzie took a deep breath and did her bidding. She smiled when she heard the applause. For goodness sake, she thought, I think they like me.

When the curtain came down on the last act, Madame Bella gathered the whole cast on stage and when the curtain went up again the audience got to their feet and cheered. The girls smiled and bowed when they heard the huge applause. Bella waited until it had died down before addressing the audience.

'Now then,' she said, 'all good things must come to an end, but I'm sure you'll agree that this young talent was more than good. I'm proud of my girls and, from what you've seen tonight, I'm sure you are too.' She turned and smiled at the girls. 'Mr Chapman certainly enjoyed the show and has decided to audition some of you for his production of *Babes in the Wood*.' The girls jumped up and down with excitement. 'You'll find a list of the lucky ones on the noticeboard. Now off you go.'

They almost fell over each other as they hurried from the stage.

Alice nudged Peggy. 'Did ye hear that?'

Her sister nodded. 'Yes, and Ah think Lizzie's in with a chance.'

'In with a chance! Is that what ye think?'

'Shut up!' said Peggy. 'Madame Bella's speaking.'

'And I'd like to thank you all for your enthusiastic support in the run-up to this successful evening,' Bella was saying. 'Your help with costumes, props and transport has been more than generous. And now please make your way to the ballroom and enjoy our special Showcase buffet.'

Immediately Mrs Rooney jumped up and made a beeline for the exit. Caught a little by surprise, the rest of the family followed behind, making their way to the big room at the other end of the building. It was often used for dancing, with its well-worn but solid wooden floor and its small stage at the far end, but tonight it was given over to catering for the performers and their supporters in the audience. Jack looked round for Alice and Lizzie, but they were nowhere in sight. Mrs Rooney was already helping herself at the buffet, filling her plate to capacity. How embarrassing, he thought, let's hope she eats herself to death.

Peter, Annie and Ena were talking twenty to the dozen when Jack went over to see his side of the family. He put his arm around his mother. 'You look worn out. Let me get you a drink.'

'Joe's just getting them, Jack. But what have you got to say about your daughter? You can see she's got talent, can't you?' Mrs Wood dabbed her eyes, overcome with pride.

'She's certainly a canny little dancer, Mother, but I'm worried she might get carried away. I don't want her to think of dancing as a profession. So please don't encourage her. I don't think building up her hopes of a career in the theatre will be good for her. If she wanted to be an actress it might be different, but you get all kinds hanging around dancers, it's not respectable for a girl of her sort. Mind you, you were right when you said the Academy would give her independence – I can see a change in her already.'

Joe waved at Jack. 'Over here!' he called, and pointed to a table. 'This should do – let's grab a few chairs while there's still a queue at the buffet.'

Annie and Ena fussed around Mrs Wood as they settled her onto a chair. 'It's been a long night,' said Ena, 'you must be exhausted. And what did you think of your granddaughter? Didn't she do well? And it's all thanks to you that she got into the Academy.'

But Mrs Wood looked crestfallen. 'I hope I've done the right thing, girls. She's taken to dancing like a duck to water but I'm afraid our Jack doesn't want her to take it up professionally.'

Annie put her arm around her. 'I'm sure he hasn't made his mind up just yet. And Lizzie's very young – who knows what she might decide to do.'

341

'Hush, Annie, Jack and Peter are on their way over with some more chairs.'

'Put one doon here!' They turned to see Mrs Rooney stumbling towards them with a plate spilling over with food. 'Ye'd better hurry up, Jack,' she said, 'or there'll be nowt left.'

It wouldn't surprise me, he thought, she's already got half the buffet on her plate.

As he turned to pick up another chair, he saw Alice and Peggy hurrying towards them. Alice was flustered and out of breath. 'Just wait till you hear the news, Jack!'

He glared at her. 'Where on earth have you been, Alice? And where's Lizzie?'

'Mr Chapman picked her for the audition and he's comin' here to try her out next week! Lizzie's name was on the noticeboard.' She could hardly contain her excitement.

'Never mind the noticeboard, Alice,' snapped Jack. 'Apart from your mother, we're all hungry.' He turned away from them and headed for the remains of the buffet.

Jack scrutinised the food. There wasn't much left to choose from. He took a plate and helped himself to two slices of cheese and onion flan, a few salmon sandwiches and a couple of Eccles cakes and went back to the table. He placed the plate in front of his mother and bowed low. 'Dinner for two, Madam,' he said, as he handed her a paper napkin.

Mrs Rooney burped loudly and took out her snuff box. 'Quite the little gentleman, aren't we, Jack?'

He stared at the snuff box. 'Not at the table while Mother's eating, Mrs Rooney.'

'Pardon me for livin'!' She snatched up her bag and left the table.

'Sorry about that, Mother, but the woman's been driving me mad all night.' He sighed. 'And we haven't seen hide nor hair of Lizzie since the final curtain fell. I suppose they're nattering about the pantomime auditions somewhere. But at least I'd like to know where she is. She can't be far away, I'm going to look.' Jack felt nettled as he set off down the corridor. If this is how they go on at Madame Bella's Academy, then it's not the place for my daughter, he thought. She must be hungry. I hope she's had something to eat. He stopped when he heard laughter coming from one of the rooms. The door was slightly open and he knocked.

'Come in whoever you are!' called a merry voice. He pushed the door open and stepped inside to see a bunch of excited children chattering twenty to the dozen and Lizzie was one of them. A plump lady was trying to call them to order. Even with her back to him, there was no mistaking it was Madame Bella. Although she had discarded her sequinned costume in favour of a slightly less outrageous dress, her ample shape and distinctive mop of red hair marked her out immediately.

Jack coughed and she spun around. 'Hello! And what can I do for you?'

'I'm Mr Wood, Lizzie's father.'

'Just a moment please, while I release the girls. That's all for tonight,' she said, 'now join your mothers in the green room.'

Lizzie waved when she saw her dad and smiled as she left the room.

Bella pointed to a chair. 'Please sit down, Mr Wood, and excuse me while I give my feet a break.' She kicked off her red, patent-leather shoes, sank into a chair and hoisted her feet on to a table. 'Just look at the poor things! I'm ashamed of the way I treat them!' She gave her toes a rub. 'That's better, Mr Wood! So what can I do for you?'

Jack was speechless. He'd never seen anyone like her and had almost forgotten why he'd come. 'It's all right now, Madame Bella, I was simply looking for Lizzie. I had no idea where she was.'

'It's out of hours,' she said, 'why don't you call me Bella? I'm sorry if you were worried, Mr Wood, but your wife did know where Lizzie was.' She treated him to an affectionate smile. 'So, I hope you enjoyed Lizzie's first showcase? Mr Chapman was very impressed with her and, who knows, she might be lucky at the audition.'

'We'll have to see about that, Madame Bella.' Jack paused awkwardly. 'But please let me congratulate you on the show – the girls were a credit to you and that includes Lizzie, of course.'

Bella beamed at him. 'I'm glad you enjoyed it. Your daughter has a lot going for her. We must meet and talk about her sometime.'

'Of course,' he said, 'but now I had better go and find her.'
He stood up hurriedly and held out his hand. 'A pleasure to
meet you, Madame Bella.'

'And you too, Mr Wood. Please pop by when you've got
the time.' She gave him a wicked smile.

Jack hurried along the corridor, looking for Lizzie.
There were signs on all the doors, but none of them said
'green room' and he was beginning to wonder if he would
ever find her when a young girl came skipping round
the corner towards him. 'You look lost,' she said. 'Can I
help you?'

'I'm looking for the green room, pet. I'm Lizzie Wood's
dad – Madame Bella said that's where I'd find her.'

'You've just missed her, Mr Wood, they've all gone to
the buffet.'

Jack rushed back to the ballroom. He pushed his way
through the crowd – there was no sign of Lizzie or Alice,
but he caught sight of Peter and waved him over. 'Where is
everybody?'

'Don't ask,' he said, 'it's been like bedlam here. Thank
God Joe and Annie took Mrs Rooney home with poor,
suffering Peggy. We'd given you up for lost! We were just
about to take Mother home – she's got a headache from
listening to Alice.'

'Where is Alice anyway?'

Peter pointed her out across the room.

'And have you seen Lizzie? I've been searching for her
all over the place.'

'Here I am, Dad!'

Jack spun round just in time to catch Lizzie as she threw herself into his arms. 'So what did you think, what did you think, Dad?'

'I thought you were the loveliest thing I'd ever seen and I was proud to be your father.'

'But was I really all right?'

'You were more than all right, pet.'

'And did you like Madame Bella, Dad? Isn't she lovely?'

'She's a very nice lady, Lizzie. Now calm down while I say goodbye to Grandma. Uncle Peter and Auntie Ena are waiting to take her home.'

When he got to the table, Alice gave him a sheepish smile. 'Ah'll bet you've bin wonderin' where Ah've bin, Jack.'

'I'm sure you'll tell me, Alice, but there's plenty of time. Let's wait until morning – there's one or two things I've got to say to you after I've had a good night's sleep.' He turned to his mother. 'Just look at you,' he said. 'You can hardly keep your eyes open.'

'Don't worry,' said Ena, 'it's nothing that a bit of TLC won't cure so we're taking her home with us tonight.'

Lizzie cuddled Mrs Wood. 'Thanks for everything, Grandma – all those Saturdays carting me off to dancing class and then getting me in to Madame Bella's. I won't let you down.'

'Ah'm sure she won't,' said Alice, 'especially as you're payin' the fees, Mother.'

Peter, who was holding Mrs Wood's coat, shook his head and Jack's face was white with rage. He kissed his mother and glared at Alice. 'Put your coat on and get the bairn's things. We're going home.'

Ena took him aside. 'For the bairn's sake, Jack, don't say anything tonight.'

He gave her a baleful look. 'Don't worry, Ena, I wouldn't trust myself.'

ᘐ

Next morning, after Lizzie left for school, the atmosphere was chilly. Alice watched Jack warily as she cleared the table. Business was thriving again, and he was never late for work, but here he was, pouring himself another coffee. She put the last dishes by the sink, but as she came to pick up the salt cellar, Jack took hold of her wrist. 'Sit down,' he said, 'I want to talk to you. I was humiliated by you and your mother's outrageous behaviour in front of my family last night.'

'But Ah was only tryin' . . .'

'Shut up, Alice, you'll only make things worse if you try to whitewash over your carry on. Last night was meant to be Lizzie's night and it could have been until your ears pricked up when you heard Mr Chapman was touting for talent for his blooming pantomime.'

'And what's wrong with that, Jack? Lizzie takes after me. She's a good little dancer.'

Jack laughed. 'And do you see yourself as a stage door mother, Alice? Pushing your daughter to heights that you never reached yourself?'

'And whose fault was that?' she shouted. 'My career was nipped in the bud when Lizzie was born!'

Jack got up from the table. 'I've already heard the story of how I spoilt your chances, Alice. Now, listen to me. I hardly slept last night, thinking about what was best to do for Lizzie and I've decided that if she's offered a part in this pantomime I won't say no. But just remember, it'll be the first and last time.'

Alice breathed out loudly. She'd been expecting worse than this. 'She'll be that pleased, Jack. Can Ah tell her?'

'Please yourself.' He stalked into the hall and pulled his jacket from the peg. 'I'm off to work, Alice. I'll see you tonight.'

❧

When the big day came, they arrived at the Academy in plenty of time for Lizzie's audition. Jack stood outside the grand entrance with Lizzie while Alice picked up her case and hurried straight inside. 'My goodness,' he said, 'your mother's keen – you'd think it was her auditioning.'

Lizzie laughed. He took hold of her hand and placed his father's lucky penny inside. 'This belonged to my dad, Lizzie. Before he died he gave it to Uncle Joe, who let me borrow it for luck during the war. When you return it to him, I'm sure he'll tell you all about it. Let's hope it brings you good luck today.'

Lizzie looked at him in surprised delight but before she could think of a suitable reply, Alice poked her head around the door. 'What the hell's going on? Get inside, Lizzie, they're waitin' for us in the green room.'

'It's my fault,' said Jack, 'I was just wishing my girl good luck. Off you go, pet. Have fun and do your best. No one can ask more of you than that.'

Alice almost dragged Lizzie inside. 'And what were you natterin' about with your dad?' she demanded as she hustled her through the door. 'You're as thick as bloody thieves.'

A row of anxious mothers, with their anxious daughters, were sitting upright on the hard wooden chairs, like criminals awaiting their trial. No one spoke – they simply stared at the new arrivals. It was unnaturally quiet, except for the strains of a muffled piano coming from the adjoining room. Lizzie took her seat as unobtrusively as possible and Alice plonked herself down beside her.

Suddenly the music stopped and a sobbing girl ran out, straight into the arms of her mother.

'Ah'm sure she hasn't got the part,' said Alice, 'or she wouldn't be blubberin' like that.'

'Keep your voice down, Mam,' Lizzie whispered. 'They might hear you.'

The girls were called in one by one. Some of them came out crying and others simply looked numb. It was impossible to tell what the results were and by the time it was Lizzie's turn, she felt drained by all the emotion in the room. When at last her name was called, she stroked the lucky penny and went inside.

A large gentleman in a smart suit looked up at her from behind a wooden table. 'I'm Mr Chapman,' he said, 'and I'm pleased to meet you, Lizzie Wood. I saw you in the little sketch the other night and I thought you spoke your lines quite well.'

'Thank you, Mr Chapman. I did my best.'

'And now,' he continued, 'let me introduce you to Miss Sarah Hall, our choreographer and voice coach.'

Lizzie smiled shyly at the pretty young woman standing to his right. She didn't look much older than she was herself.

'And, of course, you know Madame Bella.' He gave a little nod towards her, on his other side.

Lizzie grinned at Bella, who was in one of her flamboyant bright dresses as usual. Nerves or no nerves, it was impossible not to feel happy when Bella was there.

Mr Chapman passed Lizzie a script. 'Here's your dialogue. Some of the lines will be spoken by Boy Babe with the principal girl. Miss Hall will read her part and you will read Boy Babe. Go along with Miss Hall and study the lines and then I'll hear you.'

Miss Hall smiled at Lizzie. 'Come on!' she said cheerfully. 'Over here!'

When they were out of earshot, Mr Chapman took a cigar from the ashtray on the table. He took a deep pull and winked at Bella. 'So tell me, what do you think of Lizzie Wood?'

Bella gave him a straight look. 'I was hoping you wouldn't ask that – she's only in her first year and it's hard to judge, but from what I've seen so far, I think she's got potential. She works hard and never complains about extra practice. And apart from that, she has a pleasant disposition – truth to tell, I like the girl.'

'Well, well, Bella, we'll have to see what she can do.'

On the other side of the room, Sarah smiled reassuringly at Lizzie. 'Don't worry,' she said, 'it's only a read-through.'

They read the lines together until Sarah was satisfied Lizzie understood the dialogue, then went back together to the centre of the echoing room.

'If you're ready,' said Mr Chapman, 'you can begin. And speak up, Lizzie, so we can all hear you.'

She stood opposite Sarah and they read the script together. She does this so well, thought Lizzie, the words seem to lift from the page. In contrast, she felt very awkward and was aware of her voice trembling over the first few lines. But then she got caught up in Boy Babe's story. He'd been lost in a big forest and Lizzie somehow knew exactly how frightened and alone he'd felt. She began to bring meaning into the part and before she knew it, the audition was over. She sighed with relief and handed the script back to Mr Chapman.

'Thank you, Lizzie, that wasn't bad at all.' She watched his face carefully for any sign of how she had done, but it was like a mask. 'You can go now,' he said. 'Madame Bella will let you know our decision later.'

It was very disappointing to have no reaction. Lizzie tried not to look too crestfallen as Sarah took her hand and led her to the door. 'Cheer up,' she said, 'you did quite well and the part's still up for grabs.'

Alice pounced on Lizzie as she came into the green room. 'How did ye get on, pet? Have ye got a part?'

Oh my God, thought Lizzie, she's started already. 'They don't make their mind up on the spot, Mam. We won't know until they've talked it over. I'm not the only one they've seen.'

Alice's face tightened. 'They must've said somethin', Lizzie, ye've bin in there longer than the others. Didn't they give you a hint? Ah can't believe they said nothin'.'

There were four mothers with four tired children in the room all in the same situation as Lizzie; they'd all been told, 'Madame Bella will let you know.' There was a clock hanging on a wall and its ticking seemed to grow louder as the room grew stuffier. Lizzie wondered how her mother would behave if she didn't get a part and who would she blame? If she thought Madame Bella was to blame, she might put an end to the Academy – and what then?

Lizzie was desperate to leave the room. Her opportunity came when Bella called her outside into the corridor. She seemed even more excitable than usual. 'I couldn't wait to give you the good news, Lizzie. You've passed your audition with flying colours and you've got the part. They haven't decided on the Girl Babe yet and, until they do, please keep it to yourself. Of course, you may tell your family if you wish.'

Lizzie's mouth fell open and she stared at Bella. 'Are you sure?'

Bella smiled and nodded her head. Lizzie threw her arms around her. 'It's you I have to thank, Madame, and I'll always be grateful.'

Bella swallowed hard. 'Nothing's gained without work, Lizzie, and you certainly deserve the part. You and your mother will be expected at the theatre next Sunday. In the meantime, your contract and all other details should arrive in a day or two. Now off you go, and congratulations, dear.'

When they got home, Alice went straight to the kitchen to fill the kettle.

'When will ye hear?' she asked. 'About the audition?'

Lizzie took a deep breath. 'Actually, Mam, I've already heard.' The kettle fell into the sink with a clatter as Alice turned and stared at her. 'Ye've got a part, haven't ye? Go on, go on then! What part are ye playin'?'

'Boy Babe, Mam. Are you happy?'

'Am Ah happy? What do ye think? You're a clever girl, Lizzie! Ah knew ye'd get the part because yer better than the whole bloody lot of them, put together! Are ye hungry, pet, shall Ah nip out and get ye a fish supper?'

'Thanks for asking, Mam, but I'm tired and I'm all sweaty. I'd rather have a bath and an early night if you don't mind.'

'Get yersel' upstairs, hinny – there's plenty of hot water. And canna do owt else for ye?'

In for a penny, in for a pound, thought Lizzie, I'll strike while the iron's hot. 'There is, Mam. When Dad comes home could you ask him to go to Auntie Ena's? Grandma Wood is staying there tonight and I want him to give her the good news.' She held her breath as she waited for the reply.

'Don't worry, pet, of course Ah will.'

Blimey, thought Lizzie, wonders never cease. She climbed the stairs and pinched herself, hoping it wasn't all a dream. At the moment, she felt more like Cinderella than Boy Babe. But what if the shoe doesn't fit, she wondered. Will Mam turn back into the wicked stepmother?

Lizzie undressed, put on her dressing gown and was on her way to the bathroom when she heard Alice shouting from downstairs. 'Is the water hot enough, pet? Ah can put a kettle on if it's not.'

Never mind about Cinderella, she thought, I'm beginning to feel like Alice in Wonderland.

'Thanks, Mam,' she called, 'but it's just right.'

She ran a bath and poured the last of her bath salts into the hot, steamy water. It smelt so good. She put her foot in and quickly pulled it out again. It was much too hot, so she knelt by the bath and said her prayers while it cooled. 'Dear loving God, thank you for all the many blessings you bestow upon me, especially my part in *Babes in the Wood*. I'm not out of the woods myself, yet – I can't understand the sudden change in my mother. She's killing me with kindness and, as you know, that's completely out of character, so I'm turning my problem over to you and your care and let your will be done. I promise to keep an open mind over my mother's unusual behaviour, for who knows, it could be another miracle! Love from Lizzie'

Chapter 21

On Sunday, Jack took Alice and Lizzie to the Theatre Royal and guided them to the stage door. He kissed Lizzie on both cheeks. 'Break a leg,' he said, 'isn't that what they say?'

'Yes Dad, but it means much more when it comes from you.'

He laughed. 'You're only saying that because you mean it! And why shouldn't I, pet?' He leaned over to hug her. 'I'll be off now, see you tonight.'

'You bet, Dad.' She waved until he was out of sight, hardly able to believe she was really here. This was the premier theatre in Newcastle, maybe in the whole north-east of England, and she was to be performing on its stage. She'd been taken to see a show here when she was younger and had been overwhelmed by the grandeur of the place: the wide foyer with its huge marble pillars and high ceilings, embossed in gold leaf.

It was a vast place; she had been told it could accommodate an audience of well over a thousand. She tried to put that to the back of her mind. Anyway she wasn't going in through the main entrance now, but through the stage door instead, around the corner in Shakespeare Street.

Alice dragged Lizzie inside. Immediately to their left was a painted wooden door with a window in it and a sign that said, RING FOR BILL. Lizzie was just about to press the bell when the window opened and an old man popped his head out.

'What's your name, girlie?'

'It's Lizzie Wood.'

He placed a large leather-bound book on the counter. 'My name is Bill and I'm the doorman.' He had a patch over one eye and as he opened the book, Lizzie's eyes were drawn to the two missing fingers of his left hand. He passed her a pencil. 'You will sign in when you arrive and sign out when you leave.'

After signing her name, she stepped back to let Alice through.

'And what's your name, Missus?'

Alice straightened her back as she looked Bill up and down. 'Ah'm Mrs Wood, Lizzie's mother and chaperone.' She stared at Bill's missing fingers. 'Looks like ye've bin in the wars, hinny, and what's the matter with yer eye?'

Bill leant forward and glared at her. 'I left it in the battlefield with me fingers in the First World War! Now sign the book and come with me. Sarah Hall's waiting for your daughter.'

They followed him up a flight of stone steps that led to a corridor with doors on either side. 'These are the dressing rooms,' he said, 'and here's yours, pet.' He knocked on number 3 and showed them inside.

Sarah, looking younger than ever, hurried forward to meet them. 'Nice to see you again, Lizzie, and this must be your mother. Pleased to meet you, Mrs Wood.'

Sarah held out her hand and Alice shook it limply. 'How long are we supposed to stay today?' she asked curtly. She glanced around the place, noting that it was at least better appointed than the backstage rooms at the Academy, which were basic to put it mildly.

But before Sarah had time to reply, Alice's eye was drawn to a woman with a little girl sitting at the far end of the room. 'And who's that over there? Ah haven't seen them before.'

'Oh how rude of me, Mrs Wood! Come with me and let me introduce you. This is Mrs Crawford and her daughter, Beryl.' Sarah turned to Lizzie. 'Beryl will be your partner in crime. She's playing Girl Babe.'

Alice couldn't take her eyes off Mrs Crawford. She was wearing a smart suit, a frilly blouse and shoes with Cuban heels. Her hair was set in a Marcel wave, with a little felt hat complementing the tasteful outfit. Yes, she thought, she's just my type. We'll get on like a house on fire. She smiled at Mrs Crawford. 'Pleased to meet you. Ah'm Lizzie's mother. Ah expect we'll be spending a lot of time together, seeing as how we're both chaperones.'

Mrs Crawford gave Alice a pleasant smile. 'Yes,' she said, and Alice noticed her cut-glass voice. 'I suppose we will.'

Beryl was holding on to her mother's hand. 'Don't be shy, pet, say hello to Mrs Wood.'

Alice looked Beryl up and down. Well, she thought to herself, there's not much meat on her, is there, she's as thin as a rake! But at least she's got nice curly hair – I'll bet her mother puts it in rags every night.

Lizzie was standing quietly by, listening to the chitchat. How on earth will Mrs Crawford cope with Mam for the run of this show, she wondered. Maybe I'll buy her some earplugs for Christmas.

Sarah clapped her hands. 'Chop, chop, girls, Mr Chapman is waiting on stage for the read-through.'

Lizzie took Beryl's hand and they followed Sarah to the door.

'Just a minute, Sarah,' Alice shouted. 'We wouldn't say no to a coffee.' She nudged Mrs Crawford. 'Ah could just do with one, hinny, what about you?'

'Yes, Mrs Wood, that would be nice.'

'And wouldn't it be nice if we used first names?' Alice continued eagerly. 'After all, we'll be seein' each other every day. My name's Alice, what's yours?'

Mrs Crawford hesitated before replying. 'My name is Joan.'

Alice laughed heartily. 'Ah don't believe it!' she said. 'Joan Crawford! That's the name of me favourite film star! Did ye ever see her in *Mildred Pierce*?'

Mrs Crawford put her hand to her mouth and gave a genteel cough. 'No, I can't say that I have.'

'What a pity, Joan! What that woman went through! Mildred's daughter stole her mother's boyfriend and ended up murderin' him, with poor Mildred tryin' to take the blame for it. There wasn't a dry eye in the house!'

Mrs Crawford was obviously wondering how on earth to reply when the door opened and Bill came in with a tray of coffee.

'Here we are, ladies, hot and strong. Where shall I put it?'

Alice sniggered. 'Not where ye think, you auld rogue! Put the tray on that little table and behave yerself.'

Mrs Crawford flushed. 'How thoughtful of you to bring biscuits, Bill. Garibaldi are my favourites.'

'It's my pleasure, missus. Oh, and before I forget, Sarah said to tell you, the girls'll be finished in a couple of hours and could you meet them at the stage door?'

Alice bristled. 'Ah hope we're getting a lift back?'

'Don't worry, Mrs Wood.' Bill gave her a glare as if to say he'd heard it all before. 'I've already booked the cars.'

ᘐᕦ

On the journey home, Alice did nothing but grumble. She poked the driver in the back. 'Ah hope ye've got the right address, Mister.'

'Don't worry,' he said, 'I know it like the back of my hand – I'll have you there in a trice.'

When the car pulled up outside the house, Alice got out first. 'Hurry up, Lizzie,' she shouted as she rummaged in her bag for the keys and swept inside, leaving her daughter trailing behind.

Jack, who'd heard the rumpus, held out his arms. 'Come here, pet, you look fit to drop.'

Exhausted by the excitement of the rehearsal, Lizzie held on to him and he cuddled her tight.

'Are ye going to stand out there all bloody night, or what?' Alice bellowed.

They followed her in to the kitchen and watched as she filled the kettle and banged it on the stove. 'Ah'm that parched, Jack, ye'd think they'd never heard of tea in that place! Ah've drunk enough bloody coffee to sink a battleship! Ah'll be up ahl night!'

'Well, go on, Alice, don't keep me in suspense, how did it go?'

'It couldn't have gone better, Jack, and it looks as though Ah've made a friend for life!' Alice was grinning from ear to ear. 'She's Beryl's mother – the little girl who plays the other babe. Her name's Mrs Crawford and she's such a lovely woman. She told me to call her Joan, so Ah said she could call me Alice. And she's such a good listener, we're bound to be good friends.'

Jack nodded in relief and his eyes lit up as he turned to his daughter. 'And what about you, Lizzie, how did you get on, pet?'

'It's hard to tell, Dad. We went through the lines twice with the whole company, then they said we could go home.'

Alice mashed the tea. 'They didn't keep them long if you ask me! It was hardly worth going.'

'And what's Beryl like, Lizzie?'

'Well, I only met her today, Dad, but she seems very nice. And she – '

Alice butted in as she poured the tea. 'She's not a patch on Lizzie! And she's as skinny as a rake!'

Lizzie sprang to Beryl's defence. 'How can you say that, Mam? I bet you wouldn't say that in front of her mother, when you're such good friends.'

Alice banged her cup on the saucer. 'Did ye hear that, Jack?'

'Yes I did, and you can't blame the bairn for taking umbrage at your opinion of Beryl when you hardly know the child.'

Alice glared at Jack. 'Well! That's put me in my place, hasn't it?'

Lizzie cringed. Why did I have to open my mouth? Will I never learn?

Jack and Alice were staring silently at each other and she knew it would be down to her to change the mood. She stood up. 'Sorry, Mam, please forget I said that – I didn't mean it, I'm just tired. If you don't mind, I think I'll go to bed.'

'Please yourself,' said Alice, 'and Ah hope you get out on the right side of it in the morning.'

Jack shook his head. 'Come on now, Alice, the bairn's said sorry. Don't end the day on a sour note.'

As Lizzie left the room, Alice swallowed her pride and called after her. 'See you in the morning then – Ah suppose.'

❦

Lizzie's legs felt like lead as she dragged them into bed. Her body was tired, but her mind was still awake. She thought about Molly and how much she had missed her since enrolling at the Academy. At first, she had only been at the Academy after school and on Saturdays, but now she was there full time, doing all her lessons there as well as drama and dance. It was quite tiring, on top of the evening and weekend rehearsals at the Theatre Royal. She couldn't wait for the holidays when she'd only be rehearsing. She missed Auntie Marion too and remembered all the tasty treats that had kept her going throughout the war. Auntie Marion had never failed to pick her up from school either, no matter what the weather was like. And her home had been a haven from her mother's irrational behaviour. I wonder how I can show my gratitude. Yes! That's it! I'll invite them to the theatre to see the pantomime. She switched off her bedside lamp and snuggled under the blankets. And I'll send a proper invitation when I get the tickets.

⚔

Next morning, Alice couldn't get Lizzie to the theatre fast enough. Remembering how smartly her new friend had dressed, she had made a special effort to look her best in a navy blue suit and her new white blouse with a frilly collar.

She hurried to the green room with Lizzie and stood outside to straighten her seams. Lizzie pushed in front and ran straight to Beryl, who was standing next to a tall man in a smart suit. Alice watched as he kissed Beryl and turned to leave. On his way out, he nodded to Alice.

'Just a minute,' she said, 'you must be Beryl's dad. Ah'm Mrs Wood, Lizzie's mother. And where's Joan?'

'I'm afraid she's not well,' the man said in a voice even more cultured than his wife's. 'She has a severe headache and I insisted she stay at home.'

Alice tried to hide her disappointment. 'Ah'm sorry to hear that. Have you any idea what caused it?'

'As a matter of fact, I have. There seems to be something in this room my wife is allergic to, so I'll be bringing Beryl from now on. Now please excuse me, I have an urgent appointment. It was nice meeting you, Mrs Wood.'

As he left, Alice called after him, 'Be sure to tell Joan Ah'll miss her.'

Then she slumped on to a chair. What the hell could she be allergic to, she muttered. And where the hell's Sarah? Was she going to keep them waiting all day? She had a good mind to take Lizzie straight home. But just as she considered that, the door opened and Sarah breezed into the room, rolling up her sleeves.

'You look as if you've lost a pound and found a penny, Mrs Wood. Cheer up, it might never happen!' She clapped her hands. 'Come on, girls! Let's go!'

Lizzie gave her mother a little wave as she followed Sarah and Beryl out of the room. She won't like sitting there all by herself, she thought. I hope there won't be trouble later.

After they left, Alice stared around the empty room. What a waste of time that was, she thought, getting all dressed up. Why did I bother? It just goes to show, ye can't trust anybody.

She was wondering who to blame when the door burst open and Bill came in with a tray. 'Here we are,' he said. 'Coffee time!' He poured Alice a cup. 'And where's Mrs Crawford today?'

'How the hell should Ah know? Ah'm not a bloody fortune teller! But you can bet yer boots Ah'm not sitting here on me own all day.'

'Calm down, missus.' Bill looked at her stormy face and wondered how he could placate her. Then it came to him. 'There's no need to sit here on your own,' he said. 'Go up to wardrobe – there's plenty of women to chat to up there. Just tell them Bill sent you.'

'Just tell them Bill sent you? Why should Ah? Ah'm not a bloody parcel!' She folded her arms and sat back in the chair.

'Suit yourself, missus.' He didn't look as if he was bothered either way.

Oh bugger it, she thought as he turned to leave, I can't sit here all by myself. 'Where is it anyway?' she called.

'It's upstairs on the top floor – you can't miss it.'

Alice gritted her teeth. I'll see what they're like up there. She climbed the stairs two at a time and emerged into a long corridor. At the end was a room with a sign in big letters – WARDROBE DEPARTMENT. She stared at it for a long time, catching her breath and trying to work out the words, before she was convinced she'd got it right. The door was open and she looked inside. It was a huge room, and yet it still felt crowded, filled to capacity with rails of colourful costumes, sewing machines and rolls of fabric. Several women were busy on the machines, while others seemed to be sorting out trimmings. Everyone was wearing heavy jumpers as, despite being tucked away at the very top of the building, the place was freezing. Across the room, Alice noticed a tall, thin woman with an air of authority standing at one of several long cutting tables and pinning a pattern on to some bright red fabric. She saw Alice in the doorway and waved her over.

'Close the door behind you,' she called. 'Folk never remember to close it when they leave – it's like Greenland in here. My name is Mrs Dobson, I'm head of wardrobe. What can I do for you?'

'Sorry to bother you, Mrs Dobson.' Alice was on her best behaviour now. 'Ah'm Mrs Wood and Ah'm chaperone to my daughter, Lizzie. She's playing one of the Babes. Ah was sitting on my own in the green room and Bill sent me up here for a bit of company. Ah hope you don't mind.'

'Not at all. But we haven't got time for much chat – this is our busiest time. Sit over there by Mrs Stubbs – we'll be having our tea break soon.'

Mrs Stubbs smiled when she saw Alice and pointed to a chair. 'Sit down there, pet, welcome to Slave Drivers Anonymous. I'm Betty Stubbs.'

Alice stepped over a pile of trimmings and took her seat. 'Ah'm Alice Wood and my daughter's in the pantomime.'

'That's nice,' said Mrs Stubbs. 'Just look at the state of this lot! Could you pick up the end of that silver trim and wrap it around this card?' Mrs Stubbs was a plump lady with a smile that lit up her face. 'Don't listen to me!' she said. 'I love this job. I've been doing it every year for as long as I can remember.' She gave a hearty laugh. 'And my kids always get free tickets for the pantomime.'

'Ah can sort out this pile for ye if ye like,' said Alice.

'That would be wonderful, pet. If you could sort the different colours and lengths into piles you would be a real treasure.'

Alice threw herself into her task and it seemed like only moments later when there was a clatter at the door. 'Tea's up!' said Mrs Dobson and Mrs Stubbs leapt up to hold open the door. Bill was pushing a laden tea trolley and she helped him guide it into the room. The girls flocked around it, eager for the warmth of a hot drink. Despite their industry, the room was getting colder as the day wore on.

Alice was still busy sorting out the trimmings when Mrs Dobson tapped her on the shoulder. 'I think you've worked hard enough to deserve a cup of tea, Mrs Wood. I've been watching you. You're a fast worker and I'm sure Betty has appreciated the help.'

'Thanks,' said Alice, 'but Ah enjoy helpin'. It's better than sittin' in the green room and starin' at the four walls.'

'Well,' the wardrobe mistress smiled at her. 'You're welcome to give Betty a hand whenever you're free.'

Alice was excited as she hurried to the trolley. 'Ye'll never believe it, Betty, but it looks like Ah've got a job. Mrs Dobson thinks Ah'm a fast worker and says Ah can help whenever Ah want.'

Betty passed Alice a cup. 'Here,' she said, 'drink your tea and wet your whistle while you can. Mrs Dobson's nowt but a blooming slave driver – just wait, you'll find out.'

But Alice didn't care. She was going to be working in the wardrobe department, her skills had been noted and she was going to have a very important part to play.

⚶

It was the day of the dress rehearsal and Alice had invited everyone whose face she could put a name to. Lizzie was surprised she hadn't invited the milkman.

Sarah had sent a car to pick Lizzie up and Alice was glued to the window awaiting its arrival. When it pulled up at the house, she could hardly contain her excitement. She fastened the fur collar on her new coat and hurried outside.

Her mood soon changed when the driver held up his hand. 'Sorry, madam, but you won't be admitted backstage today.'

Alice turned indignantly to Lizzie and Jack, who had followed her out to the car. 'Did ye hear that, Jack? And after Ah've worked my fingers to the bone for them!'

'Calm down,' he said. 'I'll run you there with some of the family when it's time.'

Jack gave Lizzie a final hug and helped her into the car. She smiled when he said what she knew he would. 'Good luck and break a leg, pet.'

As the car pulled away, Alice went berserk. 'Break a bloody leg!' she screamed. 'Ah'd like to break his bloody neck!'

⁂

Lizzie arrived at the stage door in good time. She would be sharing a dressing room with Beryl. They had used it for a few days while it was empty, to practise putting on their stage make-up, but when she entered it this time, she hardly recognised the place. The costumes were hanging neatly on two separate rails, with the tap shoes and hoops laid out ready for their speciality number. Someone had left clean place-towels on the dressing table for their make-up, and several Good Luck cards were waiting to be opened.

The door burst open and Beryl bounced into the room, singing 'Every Little Movement Has a Meaning All Its Own'. This was the song the girls would sing while performing with the hoops.

Lizzie picked one up and threw the other to Beryl as she joined in the song. They'd rehearsed so often they almost knew the words backwords as they sang and danced together in perfect unison.

They'd just finished and were collapsing into giggles, when Mary the dresser came into the room. 'Carry on, girls,' she said, 'that was lovely! No worries about that – you sang like little angels!'

A loudspeaker in the corner of the room began to crackle. 'This is the stage manager with your half-hour call and good luck, ladies and gentlemen.'

'Put a move on,' said Mary. 'Finish your make-up and I'll be back to dress you in ten minutes.'

'Oh bother,' said Beryl as she struggled with the hairbrush. 'How can I hope to tie a bow in this lot?'

Lizzie took the brush from her. 'Stop moaning,' she said, 'lots of girls would like to have your problem.' She brushed through the curls and tied on the ribbon. 'Take a look at this, Beryl, you look just like Shirley Temple!' They were so caught up in the preparations that any nerves they'd had earlier simply vanished.

Mary came back to the dressing room just as the orchestra began to tune up. 'This is it, girls, let's get you into your costumes!'

'I've already dressed myself, Mary.' Lizzie twirled around, showing off her red silk shirt and velvet shorts.

'That's a clever girl, Lizzie. Come here, Beryl, and let's sort you out.' Beryl's costume was much fussier, with bows and frills and a little wicker basket to be carried as well.

When they were ready, Mary pointed to the long mirror. 'Go on,' she said, 'take a look at yourselves.'

As they stared at their reflections, Lizzie frowned. 'Just look at my skinny legs in these short pants, Mary. What a sight!'

'Don't be daft, girl, there's nothing wrong with your legs! Just wait till you get to my age, then you'll have something to grumble about.'

Lizzie glanced at Mary's sturdy legs and wondered if she should say something nice about them. She was saved from her dilemma as the tannoy crackled into life. 'Overture and beginners, please.'

'Hurry up, girls,' Mary said, 'or you'll miss your cue.'

Lizzie took one last look in the mirror and followed Mary out of the room.

⚜

The orchestra was playing and the lights were already dimmed as Jack struggled to sort out the seats. He'd managed to get Alice, Mrs Rooney and Peggy in the car with only a minimum of bickering, so that was a good start. Ena and Peter were sitting in the same row, with Annie and Joe, and as the curtain went up, Alice glared at them. 'Remember,' she said, 'when Lizzie's onstage, there'll be no talking or eating sweets – have Ah made myself clear?'

They nodded their heads as the lights went down.

The red velvet curtain opened in the usual pantomime way to reveal the chorus and juveniles merrymaking in the town square, waiting to welcome the principal boy. The music was infectious and the costumes were a credit to the wardrobe department. Alice whispered in Mrs Wood's ear, 'Look, Mother, Ah helped to sew those sequins on.'

Mrs Wood smiled and squeezed her hand.

At the end of the extravagant and colourful first scene, the mood suddenly changed as the curtain went up on a dimly lit stage. A single tree stood in the centre, illuminated by a spotlight focused on a pile of leaves around its trunk.

'What the hell's this?' said Mrs Rooney. 'Ah can hardly see a bloody thing!'

'Shut up,' said Peggy, 'the leaves are movin'!'

The audience gasped as two little heads popped up from beneath the leaves and yawned. Alice could hardly contain herself. 'Look!' She dug her elbow into Jack's side. 'It's our Lizzie!'

Jack looked around at the family, nudging and grinning at each other. Even Mrs Rooney smiled at the sight of the girls dressed as babes in the wood. They were all spellbound as Lizzie and Beryl played out their parts.

As far as Alice was concerned, the dress rehearsal went off without a hitch. But then, to her annoyance, the cast was kept behind for notes. Jack organised the exodus of the family, while Alice stayed behind to wait for Lizzie. She settled herself in the front row of the stalls. It was warm and she felt tired. She leaned back and kicked off her shoes. Her eyelids were heavy. Just a little snooze wouldn't do any harm.

'Mrs Wood? Mrs Wood?'

Alice jumped to her feet. 'Bloody hell, is there a fire?'

Bill was standing over her. 'Don't panic, missus, Ah've just come to tell you, Mr Chapman's let them go.'

'Ye nearly frightened the life out of me! How long have Ah been asleep?'

'Nearly an hour. Now you'd better hurry up – Lizzie's waiting for you in the car.'

'And about bloody time!' said Alice. 'The bairn must be on her knees!'

ঞ৶

Jack heard a car pull up outside the house and hurried to the window. Thank God, he thought, as he watched the driver help Alice and Lizzie from the car. He opened the front door and stood on the step. It was snowing outside. 'Hurry up, you two,' he called, 'you look frozen to the marrow.'

They walked wearily indoors and Jack helped them off with their coats. Alice's beautiful new fur collar was covered in snowflakes. 'I've just stoked the fire up in the sitting room, Alice. Warm yourselves up while I get you a hot drink. Then you can tell me why they kept you so blooming long.'

Alice and Lizzie sank on to the sofa and warmed their hands in front of the fire. When Jack came back with two mugs of cocoa, Lizzie was almost asleep. Alice nudged her. 'Wake up, pet, Ah'm sure yer dad wants to tell ye how good ye were.'

'Can't you see the bairn's tired, Alice?' He passed Lizzie her cocoa. 'Go to bed, pet, and we'll talk about it in the morning.'

She hadn't been in bed long before the sound of angry voices drifted upstairs. She knew what the subject would be and wondered if being in pantomime was really worth it. And yet being on that stage, with the enormous auditorium before her, had made her feel more alive than she'd ever known.

❦

Lizzie woke up next morning and was surprised at how quiet it was. She threw on her dressing gown and hurried downstairs. Her father was just finishing his breakfast, but there was no sign of her mother.

'Mind if I join you, Dad? Where's Mam?'

'She's gone shopping. You'll find your breakfast in the oven.'

'I'm not hungry, I'll just have a cup of tea.'

He poured her a cup and passed the sugar. 'Now, let's get down to brass tacks. In my opinion, Mr Chapman has a winner on his hands and it wouldn't surprise me if the pantomime is already booked up for the season. I was proud of you, Lizzie. You played your part convincingly and your voice could be heard at the back of the stalls.'

Her face lit up. 'Thank you, Dad. Coming from you, that means a lot.'

'But,' he continued, 'there's something I have to tell you, dear. This will have to be your last pantomime. Your mother is pushing you in a direction that I disapprove of – putting ideas in your head that are miles from reality. Sometimes I find it hard to believe it's you she's talking about and not some little puppet. I won't allow her to pull your strings. I'm sorry, but after this, there will be no more professional dance engagements.'

Lizzie shifted uneasily. 'Can I say something now, Dad?'

'Go ahead, pet, I need to know how you feel.' He took a sip from his own tea.

'Well, the whole thing seemed to creep up on me. I was happy at Madame Bella's until Mam saw the showcase. She thought I was the star and began to behave as though I was special. I was given lots of treats and, best of all, she didn't nag me so much. But then, when I got the part of Boy Babe, she practically took over the theatre. People would hide when they saw her coming. I don't want to perform like a puppet and I don't like Mam showing me up, but I won't pretend I don't want to go on the stage, because I do.' She paused to see his reaction. 'I want to be an actress.'

He smiled and took her hand. 'There's nothing wrong with that, pet. If that's what you want, I'll send you to drama school when you're old enough. I don't want you to be a dancer, but, if you really want to study to be an actress, I won't stand in your way. So, you can continue at Madame Bella's. I know you're happy there. In any case, your grandma has already paid next year's fees.'

A worried look crept across Lizzie's face. 'But it's so expensive, Dad!'

'You're not supposed to know, Lizzie, for goodness sake don't let on I've told you. Grandma wants to surprise you on your birthday.'

She threw her arms around him. 'I won't say a word, Dad, I promise. But what about Mam?'

'Don't worry, Lizzie, she won't mind as long as it's not her paying.'

❧

Lizzie was excited. She had invited Mrs Brown and Molly to the last night of *Babes in the Wood*, with an invitation to the party afterwards. She couldn't wait to give them the tickets.

She had arrived at the theatre early and was already in her red shirt and velvet shorts, long before the half-hour call. She was lacing up her boots when she heard Bill calling from the corridor outside the dressing room.

'Are you decent, Miss Wood? You've got visitors.'

The door swung open and Molly ran in, followed by her mother.

'What a charming man, Lizzie. He gave us a free programme, didn't he, Molly?' Mrs Brown was wearing her best coat. It was double-breasted, with large bone buttons and did nothing for her more-than outsize figure. She looked bemused but delighted to be backstage in this splendid theatre.

'Yes,' Molly said, as she stared at the costumes and make-up. 'Wow! This is better than our old dressing up box at home.' She took a dress from the rail and held it up. 'Just look at this, Mam!'

Mrs Brown lost her composure. 'What do you think you're doing, Molly? Put that back and behave yourself.'

To ease the tension, Lizzie pressed an envelope into Mrs Brown's hand. She opened it to find a card covered in fancy print and two tickets for the stalls.

'What's on the card, Mam?'

'It's an invitation!' She turned to Lizzie. 'Are you sure? Will they let us backstage afterwards?'

'Of course they will! Mr Chapman said you could come. It's the end of show party – there'll be lots of food and a little drink if you fancy it. But you'd better go now, Auntie Marion, the dresser will be here in a minute. When the curtain comes down, stay in your seats and I'll come out and get you.'

Mrs Brown hugged her. 'Thank you for the treat, dear. We're so grateful.'

'That's for sure!' said Molly. 'Break a leg, Lizzie!'

⁂

Lizzie was filled with nostalgia as the curtain went up for the last time. She stood in the wings with Beryl while they waited for their entrance. The stage resembled a fairground: in pride of place stood a merry-go-round, with a steam organ belting out cheerful music. The juveniles sat on colourful horses that moved up and down while the dancers spun around with their partners.

The children clapped and shouted as the magician came on stage and produced a rabbit from nowhere. The hubbub got even louder when the clowns came on with bunches of balloons, purposely allowing them to escape into the audience of delighted children. This is a night to remember, thought Lizzie. Dad's right, I need to make the most of it.

When the red velvet curtain finally came down, Lizzie hurried to her dressing room and changed before collecting Mrs Brown and Molly. It was a relief to get back into normal clothes. She ran along the corridor and almost collided with her mother.

'What's the bloody hurry?' said Alice. 'Have ye got a train to catch?'

Lizzie didn't want to divulge who she was meeting and crossed her fingers before she spoke. 'I just want to say goodbye to someone, Mam, I won't be long.'

'Well just make sure yer not, madam. Yer belongings won't pack themselves.'

When Lizzie reached the stalls, Mrs Brown was waiting with open arms. 'Come here,' she said, 'you're a little star and make no mistake! We're very proud of you, aren't we, Molly?'

'Yes we are!' she said as she pointed to the stage. 'Look, Lizzie! Your mam's up there. Does she know we're here?'

'What if she does? You're my guests and we're going to have a good time! Come on, follow me.'

They stayed close to Lizzie as she guided them on to the stage, where the party was taking place. Mrs Brown hesitated. 'Are you sure it's all right, pet? We wouldn't want you to get in trouble for inviting us.'

Lizzie took her hand. 'Relax, Auntie Marion, Mam's too busy making a nuisance of herself to even notice you. She'll be talking to all the new friends she's made in the wardrobe department. Anyway, let's get something to eat, I'm starving.'

The management hadn't stinted. The buffet table was groaning with food and the bar was stocked with enough booze to sink a battleship. People were milling around helping themselves, some still in their costumes from the final act.

'Come on,' said Lizzie, 'let's get to the food before there's a queue.' She dodged around two clowns.

Molly took a plate and scrutinised the savouries. 'What's devilled chicken, Mam?' she asked.

'You wouldn't like it, pet, it's far too spicy.' Mrs Brown made a face.

Lizzie laughed. 'Your mother's right! A mouthful of that and you wouldn't know what had hit you! Try the open sandwiches – they look scrummy!'

Mrs Brown nudged Lizzie and pointed. 'I think that's an empty table over there, pet.'

'Well spotted, Auntie Marion, I'll nip over and nab it!' She ran to bag the table as there were hardly any left. Everyone was desperate to sit down now the excitement had worn off; the run of shows had left them all exhausted.

Alice was at the bar topping up her drink, and not for the first time, when she heard Lizzie shout, 'Come on you two, put your skates on!' She turned and stared in disbelief to see Mrs Brown and Molly on their way to Lizzie's table. What the hell are they doing here, she wondered. Well, we'll just have to find out, won't we? She picked up her glass, took a stiff drink and flounced off to the table.

'Well, well!' she said, glaring at Mrs Brown. 'Fancy seeing you here! Is this a private party or can anyone join in?'

Lizzie's face turned the colour of beetroot. 'We didn't see you, Mam, or we would have asked you to join us. There's a spare chair; why don't you sit down?'

'Ah think Ah, will' she said, 'as long as that's all right with you, Mrs Brown? Ye don't mind a spare, do ye?'

Molly looked worried as Alice sat down, not entirely steadily. She nudged her mother under the table.

Mrs Brown squeezed her hand and smiled at Alice. 'Have you tried the buffet, Mrs Wood? It's top notch! There was such a selection, we hardly knew what to choose!'

'Let me recommend the coronation chicken,' said a deep male voice behind them.

Lizzie turned to see Mr Chapman sauntering up to the table.

'Sorry to intrude, ladies, but I couldn't leave without congratulating Lizzie.' He shook her hand. 'You did well, dear. How would you like to join the company again, this year?'

Alice grinned proudly and nodded her head. 'Don't worry,' she said, 'she'll be there all right!' She nudged Lizzie. 'Well? Aren't ye going to thank him?'

Lizzie swallowed hard. 'Thank you, Mr Chapman,' she said, almost in a whisper, 'I'll let you know.'

He doffed his hat. 'It's a pity I can't stay for the party, I'm just off to catch a train to London. No rest for the wicked, eh? Look forward to seeing you at the Academy Showcase, Lizzie.'

Lizzie looked down at her feet. She wasn't sure what to say without giving away her father's edict.

Oblivious to everyone looking at them, Alice took Lizzie by the shoulders and almost shook the life out of her. 'And what the hell do ye think yer playin' at, girl, with "Thank you, I'll let you know"?' Her voice carried effortlessly across the stage and into the stalls.

Molly began to cry. Mrs Brown hugged her. 'It's all right, pet, we're going home. If I stay here any longer I'm afraid of what I'll do.'

Alice bristled. 'That's right, bugger off! Ye shouldn't have been here in the first place!'

Mrs Brown stood with dignity, took Molly's hand and turned to Lizzie. 'Thanks for inviting us to the party. I'm sorry your kindness has caused so much trouble. Take care, dear, and don't be a stranger.'

Tears ran down Lizzie's cheeks as she watched them walk away. 'Wait for me, Auntie Marion!' she called. 'You'll never find your way out on your own!'

꧁꧂

Lizzie returned to an empty table. There was no sign of Alice, but there was no mistaking her voice, which was clearly recognisable above the hubbub of the crowd. There she was, talking to Mrs Crawford. Beryl was with them and she was crying. Alice caught sight of Lizzie and waved her over.

'Come here,' she said, 'say hello to Beryl. She's upset because ye've been asked to come back and she hasn't.'

Lizzie put her arm around Beryl. 'Why did you have to tell her, Mam? Please don't cry, Beryl, because it's not true. In any case, I promised Dad not to be in any more pantomimes.'

Oh my God, she thought, what have I said? A chill ran through her when she saw the look on her mother's face. Silence fell around them as the remaining cast members and friends sensed that something was about to happen.

'So!' said Alice, after a lethal pause. 'You and your dad have worked things out, have ye?' She suddenly raised her arm and struck Lizzie, who fell backwards.

Mrs Crawford gasped. 'That's enough, Mrs Wood!'

Several members of the cast had gathered around the commotion. A perturbed young woman in a sequinned dancer's costume stepped forward and helped Lizzie to her feet. 'Are you all right?' she said. 'Can I do anything?'

'Yes you can!' shouted Alice, turning on her immediately. 'Ye can mind yer own bloody business.'

Mrs Crawford pointedly put Beryl's coat on and turned to Lizzie. 'We're going now, dear. Mr Crawford's waiting in the car – would you like to come with us?'

Lizzie, still shaking from the force of her mother's blow, said nothing, knowing that to accept would only mean further trouble down the line. She wished the ground would open up and swallow her but there was no escaping the sight of Alice's enraged face.

An authoritative voice broke in. 'All right, break it up! Show's over!'

Alice was indignant. 'Who the hell are you, shoutin' the odds, anyway?'

Bill the doorman pushed through the crowd. 'This is Mr Bentall, the stage manager, and you'd better listen to what he has to say.'

'Why should Ah?' she demanded belligerently.

Mr Bentall took her arm. 'Because you've said enough, Mrs Wood, now kindly leave the stage.' He nudged Bill. 'Put them in a taxi and make sure that Lizzie's all right.'

'Just a minute!' said Alice, but he had already left. She glared at Bill. 'Bloody cheek! Who the hell does that man think he is?'

'He's my boss, Mrs Wood, that's who he is. Now come with me.' Bill winked at Lizzie and slipped his arm around her. 'Don't worry, pet, you'll soon be home.'

For once, Alice remained silent as she followed them to the car. Bill helped them inside and waved until they were out of sight. Poor kid, he thought, what a dreadful life she must have with a mother like that.

It wasn't long before Alice vented her spleen about Mr Bentall. 'Ah'd like to know who he thinks he is!' she said. 'Talking to me like that when he knows Ah'm your mother! Ah've a good mind to report him to Mr Chapman when Ah see him!' She yawned. 'This carry on's knocked the stuffin' out of me! Ah think Ah'll close my eyes and have forty winks.'

Was this the calm before the storm, Lizzie wondered. If only I hadn't told Beryl my promise to Dad. What will he think of me? I've given Mam enough ammunition to start a war.

Chapter 22

On the first day of the new term at the Academy, Lizzie joined a crowd of girls in the large hall. They were falling over each other as they tried to reach the noticeboard. Lizzie's heart sank as she got close enough to read her name and even though she was shivering with the chill of the day, her face flushed hot in nervous anticipation. 'Please report to Madame Bella's office on arrival.' I bet a pound to a penny this'll be about Mam's outrageous behaviour at the party, she thought. Oh well, whatever it is, here goes!

She knocked on the door. 'Come in!' said Bella. 'It's open!'

Lizzie gasped at the sight of her. Bella was sitting at her desk, resplendent in a scarlet cardigan even more vivid than her hair. She was devouring the biggest cream horn Lizzie had ever seen. 'Sit down, while I get rid of the evidence,' she said, as she wiped the cream from her mouth and licked her lips. 'I don't make a habit of this, you know, so mum's the word, dear. I suppose you're wondering why I asked to see you?' She paused. 'Well! It's good news!'

Lizzie wondered how there could be good news after the way her mother had carried on at the party. Surely Madame Bella had heard about it?

Bella put on her serious face and leaned forward over her desk. 'Now Lizzie, what I'm about to say is for your ears only and, just for now, that includes your parents. Mr Chapman has already decided on this year's pantomime. It's *Little Red Riding Hood* and he's got his eye on you for the part. What do you think about that?'

Lizzie's heart was pounding as she stared open-mouthed at Bella. What can I say, she wondered. I'll have to tell her the truth.

'Well,' said Bella, 'aren't you going to say something?'

Lizzie's eyes were fixed to the floor as she spoke. 'It's very kind of Mr Chapman to think of me, but please can you tell him I can't do it?'

'Stop fooling around,' said Bella, 'this is serious.'

Lizzie looked up from the floor and met Bella's eyes. 'So is my dad, Madame, and he's against me playing in any more pantomimes.'

For once Bella was lost for words. She opened the drawer of her desk, took out a box of chocolates and devoured three orange creams, before inviting Lizzie to help herself. 'That's better!' she said. 'I'm a great believer in cocoa – they say it's very good for the nerves.'

Lizzie chose a truffle and a lemon cream and passed the box back to her.

'Now,' said Bella, having had a moment to think things through. 'Far be it from me to question your father's decision, but I find it hard to understand his reason for it. He was proud of you in the Academy Showcase and even more so at the Theatre Royal. Is there something you're keeping from me? My mother always said a trouble shared is a trouble halved – surely things can't be that bad?'

For a moment, Lizzie lost her composure. 'How would you know? You don't have to live with my mother!' Then, instantly regretting what she had said, got to her feet and made as if to go to the door.

Bella stood up too, drawing herself up to her full height, undaunted by this outburst. 'And where do you think you're going to, young lady?'

Unable to hold back any longer, Lizzie burst into tears. 'Why should you care?' she sobbed. Her shoulders shook in their thin jumper.

'Because I think you need a friend, dear.' Bella opened her arms and Lizzie fell into them. 'Will I do?'

Lizzie nodded her head and sighed. Bella was the best friend she could possibly have.

'I'll take that as a yes then, and as a friend I suggest having got that off your chest, you go home and rest. Tomorrow's another day – let's make it a good one, shall we?' She drew back and held her at arm's length, gazing steadily at her. 'I mean it, Lizzie.' After a moment she let her go.

On her way out, Lizzie stopped and turned around. 'I won't forget your concern over my problem, Madame, and I'm sorry about Dad's decision over the pantomime.' She shrugged reluctantly.

Bella winked. 'Well you never know, Lizzie, he might change his mind.'

The moment Lizzie left, Bella hurried back to her desk. This is the only way, she thought, as she opened a drawer and brought out her writing paper. I'll send Mr Wood a letter – it's much better than a phone call. I can't have one of my most promising students denied her chance.

After several attempts, she finally decided on the text.

Dear Mr Wood,

Let me come straight to the point, I'm very concerned about Lizzie. As you must already know, I had to send her home on the first day of the new term. She seemed troubled over something and, unlike the girl I know, simply skirted around the subject until she ended up in tears. If you have the time, it would be helpful for the two of us to meet to discuss the problem.

Yours sincerely,
Bella Bainbridge

Bella reached across the desk and lifted the lid from a cake box. Inside were two chocolate eclairs, a Danish pastry and an Eccles cake. Mr Wood'll be spoilt for choice, she thought as she closed the lid.

In fact, it took Jack a whole two weeks to reply to her letter. Bella had almost given up hope, when his response came unexpectedly in the morning post. She read the letter eagerly.

Dear Miss Bainbridge,

Thank you for your concern over Lizzie's welfare. I'm sorry to have taken so long to reply, but we've had a few problems on the home front. If it's convenient, I could come to the Academy around three o'clock on Saturday. My office number is 188972.

I'm looking forward to seeing you.

With heartfelt thanks,

Jack Wood

Well, he seems like a decent enough man, she mused, and he certainly seems concerned about his daughter. He said he'd get here around teatime and I'll bend over backwards to make sure he really feels welcome.

She tidied her office and removed the wrapping from the flowers she had bought on the way in. You can't beat roses, she thought, as she arranged them in her favourite antique jug. She poured herself a coffee and looked in the cake box again – the eclairs looked so tempting. She was just about to take one when her conscience pricked her. How could I think of it? she thought. Sacrifices must be made! She was about to close the box when a knock on the door made her jump.

'Come in!' she said as she struggled with the lid.

Jack stood in the doorway. 'Can I be of any help?'

'Oh, it's nothing,' said Bella, smiling cheerily as she put out her hand. 'I'm glad you could make it, Mr Wood. Please sit down and make yourself comfortable.'

He looked around the room and smiled at this lady he thought larger than life. She was wearing a green satin kimono embroidered with multi-coloured birds.

'That's a bobby dazzler!' he said.

Bella turned around to show off the back. 'Thank you, Mr Wood. I'd like you to know that I once wore this garment in a Noel Coward play at the Haymarket Theatre in London.'

Jack looked surprised. 'I didn't know you were an actress, Madame Bella.'

'Well, I suppose you could say I'm an all-rounder. And by the way, you can call me Bella if you like – after all, it's out of hours. Now, shall we get down to brass tacks, Mr Wood?'

He nodded his head. Now he could see that some of the many photographs hanging on the walls were of Bella herself in various costumes – a younger, slimmer Bella but definitely the same woman. From the looks of it she had known plenty of famous people in the theatre world.

'Your daughter was one of the most ambitious and moti-vated girls in the Academy until this term.' She folded her arms. 'But I'm sorry to say, through sheer lack of concentration, her work has plummeted below standard. Can you think of a reason for this sudden change in Lizzie? I'm very fond of her, you know.'

Jack lowered his eyes. 'I hope I can speak to you in confidence, Madame Bella?'

She stiffened. 'Whatever is said in this room stays in this room, Mr Wood, please remember that.'

'I'm sorry,' he said, 'it's a delicate subject and I had to ask, but please let me come straight to the point. Ever since the pantomime ended, Lizzie and her mother have been at loggerheads. To tell the truth, they were never that close in the first place, but now it's like a war zone. It wasn't so bad during the pantomime – Alice helped in the wardrobe department and considered herself part of the company. She did a good job, too, so I hear and best of all, there was peace in the house. But now she's unoccupied again all the old troubles have resurfaced and Lizzie bears the brunt of it.'

Bella got up from her chair. 'It seems you've got quite a problem on your hands, Mr Wood, but as my mother always said, a problem shared is a problem halved. I once said that to Lizzie, but I'm afraid I can't repeat what she replied. Now please excuse me while I put the kettle on and bring out the treats!'

Jack watched as Bella took a fancy cake stand and a box advertising Brenda's Bakery from a shelf behind her desk. He was fascinated by the careful way she opened the box and arranged the fancies on the stand. She's no novice at this ritual, he thought, as she took a kettle from a cupboard and plugged it in. She set the cakes in front of him, pulled out a small brown teapot and spooned the leaves into it.

'It won't be long now,' she said. 'Please help yourself to a cake while I mash the tea.' She winked at Jack. 'I enjoy the occasional indulgence – what about you, Mr Wood?'

Jack was flummoxed by this lady and hoped she would change the subject. After all, he thought, I'm here to talk about Lizzie.

'Well, what about you?' she repeated. 'Have you got a sweet tooth, Mr Wood?'

'Not really,' he said, 'but I'm quite partial to a drop scone.'

Bella poured the tea. 'Help yourself to milk,' she said and leaned forward to pass the sugar.

Jack was stirring his tea as she moved slowly closer.

'I hope you don't mind me asking,' she said, 'but I was wondering if you think persuading Lizzie not to appear in pantomime has anything to do with this sudden change in her?'

Bella's candour and proximity caught him off guard and he couldn't think how to reply.

'Believe me, I'm not criticising you, Mr Wood, I'm simply trying to find a reason for this change in Lizzie.'

For a moment, Bella saw an anxious look flit across Jack's face. 'During the war,' he said, shifting uneasily in his seat, 'save for the occasional leave, I was away from home for almost six years – six formative years for Lizzie. I won't go through an inventory of how she suffered during my absence, but know that, without the constant help of my mother, things for Lizzie could have been a lot worse. It was my mother who persuaded Alice to agree to Lizzie's first dancing lesson and, although she was no spring chicken, she never failed to take her every Saturday. Let's not forget, it was her idea to send Lizzie to this Academy and it has been a godsend. I thank you for taking her in the first place – I know she's happy here.'

'Thank you for giving me an insight into Lizzie's background, Mr Wood, but let me assure you, it was the potential I saw in Lizzie that decided me to accept her and my reward has been to watch her constant progress.' Bella took a deep breath. 'Speaking entirely in confidence, Mr Wood, there's something I think you should know: Mr Chapman has Lizzie in mind for the part of *Little Red Riding Hood* at the Theatre Royal this year.'

'Are you sure? Lizzie hasn't mentioned it.'

Bella smiled. 'Of course she hasn't! She loves you too much. She wouldn't want you to know how disappointed she'd be if it was offered to her and she had to turn it down. She's a lovely girl and you're a lucky man to have such a considerate daughter.' Bella took an eclair from the cake stand and turned to Jack. 'Are you sure I can't press you to a cake, Mr Wood?'

What's she getting at, he wondered. Next thing I know, she'll have me cast as the big bad wolf!

Bella opened a cupboard in her desk and brought out a bottle and two glasses. 'You look quite pale, Mr Wood. Can I offer you a drink? I always have one around this time.'

Why not, he thought. I could do with one.

'It's a very special brandy – I pick it up from a local vineyard when I visit a friend in France.' She poured out the drinks and held out her glass. 'Here's to Lizzie and success in whatever you decide she should do.'

Jack wasn't sure how to take Bella's last remark. To please her, he clinked glasses and took a sip of brandy. Then he took a deep breath and threw diplomacy aside. 'I think you've got the wrong end of the stick, Madame Bella. It was never my plan to deny Lizzie something she has set her heart on. She wants to be an actress and I've agreed to send her to drama school when she leaves the Academy.'

Bella was staggered by Jack's unexpected news and, for a moment, she was speechless.

'Well,' said Jack, 'what do you think about that?'

Bella placed her hand on her chest. 'You've taken my breath away, Mr Wood, and I apologise for any misunderstanding between us. When it's time for Lizzie to audition for drama school, please let me know if I can help.'

'Thank you,' he said, 'I'm sure she will appreciate your offer.' It's time to change the subject, he thought. 'I'm taking her to the Alhambra to see a Bette Davis film tonight.'

'I hope she enjoys it, Mr Wood, but I'm afraid Bette Davis won't cure this sudden change in her behaviour. However, I have a suggestion. If Lizzie's offered the part of Little Red Riding Hood, why not let her accept it? After all, it requires a little actress and isn't that her ambition?'

'Slow down,' said Jack. 'Lizzie promised not to take part in any more pantomimes.'

'Of course she did, Mr Wood, because she wanted to please you. But can't you see that this is something special? In fact, it's a part that every girl in the Academy would die for. And besides, you would benefit too, with Lizzie on stage and Mrs Wood in wardrobe – just imagine the peace in your house!'

Jack stood up. This was all too much, too soon. 'I really must go now or I'll be late for Lizzie.'

Bella followed him to the door and held on to his arm. 'Please don't make your mind up yet – we both know what Lizzie really wants. You could make her a very happy girl, Mr Wood.'

He felt his eyes sliding away from her gaze and pulled his arm free. 'All right,' he said, 'I'll think about it.'

Bella called after him. 'And please don't tell Lizzie I mentioned the pantomime!'

Watching him stride down the corridor, she gave a sigh of contentment and poured herself another drink.

⁂

Bella was in a quandary. Am I doing the right thing, she wondered. Lizzie will be here any minute – if I want to gain her trust I'd better be careful what I say. I know

Lizzie – she'll be off like a shot if she thinks I'm doing her a favour.

She was wondering if she had time for a quick chocolate, when there was a timid tap on the door and Lizzie's head appeared around it.

'Come in,' she said, 'and close the door, dear.'

Lizzie did Bella's bidding. 'I was told you wanted to see me, Madame.'

'That's right. Please sit down and let me explain.'

Lizzie sat twiddling her thumbs as she waited for Bella to speak.

'It's about the junior prep classes on Saturday. We had rather an influx of tinies this year and Miss Dixon finds it difficult to cope on her own, so I suggested you might like to help her out.'

Lizzie gasped in surprise. 'Why choose me, Madame? There are lots of girls in third year who'd be glad to do it – girls far more experienced than me.'

'Please don't underestimate yourself – Miss Dixon and I both agree that you'd be perfect for the job. And it is a job. We have three classes every Saturday and I pay five shillings a session.'

'Thank you for asking, Madame, but I don't think my mother would allow it – I always help her with the shopping on Saturdays.'

Bella pressed on. 'But you'd be finished by two o'clock. Couldn't you help her then? I'm sure she wouldn't mind.'

Lizzie shifted in her chair. 'Like I said once before, Madame, you don't know my mother.'

No, but I've got the measure of her, Bella thought. 'You're right,' she said, 'but at least you could impress her with my offer.'

Lizzie looked sadly at Bella. 'I'm sorry but I can't accept your offer. Now I'd better get back to class – it's improvisation, my favourite.'

Bella sighed. There'll be other times, she thought, as she watched Lizzie drag her feet to the door. She called after her. 'I hope your mother knows how lucky she is to have a daughter like you, dear.'

⚜

'Hurry up!' said Alice, as she struggled indoors with the shopping that weekend. 'And be careful with that basket, Lizzie, it's got eggs in it. Put the kettle on – Ah'm fit to drop!'

Lizzie sat the basket down on the kitchen table and filled the kettle, while Alice slumped on to a chair and took off her shoes. 'Just look at my feet,' she moaned, 'they're like bloody balloons! Hurry up with that tea.'

Lizzie picked up the caddy and spooned the tea in to the pot. She set the kettle to boil, then turned to stare sympathetically at Alice. 'You look all in, Mam. I'm glad I refused that Saturday job or I couldn't help you with the heavy shopping.'

Alice stopped rubbing her feet and gave Lizzie a quizzical look. 'And what job was that, then?'

'It was nothing much, Mam. Madame just wanted me to help with the little ones on Saturdays.'

'Are ye tellin' me the truth, Lizzie?'

'Yes! Madame said she'd pay me fifteen shillings to do three sessions every Saturday, but don't worry, I told her – Saturday is our shopping day.'

'Never mind the bloody shoppin'!' Alice spluttered. 'If she pays that much it'll save me forkin' out on all those fancy clothes and fripperies you keep askin' for. Tell her ye'll take the job!'

Lizzie could hardly believe her luck. 'But are you sure you can manage the shopping on your own, Mam?'

'What have Ah just said?' Alice shouted. 'Tell her ye'll start next Saturday. And mind, ye needn't think yer keepin' all that money to yerself, either. Now hurry up with that tea!'

Lizzie poured it out and got on with unpacking the groceries. If only Mam knew, she thought, it's not the money that matters. I know my work has suffered this term – but it's great to know that Madame still trusts me.

❧

Bella helped herself to another chocolate and passed the box to Jack. He shook his head. 'Please don't tempt me, Madame Bella, I need to lose a few pounds.'

'What nonsense! You're a fine figure of a man!' She looked at him appreciatively. 'You know, I really enjoy our little chats when you pick Lizzie up on Saturdays and I was thinking that, after three months, maybe it's time to use first names, if that's all right with you.'

'I assure you, it's more than all right,' he said. 'You know, Bella, it's strange how some of us set off on the wrong foot. I certainly did with you and I apologise for mistrusting you.'

'Don't be silly – '

Jack interrupted. 'No, please hear me out. Apart from my mother, you've been the most encouraging influence in my daughter's life and trusting her to teach the little ones on Saturdays has boosted her confidence beyond belief. I don't know how to thank you, Bella.'

How can I ignore this opportunity when it's handed on a plate, she thought. If I handle the problem with sensitivity we could be in with a chance. She cleared her throat. 'Thank you, Jack, but I don't need thanks for anything I've done for Lizzie. Her achievements have come from hard work and dedication. I know some of the hurdles she's had to face and I respect the way such a young girl has tackled them. Don't you think it's time we acknowledged her efforts?'

'You're right,' he said. 'Do you have something in mind?'

'Yes, as a matter of fact I do. It's a sore subject, but please be patient and hear me out. I won't beat about the bush, Jack. You'll remember that we spoke about Lizzie playing Little Red Riding Hood in the pantomime and you promised to think about it. You've never mentioned it again – '

'That's because I really don't like the idea of it,' said Jack. 'I want Lizzie to have her feet on the ground, not thinking about musical fairy stories.'

'That's a great shame,' said Bella. 'I remember when you said it was never your plan to deny Lizzie something she had set her heart on. You and I both know how much she would love to play this role. And, goodness knows, she has enough troubles to contend with. Don't you think she deserves some fun?'

Jack turned his face away from Bella's gaze. Would one more panto do his daughter any harm? For one thing, it would shut Alice up – she hadn't stopped nagging him about *Little Red Riding Hood* for weeks. All she wanted was to be back in the wardrobe department. He took a deep breath. 'You're very persuasive, Bella.'

She jumped to her feet. 'Does that mean yes?'

Jack sighed. This eloquent woman was impossible to oppose. 'I suppose it does.'

Bella leaned forward and kissed him on the cheek. 'I think we have cause to celebrate!' She reached into the cupboard and took out her special brandy and two thick glasses.

She was about to fill them, when there was a tap at the door and Lizzie's head appeared around it. Bella smiled at her. 'You're just in time, Lizzie. Your dad and I are just about to celebrate!'

Lizzie laughed. 'Don't tell me he's won the pools!'

'I'm afraid not,' said Bella, 'but he does have something important to say.'

Lizzie held her breath as she waited for him to speak.

'You can remove that worried look from your pretty little face,' he said. 'It's good news. After talking things over with Bella, I've agreed you should play Little Red Riding Hood.'

Lizzie threw her arms around him. 'Thank you! Thank you both! And you won't regret it! But what about Mam?'

'Don't worry about Mam,' said Jack. 'She's been bending my ear about this pantomime for weeks. Nothing would make her happier than to work in the wardrobe department again.'

Bella poured out the brandy and passed Jack a glass. He held it up and smiled at Lizzie. 'Here's wishing you luck for the pantomime and don't worry about the big bad wolf while I'm around, pet.'

Bella clinked glasses with him. 'All's well that ends well,' she said, 'and here's to a bright future.'

Lizzie's eyes were filled with tears as she threw her arms around her benefactors. 'Thank you,' she said, 'but it couldn't be brighter than it is right now.'

❧

Lizzie's heart was racing as she stood outside the stage door. The first day of rehearsals was always the worst, and even though she was familiar with the Theatre Royal and knew her way around this time, it didn't make it much easier. Will they think I'm good enough? she thought. It's a big part and will I forget my lines?

Alice pushed her. 'What're ye waiting for?' she said eagerly. 'Get inside!'

Lizzie stepped up towards the big wooden door and pressed the brass bell. It opened almost immediately and Lizzie smiled as she saw Bill's familiar face – another year older but still the same old Bill.

'Well, I'll eat my hat,' he said, 'if it's not little Lizzie Wood. I've been expecting you. I've seen the poster!'

'It's good to see you again, Bill. I'm glad you're still here.'

'Where else should I be, pet?'

Alice pushed in front. 'Ah've no idea where ye should be, but Lizzie's due onstage in a minute, so hurry up and sign us in.'

Bill opened the book and gave her a pencil. Alice signed her name and passed the pencil to Lizzie. 'I'd better get up to wardrobe,' she said, 'or they'll be wondering where I am.'

When Alice was out of sight, Bill pulled a face. In all his years of watching pushy parents, she was up there with the worst. Still, it was all in a day's work for him.

༕

Lizzie made her way to the stage and stood in the wings. She looked out at the massive auditorium with its hundreds of seats, the high, ornate ceiling and the opulent red boxes on each side, and she felt a little flutter of fear mixed with exhilaration. The stage was milling with people, but there was not a single soul she recognised. She took a deep breath – it was too daunting to go out there on her own.

'Well, it if isn't Little Red Riding Wood!'

Lizzie spun around, delighted to hear the familiar voice. 'Sarah! Please say you're choreographer this year!'

Sarah laughed. 'Well, I was offered a Hollywood contract, but when I heard you were playing Little Red Riding Hood, I turned it down. Now let's go onstage and see if we know anyone – Mr Chapman will be here in a minute.' Sarah looked around. 'By the way, where's your mother?'

'Don't ask,' said Lizzie, 'I think she's gone to wardrobe to claim her old job.'

Wow, that should be interesting, Sarah thought. News had spread about Alice's behaviour at the last end-of-show party and the choreographer couldn't imagine she would be getting a warm welcome this year. She shook herself out of her reverie as a stirring of the people behind her indicated that something was about to happen.

A hush came over the stage as Mr Chapman walked in.

'Welcome, fellow thespians,' he said in a loud, articulate voice.

Wow, thought Lizzie, he'd be heard at the back of the stalls all right.

He took off his coat, rolled up his shirt sleeves and held up the script. 'Now ladies and gentlemen, with your help, this is going to be a winner. So let's get down to the read-through. You can dismiss the dancers, Sarah, and call the principals. Oh, and get the ASM to bring some chairs.'

Lizzie opened her script, with pencil poised, ready to take down Mr Chapman's notes. She was concentrating hard when she overheard a catty remark from one of the dancers. 'It's all right for Lizzie Wood, she's Mr Chapman's pet and always gets the best parts. And you should see her mother! Pushy's not the word for it!'

Lizzie glared at the girl. 'I heard that. Why don't you complain? Who knows, with your two left feet, Mr Chapman might cast you as a clown and treat the audience to a laugh.'

As Lizzie turned away, the girl shoved her in the back, causing her to drop her script. She panicked and bent down to retrieve it, just as Mr Chapman called out her name.

'If you're ready,' he said, ignoring the fuss, 'we'll read the first scene. Red Riding Hood and her mother are in the kitchen packing a basket for Grandma. All right? Now, can we get on with it?'

⟡

The sewing machine stopped as Alice rushed into the wardrobe department. 'Here Ah am!' she said. 'Ready, willin' and able.'

Mrs Dobson dropped her scissors on the cutting table when she saw her. 'Carry on, ladies, I'll see to this.' She took a step towards Alice. 'Well, Mrs Wood, I hadn't expected you to show your face!'

She moved to stand in front of Alice, barring her way into the room. She was wearing the same thick cardigan as last year and Alice could feel the familiar chill in the air. She looked over Mrs Dobson's shoulder at the other women, all busily working away, as though they weren't straining their ears to overhear the conversation.

Alice squared up to Mrs Dobson. 'And what does that mean?'

'If you don't already know, then there's no point in my explaining. Surely you haven't forgotten the end-of-show party, Mrs Wood?'

'What about it?'

'What about it? Surely you remember shouting at every-one within earshot? And showing up your daughter in front of the whole company?'

'So what? That's none of yer bloody business!'

Mrs Dobson glared at her. 'I'm sorry,' she said icily, 'but you've had a wasted journey, Mrs Wood. I won't be needing you this year.'

For a moment Alice was too outraged to speak. Then she found her voice. 'Well!' she exclaimed. 'Is that the thanks Ah get for working me fingers to the bone last year and never askin' for a penny? How can ye stand there and say Ah'm not wanted? And what about you, Mrs Stubbs? After the miles of bloody silver trim Ah've unravelled for ye, why don't ye stand up for me?'

Alice moved towards her former colleague.

'That's enough!' said Mrs Dobson. 'I'm in charge and I can tell you this, I wouldn't dream of taking you back! I'm sorry for your daughter, she's such a lovely girl, but with a mother like you, I'm glad she's old enough not to need a chaperone this year. I'm sure you must have been an embarrassment to her.'

Alice's temper boiled over. 'Who do ye think you are, ye stuck-up bitch? I know yer type – fur coat and no knickers, that's you! And don't think ye've heard the last of this!'

She stormed out, slamming the door behind her.

⌘

Jack was reading the evening paper when a breathless Lizzie ran into the kitchen.

'Whatever's the matter?' he said. 'Sit down, pet, you look as though you've been chased by a banshee.'

'Where's Mam?' she gasped. 'I was supposed to meet her in the lunch break but she didn't turn up and she was still missing when the car came to take me home.'

'Calm down, Lizzie, your mother's here. She was just a bit upset at the way she was dismissed from the wardrobe department, that's all.'

Lizzie stared at him in disbelief but before she could ask what he meant, there was the sound of a footstep from the corridor.

'Just a bit upset!' Lizzie spun round to see her mother in the doorway. 'Is that what ye think, Jack? After Mrs Dobson showed me up in front of the whole bloody workroom? But don't worry, she won't get away with it!'

Lizzie stood up. 'I'll put the kettle on, Mam, you look as though you could do with a cup of tea.'

Alice ignored her. 'And what about Mrs Stubbs? Ah thought at least she'd stick up for me, but, oh no, the way she turned her back on me, ye'd think Ah was a bloody leper!'

'That's enough!' said Jack. 'The bairn doesn't need to hear all this – she must be tired after rehearsing all day.'

Lizzie shifted from foot to foot. 'Shall I make the tea, Mam?'

'Never mind the bloody tea!' snarled Alice. 'Did ye know ye've got a fan, Lizzie? Mrs Dobson said yer a lovely girl and she didn't mince her words either when she said Ah was just an embarrassment to you!'

Jack stood up. 'It's got nothing to do with Lizzie, it's not her fault.'

Alice looked daggers at him. 'That's right! It never is, is it? Ah break me back keepin' this house clean and puttin' food on the table and what does she do, apart from prancin' around in that bloody Academy all day?' She glowered at Lizzie. 'Ye might as well know, Ah've got other plans for you, lady, so think on! This will be your last bloody pantomime!'

'All right, that's enough,' said Jack, 'you haven't got a kind word to say to the bairn. You're eaten up with jealousy, just because you've had your nose put out.'

Lizzie could tell this was going to get nasty. 'Dad,' she said, 'if it's all right with you, I'll be off to bed now. I'm tired and I've got a few lines to learn for tomorrow.'

'But you've had nothing to eat, pet. Shall I bring you something up?'

'Stop fussin', Jack,' said Alice, 'she's a big girl now and she's got a mind of her own.'

Lizzie could see where things were leading. 'Mam's right,' she said, 'I'm not a child any more. I'll be off to bed now, see you both in the morning.'

She hurried upstairs and wrapped herself in the silence of her room, but it wasn't long before angry voices invaded her solitude. Just like old times, she thought. Nothing ever changes.

❧

When the curtain came down on the last night of *Little Red Riding Hood*, the whole cast assembled onstage to take their call. It was different for Lizzie this time and her heart was racing as she stood in the front line with the principals. There was no question in her mind: this was where she belonged. There was nowhere else she'd rather be than on the stage.

The curtain went up again to overwhelming applause and, in the traditional way, the dancers guided the juveniles from the stage while the rest of the cast took their bows in turn. Then the principal boy and girl made their entrance, dressed in their wedding costumes, while Lizzie, acting as bridesmaid, sprinkled confetti over the happy couple. The applause almost hit the roof when the cast encouraged Lizzie to take her bow. She was just about to curtsey when she heard a familiar voice shouting from the stalls.

'That's right, hinny, show them what yer made of! Ah always knew ye had it in ye!'

Lizzie squinted over the footlights to see Peter and Ena almost lift Mrs Rooney from her seat. Oh no, thought Lizzie, she's drunk again. She watched in horror as Peggy tried to grab her mother's arm, but then staggered away. It looked like Mrs Rooney had kicked her in the shin. Peggy fell backwards on to the knee of an irate-looking man. Lizzie could hear him objecting, but couldn't quite catch what he said.

The cast took their final bow and when the curtain came down Lizzie ran all the way to her dressing room. Tears welled up in her eyes as she went inside. She couldn't believe that her family had humiliated her on the last night.

Grandma Wood was waiting with arms outstretched. 'Come here, pet,' she said, 'this is where you belong.'

Lizzie flew into her arms like a homing pigeon and sobbed her heart out.

Mrs Wood patted her on the back. 'There, there now, don't allow that lot to spoil your fun. But watch out, pet, I've just seen your mother and I'm warning you, she's got a face like thunder, so don't rub her up the wrong way. She's just looking for trouble.'

There was a knock at the door and the dresser came in. 'For goodness sake, Lizzie, you're still in your costume! Let me help you out of it.' She began to brush away the sprinklings of confetti that clung to the girl's shoulders.

'I'm afraid it's my fault,' said Mrs Wood. She hugged Lizzie. 'I'll see you downstairs, pet, and don't forget what I said.'

As if I could, thought Lizzie. I'll just get dressed and dodge the bullets. She put on her special dress and looked in the mirror. It was pale blue with a dark blue sash and a sweetheart neckline. She tried on the necklace her father had given her for Christmas and it was just right. She went to her make-up box and took out a pale pink lipstick. In for a penny, in for a pound, she thought, as she applied it sparingly. She looked in the mirror again, decided she was looking as good as she could manage, then took a deep breath and made her way downstairs.

She was surprised to see Ena and Annie waiting at the bottom of the stairs with Joe, her mother and father standing a little back behind them.

'Here she is,' said Annie, 'the star of the show!'

'Oh please, Auntie Annie, don't exaggerate!'

'Who's exaggerating,' said Ena, 'you're a little star!'

'I'll second that,' said Joe.

Alice scowled. 'Well, well,' she said, 'if it isn't Lizzie and her fan club!' She turned to Ena. 'Aren't ye layin' that on a bit thick?'

The words had hardly left her mouth when she noticed Lizzie's lipstick. 'And what the hell's that ye've got on yer face, girl? Get it off!'

Lizzie flushed.

'Leave her alone,' Annie said. 'It's so pale you can hardly see it.'

Ena glared at Alice. 'Many a mother would be proud to have such a lovely, talented daughter.'

'Well, how would ye know, since ye've never had a bairn!'

Jack raised his voice. 'That's enough, Alice! This is Lizzie's night and don't forget it! Ignore her, Ena. Why don't you see how Peter is coping – he's been stuck with Mrs Rooney and Peggy since the curtain came down.' He took Lizzie's hand. 'Come on, pet, you must be hungry, let's find the buffet.'

When they reached the food, they were surprised to see Mrs Wood, sitting in a comfortable chair, talking to Mr Chapman. He stood up when he saw them. 'Good timing!' he said, putting his arm around Mrs Wood. 'I have this woman to thank for having the insight to encourage Lizzie in what I hope will be her chosen profession. I've been watching her over the last two years and, in my opinion, she has a future in the theatre. Thank you, Lizzie, for helping to make this production the success it has been. You're a great little trouper. Now, if you'll excuse me, I'd better mingle.' He patted Mrs Wood once more and made his way across the room to where the principals had gathered.

'Here comes Peter,' said Jack, 'with Peggy and Mrs Rooney.'

Oh my God, thought Mrs Wood, just look at the sight of her! In that moth-eaten coat and the shabby hat that could find its own way to a funeral! If it weren't for Peter she'd be falling over – she's surely the worse for drink.

'Away the lads!' Mrs Rooney shouted, as Peter sat her on a chair.

He laughed. 'I didn't know she was a Newcastle supporter!'

'Ah'm sorry,' said Peggy, 'but ye know what she's like when she's had a few.'

Mrs Rooney grabbed Lizzie's hand. 'Yer a clever little bugger, Ah'll say that for you!'

Lizzie pulled her arm away. 'Can we go home now, Dad? I'm not hungry.'

Peter nodded. 'That's the best idea I've heard tonight, Lizzie.'

'Is that right?' said Alice. 'Well, Ah've got a better one!' She waited while they all fell silent, savouring the moment.

Ena's ears pricked up. What has she got up her sleeve this time, she thought. 'Go on, Alice, don't keep us in suspense.'

'All right. Ye may as well know, Ah've made up my mind about Lizzie's future and it won't be on the bloody stage!'

Mrs Wood got up from her chair and faced her. 'Surely you can't mean that, Alice, after hearing Mr Chapman's opinion?'

Lizzie reached out and squeezed Jack's hand, not sure where this was leading.

'Don't worry,' he whispered, 'we'll sort this out.'

Peter stepped forward. 'How can you do this when you know the girl's heart is in the theatre?'

Alice turned to her brother-in-law and laughed in his face. 'Don't worry, Peter, she'll be in a theatre all right – a bloody hospital theatre!' Then, turning back to her daughter, 'You can finish school since your grandma has already paid for it, then as soon as you're old enough, you're enrolling as a student nurse!'

Lizzie felt the ground tilt as if she'd been struck. This couldn't be true. It had to be one of her mother's tasteless jokes. Gasping, she ran to Mrs Wood and threw her arms around her. 'If you take me home with you, Grandma, I'll be as good as gold, I promise!'

'There, there,' said Mrs Wood, as she struggled to contain her tears. 'Never say die, pet. Have a little faith – we'll put this right.'

Ena took Jack aside. 'How long do you intend to let your wife get away with this? For Lizzie's sake, why can't you put your foot down?'

Jack couldn't meet her eyes.

'Oh Jack,' said Ena, 'she hasn't already pushed you into agreeing with this, has she?'

'Mind yer own business!' Alice shouted. 'Get the coats, Jack, we're going home!'

Ena grasped Jack's arm. 'You haven't said yes to this, have you?'

Jack lowered his eyes and turned away.

❧

Lizzie hung her coat in the hall and tiptoed to the bottom of the stairs. She was halfway up, when Alice shouted, 'Where the hell d'ye think yer going? Yer dad wants a word with ye!'

'But we've just got home, Mam. It's been a long day and I'm tired.'

Alice ignored her protests as she dragged her to the kitchen and pulled her inside. 'Here she is, Jack! Now tell her!'

'All in good time,' he said, 'the bairn looks exhausted.'

Alice glared at him. 'Ah thought ye had something to say to her!'

'Yes I have, but she looks hungry. She hasn't eaten all day. Maybe you could make her a sandwich, Alice.'

'Ye've got a short memory when it suits ye, Jack! She made it quite clear she wasn't hungry at the party!'

Lizzie stood up. 'Stop it, the both of you! I'm sick of playing pig in the middle! I'm going to bed now – and you may as well know, I'll never be a nurse, so put that in your pipe and smoke it!'

Alice's mouth dropped open and she stared at Lizzie in disbelief. 'Did ye hear that, Jack?' she shouted.

Lizzie turned to leave, but Alice grabbed her arm and pulled her back. 'Now you listen to me,' she said, 'yer dad's got something to say to ye and it won't wait. Go on, Jack, get on with it!'

He turned to Lizzie and lowered his eyes. 'I'm sure we can work things out, just let me explain.'

Lizzie's heart sank. She stared coldly at her father. 'Go ahead, Dad, I'm listening.'

'You might not like what I'm about to say, pet, but please hear me out. If you do what your mother wants and you really don't like it, I promise you won't have to finish the course. Mam just wants you to give it a try, that's all.'

'That's right,' said Alice. 'Now that's not too much to ask, is it?'

Lizzie glared at Jack. 'You don't mind who you have to sacrifice to keep your wife happy, do you?'

'That's enough,' he said, 'I don't want to hear any more. Remember, she is your mother.'

'How can I forget, Dad? You were the lucky one during the war – I had to cope with her for six years! It's a miracle I'm still here!'

'Did ye hear her, Jack?' Alice shouted. 'The cheek of her!'

Lizzie held her ground. 'You know it's true, Dad.'

'Lizzie – '

Something in her snapped and she cried out in anguish. 'Don't do it, Dad! Don't let her win this time! I can't be a nurse, I can't!'

Alice folded her arms. 'Ye'll do exactly what yer told, young lady!'

'No I won't!' said Lizzie. 'Dad – '

Jack stepped forward as if to hug her, but Lizzie recoiled as if stung.

'We can't go on like this,' he said.

'You mean Mam will make your life a misery if you don't do what she wants! That's it, isn't it, Dad?'

Alice took a step towards her. 'One more word from you and ye'll feel the back of my hand!'

Lizzie looked at her father as though she was seeing him for the first time and knew there was no hope. All the joy of her final performance faded away to nothing – all the applause, the excitement, the sense of being truly alive. It had been an illusion. 'All right, Dad,' she said, 'you'll get your peace. I'll go like a lamb to the slaughter. I'll go and live in the nurses' home as soon as they'll let me, then you can have Mam all to yourself – and good luck to you both!'

PART 4

Chapter 23

Gateshead, 1950

Lizzie stood outside Sister Joblin's office and straightened her uniform. It was her first day on a ward and, although she hated the very thought of nursing, she still wanted to make a good impression.

Her first days had been spent under the instruction of Sister Tutor with the rest of the new intake, trying to absorb all the new information. She thanked God for her good memory; there seemed to be endless amounts to learn and it all had to be perfect. People's lives were at stake.

The only bit she had liked so far was moving into the nurses' home, where she had her very own room. The block was newly built, and she was well aware that she was lucky; some hospitals made their nurses share rooms and they were awful, draughty places. But here, at Sheriff Hill Isolation Hospital, all the rooms were singles and came ready furnished with all she could reasonably need. It had been impressed on them that they were expected to keep their rooms as clean and tidy as the wards themselves: beds made with proper hospital corners, clothes hung up and tidied away. There had already been one inspection and Lizzie had been reprimanded for leaving her shoes lying on the floor rather than at the bottom of the narrow wardrobe.

She was about to knock on the door when a young nurse with frizzy brown hair and a pale complexion came rushing out. Her uniform indicated she had been there longer than Lizzie. She skidded to a halt when she saw her. 'You must be Wood,' she said, 'Sister's expecting you. I'm Poole – you'll be working with me today.'

Lizzie hesitated. She wasn't sure what to make of this energetic young woman.

'Go on,' said Poole. 'She doesn't like to be kept waiting.'

Gathering her courage, Lizzie tapped lightly on the door. 'Come in, Nurse.'

She pushed it open and stepped nervously inside. Sister was a tiny woman, with sharp features and bird-like eyes. Her uniform was so starched, Lizzie wondered how she could move in it, but evidently she could. She got up from her desk and moved forward to shake Lizzie's hand.

'Welcome to Sheriff Hill Isolation Hospital, Wood.' The woman's voice was firm. 'As a student nurse, you will have the privilege of working on the wards for five hours each day, as well as continuing your instruction from Sister Tutor. And today you will work with Nurse Poole on my ward. This is the female ward for patients with spinal problems and, as their movements are restricted, they need lots of attention.' Her eyes never left Lizzie's, as if she were waiting to see any flicker of doubt or weakness in her newest trainee. 'Recovery is a long one – some of our patients have been here for months. Nurse Poole has been on this ward for some time and will guide you through the procedures. Now run along, Nurse, and familiarise yourself with the patients.'

Lizzie nodded. She knew that this hospital specialised in infectious diseases which couldn't be treated in other institutions. Somehow she had to learn to care for patients with scarlet fever, polio, smallpox, diphtheria and the dreaded scourge of tuberculosis. Inwardly quaking, but determined not to show it, she left the room to find Poole pacing up and down outside. 'Hurry up,' she said, and she strode off down the corridor. Lizzie had to almost run to keep up with her.

Suddenly Poole stopped outside a set of double doors. 'This is it,' she said, as she pushed them open. Lizzie followed her into the ward, a vast room with high ceilings, but from where she was standing it was difficult to see the patients, for they were stretched out in plaster casts resting on wooden boards fixed to the bed. A mirror was attached to the front of the cast to help them see their surroundings. Poor things, Lizzie was thinking. If it wasn't bad enough to have TB they were stuck in those casts as well. They looked like mummies from a museum, balanced on their wooden racks. Her thoughts were interrupted when a patient called out, 'I've dropped my pen, Nurse, can you pick it up please?'

Lizzie turned to do her bidding but Poole took her by the arm. 'Ignore her,' she whispered. 'This lot will have you at it all day if you let them. We don't call this the pick-up ward for nothing.'

Lizzie gave Poole a look of disapproval. 'How would you like to be confined in one of those coffin-like contraptions for months on end,' she said. 'I feel sorry for them.'

'And who do you feel sorry for, Nurse Wood?'

Lizzie froze and turned to see Sister Joblin standing behind her. This bird-like woman seemed to move with complete silence, which made her even more unnerving.

Poole spoke up. 'Nurse Wood thinks the plaster bed is like a torture chamber.'

'Oh dear,' said Sister. Neither her expression nor her voice held any trace of sympathy. 'Well, let me assure you, these plaster casts are made with the utmost care to fit the patient like a second skin. But I won't go into the details when you can see for yourself.' Her face broke into a smile and Lizzie couldn't tell if this was a good or bad thing. 'Our technician is working on a cast today and, to put your mind at rest, you can assist him.' She turned to Poole. 'Please escort Nurse Wood to Mr Evans' studio after break and let's hear no more about torture. But first, kindly show her the sluice.'

As soon as Sister Joblin was out of earshot, Lizzie nudged Poole. 'What's a sluice?'

Poole raised her eyebrows. 'This is your lucky day, Wood. Follow me to the bowels of the ward and you'll soon find out.'

She set off at a pace and Lizzie hurried behind until Poole stopped and pointed to a door. 'This is it,' she said, as she pushed it open.

Lizzie's eyes widened as she went inside. It was another high-ceilinged room, much smaller than the main ward and much colder. There were bedpans stacked in neat rows and kidney-shaped bowls hanging from the walls. 'What are those?' she asked.

Poole replied with brutal honesty. 'They're for the patients when they need to vomit.'

Lizzie pulled a face. 'How gross,' she said. 'And what are those rubber tubes for?'

'They are used in a procedure when the ladies need an enema. You know what one of those is, don't you? They suffer from constipation from being on their backs so long. Anyway, come over here and meet Big Bertha. I don't know what we'd do without her.' Poole bounded across to a contraption with her usual enthusiasm.

Lizzie, wondering what was in store for her now, followed her to what looked like a giant lavatory. 'Now watch this,' said Poole, as she placed a bed pan into a special slot and pulled a lever. Lizzie gasped as water poured into the bedpan, sluicing it out before guiding it on to a special drying rack.

'There you are, Wood! Now you know what a sluice is for.' Poole rubbed her hands together. 'Clever, isn't it?'

'But how can a patient sit on a bedpan when she is stuck in a plaster cast?' Lizzie didn't want to imagine what might happen.

'That's simple,' said Poole. 'Remember the wooden frame under the plaster? Well, the bedpan fits into a special slot. Don't worry about it – you'll get the hang of it in time.'

Oh my God, thought Lizzie, that's what she thinks! I'd rather be a lavatory attendant – at least I wouldn't have to wipe the customers' bums and pull the chain!

'Anyway,' Poole continued, 'you'll see Mr Evans doing his stuff today.' She looked at the watch pinned to the starched bib of her uniform. 'Ooh good,' she said, 'time for morning break. Hurry up, Wood, I can hear the trolley. Grab two teas while I bag a couple of chairs in the rest room. You never know, Sister might have left us some biscuits!'

Lizzie hurried back down the ward and out into the corridor, and, sure enough, there was the trolley. Nurses in their various uniforms were converging on it, but she managed to get there first. Somebody behind her tutted loudly but she ignored them. An attractive young man beside the trolley smiled at her. 'And what can I get you?' he said.

'I'd like two cups of tea with sugar,' she was saying, when someone pushed her in the back.

Lizzie spun around to see an angry face staring at her. 'You're Wood, aren't you?' she said. 'Well, I've been here longer than you, so shove over! I'm Nurse Aitken and I've been here for six months. You might be new at the moment but you'll learn to respect seniority soon enough. That means I get served before you, and you have to wait your turn.'

Lizzie felt the urge to wallop her, but after looking her over, she changed her mind. Aitken was taller than her and twice as wide, so she considered it politic to stand aside. She stood back and gave way to Aitken, then watched as her large frame disappeared off down the corridor, her uniform nearly bursting at the seams. The attractive young man raised his eyebrows and smiled as he poured out the tea.

'Don't worry,' he said, 'they come in all shapes and sizes, don't they?'

Lizzie smiled back, vowing to time her refreshment break more carefully from now on. 'Could you tell me where the rest room is?'

'Certainly, Nurse. It's down the corridor behind you, first on the left.'

Lizzie followed his directions, trying not to spill the tea as she walked to the door and pushed it open.

Poole was alone in what might well have been the shabbiest room in the entire hospital, resting on a well-worn sofa with her feet up. 'Where have you been, Wood? I'm half parched.'

'What did your last servant die of?' said Lizzie. 'It's still hot, isn't it?' She grinned and joined her mentor on the sofa. The nap on the armrests was so ancient it was shiny.

They sipped their tea and Poole passed her a biscuit. 'That wasn't so bad, was it?' she said.

'You didn't see what happened to me in the corridor,' Lizzie replied grimly. 'This oversized excuse for a nurse practically threw me out of the way when I was getting the drinks. Who does she think she is?'

'Let me guess.' Poole grimaced. 'Straight dark hair, red face, looks like she's spent all morning sucking on a lemon? That'll be Nurse Aitken. Don't take it personally, she's like that with everybody. God only knows why she wants to be a nurse. Don't let that big heap of misery ruin your day.'

'Can't say I'll be sorry if I don't see her again,' Lizzie said, realising she was lucky to be paired with the no-nonsense Poole. She drained her tea.

'Come on,' Poole said, getting up with difficulty from the sagging cushions of the old sofa, 'or you'll be late for Mr Evans.'

She guided Lizzie down a maze of corridors which all reeked of strong disinfectant and eventually stopped at a large double door, with the windows covered and a prominent sign reading, MR EVANS' STUDIO.

'Here we are,' she said.

Lizzie looked up at the ominous doors. 'What does Mr Evans do in here?'

'He takes the new patients and builds the casts to fit them.'

'Oh dear,' said Lizzie, 'I suppose the casts help them, but don't they feel claustrophobic?'

'Yes, but it's worth it in the end,' said Poole encouragingly.

Lizzie sighed. 'Do you like being a nurse, Poole?'

'I've always wanted to be a nurse – ever since I was a little girl.' Poole obviously meant it – she looked as if she was in her element, bedpans and all.

Lizzie's eyes filled with tears. 'It's not what I want to do at all. I hate to think of all of those people trapped in their plaster casts for months on end and all the other patients suffering in all those different ways. I do understand how good it is to help them, but I had other dreams.'

'Well,' said Poole briskly, 'dreams aren't for the likes of us, are they? We have to live in the real world. And the real world is in that ward – you'd better go in and get on with it.'

Lizzie wiped her eyes. 'You know, nursing will never be my profession,' she said, 'and, mark my words, it won't be long before I leave.'

'Time will tell, won't it?' said Poole. 'But now you'd better pull yourself together and get inside. He doesn't like to be kept waiting. I'll see you later.'

She passed her a handkerchief as she left.

Lizzie took a deep breath and put her head around the door. At the end of the room, a man with thinning grey hair and wearing a white coat was leaning over a patient. When he saw her he called, 'I'm Mr Evans, you must be Nurse Wood. Hurry up, I'm waiting. You are to be my assistant today, Sister Joblin informs me.'

As Lizzie drew nearer, she could see exactly what it was she would be assisting with and she froze at the sight. A man in his birthday suit lay face down on a wooden board. Blood rushed to her face and her cheeks grew hot.

Mr Evans raised his voice. 'We haven't got all day, Nurse, we are working with fast-drying plaster, so time is of the essence. Now pay attention,' he said as he smoothed a jelly-like substance on the patient's back. 'This is to allow the plaster to slip off easily once it has set. Now watch this carefully, Nurse. This is what I want you to do.' He soaked a large strip of plaster in a tub of cold water from a table beside him and moulded it on to the patient's back.

It didn't take Lizzie long to get the hang of it. She did the soaking while Mr Evans smoothed and shaped the quick-drying plaster. Her hands grew colder and colder and she could only begin to imagine how unpleasant it was for the patient, who now and again shivered on his board. When at last it was over and the patient's back was completely covered, Lizzie breathed a sigh of relief. This must mean her job was finished.

'Now, Nurse Wood, help me to turn this patient on to his back.'

'On to his back?' said Lizzie in horror. 'Forget it, Mr Evans, I've seen enough! I don't want to see his private property!'

Mr Evans was not impressed. 'And who do you think you are, Nurse?' he said. 'I've a good mind to report you to Sister.'

'Do what you like!' Lizzie cried. 'I don't want to see the rest of him!'

She took to her heels and fled outside.

※

Sister Joblin had not been impressed by Lizzie's behaviour with Mr Evans – she had been given a strict talking to and told she had to perform any task required of her, so Lizzie approached the other wards with some trepidation. But so far, nothing had been quite so shocking. And then, after learning the ropes on the adult wards, she was assigned to work with the children. Poole had broken the news to her.

'Lizzie,' she'd said, 'you lucky thing! I love that ward! It's full of little children with serious problems.'

She had taken Lizzie's arm, led her to a window and pointed to a long, low building across a patch of green. 'There's where you'll be. You'll enjoy it over there.'

Now Lizzie gasped as she went inside. It's not in the least like Sister Joblin's ward, she thought, as she walked along the corridor, counting the rooms on the way to the office. There were six rooms, all with round observation windows in the doors. It reminded her of portholes on a ship.

She eventually came to the end of the corridor and knocked on the office door.

'Come in,' called a cheery voice, 'it's open!'

Sister Fosbrook was attractive, with pale blue eyes and shiny black hair tied in a neat bun. Lizzie walked up to her desk. 'I'm Student Nurse Wood, reporting for duty.'

Sister's smile lit up her face and Lizzie felt instantly comfortable in her presence. Her voice was soft and gentle as she spoke. 'Nice to have you on board, Nurse. As you must have noticed, this unit is different from the rest of the wards. It is our privilege to treat very sick children in these isolation units. Some of them have almost forgotten what it's like to be held in their mother's arms after being in isolation for so long. Their mothers also need support, so a kind word from time to time will not go amiss. Your duty will be to make sure that these children are comfortable and free from any kind of distress, such as wet beds, sore bottoms and boredom. A staff nurse will teach you how to prevent any discomfort, such as bedsores and chafing. And, as a mother's only view of her child is through the viewing glass, we must make sure it is clean at all times. I think that's enough to take in for now, so come along and meet some of our little charges.'

She led Lizzie in to the first room, where a tiny baby lay motionless in a cot. At the foot of the cot was a chart, with the baby's name and treatment record.

'What's wrong with the poor little thing?' she asked.

Sister ushered her from the room. 'You don't have to be concerned about Thomas – a senior nurse will attend to him.'

She showed Lizzie into the next room, where a small girl was tugging at bright purple bandages on her arms. 'This is Mary,' said Sister. 'She's two years old and, apart from her other problems, she has scabies.'

'What's that?' Lizzie asked.

'It's a contagious skin disease. It causes serious itching from small raised spots caused by the itch mite. We try to keep Mary's arms covered, as scratching can break the skin, but I'm afraid it's a losing battle.'

'And what's that purple stuff on the bandage, Sister?'

'It's called Gentian Violet,' Sister told her. 'Now come along to meet Henry. He has curvature of the spine and has just been prepped for his surgery this afternoon.'

Sister looked through the window in the door and put up her hand. 'He's fast asleep, Nurse, best not disturb him. Let's look in on little Barbara.'

The lights in Barbara's room were dimmed and, as Lizzie moved closer to the bed, it was clear to see why. The little girl's head was swathed in a bandage, supporting a dressing on her left eye. Lizzie gave Sister a worried glance.

Sister shook her head in frustration. 'Damned fireworks, Nurse! You'd think that parents of a four-year-old child would have the sense to keep her inside on Guy Fawkes night.'

Lizzie swallowed hard as she turned to Sister. 'Some people don't deserve to have children, do they?'

'Well, at least we saved her eye, Nurse, and that's the main thing. Now come along and let her sleep.'

They moved on to the next room and Sister looked through the window. 'We won't go in,' she said. 'Paul had a lumbar puncture this morning and he's still sleeping. We won't disturb him. Let's look in on little Christopher.'

As they reached the last room, loud crying could be heard from inside. Sister beckoned to Lizzie and they went in. 'This is Christopher. He's eighteen months old and, on top of everything else, he's retarded.' She gently picked him up and patted his back. 'Christopher has been with us for three months and needs constant attention. There, there, Christopher,' she said, 'Nurse is coming to change you soon. Christopher is a special case and so I'd like you to spend as much time with him as possible. Get him interested in his toys – and sing to him, he seems to like that.' She settled Christopher in his cot once more and gestured to Lizzie. 'Come with me, Nurse, and I'll show you the linen room.'

Sister quickened her pace as she led Lizzie back down the corridor and through an archway. An arrow pointed to a sign: LINEN ROOM THIS WAY. BEWARE OF TROLLEYS. 'This is it,' she said, as she opened the door and beckoned Lizzie to follow. It was a huge room with shelves displaying neatly folded linen. Each row was clearly marked: draw sheets, pillow cases, counterpanes, mattress covers and nappies. Lizzie nudged Sister. 'There's enough linen here to serve an army!'

'Maybe so, Nurse Wood, but at least on my ward there will be no need for any child to have soiled sheets or dirty nappies. They have enough to cope with already. Now come along and meet the nurse you will be helping today.'

Sister led Lizzie to an annex at the back of the room where a nurse was loading a trolley with clean linen. Lizzie gasped when she saw who it was. My God, she thought, as Nurse Aitken turned round and glared at her. What have I done to deserve this? Trust me to be lumbered with Bossy Boots.

Sister turned to Aitken. 'This is Nurse Wood. She is assigned to this ward as temporary help.'

Aitken smiled ingratiatingly. 'We've already met, Sister. In fact, just recently we had tea together.'

Lying cow, thought Lizzie.

'As you can see,' said Sister, 'Nurse Aitken has already loaded the trolley so take first tea break and relieve her when you return. Carry on, Aitken, and come with me, Wood.'

Lizzie, avoiding Aitken's gaze, followed Sister into the nurse's rest room. It was much smaller than the one on Sister Joblin's ward and brighter too. There was a small tea urn, a tin of biscuits and comfortable chairs. This is more like it, Lizzie was thinking when her eyes were drawn to a large noticeboard fixed to a wall. It was covered in pictures of young children, each one marked with the date and a child's name. Sister placed her hand on Lizzie's shoulder. 'I expect you're wondering who these children are?'

'Yes, Sister, I didn't see them on the ward.'

Sister's voice grew solemn. 'These are some of the little ones who didn't make it – gone, but not forgotten by the staff who nursed them.' She let her eyes wander along the photographs, some now dog-eared and worn.

Lizzie tried hard to control her tears, but to no avail. They ran down her cheeks uninvited. Sister passed her a piece of gauze. 'Here,' she said, 'dry your eyes with this and get on with your tea break. We don't want to keep Nurse Aitken waiting, do we?'

Sister Fosbrook turned to go, but then paused on her way out. 'And by the way,' she said, 'I believe in a power greater than myself. He helps me to accept the things I cannot change, gives me courage to change the things I can, and wisdom to know the difference. Please try to control your emotions, Nurse, and think of the child who may need your care and attention. You might be surprised at the results.'

As Sister closed the door behind her, Lizzie looked at the pictures once more. Dear God, she thought, I didn't choose to be a nurse. After all, it was my mother's idea. I believe nursing should be a chosen vocation, but even though it's not mine, I promise to do my best while I'm here.

She finished her tea and went back to the ward.

The linen trolley was standing outside Christopher's room. Loud sobbing could be heard from inside. Lizzie pushed open the door to see Christopher standing shivering and naked in his empty cot, clearly terribly upset, and Nurse Aitken standing over him. She took a moment to register the scene, so different to when Sister Fosbrook had cared for the little boy. 'What the hell's going on?' she demanded. 'And what's that smell?'

Aitken turned on her, her expression one of distaste. 'It's Christopher,' she said. 'He's led me a merry dance. I had just put him into his clean cot when he shat all over it.'

Lizzie looked at the hysterical child and glared at Aitken. 'He's only eighteen months! He can't help it. We'd better change it again.'

Aitken huffed in contempt. 'What, so he can shit all over it as soon as our backs are turned? It's not worth bothering with some of them, you'll learn that when you've been here as long as I have.'

Lizzie gasped in shock. 'You can't let him lie in that all afternoon! He'll get infected!'

'You don't know what you're talking about.' Her voice was menacing now.

'You're not fit to work with children!' Lizzie shouted.

'Mind your own business!' Aitken snapped. 'Anyway, he seems to like the feel of it on his skin.'

434

It was the last straw. Lizzie lost control and picked up the soiled sheet. 'Now let's see how you like the feel of it!' she said as she wrapped the sheet around Aitken's head.

Christopher screamed and so did Aitken. The combined volume was enough to wake the dead. Sister appeared in the doorway just in time to see Nurse Aitken struggling to remove the soiled sheet as Lizzie was trying to tighten it. 'Stop it, Nurse Wood!' Sister shouted. 'Unwrap Aitken at once! What have you done to her?'

Lizzie turned to explain.

'Be quiet, Nurse! Clean yourselves up! I'll see to this poor little boy.' Sister immediately turned to Christopher, settling him back into a clean, fresh bed.

Lizzie hurried to the nurses' rest room and locked herself in the toilet. She removed her soiled apron, scrubbed her hands and tidied her hair, before pinning her now-crumpled cap back on to her dark curls. Part of her wanted to stay in this sanctuary for the rest of the afternoon but she knew that would serve no purpose and she had better report back to Sister now she was calmer again. Making her way to the office, she tried to compose herself. She knocked on the door and went inside, only to find that Aitken had got there first. Typical, she thought, I wonder what lies she's told already.

'Come in,' said Sister. All the warmth had gone out of her eyes. 'I've been listening to Aitken's account of your outrageous behaviour in poor little Christopher's room. Please be kind enough to give me your version.'

'Yes Sister, I will.' Lizzie could feel her temper rising again. 'But I think it would have been fairer had you waited until I was present before hearing Aitken's side of it.'

Sister stiffened. 'How dare you tell me how to carry out an enquiry on my own ward! Why did you try to suffocate Nurse Aitken with a soiled sheet?'

Lizzie pointed at Aitken. 'Because she had the child in hysterics, just because he dirtied his sheets again! I'm sorry I didn't suffocate her! If I were Sister on this ward, I wouldn't trust her as far as I could throw her! And, as she's grossly overweight, that wouldn't be far!'

'That's enough!' said Sister. 'Control yourself! Apologise to Aitken for that hurtful remark. And to me for your bad language.'

Lizzie smiled at Sister. 'I apologise to you. But I won't apologise to Aitken. I expect you believe every word she said!'

Sister raised her voice. 'That's enough, Nurse Wood! Since there were no witnesses, you will both report to Matron in precisely thirty minutes' time and we'll see what she decides.'

'Why bother,' Lizzie scoffed, 'when you already blame me and believe Fatty!' She ran from the room, her head spinning with the injustice of it all.

❧

When Lizzie arrived outside Matron's office, Aitken was already there with her arm wrapped in a sling. That's right, she thought, exaggerate your injuries. She was about to grab Aitken when the door opened and Sister Fosbrook came out. 'Hurry along,' she said. 'Matron will see you now.'

Lizzie followed Aitken inside to see a woman sitting at her desk, ramrod straight, as though ready to charge her victims. Her face was expressionless as her piercing blue eyes focused on Aitken's sling. Her thin lips tightened as she pushed back her chair and stood up. 'I'm very sad to see two of my student nurses standing before me on two counts. One of child cruelty. And the other of violence.'

Lizzie, still upset after the events of the past couple of hours, misunderstood. 'Thank you for your verdict,' she said. 'You got that right, Matron! Aitken is guilty of child cruelty! I've got no intention of denying my actions. Thank God for justice at last!'

Matron looked at Lizzie in disbelief. 'I did not accuse Aitken of child cruelty. As there are no witnesses to this dreadful affair, I am unable to pass judgement. However, Sister did see you trying to suffocate Aitken with a soiled sheet. And she suffered a great deal of pain in her arm when you pushed her. Do you deny this?'

'No Matron, I don't. I always tell the truth. I saw Aitken being cruel to little Christopher and that's why I laid into her. I only wish I'd suffocated her because she's not fit to be trusted with children.' Lizzie was completely beside herself.

'All right,' said Matron, 'have you finished?'

'Yes I have, and I've finished with this hospital as well. You can ask me to leave if you like.' Lizzie was shaking with emotion.

Matron looked at Aitken. 'You may go now. I wish to talk to Nurse Wood in private.'

Shifting her arm in her sling in the most obvious way she could, Bell smiled with satisfaction as she left the room.

Matron turned to Lizzie. 'Now then,' she said, and Lizzie would have seen her expression was a fraction less stern if she had only been calm enough to notice, 'this is no time to make rash decisions. I have no intention of asking you to leave. Sister Tutor tells me that you are one of her brightest students. However, your fiery temper has been the cause of two warnings and now I'm giving you another. Please make it your last. I would hate to lose you.'

Lizzie opened her mouth to speak but Matron got there first.

'Hush, Nurse. Try to leave this room without any further remarks. That would be a good start. Now, carry on.'

Chapter 24

Newcastle upon Tyne, 1950

Lizzie paced up and down outside the house she had once called home. It was her first visit since being frogmarched into nursing and she was dreading it. It was only a few weeks since she had left, but to Lizzie it seemed like a lifetime. Never mind, she thought, in for a penny in for a pound. She plucked up courage and was about to knock when the door swung open. Jack stood there with his arms outstretched and Lizzie fell into them.

'I saw you loitering, pet. Come in and I'll put the kettle on.' He looked the same as ever, which felt strange as so many new things had happened to her. How could life at home have stood so still?

She followed him into the kitchen. 'Mam's out shopping,' he said. 'She's making a special dinner for you. Sit down while I make the tea.'

Lizzie sat at the table and looked around the room. Nothing's changed, she thought: a place for everything and everything in its place. Her eyes fell on the kitchen dresser. And does she still hide her chocolate in the drawer, she wondered.

'So tell me, Dad, how are things on the home front?'

'Don't ask, pet. Thank God I'm at work all day. And when I'm home, I manage to dodge the bullets. But don't worry, I'm sure she won't start on you.'

He turned up the gas under the kettle and warmed the teapot. 'Anyway, she's as pleased as punch to have a nurse as a daughter – she can't wait to show you off.'

Lizzie caught him smiling as he mashed the tea.

'What's the joke, Dad?'

'I was just thinking of your grandma. She always said, "a waiting kettle never boils".'

'How is she, Dad? I can't wait to see her!' Lizzie knew her grandmother had moved to a small, neat cottage not far from The Lilacs. It had been a wrench for her, but the new house would be much easier for her to manage.

Jack's face fell. 'Well, pet, you're bound to find out sooner or later. I'm afraid your grandma's not well.'

'What's the matter with her, Dad? I hope it's nothing serious.'

'She's had some tests, Lizzie, and they suspect it's gallstones.'

'What on earth's that, Dad?' Lizzie felt slightly guilty that she didn't know, but it wasn't one of the conditions they treated at Sheriff Hill.

'I looked it up in the dictionary, pet. It's what they call "crystals" in the gallbladder. But don't worry, Aunt Ena's with her most of the day and Uncle Peter joins her after surgery. It's handy having a doctor in the family, isn't it?'

'It's a godsend, Dad! What would we do without Aunt Ena and Uncle Peter? They're the salt of the earth.' She looked up to smile at him, but her expression changed as she heard footsteps outside, accompanied by a burst of song.

'Hush, Lizzie, your mother's back and it sounds like she's in a good mood. I haven't heard her sing in years!'

Alice pushed the kitchen door open with her foot, dropped her heavy carrier bags on the floor and glared at Lizzie. 'And why aren't ye wearing your uniform, Nurse Wood?'

Oh my God, thought Lizzie, not even through the door and she's started already. Well, she can't show me off now. 'Sorry, Mam, but I'm not allowed to wear it on home leave. After all, it's an isolation hospital and you wouldn't want me to put the public at risk, would you? I'd be a walking time bomb!'

Alice smiled. 'Quite right,' she said, 'yer a thoughtful girl. Now, tell us what it's like to be a nurse.'

'That's easy,' she said, 'I hate it! And I hate the things they expect me to do. You've always warned me about men, Mam, but I didn't expect to see one in his birthday suit! It was horrible!'

Alice gasped, her shopping forgotten. 'What's that?' she said.

'For goodness sake,' said Jack, 'let her settle in before you give her the third degree.'

'It's all right, Dad, Mam has a right to know.' Lizzie was taking a perverse delight in building up to the punchline of her story. 'Anyway, it wasn't so bad until he was rolled over on his back, showing all his private bits. That's when I got up the courage to run from the room, Mam!'

Alice's face was white with rage. She turned to Jack. 'Did ye hear that?'

'Yes, I did, and in my opinion, it's no place for a girl like Lizzie, especially after the way you've brought her up.'

Alice's lips tightened. 'Ah know what you're up to,' she said. 'And if you think she's leaving, ye've got another think coming. You leave it to me – I'll soon sort it out!'

Lizzie forced a smile. 'At least one good thing has come out of this, Mam. It's put me off men for life!'

Alice began unpacking her shopping with a vengeance. She picked up a tin of condensed milk and banged it on the table. 'Now then,' she said, 'are ye sure ye saw everythin', Lizzie? Ye'd better not be lyin' so you can leave that hospital!'

'Give it a rest,' said Jack. 'The bairn's just got here, for God's sake.'

Lizzie picked up her overnight bag and sidled towards the door. 'I'll just freshen up before I see Grandma. Dad's already told me she's not well.'

Alice glared at Jack. 'What did ye tell her that for? There's nowt wrong with her, Lizzie. She's been a bit poorly, but yer Aunt Ena's seeing to her.'

Lizzie stuck to her guns. 'Neverthless, I'd like to see her if it's all right with you, Mam.'

'Bloody hell, Lizzie! You've only been here five minutes and you can't wait to leave!' Alice continued to throw her groceries into the cupboard.

Jack clenched his fists behind his back. 'Go on,' he said, 'let her go, it'll do Mother good to see her.'

Alice's face reddened. 'Well, ye heard what yer dad said! So bugger off – at least Ah can see where Ah stand!'

Why did I expect anything different, thought Lizzie. Just look at poor old Dad with his tail between his legs. He deserves a medal for endurance!

'Well,' said Alice, 'what're ye waitin' for? Never mind about me, don't keep your grandma waitin'.'

Lizzie swept up her bag and opened the door. 'Don't worry, Mam, I won't. And don't expect me back for lunch either!'

❦

Lizzie's heart was pounding as she stood at the cottage gate. Thank God I made it, she thought, as she straightened her coat and tidied her hair. She pushed open the freshly painted white gate and hurried down the curving path to find Ena cleaning the cottage windows. 'Auntie Ena!' she shouted. 'It's me!'

The shammy leather fell into the bucket as Ena held out her arms. 'Come here, canny lass, let's look at you!' Ena hugged Lizzie tight, then pulled a face. 'Why, you're nothing but skin and bone, pet! I hope they're feeding you at that hospital.'

'I'm all right, Auntie, it's Grandma I'm worried about. Dad says she's got gallstones and she's having tests.'

Ena nodded. 'That's right, Lizzie, but we're not going to worry until there's something to worry about. Your Uncle Peter is keeping an eye on things. Now let's go inside, I can't wait to hear about the latest perils of Pauline.' She put her finger to her lips. 'Shh, now, be quiet, Uncle Peter moved Grandma's bed into the sitting room so I can keep an eye on her, so let's tiptoe into the kitchen and have a glass of her elderberry wine.'

'Do you think I should, Auntie?'

'Why not, your mam won't know.'

Ena opened a bottle and winked at Lizzie. 'Sit down at the table, pet, and I'll get the glasses.'

Lizzie pulled up a chair and sat at the familiar kitchen table. It looked just as warm and welcoming here as it did in The Lilacs. Ena put a glass in front of her. 'This is guaranteed to loosen the tongue,' she said as she poured the wine, 'so tell me everything.'

'All right, but I hope you can take it, Auntie Ena, it's pretty sordid!'

Ena beamed in anticipation. 'Then carry on, pet, I can hardly wait.'

'Well if you say so, Auntie, here goes! I wasn't in that hospital five minutes before I was drawn into the most embarrassing situation you can imagine! I was ordered to assist a technician with a plaster cast for a man with a TB spine. When I got to the workroom, I couldn't believe my eyes! There was a naked man lying on his stomach waiting to be covered in plaster and I had to help!'

Ena laughed. 'You've always been a great little storyteller, Lizzie.'

'This is no story, Auntie! I carried on with this embarrassing task until the technician told me to help him lift the man on to his back, exposing all his private parts! It was then I ran from the room as fast as I could! And can you blame me? So, there you are, what do you think about that, Auntie Ena?'

Ena poured herself another drink. 'Have you told your mother, Lizzie?'

'Of course I have! I thought it might get me out of nursing, but no such luck! It's more important to Mam that I'm out of the way.' Lizzie was warming to her theme but suddenly she halted as Ena held up her hand.

'Just a minute,' she said, 'did you hear that? I think your grandma's awake. Come with me, pet.'

Lizzie followed Ena into the bright sitting room and watched as she plumped up her mother's pillows.

'Let's sit you up,' she said, 'look who's here!'

When Ena stood back, Lizzie was shocked at the change in her grandma. Gone were the chubby pink cheeks and the smile like a Cheshire cat. She looked frail and tired as she held out her arms. 'Come here, pet, and give your grandma a cuddle. How's your dancing coming along? And how's Madame Bella?'

Lizzie glanced quizzically at Ena, who put her finger to her lips and shook her head. When the penny dropped, Lizzie tenderly laid her head on Mrs Wood's chest. 'I've missed you, Grandma – I've been busy rehearsing for the end-of-term show. I've already reserved you a good seat.' Clearly Mrs Wood had clean forgotten she had left the Academy and gone to train as a nurse.

'That's a good girl. And how's your mother? I haven't seen her for such a long time – I expect she's busy.'

That's right, thought Lizzie, busy making everyone's life a misery! She's got a short memory when it suits her. And after the way Grandma put up with her during the war, you'd think she'd show some concern for her welfare.

Mrs Wood pointed to an ornately carved wooden box on a table by the side of her bed and held out her hand. 'Pass that to me, pet.'

She did her grandma's bidding and placed the box on her lap. As Mrs Wood lifted the lid, a familiar tune rang out and childhood memories came flooding back for Lizzie. Mrs Wood put her hand inside the music box and took out an amber necklace. 'This is for you, Lizzie, you're a big girl now and I know you'll look after it. Granddad gave me this on our wedding day.'

Lizzie glanced at Ena.

'Go on, pet,' she said, 'it's all right, Mother always wanted you to have it.' She took the necklace and fastened it around Lizzie's neck.

Lizzie looked in the sideboard mirror. 'Oh Grandma,' she said, 'it's lovely!'

'Not half as lovely as you, my darling. Wear it in good health.' She yawned. 'Now, I think it's time I had forty winks. So run along, pet, and don't keep Bella waiting.'

Lizzie swallowed the lump in her throat as she kissed Mrs Wood goodbye.

'Come on,' Ena whispered as she ushered her niece from the room, 'don't make it worse by dragging it out – you must have things to do on your weekend home.'

'Well I promised Bella that I'd pop in to the Academy, but I don't feel like it now.' Lizzie paused at the front door, uncertain what to do.

'Don't be silly, Lizzie, you can't disappoint her, she'll be glued to the window. Off you go and have a good old chinwag, it'll do you good.'

'I suppose you're right, Auntie, I'll pop in on the way home.'

Ena threw her arms around her. 'Now don't be a stranger, pet, you know where we are.'

❧

Lizzie held the amber beads close to her chest as she stood outside the Academy. The front door was open and, like a homing pigeon, she flew straight to Bella's office. Bella was waiting with arms outstretched. 'I saw you from the window,' she said, pulling Lizzie to her ample bosom.

Lizzie clung to her like a drowning woman. 'You'll never know what I've been through!'

'Of course I won't, darling, not unless you tell me,' Bella said. 'The tea's ready, now get the biscuit tin out while I pour. You're as skinny as a rake. Open the tin and help yourself – there's a few chocolate ones left.'

Bella put the cups on the coffee table and patted the sofa. 'Now sit down, Lizzie, and tell me all about it.'

'What's the use, Bella?' Lizzie's head drooped. 'I'll never get out of nursing. I know when I'm beaten – Mam's determined to get her own way and Dad's not much help. I can't fight the two of them!'

Bella clapped her hands. 'What a performance, Lizzie! You deserve an Oscar for that! Or is it just a case of the "poor me's"? Now, if this was pantomime, I could wave my magic wand and get an instant solution, but in real life happy endings are something we have to work for ourselves. Have you ever heard the expression, "life is what you make it"?'

Lizzie nodded.

'Well, first of all, I see this problem as a struggle of wills. Your mother insists you become a nurse while you want to work in a profession you love and have been training for. So, against your will and to please your mother, you'll give up all hope of entering the theatre? I'm sorry, but the girl in this story doesn't sound like the Lizzie Wood I know. She would never give up so easily.'

Lizzie's eyes filled with tears. 'But you don't understand, Bella. You haven't lived with my mother. She always gets her own way and just for peace, Dad always agrees with her.'

'To hell with my diet,' said Bella, 'pass the biscuits.' She rummaged through the tin until she found the last chocolate one and took a bite. Her expression grew thoughtful and she took a few moments before she continued. 'Suppose I got an audition for you in London, Lizzie. How would you feel?'

Lizzie stared at her old mentor. 'How would I feel?' she said. 'I'd feel I'd died and gone to heaven!'

'Well, I don't want to build your hopes up, dear, but I have a friend who may be able to help. As young girls, we toured together and became best friends. She's a successful choreographer now and highly thought of in London's West End. That's her there on the wall – next to the window, the one in the wooden frame. That other girl is me, now you wouldn't think it, would you?' Bella laughed at Lizzie's reaction. 'I'll have a word with her on condition that you accept the things you cannot change at the moment and face up to life a day at a time.'

Lizzie threw her arms around her. 'How did you become so wise?' she asked.

Bella laughed. 'It was the day I looked in the mirror and realised I wasn't. Who knows, it might happen to you one day. Now off you go and enjoy your weekend.'

Lizzie hugged her even more tightly. 'Thank you,' she said, 'you've thrown me a lifeline, Bella. Nursing may be the pits, Mam may never change and Dad may never find a way to stand up to her, but you've given me hope and strength to believe in myself. Whatever happens, I'll never let you down.'

Chapter 25

Gateshead, 1950

Lizzie turned the key in the lock, pushed open the door and threw her bag inside. Who would believe I'd be glad to get back to this place, she thought, as she flopped into the one comfy chair. But be it ever so humble, there's no place like home and at least this is better than the one I left behind. She gazed around her small room. She had begun to make it feel like her own, with a few pictures of the Wood family, and one of Molly from their schooldays, framed on her windowsill. Her navy blue nurse's cloak hung from its peg on the door. Despite its basic furnishings, she felt safer here than she had in her bedroom at home.

The door flew open and Poole bounced inside. 'Can I come in? I can't wait to hear about your weekend!'

'You're already in,' said Lizzie, 'but I'm too tired to talk about it now. I could sleep for a week after what I've been through!'

Poole moved in closer. 'Go on,' she said, 'you know what they say, a problem shared is a problem halved.'

Lizzie took off her shoes. She began to relate all the trials of her visit home, exaggerating for her friend's amusement, but leaving out the bit about the audition. Then she grew thoughtful.

'I hope you don't mind me asking, but what's your religion, Poole?'

'That's a funny thing to ask,' she said, 'but as it happens I haven't got one! My mam just put down C of E when she filled in the form. But I haven't been inside a church since I was christened. What about you?'

'Oh, I'm a reluctant Catholic and my mother's a religious maniac. She sits in church looking as though butter wouldn't melt in her mouth and cheese couldn't choke her. And she has the nerve to take Holy Communion even when she hasn't seen the inside of a confessional. My mother doesn't know the first thing about Catholicism! She can't wait until mass is over so she can have a good gossip! I'm not religious, Poole, but I believe in God. He's my friend and confidant – I tell him things I could never tell anyone else.' Lizzie raised her voice. 'And I don't need to go to church to do it, either!'

Poole was surprised at Lizzie's outburst, but it was clear to understand the anger in her voice. She put her hand on Lizzie's shoulder.

'Sounds as if you're better off staying here,' she observed. 'Nobody's going to ask you about any of that as long as you do your job and pass your exams.'

'Suppose so.' Lizzie had calmed down and all the energy had left her. 'Sorry,' she said. 'I'm shattered and I can hardly keep my eyes open.'

'What am I thinking of?' said Poole. 'When it's as clear as day to see you're exhausted.' She covered Lizzie with a blanket. 'There we are,' she said, 'that's better. Have forty winks and I'll come back later.'

Lizzie snuggled under the blanket. 'Thanks,' she said, 'you're a real friend.'

Poole had a lump in her throat as she left. Why the hell does Lizzie put up with that excuse for a mother, she wondered as she tiptoed from the room.

❧

Lizzie's sleep was interrupted by an ambulance screaming its way to Emergency. She sat bolt upright and looked at the clock. For goodness sake, she thought, that can't be the time. It's nearly six! I've missed the rest of the afternoon, it's grown dark. She got out of bed and put on her shoes. What am I doing tomorrow, she wondered. I might as well look at the list. She hurried down the corridor to check the noticeboard. There were several new notices, but one of them stood out like a sore thumb. 'Sister Tutor will meet the following nurses outside the mortuary at 10 a.m.' My God, she thought, my name is on the bloomin' list! She turned on her heels and ran straight to Poole's room.

'Anyone here?' she shouted.

Poole came out of the bathroom with a towel around her head. 'What do you want?' she said. 'I'm trying to wash my hair.'

'Have you seen the noticeboard? They've got me down for a post-mortem!'

'So what?' Poole couldn't see what the fuss was about.

'So what? I'll tell you so what! I'm not going! I can't stand the sight of blood!'

'Don't be silly,' said Poole. 'There's hardly any blood. In any case, you can always close your eyes and pretend to look. Anyway, it's late and I have to wash my hair. I'll tell you all about it at breakfast.'

'No thank you, Nurse Poole, I don't want to hear about it while I'm eating. Goodnight!'

A fat lot of help she was, thought Lizzie, as she hurried back to her room. She shut the door behind her and breathed in deeply. Oh dear, a post-mortem. How would she cope? There was only one thing for it. She sank down on her knees and put her hands together.

'Dear loving God,' she said, 'I feel sick at the thought of what I'm expected to watch tomorrow. They'll be cutting up some poor soul in front of an audience – and without his permission! I don't know what to do. I can't ask Poole – she's my best friend, but she's as tough as old boots, so she's no help. You are my only hope, so once more I turn to you for guidance. Please let it be all right tomorrow. Love as always, from Lizzie.'

⚘

The mortuary was a long, grey stone building, sitting at the edge of an abandoned field. Lizzie shuddered at the thought of what could be inside. It was a cold, damp day and her shoes squelched as she walked over the soggy grass. To make matters worse, the sky was grey and it looked like rain – Lizzie hoped there wouldn't be a downpour. Pulling her warm cloak around her she ran the rest of the way and joined several other nurses already standing outside the mortuary. They were laughing and giggling. For goodness sake, she thought, you'd think they were queuing up for the pictures! Have they no respect for the poor person about to be cut up?

Sister Tutor appeared without warning and glared at the giggling students. 'May I share the joke?' she said.

The girls were shocked into silence.

'That's better,' said Sister. 'There won't be many laughs when you get inside, I can assure you. Now, is everyone here?'

The nurses responded in perfect unison. 'Yes, Sister.'

'Very well. Now listen carefully, once you are inside there will be no talking. You will be shown where to stand and will remain there until you are asked to leave. If that is clear, follow me inside.'

Without further ado, she marched them through the mortuary's gloomy entrance.

Lizzie remembered Poole's advice and found a place at the back. There was an unfamiliar smell in the room, a mixture of strong disinfectant and something almost rotten that made her feel sick. She turned to see how the nurse next to her was coping and her heart sank. It was Bell. Even though they had been forced to be civil to one another since the incident in little Christopher's room, Lizzie still couldn't pretend she enjoyed her company.

Bell nudged her and pointed. 'Look!' she said. 'That's the victim!'

Lizzie squinted her eyes and pretended to look over the heads of the other nurses in front. Typical of Bell, she thought, trying to make me look at all the gruesome details. She seems to enjoy other people's pain.

'Pay attention, Wood,' said Sister, 'you won't see anything with your eyes shut.'

'Come over here,' said Bell. 'Swap places with me and you'll get a better view.'

Lizzie opened her eyes and shuddered. There was a body lying face up on a metal table, partially covered with a sheet.

Bell sniggered. 'My, my,' she said, 'he's a big boy! Come on, Lizzie, swap places! You don't want to miss anything!'

Lizzie was saved from having to reply as the house surgeon came into the room. He stood at the metal table, while his assistant whisked the sheet from the body of a very large man with a head of magnificent black curly hair.

Bell dug Lizzie in the back and giggled. 'Now you see it, now you don't!'

Lizzie wasn't puzzled by her remark for long – the assistant shaved off what must have been the man's pride and joy, leaving nothing behind but a shiny dome.

'Now pay attention,' the surgeon said, as he placed a metal band around the barren head and tightened the screws. 'This subject died from a brain tumour and I shall begin by removing the top of the skull.'

He picked up what looked to Lizzie like a small, sharp saw and began to cut through the bone like it was butter. The noise was deafening – it set Lizzie's teeth on edge. She covered her ears and closed her eyes, but Sister nudged her again.

'Pay attention,' she snapped, 'or you'll miss something.'

At that moment, the surgeon prised the top of the man's skull clean off, just like topping a hard-boiled egg. Lizzie's eyes almost popped from their sockets as she stared at the cerebral matter. Then everything began to blur and before she knew it she sank to the floor.

❦

The next thing Lizzie remembered was waking up in a chair with her head between her knees. She tried to stand up. 'Where am I?' she asked.

'It's all right,' said Sister, 'you've only fainted. You're in the doctor's office. Now sit back in the chair, there's a nice cup of tea on its way.'

Lizzie did as she was told as Sister took her pulse. Even though she still felt woozy, she couldn't help noticing that the doctor had a very different office to the senior nurses. She was dimly aware of old dark wood and chairs of soft red leather. She was just thinking that she could get used to this when Sister Joblin burst into the room. She held her chest, trying to catch her breath. 'Could I have a private word?' she said. 'It's urgent.'

Sister Tutor took her arm and helped her into the adjoining doctor's changing room. 'Sit down,' she said, 'and get your breath back.'

Sister Joblin slumped into a nearby chair. 'How's Nurse Wood?' she said. 'I've heard all about the rumpus. But I haven't come because of that.' She held her chest again. 'Oh, Sister, I'm afraid it's bad news. I ran here after receiving an unexpected call from Wood's father.'

'What is it, Sister?'

'Nurse Wood needs to return home as soon as possible – there's been a death in the family. I'm afraid her grandmother has died.'

⁂

Lizzie's heart was pounding as the driver of the taxi that Sister Tutor had hurriedly called for her drew up outside her parents' house. 'Are you all right?' he asked as he helped her from the car. 'I see you're wearing a black armband and your front curtains are closed – it looks like there's been a death in the family.'

She nodded her head, unable to take in what was going on.

'I am sorry, pet.'

'Thank you,' she said as she fumbled in her purse for change. It was only a few miles from the hospital to her house but she couldn't think clearly enough to find the right money.

'Lizzie!'

She turned to see Uncle Peter hurrying down the path towards her.

'Let me get that,' he said, as he leaned into the cab and handed the driver five shillings. 'Keep the change,' he said. 'She'll be all right now.'

As the cab pulled away, he turned back to Lizzie. His face was pale. She dropped her bag and he held out his arms as she ran to him. 'It's so good to see you, Uncle! I can't believe I wasn't here when Grandma left us!'

'There, there, pet, it's all right. Auntie Ena was with your dad at her bedside. She was very peaceful at the end. And wherever she is, she will never be far from you. You were the light of her life – never forget that.'

Lizzie wiped her eyes. 'What about poor Dad, how is he coping?'

'He's not so bad now, Aunt Ena's with him. I dropped her off before surgery. They both took it badly, so I'm glad you're here. It will make all the difference. Uncle Joe and Auntie Annie will pop in later – they can't wait to see you.' He leaned down and kissed her on the forehead. 'I've got patients waiting so I'll have to leave, but don't worry, pet, I'll be back later. Now, go straight inside, they're expecting you.'

Lizzie stood frozen to the spot as she watched Peter start his car and drive away. Her legs felt like lead as she dragged them along the garden path on her way to the back door. Well, this is it, she thought, as she lifted the latch and went inside.

She found Jack and Ena at the kitchen table, nursing cups of tea. She ran to her father and threw her arms around him. 'Oh, Dad!' she cried. 'I'm so sorry!'

Jack swallowed hard. 'It's all right, pet, she didn't have any pain. Her passing was peaceful. I'm sorry I couldn't pick you up from the hospital, but I had to wait for the death certificate. We couldn't get on with the funeral without it.'

Ena raised her voice. 'Now, Jack,' she said, 'the bairn doesn't need to get involved in the details. Get her a cup of tea – by the looks of her, that's what she needs.'

Lizzie looked around her. 'Where's Mam?' she asked.

'Don't worry,' said Ena, 'I haven't done her in. She's upstairs getting your bed ready.'

As if on cue, the kitchen door swung open and Alice staggered in with an armful of dirty sheets. She dropped them on the floor and turned to Lizzie. 'Ah'm glad to see you made it, then.'

Ever the diplomat, Jack stood up. 'I was just about to make Lizzie a cup of tea.'

'That's a good idea,' said Alice. 'Ah could do with one meself.'

'For goodness sake,' said Ena, 'the bairn hasn't taken her coat off yet and all you can think about is yourself!' She helped Lizzie off with her coat and cringed when she saw the amber necklace proudly displayed around her neck.

Alice's eyes were like hot coals. 'Well, Lizzie!' she said. 'I see you couldn't wait to wear your inheritance.'

Jack raised his voice. 'The tea's ready, shall I pour it out?'

'Leave it to me,' Ena said, her voice tight with rage. 'I'll see to it.'

She turned to Lizzie. 'We'll just have a cup of tea, pet, and then we'll be off to the undertakers while you unpack and settle in.'

Lizzie glanced doubtfully at her mother's stormy face and Ena caught the look. 'Or you could go and see Madame Bella? She sent her condolences and said you should visit as soon as you're up to it.'

Lizzie felt the weight lift from her shoulders. 'That's a good idea,' she said, 'thank you, Auntie Ena.'

'Don't think about staying here to share a few minutes with your mother, then,' Alice scoffed. 'It's not as though you make a habit of it, is it?'

Ena's hands trembled as she poured out the tea. She passed Alice a cup. 'Will you be coming to the undertakers with us?'

'What do you want me there for, Ena, when you'll have planned the whole bloody thing yerselves?'

'Well in that case, Alice, we'd better set off now, we don't want to be late.' She turned to Lizzie. 'Would you like to go to Bella's now? We can give you a lift if you like.'

Lizzie almost leapt to her feet, her tea untouched. 'Thank you, Auntie Ena, that's very kind.'

⁑

Stepping into the Academy was like coming home again and at a time like this, there was no other place she would rather be. As she walked through the imposing hallway, she recalled the very first time she had come here, how nervous she had felt and how her beloved grandma had supported her every step of the way. Her heart gave a sharp pang as she thought of it. As far as Grandma was concerned, there was never any doubt about Bella accepting her.

It was hard to comprehend that Grandma Wood was gone and the pain of her loss was beginning to take its toll. She quickened her pace as she set off down the corridor to Bella's office – just as she had expected, the door was wide open.

Bella ran to her and squeezed her like a lemon. 'Can you feel that?' she said. 'That's strength – and I have enough for two!' She patted the sofa. 'Sit next to Bella and we'll put the world to rights. First, you don't need to talk about your nightmare this morning – Sister Joblin told your Auntie Ena the whole story and she has already told me. And I don't need much imagination to guess what your welcome home was like, either. So let us speak only of things that matter.'

She took a large cut-glass jug from the sideboard, poured out two helpings of homemade lemonade and clinked glasses with Lizzie. 'Here's to the memory of your wonderful grandmother, without whom we might never have met.'

Lizzie's eyes filled with tears. 'Remember how she came with me on my very first day, Bella. It was her idea to get me into the Academy in the first place. I don't know what I would have done without her – or you for that matter.'

Bella put down her glass and hugged Lizzie tight. 'She was your lifeline, dear, there's no mistaking that.'

Lizzie's tears spilled over. 'I can't tell you how much I miss her. If only I'd had the chance to see her before she died. Now she'll never know how much I miss her or understand the depth of my gratitude for everything she has done for me.'

Bella patted Lizzie's back. 'Now, now,' she said, 'not so sad. Your grandma knew how much you loved her and how very grateful you were.'

'I do hope so, Bella, I really do.'

'It may not feel like it at the moment,' she said, 'but one day you'll take comfort in knowing that your grandma will live on in you – in your memories and in all the ways you will be different through the influence she had on you.'

'Had is the right word,' said Lizzie. 'The only influence I have now is my mother frogmarching me into the nursing profession. I'm incarcerated in that bloomin' hospital and I can just see myself wiping dirty bums for the rest of my days! I can't bear the thought of it!'

Bella took her gently by the shoulders. 'There's something I have to tell you, dear, something that could change things for the better. So dry your eyes and trust me. I had a call from Jenny earlier today – she's holding auditions in London.'

Lizzie's eyes widened. 'Auditions for what, Bella?'

'Well, as far as I can tell, she's replacing some of the dancers at Murray's Cabaret Club before the new show starts rehearsing in two or three months.'

'What's Murray's Cabaret Club?'

Bella laughed. 'Only the most famous nightclub in London, that's all! You practically need a title to get in!'

Lizzie gasped. 'And do you think I should try, Bella?'

'It's better than that,' she said, 'Jenny has specifically invited you to attend.'

'That's amazing!' said Lizzie. Then her face fell. 'But it's not just a favour to you, is it? I hope it's not part of the old pal's act?'

'Not at all,' Bella said, 'you're a very talented dancer and this is all on your own merit. Jenny's very keen for you to audition. She's happy to fit you in when the funeral is all over. Isn't that wonderful news?'

Lizzie thought her heart would burst with excitement, but then reality struck home and her face fell again. 'It is wonderful,' she said, 'but isn't there something we've both forgotten?'

'And what is that, Lizzie?'

'My mother, of course. She would never let me audition – not in a million years.'

Bella grinned. 'Oh Lizzie, did you think I'd forget your mother? To be forewarned is to be forearmed, my dear, and I've worked the whole thing out with your father. Believe me, if your grandma was here, she would split her sides laughing with what we have in mind.'

'Well go on then, Bella, I could do with a good laugh.'

'Well,' Bella said, 'as you know, your grandma will be buried in our local churchyard and, as it's so close to the Academy, I suggested we hold a reception for her loved ones right here. What do you think about that, Lizzie?'

'It's a lovely idea, Bella, but how does that help with Mam?'

'Well apparently, she's all for holding the reception here – your father thinks she's happy to let someone else do the catering. And, as for the rest, just leave that all to us.'

Lizzie pouted. 'I don't know what you're up to, Bella, but I do know my mam. And I'll never meet anyone to best her. What if your plan doesn't work?'

Bella put on her serious face. 'Then, I'm afraid, you'll just have to go back to the hospital and suffer.'

Lizzie gasped. 'So what do you want me to do, Bella?'

'That's better,' she said, 'you just follow instructions. The audition will be just after the funeral, so you need to pack your bag and leave it here at the Academy. Then, if all goes well, you can spend the night with me and catch the London train in the morning. In the meantime, you need to swallow hard and act like a loving daughter.'

Bella took a bunch of deep pink peonies from a vase and shook the water from the stems. She pulled open her desk drawer, took out some colourful paper and wrapped it round the flowers. 'Give these to your mother,' she said, 'it's always good to surprise the enemy.'

⚮

Bella paced up and down in the practice room. It was a bright day and the wall-to-wall mirrors reflected the tasteful buffet she had lovingly interspersed with forget-me-nots. How befitting, she thought, I couldn't have made a better choice! She glanced in the mirror and gave a little twirl. Yes, the dress is quite suitable, too, and although brown has never been my colour, I think the cream lace gives it elegance.

She went to the cheeseboard and sampled the Brie, before uncorking the Burgundy. She examined the label and smiled. 'Don't worry,' she said, 'I'll give you time to breathe before Mrs Rooney gets her hands on you.'

She was about to test the wine when she heard cars pulling up on the gravel driveway. She put down the bottle and hurried to the window. Two black limousines were drawing to a stop outside the Academy. Well, speak of the devil, she thought, as she watched Mrs Rooney stumbling from a car in unseemly haste, clutching her old fur collar. Peggy, smart in a navy belted coat, stepped out after her, and attempted to grasp her arm, but Mrs Rooney shrugged her off.

466

What a way to behave, Bella thought, but I'll have to go and welcome her, nevertheless. She hurried to the hall to find Peggy and her mother already there.

Bella took Peggy's hand. 'It's so nice to see you, dear, after all this time. I hear you're married and living in Portsmouth? I'm so glad you could make it to the funeral – I know how fond you were of Mrs Wood and she always had a soft spot for you, dear.'

Mrs Rooney pulled a face. 'Me feet are killing me. Ah'm that parched, Ah could drink through a shitty nappy!'

Peggy's face turned bright red.

'Now, we can't have that,' said Bella. She turned to Peggy and winked. 'The reception is in the practice room, Mrs Rooney, I'm sure you'll find what you need in there. Now please excuse me while I see to the rest of the family.'

❦

Lizzie stood outside the Academy and waved to Bella, who was already waiting in the doorway. It had been a very difficult morning and it was a relief to see her friendly face. Thank goodness for Bella, she thought, and for Molly too. I'm so pleased she came to the funeral with me.

As if on cue, Molly climbed out of the car and took Lizzie's hand. 'Are you sure I'm invited to the reception?' she said. 'Your mam didn't seem too pleased to see me today.'

'Never mind about her, Molly. You're my best friend and Grandma would want you here.'

Molly glanced back at Jack as he helped Alice from the front seat. 'Look, Lizzie, your mam looks like she's lost a pound and found a penny, and your dad's face looks like thunder.'

'Leave them alone to sort themselves out, Molly. Come on, let's go and say hello to Bella.' She linked arms with her best friend and headed towards the imposing entrance.

Jack watched the girls walk across the drive and grasped Alice's arm. 'I hope you're proud of yourself,' he said. 'The way you treated Molly was unforgivable. Try to keep your hurtful comments to yourself, especially on a day like this. Or have you forgotten that I've just laid my mother to rest?'

Alice threw her head back. Didn't he care she was heartbroken too? She marched off towards Bella.

Jack sighed. If he couldn't rely on her to be understanding on a day like this, when could he?

He turned towards the second car and smiled with relief as he saw Joe and Annie walking towards him. Joe waved. 'Wait for us, Jack!'

You bet, he thought, I'd rather be with you than with my wife right now.

Behind them, he could see Ena and Peter getting out of the car. Ena noticed his strained face and ran to throw her arms around her brother. 'Come on now, Jack,' she said, 'pull yourself together. We don't want to keep Bella waiting.'

'We certainly don't,' said Joe. 'That woman deserves a medal as big as a frying pan.'

'You're right there,' said Annie, 'her kindness knows no bounds.'

⚜

Bella stood at the entrance with arms outstretched, waiting to welcome the family. After hugs and condolences, she guided them straight into the practice room.

Jack looked around the beautifully decorated room. 'What a woman,' he said, 'just look at the spread. Is there no end to her talent?'

Mrs Rooney turned towards him and Jack noticed a sway in her step. For goodness sake, he thought, the woman's well-oiled already.

'"No end to her talent",' she repeated with a sneer. 'Well, you should know, Jack, you were never away from this bloody place!'

Peggy nudged Mrs Rooney in the back, causing her to spill the last drops of gin down her blouse.

'Just look what ye've done!' she shouted.

Peter stepped forward and dabbed her blouse with his handkerchief.

'Get yer bloody hands off!' she said. 'Ah'll not be tampered with!'

What a nightmare, he thought as he took her arm and led her to the hospitality table. 'You'll feel much better after a drink, Mrs Rooney. What can I get you?'

'Ah'm not paralysed!' she snapped, as she picked up a tumbler and helped herself to the gin.

Ena sidled up to Peter. 'Don't encourage her, dear, she looks as though she's had enough already. Keep an eye on her while I have a word with Lizzie. It can't have been easy for her today. I'm glad she bought Molly with her.'

She turned to look for her niece and caught sight of Joe staring at Jack.

'Just look at our brother,' Joe said. 'I've never seen him look so desolate.'

She touched his arm. 'Don't worry, dear, it looks as though Bella's taken him in hand. Look, I think she's about to say something.'

Bella stepped forward and clinked her glass with a spoon. 'If I can have your attention for a moment,' she said. 'I'd like to thank Mrs Alice Wood for her kindness in allowing me to arrange her mother-in-law's reception.'

Ena nudged Annie. 'What's the matter with that woman? Can't she see that the last thing Alice wanted was to be bothered with the catering?'

'I'm glad to see you all here today,' Bella went on, 'especially Peggy, who made the effort to travel all the way here from Portsmouth. Now please help yourselves to the buffet while the gentlemen pour out the drinks.'

Annie followed Ena to the groaning table. 'Well,' she said, 'Bella's certainly done your mother proud.'

Ena helped herself to some salmon fancies and a portion of apple and cucumber salad. 'You're right there, it's very tasteful. I wish Mother could have seen it.'

Jack made a beeline for the roast beef and horseradish sauce.

'That'll stick to your ribs,' said Joe, 'real home cooking, aye?'

Ena noticed Mrs Rooney swaying and hastily fetched a chair. Molly giggled as she filled her plate.

'What are you laughing at?' Lizzie asked.

'Look over there! Your grandma's drunk!'

'So what's new, Molly? Let's find somewhere to sit. Look, Aunt Peggy's over there and she doesn't look too happy.'

'Well, with a mother like hers I'm not surprised, Lizzie.'

Peggy's face lit up as she saw the girls approach the table. 'It's so good to see you both,' she said. 'Ah've missed you, Lizzie. Ah've heard all about that sister of mine and her shenanigans – sending you off to be a nurse when she knew yer heart was in the theatre. Yer grandma would turn in her grave if she knew what she'd done.'

'Don't worry, Auntie Peggy, nothing stays the same. You never know what's around the corner.'

'What optimism, Lizzie. Ye must have got that from yer Grandma Wood.' Peggy smiled at her fondly.

'Yes, Peggy, and I got a lot more than that, so please don't worry about me.'

Alice drifted up to their table like a black cloud. 'Well, well,' she said, 'is this a private party or can anyone join in?' She turned to Lizzie. 'And have ye been sharin' yer good news with Peggy?'

No, she thought, but if only I could – share my real good news – it would make her day.

'What's that?' asked Peggy.

'Go on,' said Alice, 'don't be shy – tell her.'

'It was nothing, really, I got a first in anatomy, that's all.'

'That's all!' said Alice. 'It wouldn't surprise me if you ended up running that bloody hospital! Just keep on passin' those exams, girl!'

Peggy looked surprised. 'Have you changed your mind, Lizzie? Do you like being a nurse, then?'

Before Lizzie had time to reply, Molly spoke up. 'No, she bloomin' hates it! She wants to go on the stage!'

'That's enough!' said Alice. 'Yer nothin' but a little troublemaker! Ah never wanted to bring ye in the first place!'

Across the room, Peter turned to Joe. 'Give Bella a wave,' he said, 'it's time to make the tributes.'

Joe signalled to Bella and she hurried forward. Pausing dramatically she waited for everyone to fall silent before speaking in her melodious voice. 'I met Mrs Wood for the first time when she brought Lizzie to audition for a place in the Academy. I'll never forget the smile on her face when I accepted Lizzie and pinned the Academy badge on her jacket. She couldn't have been happier if she'd won the pools. She was a kind woman, a woman of wisdom and foresight, but other people knew her better than me and now I would like the family to make their tributes.' Gracefully she moved back.

Joe stepped forward. 'Well, there's not much you don't already know about my mother. She was kind, patient and generous to a fault. My port in a storm whenever I needed it. I remember, when our father died before his time, she took in paying guests to help fund our education. I shall be forever grateful for her undying support and understanding.' He held up his glass. 'To my mother – may she rest in peace.'

Annie passed Ena a handkerchief. She dried her eyes and swallowed hard before managing to speak the words she'd prepared. 'Mother was the backbone of the family, with a heart of gold, filled with compassion and sympathy for those in need of it. My little niece was her pride and joy. Mother was walking on air when she was accepted into Bella's Academy. We will all miss her love and generosity.'

'Not more than me,' said Lizzie. 'She was a tower of strength in my darkest days.'

Tears welled up in Ena's eyes once more. Lizzie put her arms around her. 'Don't cry, Auntie, Grandma has gone to her reward. And by the way she lived her life, I bet it's a big one.'

'What else could it be?' said Jack. 'She was the salt of the earth. Mother never shirked her duty when it came to keeping an eye on Alice and Lizzie while I was away during the war.'

'So that's what she was doin'!' said Alice. 'And here Ah was, thinkin' she came to enjoy her Sunday dinner!'

Annie for once raised her voice. 'Well you were wrong, Alice! Mother only came to keep an eye on the bairn!'

Alice turned to Jack. 'Did ye hear that?' she shouted. 'Are ye goin' to let her get away with it?'

'He will if he's got any sense!' said Ena.

Joe weighed in. 'Why don't you control that excuse of a wife, Jack?'

'That's right!' said Annie. 'Has she forgotten why we're here today?'

Mrs Rooney searched in her handbag and took out her snuff. She took a healthy sniff, sneezed and wiped her nose on her sleeve.

'Dirty bitch!' said Alice. 'Yer not fit to be let loose!'

Mrs Rooney showed a fist. 'And yer not fit to be a mother, ye lazy cow! Yer jealous of yer own bairn, sendin' her to that bloody hospital!'

Alice pushed Jack in the back. 'Well, isn't it time you said something?'

'I think enough's been said already, woman. Anyway, Bella's about to tell us something.'

Bella held up a letter and gestured to Lizzie. 'I received this letter yesterday and, as it concerns you, I think I should read it.'

'Just a minute,' said Alice, 'Ah'm her mother – give it to me!'

She tried to grab the letter, but Peggy pushed her aside. 'That's enough!' she said. 'Go on, read it, Bella!'

Bella turned to Lizzie. 'Is that all right with you, dear?'

Lizzie nodded her head in approval.

'I received this letter from an old friend of mine. She's a choreographer in London. I hope you don't mind, Lizzie, but I wrote to her on your behalf. But if I was wrong and you are happy in your nursing career, then I apologise.'

The family watched in silence as Bella took the letter from the envelope and began.

'Dear Bella, I thought I'd let you know that I'm replacing some of the dancers at Murray's Cabaret Club before the new show starts rehearsals. In the meantime, as you speak so highly of Lizzie Wood, I'd be happy to see her if she is still interested.

'You ask how things are going with Charles – well, I'm sad to say, there's still no sign of a ring. The story of my life. Looking forward to hearing from you and we can have a good old natter.

'Your loving friend, Jenny.'

The room was so quiet you could hear a pin drop as Bella handed the letter to Lizzie.

Annie whispered in Ena's ear, 'Watch out, it looks like trouble.'

Alice was frozen to the spot, her eyes fixed on Bella.

Peggy took Lizzie's hand. 'Come with me,' she said, drawing her niece to one side for safety.

Joe put his arm around Bella and led her away. She was trembling. 'What have I done, Joe?' she asked.

'What have you done? You've probably saved Lizzie from a fate worse than death, that's what you've done.'

Alice made a beeline for her mother, who'd been watching the proceedings with keen interest, from her place at the buffet table. 'This is all your doing, you auld bugger!'

'Shut yer gob, Alice, Ah never stopped you from being a dancer! So why should you stop the bairn, when it's in her blood?' The old woman grabbed a fork and stabbed a sausage.

Ena stepped forward. 'That's right, Mrs Rooney, we all helped Alice to continue with her competitions when the bairn was little and we never complained when she took advantage.'

'Absolutely!' said Peter, striding over. 'Many a time I asked Ena to refuse after Alice made a habit of leaving the bairn overnight.'

'Come off it,' said Alice, 'Ena couldn't get enough of Lizzie! You were just jealous, because you couldn't give your wife her own bairn!'

Mrs Rooney glared at Alice. 'That's a bloody awful thing to say to the lad, ye should wash yer bloody mouth out with soap!'

'And ye can mind yer own bloody business, Mother!'

Alice turned to leave when Ena grabbed her arm. 'Just a minute,' she said, 'I've waited a long time to put you straight and I won't mince my words. When I look at Lizzie I often wonder how she managed to survive for six years during the war with a mother like you. We never knew what went on behind closed doors, but by the way you behaved, it didn't take much imagination to guess what Lizzie went through. And I'm damned if I'll let you prevent her from choosing her own future.'

Alice turned on Ena. 'Well, Mrs Busybody, aren't ye forgetting who Ah am? Ah'm her mother and Ah will decide her future!'

'And I'm her father!' Jack shouted. 'And I think it's time we left! We can discuss the matter in the morning.'

'Come on, Lizzie,' Alice shrieked across the room. 'We're going!'

'No she's not!' said Peggy. 'The bairn's exhausted!'

Bella crossed her fingers and smiled sympathetically at Alice, while taking centre stage once more. 'You look all in, Mrs Wood, it's been an emotional day. Why not let Lizzie stay here for the night? It would give you and Mr Wood some private time together to decide your plan for Lizzie.'

'Bella's right,' said Jack, 'we can discuss this at home.' He took Alice's arm.

'We can discuss it till the cows come home, Jack, but she'll be back in the hospital in the mornin', Ah'll see to that!' Alice wasn't going to budge.

The family parted like the Red Sea as Jack finally led Alice to the door.

Lizzie followed and squeezed Jack's hand. He winked at her. 'Sleep well, pet,' he said. 'See you soon.'

'And don't be late, I'm not keeping your breakfast hot,' Alice shouted as she slammed the door behind them.

A hush fell over the room, until Peggy broke the silence. 'If you don't mind, Bella,' she said, 'I'll take Mam home now, she looks worn out.' Peggy put her arm round Mrs Rooney. 'I was so proud of you today, Mother, your words hit the nail right on the head.' She helped her on to her feet.

One by one the others made their excuses and prepared to go.

'I can't blame you for leaving so soon,' said Bella. 'I'm sure we're all exhausted after the unexpected behaviour on today of all days. But at least let me leave you with hope for Lizzie's future. Come on,' she said, as everyone gathered around, 'give them the good news, dear.'

Lizzie was a bundle of nerves. She looked at Bella and squeezed her hand. 'I've already got an audition in London. It may come to nothing, but I'm going to try my best. I'm staying with Bella tonight and I'm leaving in the morning, so please wish me luck.'

'And there's another thing,' said Bella. 'If she gets the part, she will start rehearsals right away, so there's a chance she might stay in London.'

Mrs Rooney clapped her hands. 'Ye don't need any bloody luck, pet! Bella's a good judge and if she thinks yer ready, ye've already got the job. Ah can't wait to see Alice's face in the mornin' when she finds out ye've done a runner!'

Joe began to applaud and the family joined in. He held up his hand. 'Just a minute,' he said, 'let us not forget who we have to thank for Lizzie's opportunity. I'm sure I speak on behalf of all of us when I say thank you to a wonderful woman. Without her love and encouragement, goodness knows where Lizzie could have ended up.'

'Joe's right,' said Ena. 'My brother and I can't thank you enough for all you have done. God bless you, Bella.'

Annie came back with the coats and called to Molly. 'Say goodbye to Lizzie, pet, we'll be off in a minute.'

Molly tried to swallow her tear. 'I have to go now, your Uncle Joe's giving me a lift. I hope you get the job, Lizzie, you deserve it.' She threw her arms around her best friend. 'As they say – break a leg' she said.

Annie helped Molly on with her coat. 'Come on,' she said, 'we're leaving now.'

Lizzie's eyes filled with tears as she wondered when she would see her best friend again. She waved until Molly was out of sight.

'Just look at you,' said Ena as she took Lizzie in her arms. 'Grown up and travelling to London all on your own. I can come with you if you like, pet.'

Lizzie was moved by her concern. 'That's a tempting offer, Auntie, but I have to grow up sometime. Anyway, if I fail the audition, I could be home by tomorrow night.'

Joe put his hand in his pocket. 'Well just in case you're not, pet, take this to tide you over in an emergency – it's just a few pounds.'

Lizzie's eyes misted over again. 'What did I do to deserve all this caring?'

Ena hugged her. 'If I told you why, dear, it would take all day.'

Peter stepped forward, with Mrs Rooney and Peggy. Lizzie smiled as she remembered Mrs Rooney's words: Bella's a good judge and if she thinks you're ready, you've already got the job. Lizzie hugged her and kissed her on the cheek. 'Thank you for your kind words, Grandma, they mean so much to me.'

Mrs Rooney smiled. '"Grandma"!' she said. 'Looks like Ah've been promoted! Now look out in London, Lizzie, and don't forget to keep yer hand on yer penny!'

Ena wiped her eyes. 'Let's go, Peter, before I start blubbering.'

Peggy put her arms around Lizzie. 'Good luck, pet, I know you've got it in you.'

As they moved towards the door, Bella called after them. 'Thank you for your support, it made all the difference.'

Lizzie sighed with relief as the room emptied. Have we got away with it, she thought. But supposing I fail the audition, what then? And what about Dad? I wouldn't like to be in his shoes when I don't turn up for breakfast.

Bella opened her arms and Lizzie fell into them. 'Dear girl,' she said, 'you look tired. And we don't want you turning up at the cabaret club with bags under your eyes. Off you go, have a nice soak in the bath and I'll bring your supper up on a tray. It's an early night for you, dear, your train leaves at 8.30 in the morning and you can't afford to miss it.'

Chapter 26

Lizzie hurried along Regent Street carrying her practice clothes in the old silk bag her grandma had made for her first dancing lesson. She stopped and read Bella's directions again. 'Turn left at Lawley's and you can't miss it.' She tried to concentrate and blank out the noise of everything around her – the teeming streets, the crowds, the constant racket of more traffic than she'd ever seen. She'd thought Newcastle was bad on a Saturday afternoon but it was nothing compared to this. She didn't care though. She was here at last.

She hadn't walked far when she saw the sign: LAWLEY'S EXCLUSIVE CHINA: BY APPOINTMENT. The club was just a few yards down on the opposite side of the street, but Lizzie hesitated before crossing the road. She could see the sign from where she stood and wanted to savour the moment. It said, CABARET CLUB in big gold letters and then, more delicately, MEMBERS ONLY.

The building was smaller than Lizzie had imagined, but the entrance was impressive. There was a big, studded door with a long, fringed canopy stretching to the kerb. Lizzie imagined it was to keep the glamorous ladies dry when they stepped from their chauffeur-driven cars.

She was standing by the entrance when a girl came out and smiled at her. 'If you've come for the audition, it's down there, darling, but I think they've finished now.'

Lizzie summoned up her courage, tiptoed downstairs and stood outside a door with a sign saying QUIET PLEASE. She pushed it open to see a huge room surrounded by bare tables. It all looked disappointingly drab, but she remembered Bella saying that it was a very exclusive establishment. She half-closed her eyes and imagined the tables dressed in fine covers, with sparkling cutlery and candlelight. She bet it would look lovely once it was all ready.

She spotted the stage and was about to investigate, when someone shouted, 'Hello, you must be the Geordie girl! Lizzie Wood, isn't it?'

'Yes,' she replied, in a voice that was close to a whisper.

A lady wearing a leotard was sitting at a table marking papers. 'Don't look so worried, dear, I'm Jenny, choreographer and general dogsbody around here, and I don't bite. Sit down and tell me about yourself, Lizzie.'

'Well, there's not much to tell. As you know, I trained at Madame Bella's Academy in Newcastle and performed in the end-of-term productions. I excelled in tap and musical comedy. I believe Bella sent you my report?' Lizzie tried to sound businesslike despite her nerves.

Jenny nodded. 'Anything else, Lizzie?'

'I wasn't too bad at drama and ballet either. I had my first professional engagement at the Theatre Royal in Newcastle and was fortunate to be invited back for pantomime.'

Jenny laughed. 'They must have liked you. How old are you?'

'Seventeen and three quarters.'

Jenny smiled. 'Well, that's very specific,' she said. 'Now, let's see what you've got for us.' She pointed to the changing room. 'Get into your practice clothes, Lizzie, then give Mr Bampton your music.'

She gestured towards the stage and Lizzie peered through the gloom. In the corner was a piano and she could just make out a small, hunched figure of a man puffing on a cigarette, his greasy hair hanging over a newspaper he was struggling to read.

Lizzie dashed to the changing room and changed in record time. She put her hands together. 'Dear God,' she said, more hastily than she would have liked, 'please let me get this job. If you do, I promise never to ask for anything again.'

She yanked open the changing room door and sped back down the corridor. She burst into the audition room, remembering the QUIET PLEASE sign as the door crashed back into the wall and Jenny looked up sharply from her papers.

'I've got my music,' she said, waving the papers at Jenny. 'Oh, yes, you said to give them to Mr Bampton, didn't you?'

She was gabbling – this was awful. She could see that Jenny wasn't impressed. She hurried to the stage, stumbling slightly as she climbed the steps. Calm down, calm down, she told herself. She took three deep breaths and looked over at Jenny again. It was hard to read her expression from here. Oh dear, there was nothing for it but to start. She walked across the stage and handed Mr Bampton the music with trembling hands.

He glanced down at it. 'Not this again!' he said. 'We've had this three times already today!'

Lizzie's heart sank.

Mr Bampton glanced over her music while she limbered up nervously at the bar. When she was ready, she walked to the centre of the stage and nodded to him. She placed her feet in third position and her arms in first as he began to play the opening bars of the familiar music. Her arms were shaking. Oh dear, this wasn't good. But the music calmed her a little. She began the movements she had known so well all those years ago, but they now felt awkward and unfamiliar. Oh dear, she was definitely rusty – all those wasted months training to be a nurse when she could have been dancing! She hoped her lack of recent practice wasn't too obvious to Jenny. But she couldn't let that distract her – she had to give this audition her very best shot.

Her first arabesque went as well as she could hope, her balance was good and her body perfectly arched. As the tempo of the music increased and her confidence grew, she felt less nervous and concentrated her whole being on her technique. Her *grands jetés* felt elegant and strong, and she landed neatly before taking off into the air again, one arm stretched out in front, the other held high above her head. She dared to hope this was going well – her momentum was good and she felt she was beginning to take control of the stage. And now, although it seemed like she had only just begun, she was jumping and leaping toward her last series of pirouettes, each spin ending perfectly.

By the time she finished her fifth pirouette, she was at the front of the stage, holding her pose and imagining the applause she would get had there been an audience in the house. But of course, there was no audience, just Jenny, watching her like a hawk, and Lizzie felt uncertain again as her routine ended in silence.

'Thank you,' said Jenny. 'Now let's see your tap and improvisation. We'll start with tap, shall we?'

Lizzie loved tap and was glad she had chosen 'Bye Bye Blues'. It was so zippy! She felt confident again and, nodding to the pianist, began to perform a familiar on-the-spot tap routine that had gone down well at the Academy Showcase. Halfway through, she glanced at Jenny and saw she was smiling. Lizzie's confidence grew, her speed increased and she ended brilliantly, though she thought it herself, with a cartwheel followed by the splits.

She got up from the floor and peered at Jenny, expecting some reaction, but there was none.

Jenny was holding up a towel. 'Dry yourself off,' she said, 'take a drink and get your breath back, then, when you are ready, we'll try some step variations. I will demonstrate in groups of four, then you repeat them straight after me.'

Lizzie watched nervously as Jenny strode on to the stage and began the steps. Her eyes were glued to her as she tried to memorise her movements, but the sequence was so fast, she could hardly take them in.

Jenny clapped her hands. 'Come along, Lizzie,' she said, 'your turn.'

My turn, she thought, what does she expect? Jenny's feet were like lightning!

She was nervous as she struggled to remember the order of the variations, but apart from one or two hitches, she thought she was doing all right. As she came to the end, she looked for approval, but Jenny had already started on the next variation. Lizzie didn't have time for self-doubt. Once more, she glued her eyes on Jenny and when she finished this time, there was no need to be told, 'your turn' – Lizzie was up and off, almost before Jenny had left the floor.

As she completed the last step, Jenny held up her hand. 'That'll do,' she said. 'Sit down, dear, and get your breath back.'

Lizzie couldn't wait another second to hear Jenny's reaction. 'How do you think I did, Jenny?'

Jenny shrugged slightly. 'It's not my decision, I'm afraid.' She waved towards the back of the room. 'You see that window up there?'

Lizzie peered towards the back wall. 'Yes, now you mention it.'

'That's Mr Murray's office – he's the producer and the decision is his. Just give me a moment and I'll get him.'

Jenny got up but she didn't go anywhere. Lizzie followed her gaze and saw a tall, stout man walking towards them. He was wearing a pinstriped suit and patent leather shoes, and he approached with his hand held out, inviting Lizzie to shake it.

'This is Mr Murray,' said Jenny, 'the owner of the club.' She pointed to the window at the back of the room. 'He watched your audition from up there, Lizzie.'

It was hard to know how old he was. The crown of his head was bald, but he had arranged the front in an arresting quiff. Lizzie dragged her eyes away from it, in order to meet his eyes.

Mr Murray smiled broadly, pulled out a chair and sat opposite them. 'Ah, the girl from the Tyne,' he said, in a commanding voice. 'I've heard a lot about you. Coming all this way to audition for us and highly recommended too.'

'Thank you, Mr Murray.' It was all she could do not to curtsey.

'Sit down, girlie,' he said, 'I've been watching you from the bridge.'

Jenny pulled a face. 'I don't suppose you have any idea what he's talking about, Lizzie. But when he says "bridge", he means the office with the window. Mr Murray was in the Navy and we all have to get used to his jargon.'

He pointed to a small medal on his lapel. 'See this, my dear? I got it for bravery. I was shot in the war, don't you know?'

Jenny tapped him on the shoulder. 'Shall we get on with it, Percy?'

487

'Yes, yes. Let me tell you something about our club, Lizzie. We are considered one of the best in London and are renowned for our floor show. This is a very prestigious venue, with a very prestigious membership. My girls are all hand-picked for their talent and beauty, and many have gone on to be West End stars. You look a little like one of my girls who made it right to the top. Her name was Jessie Andrews, although she's so toffee-nosed now, she wouldn't give me any credit.'

Jenny stood up. 'Please, Percy, put the girl out of her misery.'

He cleared his throat. 'All right then, Lizzie Wood, what I can say is this – I was impressed with your audition. You're extremely young, but, with hard work and dedication, you might have a successful career.'

Lizzie nodded. Yes, she thought impatiently, I know all about that, but do you want me or not? She was on the edge of her seat. Was it going to be a yes or a no?

Jenny nudged him. 'Come on, Percy!'

'Well,' he said, 'as I said, I was impressed. Despite your inexperience, that was quite an audition.'

Lizzie's heart was thumping so hard, she was sure they could hear it.

Jenny scowled at him. 'For goodness sake, Percy, let the girl know your decision.'

But Mr Murray was looking a little doubtfully at Lizzie. 'Now, girl, if you were to join our company now, you would be joining at our busiest time. The current show comes off in eight weeks. We change the cabaret every six months and start costume fittings and rehearsals for the new show in three weeks.'

Lizzie could hardly take in what he was saying.

'So, for five weeks, you'd be rehearsing most of the day and performing twice nightly. Do you think you could cope with that, a young girl like you?'

'Oh yes, Mr Murray, I'm sure I could, Mr Murray!' Lizzie shifted in her seat. Little does he know, she thought, I'd shovel coal for this job.

'Well,' he said, 'if you're sure – Lizzie Wood, it's a pleasure to welcome you on board!'

Her heart quickened and she swallowed hard. Had she really got the job or was he inviting her on to his boat? She was tempted to ask if she had heard right, but she didn't need to.

'Well,' Mr Murray asked in his booming voice, 'girl from the Tyne? Would you like to come to the big city and work for me?'

'Oh yes!' she said. 'It would be an honour! You won't regret this, Mr Murray!'

'I should hope not, girlie!'

'You won't, Mr Murray, and thank you, Mr Murray!'

❧

Before she knew it, Lizzie was back in the changing room. It was hard to believe what had happened to her. The drawstring bag her grandma had made for her very first audition was lying on the cloakroom floor. She picked it up and thought about the woman whose undying love and determination had got her here. Because of her, Lizzie's life had just completely changed. She stood stock still in the centre of the room, trying to take it all in. She would be moving from Tyneside to London, starting afresh. It was like a dream.

There'd be no more tiptoeing around, searching for the right words to prevent a tongue-lashing from her mother, no more sleepless nights from the never-ending rows between her parents. And no more nursing. It was all behind her now. Lizzie bent down and picked up the drawstring bag, holding it tight. Everything, *everything* had changed. At last the future was in her own hands.

Welcome to the world of *Melody Sachs*!

Keep reading for more from Melody Sachs, including a
sneak peek at her next book . . .

We'd also like to introduce you to MEMORY LANE, our
special community for the very best of saga writing from
authors you know and love, and new ones we simply can't
wait for you to meet. Read on and join our club!

www.MemoryLane.club

Dear Reader,

I hope you enjoyed the characters in this book as much as I did while creating them. In the end I became so involved in their ups and downs, their hopes and fears, and for some, their never-ending faith in the future that I found it hard to let them go – so I didn't, and as we speak I am writing the sequel. I hope *The Girl from the Tyne* will encourage you to continue Lizzie's journey.

Happy reading,

Melody

Read on to continue Lizzie's story with
this extract from Melody's
next book . . .

As the bridal car approached the town hall, Jenny nudged Lizzie and pointed to a colourful crowd gathered outside the greystone building.

'Look,' she said, 'they must be on their way to a fancy-dress party. See that woman in the feather jacket? She looks just like a chicken.'

Lizzie laughed. 'That's not a fancy-dress party. They're here for the wedding. See that woman in the pink-beaded dress? Well, that's my mother-in-law so be careful of what you say.'

Lizzie watched as Sadie checked Gary's buttonhole and straightened his tie. 'Look at that, Jenny, she treats him like a child.'

Gary stood frozen to the spot as the car pulled up outside the entrance. Sadie pushed him. 'Go on then – what are you waiting for?' she shouted. 'Open the door and let the girl out.'

Gary's face lit up at the sight of his bride. He held out his hands and helped her from the car while Jenny and Maria guided the dress from inside. Betty hurried forward and kissed Lizzie. 'Good luck to the both of you,' she said. 'Now let's get inside, Sadie. Gary doesn't need his mother to hold his hand.'

Sadie gave Betty a dirty look but headed inside.

Lizzie held on to Gary's arm as he led her to the registry office. He was about to open the door when it suddenly swung open from the other side. Sadie stood there, seething with impatience.

'What the hell's keeping you?' she said. 'Get inside Gary and get this thing started. There's people in there desperate to whet their whistle.'

Lizzie's face flushed as they walked into the room. Jenny and Maria glanced at each other and followed. The room was packed with ladies of indeterminate years wearing the most outrageous outfits. As far as hats were concerned, Maria's fruit-and-flowers creation looked elegant compared to the rest.

Most of the guests were in the drinks trade; mainly publicans and licensed club owners. The ladies resembled Christmas trees in their sequined dresses and flashy jewellery.

Yes, thought Lizzie. As my grandma Rooney would say, *Fur coats and no knickers.*

'No one seems to be organising this wedding. You're giving Lizzie away, Jenny, so I suppose we'd better sit up front.'

Sadie glared at them as they took their places. She nudged Betty. 'What the hell are they doing in the front row?'

'Keep your voice down,' said Betty. 'Jenny's giving Lizzie away.'

You could cut the atmosphere with a knife. Jenny was glad when the registrar made his entrance. She nudged

Maria as she watched him glide behind a large desk and clear his throat. He was a small, thin man in a well-worn suit that looked as though it had seen better days. He placed a book on the table and after adjusting his steel-rimmed glasses turned to the bride and groom.

Maria wiped away a tear. 'Isn't our girl a sight for sore eyes?' she whispered.

Lizzie and Gary took each other's hands and a hush fell over the room. Sadie nudged Betty. 'I hope he knows what he's doing,' she said. 'You know what they say? Marry in haste and repent at leisure.'

Betty squeezed Sadie's arm. 'That's enough,' she whispered.

The registrar turned to the bride and groom. 'Shall we begin?' Lizzie nodded.

He turned to the guests. 'Welcome everyone. My name is Mr Snaith and I'm your registrar. We are gathered here today to celebrate the marriage of Gary Carter to Lizzie Wood. Now, if we're ready, please repeat after me, Mr Carter: I do solemnly declare that I know not of any lawful impediment why I, Gary Carter, may not be joined in matrimony to Lizzie Wood.'

As Gary smiled and repeated the words, Lizzie felt her heart flutter.

The registrar continued. 'I call upon these persons here present to witness that I do take thee, Lizzie Wood, to be my lawful wedded wife.'

Jenny stepped forward with the ring and passed it to Gary. He looked lovingly at Lizzie as he made his vows and slipped the ring on her finger.

The registrar turned to Lizzie. 'Repeat after me,' he said. 'I do solemnly declare . . .'

As Lizzie repeated her vows, it was hard to believe this was really happening.

Sadie nudged Betty. 'Well, that's it,' she said. 'Mark my words: Gary's just made a rod for his own back.'

Before Lizzie knew it, the registrar was declaring them man and wife, and Gary was turning to kiss her. The colourful guests raised the roof with their approval and as their lips met Maria nudged Jenny and whispered, 'Just look at Sadie's face! You'd think she'd lost a pound and found a penny.'

Lizzie closed her eyes as Gary whispered, 'I love you, Mrs Carter.'

She took his arm and smiled at Jenny as he led her outside.

The merrymakers followed, almost falling over each other in their scramble to leave the room. Jenny and Maria hurried after them, but by the time they arrived outside, the bride and groom were already covered in confetti.

Sadie was holding court as her colourful friends sang her praises. 'Just wait 'til you see the cake,' she said. 'It cost me an arm and a leg, but who cares? Your son only gets married once.' She laughed. 'Let's hope I'm right!'

A photographer was busy snapping away when Lizzie caught Jenny's eye and beckoned her to bring Maria for a picture.

'Come here,' she said. 'Thank you two for everything, especially putting up with my childish behaviour this morning.'

Maria dabbed her eyes. 'I don't know what we'll do without you, Lizzie.'

'That's enough,' she said. 'Smile for the dicky bird.'

The final hurdle was over. As the newlyweds left in their limousine, the wind blew away the last traces of confetti and the guests hurried to their cars on the promise of a grand reception.

'Well,' said Jenny, 'we'd better get a taxi, I suppose.'

'Don't bother,' said Maria. 'Jimmy Langdon's waving from his limousine.'

The car pulled up and the chauffeur opened the door. 'Get inside,' said Jimmy. 'We're all going to the same watering hole.' He nudged his wife and she laughed.

'Hurry up,' she said, 'or we'll all die from thirst.'

No sooner had they settled into the car, when Maggie cleared her throat and burst into song. 'They tried to tell us "We're too young",' she warbled.

Oh my god, thought Jenny. This, on top of everything else.

The journey to the reception seemed endless as Maggie, with tears running down her cheeks, belted out what seemed like her entire repertoire.

As the car slowed down, Maria breathed a sigh of relief. 'Look,' she said. 'It seems as though we've arrived.'

Jenny looked out of the window and cringed. The entrance to the hotel was draped in fairy lights and plastic flowers with a huge sign above the door proclaiming, in luminous letters, *Gary and Lizzie's big day.*

'As if we didn't know,' said Maria. 'Sadie doesn't need to advertise!'

Jenny nudged her. 'Keep your voice down. We don't want to get off on the wrong foot. As far as Sadie's concerned, we're not even welcome.'

MEMORY LAN

If you've not read Eileen Ramsay's sweeping historical romances before, you're in for a treat with the first in the Flowers of Scotland series, *Rich Girl, Poor Girl*.

When you're chasing a dream,
does it matter where you come from?

From the slums of Dundee to the diplomatic homes of Washington D.C., two young women are drawn together by their dreams . . . and broken apart by love and war.

Upper-class Lucy Graham is expected simply to marry well, while for poverty-stricken Rosie Nesbitt just getting by is a daily struggle. Both girls share an unlikely dream – to become a doctor – and each will do anything to succeed.

Their paths cross at a party filled with eligible bachelors, and it soon becomes clear that their chosen career isn't the only desire they share . . . But meeting their match is overshadowed by the outbreak of war.

With society's conventions stacked against them and war raging on the continent, Lucy and Rosie must draw their own battle line in their fight for love, life and happiness. But can they *both* succeed

Out now in paperback and e-book

Sign up to MEMORY LANE to find out more:
www.MemoryLane.club

Introducing a new place for story lovers – somewhere to share memories, photographs, recipes and reminiscences, and discover the very best of saga writing from authors you know and love, and new ones we simply can't wait for you to meet.

A new address for story lovers

www.MemoryLane.club